TWO BY ASTLEY

Two by Astley

A KINDNESS CUP

&

THE ACOLYTE

by

Thea Astley

G. P. PUTNAM'S SONS   NEW YORK

G. P. Putnam's Sons
Publishers Since 1838
200 Madison Avenue
New York, NY 10016

First American Edition 1988

A Kindness Cup copyright © 1974 by Thea Astley
The Acolyte copyright © 1972 by Thea Astley

Library of Congress Cataloging-in-Publication Data

Astley, Thea.
Two by Astley.

Contents: A kindness cup—The acolyte.
I. Astley, Thea. Acolyte. 1988.   II. Title.
PR9619.3.A75A6   1988   823   87-19065
ISBN 0-399-13363-1

Printed in the United States of America
1   2   3   4   5   6   7   8   9   10

A KINDNESS CUP

Should auld acquaintance be forgot
And never brought to min'?
Should auld acquaintance be forgot
And days o' lang syne?
For auld lang syne, my dear,
For auld lang syne,
We'll tak' a cup o' kindness yet,
For auld lang syne.

—ROBERT BURNS

ACKNOWLEDGMENTS

The impetus for this novel came from an actual incident at The Leap, Queensland, in the second half of the last century; but this cautionary fable makes no claim to being a historical work. Liberties have been taken with places and times, and the author happily admits possible anachronisms.

Acknowledgments are made to the report of the Select Committee on the Native Police Force, Queensland, 1861.

T HIS WORLD is the unreality, he thinks between smiles and frowns over the letter.

After twenty years—back!

They'd done it after ten—a folly he'd ignored. Back to The Taws. After all these longitudes of time, what would that make them all if all of them could make it? Trembling sexagenarians, hearts pausing— but not for joy; eyes cataracted, prostates swollen or excised, livers cirrhosed, hearing dimmed.

This man pauses in his shaving to squint at the piece of paper again, razor hesitant, eye returning anxious but reluctant to the blurred letters. Who is Barney Sweetman? A name he has tried to forget. Barney . . . Sweetman? Jesus! Sweetman Sweetman Sweetman? Raintrees outside the stock-and-station agent's before the dogmatic through road eased round by the school. Where he. Under crushing dust. Velvet crushes. And the flies busy. A youngish man then. And that other youngish as well, weighing out some sort of glittering utterance with his face ju-jubed by School of Arts stained glass, frecklings of cerulean and jonquil in lamp-light. From shadow into heat and buggies, dozy cobs blinkered in shafts by a water-trough. The slipperiest of memories. Had that been Barney Sweetman, later town councillor, mayor, State member, mutton-chopped hearty? Retired now? Conniving now?

He nicks himself and the tired blood trickles a moment, stops easily these days almost before the cotton-wool sticks.

Crumples the letter that morning. Picks it out of the bin that night, hearing wind along the Moreton Bay reaches moving out of the sea into the empty passageways of his house with its too many lumps of

11

darkening furniture and the whisky bottle too handy. Smooths it out again and licks at the strange invitation a little, the liquor moist on his lip. The impersonal jargon of some bleeding go-getter, he tells himself, making a quick quid on the boosted tourist tears of returning townsfolk! Why, his bay is filled with tears and the figs of its name, the long roots stretching, groping down in laterals to weep over slight grey waters with islands humped and sand-duned and afloat. He is drenched in nostalgia here. What is the point, any point, in a return?

My filled days, he thinks ironically, my filled days. With walks along the front, a shambles to the pier and along it to the point where winds knot green swirl of sea and gull and fish and some crumbling other man casting his lines. Back to the figged park and the bottle-lollied picnic kiosk, and an hour or so beneath broad leaves pecking at book or paper. Barney Sweetman. The bastard, he says. And Buckmaster. Buckmaster and Sweetman. Knighted for milking God's earth. Knighted for handling the sugar strikes. Knighted for owning more acres of sweet grass in the north than any man had the right to control. But not knighted for that noon at Mandarana—how the names come back now!—the virtue guards with rifles kicking their unwilling horses up the runty slopes while the natives scuttled like roos from bush to bush until the high plateau. Or after. The down-curve through hot air and the body whizzing.

He closes his eyes.

"Boys," Mr Dorahy said, "let us recapitulate . . .

"I cannot believe," he continued musingly, his finger poised at a certain section of the Gallic Wars, "that men are rational beings when I observe their militaristic antics. I mean the drill protocol claptrap, of course, quite apart from the specifics of learning how to kill." His thin and rather sour face was extremely gentle. He smiled with the terrible snaggle teeth that all who had grown to love failed now to notice. "What do you think, Jenner?"

"Are you serious, sir?"

"Of course."

"But we have our own sort of drill, sir. I mean terms and classroom behaviour and . . ."

"When," Mr Dorahy interrupted, but still gently, "have I ever required a clicking to, a standing to, a goose-stepping hop to it?"

12

Jenner's round sixteen-year-old face began a small grin. "We just do it, sir."

"You miss my point, boy. You miss it." Dorahy sighed and stared bleakly past the eight faces to the school paddock, still being fenced, at workmen whacking on wood for the new school block beyond the pepper-trees.

"Close your Livy," he said tiredly. "If you'll give me all that keen attention of yours, I'll try to draw a parallel."

"Parable, sir?" a shaggy lad next to Jenner inquired with a smirk.

"If you like," Mr Dorahy said. He could feel reluctance lumping his tongue. "*If* you like. Tarquinius Sextus, as you will recall, was a bastard par excellence." The boys began to laugh quietly. "His bastardry," continued Mr Dorahy without a muscle-twitch of amusement, "entered the fields of male folly which ruined not only himself, I mean his soul, but a family line!"

He began to quote but no one understood, so he dragged himself from his chair and scribbled the Latin on the board. "Buckmaster," he said, "translate."

The clock hands were staggering. Time passed slowly in that cube of heat and flies. Clause gobbets. Literal patches of historic infinitive. Torture, Dorahy decided. Sheer mindless torture. He said, "Take over, Jenner."

Jenner bumbled for a while, testing words with his incompetent tongue. He crashed over the last sentence—". . . and there to her surprise Tarquinius found her lying unclad."

Dorahy coughed. He coughed out this dust and the dust became the expectations of three failed years.

"A little more delicately, I think: 'And there surprised Lucretia lying naked.' It was Tarquin who did the surprising in the literal sense of the word, boys. Not the unfortunate lady. Though doubtless she, too, was surprised in your sense. I'll read it to you again. 'And there the Tarquin, black and forceful, surprised Lucretia lying naked.' " He repeated the last two words softly and a terrible adolescent excitement charged the room. The angle of his vowel, that first vowel, lecherously over-toned plus the quiet refinement of the soured mouth and face made for frightful antithesis.

Outside a world of trees and umber. Flies inside drumming window-heat, taking glass for air.

"The militaristic claptrap and the insolvency of the rapist are equally sub-human—is what I mean. Is very much what I mean."

Buckmaster didn't quite scowl. He was later to sire three half-castes. "Women!" he whispered hissingly along the row. "Gins!" he whispered. And he scrawled furtively a set of parted legs on the margin of his Livy.

"If your thinking, Buckmaster," Mr Dorahy proceeded gently, "lies only in the force of your genitals, God help the world."

Buckmaster senior later said, leaning on his silver-topped riding crop, "You cannot speak to the boys like this. There are certain matters. Things such as . . . Decencies must . . ."

"In this noisome little colony," Mr Dorahy replied mildly with more sweat than usual running down the edges of his weary hair, "where masculinity is top dog, it seems to me that some occasional thought should be given, chivalrously you understand—*do* you understand?— to the sex that endures most of our nastiness."

"You're mad," Buckmaster said.

"You become that which you do."

Mr Buckmaster allowed himself a tiny bleached smile. "Any bloody teacher in this place would have to be mad."

"I meant you," Mr Dorahy said. The small scar of some long-forgotten protest whitened on his cheek. "Would you want your son to become one of the mindless, insensitive, money-grubbing bulls you see around this town and that he gives every indication of aping?"

"I'll have you sacked, by Christ!" Pulling at his crotch. His cutaway donned for the occasion—running the bejesus out of a back-town schoolie—stank in the heat. Summer was crouching all over the town.

"Please do," Mr Dorahy said. "I am so tired."

But it did not could not happen. Who else was there for a pittance in a provisional school slapped hard in the sweating sugar-grass north of the tropic?

I am single, Mr Dorahy told himself proceeding through the drudgeries of instruction. I am single and thirty-seven and in love with landscape. Even this. Other faces cut close to the heart. His assistants, say, who took the junior forms. Married and widowed Mrs Wylie gathering in the chickens for a spot of rote tables or spelling, beating it out in an unfinished shack at the boundary fence. Or Tom Willard with his combined primary forms and his brimstone lay-preaching on

14

the Sabbath. Or himself as a gesture to culture, keeping on the bigger boys of his parish, for he was priestly enough to use that word, for a bit of elementary classics and a purging of Wordsworth. It all seemed useless, as foolish as trying to put Tintern Abbey into iambic hexameters. He had come with a zealot's earnestness, believing a place such as this might need him. And there was, after all, only loneliness; he was cut off from the pulse, of the town, although, he insisted to himself rationalising furiously, he had been regularly to meetings of the Separation League and had blown only occasional cold air on their hot. He had drunk with the right men. He had kept his mouth closed. He had assumed nothing. And yet other faces, the wrong sort because they were black, had their own especial tug, the sad black flattened faces of the men working with long knives in the cane and their scabby children making games in the dust at the entrances and exits of towns. The entrances. The exits. Observe that, he cautioned himself.

He was friendly with them, as friendly perhaps as Charlie Lunt on his hopeless block of land west of the township; friendly even when they robbed his accessible larder, noting the small fires they made at the boundary fences of his shack; or when he caught Kowaha, shinily young, pilfering sugar and flour, eyes rolling like humbugs with the lie of it while he did a bishop's candlesticks—"But I gave them to you"—confusing her entirely. Bastardry not intended, he told his ironic self. Yet she asked next time, and the next, always at half-light so that the scurrilous tongues of settlers along the road were never sure of shadow or concretion.

Nort, Mr Dorahy inscribed meticulously on Buckmaster's ill-spelled prose. *Nort,* he gently offered, as Trooper Lieutenant Fred Buckmaster gave his evidence before the select committee.

Do you think, the magistrate, a bottle-coloured Irishman, had asked, you should be cognisant of the facts before you take your measures? Have you no written or printed instructions?

No printed ones, Lieutenant Buckmaster said, truculent and oiling slightly. I act on letters received from squatters.

Do you think, the magistrate pursued, hating the stinking obese fellow before him, that it is right to pursue these blacks—say a month after their depredations?

I always act immediately, Lieutenant Buckmaster said flatly, immediately I am called upon. But it is the tribe I follow. Not individuals.

You can never see the actual depredators. (Conjugate that verb, Dorahy whispered to himself. Oh, conjugate it, man!)

Mr Sheridan tapped his fingers on the edge of the greasy desk. He was not in love with his job.

Do you not think there is any other way of dealing with them except by shooting them?

Lieutenant Buckmaster smiled.

No. I don't think they can understand anything else but shooting. At least that is the case as far as my experience goes.

And your experience goes a long way, does it not? Another point, then. Tell me, are your police boys in the habit of taking the gins from the tribes . . . for whatever purpose?

Buckmaster edged slightly. His real rash irritated, but this was now a rash of the mind. It was very hot in the little court.

No. Except with my instructions.

Did they take any this way in the previous case at Kuttabul?

No. Buckmaster could not conceal his contempt. There were no young gins there. Only old ones. Later some young gins followed us up from the Kuttabul scrub.

And do they stay with you? The magistrate could not blur his wonder.

No, Lieutenant Buckmaster admitted. They only stop a night and get a piece of tobacco in the morning and go away. (Mr Sheridan raised his eyebrows at this point.) But generally we have to flog them off. They will follow the men all over the country. I have known them to follow my boys for as long as five days and I have had to flog them off in the middle of the night.

Have you indeed? Mr Sheridan inquired, unable to control himself. And watched with interest the slow red on the lieutenant's ruined face.

Dorahy had been observed by the port-nosed Buckmaster allowing some slight scrap of black flesh to depart his humpy unmolested long after sunset. So long after sunset that Buckmaster was returning from his own bodily revenge on a depressed white woman who ran an out-of-town shanty on the Mandarana road. His sexual angers were unsatisfied, not merely because of the fifth-rate partner who accepted his adulterous attentions like a necessary lash but by sighting a sleek gin

16

slipping with a sugar-bag of something from the sour schoolmaster's. "To be in charge of my boy!" he raved inwardly, kicking his horse into a canter. Its nervous rump responded quiveringly to the crop. He could have been flogging Dorahy or the gin or the woman he had just left.

All around him, however, was the benison of cane arrowing on the back roads to his farm, the beige spearhead of flower proving gentleness. Yet he was sickened by cycles of it and sometimes wondered if he really were committed to farm.

His own house was pocked with slow pools of light from the kerosene lamps along the back veranda where he found, gripping the rage within his flesh, son Fred playing a game of chess with young Jenner.

Both boys stared curiously at this unsated man who communicated distemper with his first words.

"Where's your mother?"

Fred dangled a lost pawn. It was an insolent gesture over-interpreted by the father who saw himself thus. "Sewing," Fred said. "In the front room."

His father could have been choking when he roared, "And what are you two wasting time on now? We don't keep you on at school like bloody gentlemen, you know, simply to fritter. Yes, fritter, by God! This is the last year of it and then you'll have to earn your keep. Slumped around here!" His voice was lumpy with scorn.

"It gives you a certain prestige," Fred said unwisely, "having an unemployed wastrel adult son."

"By the living Christ," Buckmaster roared, "I won't take, I don't have to take *that!*" Slamming his broad hand across the side of his son's thick head.

Young Jenner said, offering his handkerchief towards the bloody nose, "It's true, you know. My father reckons we'll do much better for ourselves. Ever so much better."

"With your piddling bits of filthy Latin! With your sexless poets, your witless grammarians!"

(He has quite a flow, Jenner commented later to Fred, for an uneducated man.) Now he said, "We can't help it, sir. We're the victims of parenthood."

Mr Buckmaster had moved to the wine-rack near the kitchen door.

17

"I am an important man in this town," he stated redundantly. "I have thirty boys working for me on the farm. I must have a son who can control, share with me, know how to handle men."

Young Buckmaster was too absorbed in blood and shame to dribble anything but snivels into this.

"Your father," Buckmaster pressed on, gulping some ferocious indigo liquid that always failed to make him feel better, and swinging on young Jenner, "is a step beyond my reasoning. The biggest property in the district. Two score of Kanaks hauling in his profits. What does it matter what his soft-haired boy does, eh? What the hell does it matter? You'll sleep sweet on a sugar-bed as long as you live and you can take this fancy education from that snot-nosed teacher of yours and whatever it does for you, for it won't do much but make you useless when it comes to dealing with men!" (He was fond of dealing with men, was Buckmaster, and could handle women in much the same way.) "So I'd thank you to keep your privileged presence and fancy ideas"—the chessboard was scattered at this point across the veranda flooring—"to yourself."

In protest Jenner cried out, "But it was for Mrs Buckmaster I called. My mother sent over a book she had asked for."

Mr Buckmaster, slowed by wine, thought this one over.

"Sewing, you said?" His son nodded sullenly. "Not reading? Not wasting the light?" He mumbled into his glass some winey incantations and, as on cue, his wife came through suddenly from the front of the house to ignore her son's bloodied face and begin stoking up the last of the fire to make tea. She was forty and ruined, not so much by her husband as by the country and the tyranny of it.

A strange woman, the neighbours said, and would continue to say for her resistance both to them and to her husband who had used her as an incubator to breed sons but extracted only daughters except for this youngest, gulping mucus and tears. She continued to read—it seemed to her husband to be a sickness with her—despite him during those hours he was away being a man among men. For his part, he respected and almost feared those sinews of character she retained, but resented them. "My wife's a great reader," he would boom among the husbands of cake-makers. It gave him cachet, he suspected, and somehow atoned for those moments when, with him biblically ranting, Old Testament sexually referring, she would laugh at him. He was a

18

violent man, but imposed restraints that threatened to burst the blood out of his facial skin.

Jenner, who at sixteen should not have understood but nevertheless did, handed him his cup of tea and sat sipping and watching from behind the light of the lamp.

Young Fred was still sulking. He could wait till death for a formal apology from his father, who was sorry but could not say so, offering instead a kind of blessing with a supper hunk of bread and cheese. Fred took slow bites before deciding on speech. Finally: "Jilly Sweetman tells me there's government troops coming up this way to flush out the blacks."

His father, who had known about this for some weeks, who had privately and quietly officially requested, said, "Now there's a man's job for you instead of this rubbishing school. They're going to clear out the lot who've been raiding the coast farms. Drive them back north and west where they came from. Shoot the thieving bastards if they catch them at it."

"They're still around," Fred said, trying eagerly for paternal favor. "The fellows have seen them out near Dorahy's place. He encourages them, he does." Oh, the lad could spill the sins of others with horrible readiness. "And old Charlie Lunt's as well. Sugar and flour and things. Tobacco. They give them, I mean."

"Do they indeed?" asked his father, who knew.

His wife was silently stirring knowledge in with sugar and tea.

"Gin lovers?" Mr Buckmaster asked shockingly of no one in particular; but his wife who could have endured any kind of lover at all said mildly, "They're kind to them. They think they're people."

"People!"

"Yes. People. Christ's skin was probably as dark as theirs."

"My God!" Mr Buckmaster cried, inspecting her handsome intransigent features for irony. Christ was the New Testament revealed once a week by a minister who viewed him joylessly. He was presented as totally pale-skinned and it was to a white man they sang their whining hymns. "My God! Up north, you know, up in the rain-forest, hunting them down makes a pleasant way of filling in Sunday." It could be done straight after addressing his puritan white god. He enjoyed watching her wince. "What's the bag, eh, mate?" he pursued. "Ten? Eleven? Not as good as last week."

19

"Leaving them to rot," commented his wife, suddenly brutal and vicious with him. "Not even a hole in the ground!"

"Ach!" Buckmaster grunted. "You're like all the other women after all." He felt unexpectedly pleased with this discovery. "Sentimental and stupid. First to squawk if a party of them raped you, though."

"I've never squawked at rape," his wife replied calmly, putting the supper cheese closer to her son's friend, understanding his subtlety.

There was a frightful silence. Young Jenner blushed. Even young Fred, thigh doodler of private and particular yearnings, was finding the scrubbed veranda floor of savage interest.

"There would not be," Mr Buckmaster said finally and heavily, "room for much else." A winner, he felt, in front of Jenner's bright intelligent eye.

But the boy gave a last embarrassed gulp at his tea and said to the waiting room, "I must be getting back now." The innocence of his red hair was startling against his newly educated face. He stood up awkwardly and walked over to the landing uncertain whether to speak again would be the ultimate refinement in this uncivil war. But the wife spoke.

"Good-bye," she said to him. "Thank your mother for me, and come again soon."

Young Jenner smiled once more, stopped smiling and said good-bye. As he cantered his horse into darkness, he understood that the blows dealt in metaphor were deadlier than the thwack of flesh on flesh. He could not ride fast enough to hear silence move in behind him while his soul lugged a new and doughy knowledge.

D ORAHY SUBMITS to this pull of fate.
    He packs a small bag, noting how one's needs in age lie in inverse ratio to the expansion of the soul.

He hopes. He boards a lumbering coastal vessel that rocks him out of his capital and, after a sea-shaken slumber, wakes after the third night to a sugarville morning of hard blue and yellow north of the tropic. From the salty deck he observes the wide reaches of blue bay water as the boat enters his destiny. Coastal scrub has thinned out its scraggy imprecision and has become the scraggier, scrubbier buildings of a town he has not entered for twenty years, which yet, as he watches the houses grow larger with approach, fills him with a nauseating nostalgia.

He has kept apart as far as possible from the other passengers all the week, but now, as they join him along the railing, he feels obliged to share the excitement and the chatter. Hands point. Voices cry out. The boat noses its rusty way from harbour to river and river docks.

There are only two others disembarking and he hopes to avoid them, knowing the town is full of pubs. Their reason for return is the same as his and already, conscious of his ambitions for solitariness, he wonders why he has come. His elderly legs wobble on this Friday morning gang-plank but they are the same legs that strolled through this town twenty years before, and he marvels that he is experiencing grief when, he supposes, rage would be the better thing. Turning his back firmly on the river and the docks, he walks steadily up the slope past the warehouses and enters the town.

The streets are busy with horses and big drays. There are people on bicycles bumping along the rough roads. Groggy from all this, he

21

stands uncertain in sunlight, his bag at his feet. One should never go back. He decides this with vehemence and wonders then is he thinking of the psychic mistake of it or his own lack of charity. One does go back, he knows, again and again. One should forgive places as much as people.

This place has much to be forgiven it.

Terrible to sense the valetudinarian legs tentative along the footpath. But up here everyone saunters. He is relieved he does not look remarkable. It is a refusal to fight the heat which already is dealing him blow upon blow; rather a yielding to it. Already steam is rising from the baking township and its slow river. Already there is sweat along his hairline, the saddened back of his neck, trickling between his breasts.

He feels reluctant to face his hotel yet, knowing its drabness already, the tired pots of fern, the bar-stink, the narrow bedroom with its spotted mirror. He walks on one hundred, two hundred yards and finds a tea-shop sluicing out the evening before. Rinsing the last stains of it, a thin girl has been doing penance with mop and bucket. She couldn't care less about this elderly man with his thin face and thinner voice demanding tea. She isn't forgiving anybody, refuses the credit of his smile, while slinging her bile across one table surface after the other with a rancid grey rag.

But he tries.

"It's twenty years," he volunteers, "since I've been here." (Where are the banners, the bunting, the tuckets sounding at left?)

She deals savagely with the counter and crashes the glass jars of sweets to one side.

"Lucky you," she says.

"It seems to have changed a lot. You notice things after that time." But what has he noticed? Bicycles, drays?

"I don't." She is grudging altogether. "Don't notice any change, I mean."

"You're young," he says. "Things happen so gradually you never see them when you're young." Except for young Jenner, he remembers. Always remembering young Jenner with terrible clarity. "Coming back after a long time makes you see, pulls the scales off your eyes." He is conscious that he is talking too much.

Young Jenner sits opposite him at the rocky table and says, "Sir, do something. Please. You'll have to do something."

22

"Of course I'll do something," he says and the girl pauses with her slop-rag and says, "What did you say?"

"Nothing," he says. "Nothing." Jenner fixes him with his terrible grey young eye and says, "You mustn't hedge. You're the only one."

"Me?" He flexes his useless arms, thin at sixty and not much better at forty. "Boy," he says, "I could never have crossed the Rubicon. Never blasted my way across the Alps given an ocean of vinegar. But you are right, of course. It's the mind that does the blasting. I must apologise, boy, for never being one of your muscle-bound footballers with their intemperate logic. I never matched up."

"You matched up," says young Jenner. "Please don't apologise."

"Would you like," the girl asks, "a couple of aspirin?"

"No," he says. "No. I—it's the heat, you know. Come from the south. Feelings run warm here." And he frightens her again, because she moves away a little distance before asking, "What are you up here for then?"

"It's Back to The Taws week," he says.

"Oh that!"

"Yes, that. We're infesting in droves, I suppose. Migratory slaters crept out from under our little rocks. Full of sentiment."

"Sentiment!" she scoffs. "Sentiment! Well, if that's how you feel . . . My mum and dad talk about it. They're part of it."

He looks up to smile his gentle gappy smile.

"There must be dozens of us."

"Oh, yes," she agrees, and is kindly for a while with the dish-rag. "Oh, yes. My family came up here fifteen years ago just after I was born. They didn't do much good, though. I feel there must be something better than this. They're hoping they'll see old friends. They had a lot they'd like to see again. Who went away, I mean."

"I didn't have many friends," he admits, horrifying her; and young Jenner says, "Rubbish! Sorry, sir."

"Not rubbish, young Jenner," he says. "Not friends who mattered."

"You'll make me ashamed of you," young Jenner says. "I thought you always said it was the saints who mattered."

"I must have been talking through my hat, boy. Wise after twenty years. It was the moneyed men who counted. The power stars. The rules makers. I had all the wrong friends."

Jenner blushes. He is still sixteen and cannot handle the unintentional insult.

23

"Yes," Mr Dorahy goes on. "All the wrong ones."

He pays for his tea and the girl watches him curiously as he sips.

The courtroom begins to shift its walls inward.

Do you ever, Mr Sheridan was pursuing with deadly interest, take any of the natives prisoner for no reason and without their consent? Would it be possible in a patch of scrub, perhaps?

No, to your first question, Lieutenant Buckmaster replied. I only act on instructions.

And the second question?

No. I don't think so. You might on a station. Have a chance, I mean.

Without shooting them?

I suppose so, Lieutenant Buckmaster said sulkily.

But you said previously that shooting was the only thing they understood?

I suppose so.

Mr Sheridan smiled. Is it not very difficult, almost impossible, for a white man to take a blackfellow?

I think it is very difficult, but on an open plain, say, you might run a blackfellow up a tree and you would soon get him then.

Mr Sheridan took off his glasses, polished them and put them on again.

I want to know whether you could take them alive.

Hardly, Lieutenant Buckmaster said before he could pause to think.

Oh, Mr Sheridan said. Indeed! And he glanced through his lenses sharply at this portly young man and hated him.

Outside the courthouse a child began to bounce a ball against the timber walls. Mr Sheridan frowned.

"Well, that's it then," Mr Dorahy says pushing his cup to one side. Nothing stands between him now and the hotel. He gives the girl another smile and this time is repaid. Taking up his bag, he goes back into the sunlight and turns automatically in the direction he must go.

Brutally the sun underscores his age and the hopelessness of this return. The shops still look like shanties, but some beneficent council has planted palms on centre islands in the main street that takes him seawards. And the sea still burns its blue acid.

Beside the hotel office there is a group of people waiting. Like the

24

remnants of some Eventide picnic, he thinks. There are faces he suspects knowing, pondering how "suspects" is the right word here. Semantic priss, he tells himself, examining cautiously the faces, the maps—boundaries changed, contours altered—of those near him. Gracie Tilburn had won first prize at the Liedertafel singing "O for the wings of a dove" which brought tears and the house down, and she is standing just ahead and to one side of him now with her blue bows and slender body vanished into rich fullness and plum silk. "How am I so sure?" he asks himself. There is an unforgettable mole that had once the magic of an Addison patch high on the left cheek bone. Nothing else is recognisable. Not to him. He hopes he is wrong, for there is still a splendour if only in his memory.

"Oh, Gracie, Gracie, Gracie," they had all warbled back at her afterwards, the choirs dispersed, the hall manager handing out weak lemon, the mothers sipping tea and crumbling biscuits.

GRACIE WAS a nice girl. She knew it. Everyone in town knew it. She had allowed only a remnant of her forces to be scattered by Freddie Buckmaster who would appear sometimes to walk her home after Sunday Bible hunts. That's what he called them, making her laugh her magnificent laugh so that her rather long nose quivered and her doric neck, which troubled Freddie deeply, would throb. He troubled her too, his loutishness, the very racketing quality of it coursing through her blood in a dangerous manner.

"And no boys, dear," her mother warned, along with a dozen other superstitious noli tangeres. "It will spoil your voice."

"Exactly what will spoil?" Gracie had inquired.

"I do not care to go into it," her mother said, but because she was superstitious felt obliged to add that, on the other hand, she had heard marriage enriched the voice, giving it darker tones.

"My voice!" Gracie admitted grudgingly, and already it was a burden. She suspected it was only a voice even though it was the best in those parts; and not until she had begun to soar her way through a jungle of butter-dish and cut-glass trophies was her assurance bolstered.

Watching young Jenner the evening of the grand eisteddfod observing her with his lucid and innocent intelligence from four rows back while she sang, ignoring the bloody pianist, some of the loutishness in her, to which without any doubt at all Fred Buckmaster's loutishness had responded, demanded more than that cool-eyed attention. For a while she returned his gaze, buffet for buffet it seemed, and felt her voice superbly detached, the head notes so effortless and purely accurate that she was conscious of some spiritual victory not only over him and all those others jammed in the hall, but also over the terrible brown and green distances eating away at the compass outside.

Afterwards she had managed to be near him in the fragmented crowd.

"That was beautiful," he said with such simplicity she could only believe him. She was surprised to feel ashamed.

"She could go far," some thin man's back was saying to her parents. Far? She had heard of cities. But she knew then he meant distances of the mind, long pilgrimages of the spirit.

"Isn't that your teacher?" she whispered to young Jenner.

"You know it is." Jenner was observing her with interest. "What do you pretend for?"

"I don't know," she admitted. "I do sometimes. Everything here seems so narrow. So small. It extends the limits." She grew muddled. "Truly, I don't know." But she did in fact. She was claiming seclusion as well, an untouched-by-the-world virginity she thought might appeal. Jenner was too young to accuse fishers of men though he came close to it. His features were assuming the carved-out look of adolescence.

"I'd like to go far," she said. "A long way from here." She kept smoothing the silk over her hips.

"He didn't mean that sort of far, really," young Jenner said. "You always take yourself." He was recalling something from his last Latin lesson and the vision of Mr Dorahy with only adumbrations of despair viewing the hideous ochre landscape beyond the schoolroom windows.

Her mother knew she had calved a winner. She was a pusher of whacking determination, prepared to ram citadels for those bell-like top A's.

"Freddie Buckmaster is nothing," she later warned. "Tim Jenner is nothing. There are other things for you." She sweated through committees until someone arranged a fund.

"I'll be leaving soon," Gracie announced to the rivals who were resenting their collision on her courting veranda.

"How soon is soon?" Freddie Buckmaster asked, being desperate to prove something to himself before she went. He scowled. It only accentuated his thickish brooding good looks.

Gracie said vaguely, "In a few months. January or February."

27

"That's too soon," Buckmaster said. He had never heard her voice even at its most exquisite.

"That's too soon," said young Jenner, who heard only her voice.

Like the blacks, she could sing off disaster for him. His mother played the piano for her on those evenings when the Tilburns visited and Gracie, carelessly posed against one side of the unbelievable French grand that had been lugged battering miles from the south, decorated the long timber living-room with sound. It made a kind of truce between them, young Jenner and Buckmaster. Her throat affected them both.

"I could swallow her whole," young Buckmaster admitted. "Keerist!"

"It's her voice I want to gulp," Jenner said.

When he told her that he scored a sort of victory. She rode over to his home more often, a lazy-daisied hat flapping upon her shoulders. They wandered through grass-drench to creek banks where they would sit idly watching tiddler stir or dragonflies hurtling across the surface. Rested her hand briefly in his.

Buckmaster sniffed them out sometimes, perched on his tall and spying chestnut. He had chucked school and had moved into the police where muscles and dad had won him preference. His horse could feel the irritation in his rider's flanks.

"You'd better be moving back," he would order, having no finesse. "We're on the track of the bunch that raided the mill. My boys are following a little way back." His buckle shone. His belt shone. Some official silver buttons shone. "Tirra lirra by the creek," young Jenner said, smiling.

"Now what the hell does that mean?" Buckmaster asked.

He was ripe for revenge.

He crept on young Jenner one evening of long lilacs and bronze as Jenner came from the School of Arts with a bundle of books. There was no provocation, no time for specious gallantry, just the old bunch of fives smashing the nose bridge, the baffled mouth, cracking the ear till it screamed with the noise of deafness. Jenner, his visions torn, felt only bones commenting on flesh and, dropping the books in the dust, fought back with every part of him until Buckmaster, thudding his whole bull weight into his stomach, dropped him to the ground. Then he kicked him, once, with perfect timing and direction, so that his whole body wound itself up like a watch spring.

Mr Dorahy, coming down a back lane in his sulky, found Jenner vomiting by the side of the stock-and-station agent's storehouse.

"You're entering the world of men," he said. "Christ was wasting his time. It would take a score of Gethsemanes."

He took him home and cleaned the muck from his face and later, seated on the little porch, they watched the flattened scrolls of landscape making proclamations until they were absorbed in a distant haze over which the moon rode clean and indifferent. Jenner kept repressing gouts of sobs which were shame rather than pain.

"Here's a man," Dorahy stated, "who might restore your faith."

A horse and buggy was clipping its way down the dirt road towards them, its driver a solid fellow and deliberate, a man from the back country who had once worked a barren and hopeless holding that he had tried to milk with half a dozen windmills. On the testimony of willow-twigs, he had believed implicitly in the presence of a great artesian source and had sunk his shafts with the same faith as a miner. In his half-finished shack he had waited the arrival of his girl. Drays drew north and then coaches and she had failed to step from either into the dream. It had been ten years and his letters did not tap her source either.

Now he had moved closer in, but his ill-luck followed. Ground he touched dried mysteriously. He had no luck with cattle, though he pumped from a creek, and his animals grew lean and ribby like the grass on which they fed. Yet he laughed from time to time, committed to help others who were luckier, begrudging them nothing he could give.

Taking tea now beside Dorahy and the boy, his chunky body was propped against the veranda steps. Moths were coming in, unsober with candle-light. Lunt lifted one delicately from his tea.

"And what were you doing in town?" Dorahy was asking.

"Just picking up a few things." Lunt drew deeply on his pipe. "A bit of tucker, some pipeline and a crank handle." But he seemed to have lost interest, even though hope still pummelled him.

He leant back to look at the boy. "How's your dad?" he asked. "He's been a great help to me over the years, did you know? Not that I like to lean. But you need a bit of a hand. That's when you sort 'em out."

"Sort what?"

29

"The real people. You see, I believed in that water. I believe in Eden. And I've tried to make one. But all the time I get the feeling the world's just a dream in God's eye."

What a hope, thought young Jenner, but he said wonderingly, "Maybe Eden's whatever you make. It's the trying."

Dorahy sighed. "Pliny had a heating system, you know, a water system, right through his farm home just a few decades or so after Christ. If he could do it then, why not you? Here. Now."

Jenner was moved by this idealism, but he could see it was mad impractical stuff. They couldn't put the water there.

"Did he now?" Lunt said with interest. "Yes. It was there all right. I only had to tap it. But it came in trickles like tears. It broke my heart when I knew there was enough of the stuff there to float a navy. A great inland sea of it. And now I'm not doing much better."

Even the landscape was isolate. Trees, floating moon.

"You should come by more often," Dorahy said, "and talk to me. God knows I need it. Is it very lonely out there? Any lonelier than here, I mean?"

"I still have mills," Lunt said simply, "sucking away at the creek. It's almost as useless as it was before, but each has a different voice and at night they yacker between themselves. Drive most people mad, I suppose, but they're good pals. They keep trying for me."

He pulled a bag out of his pocket and fished out a sandwich.

"You mind if I eat? Haven't had a bite since this morning. I'm giddy with the world."

"There's some soup going," Dorahy said. "I was just going to have some with Tim."

His kitchen lay at the back, a feverish little lean-to with a small wood stove backed up against a sheet of iron. Heat became personal here. There was a dresser with three cups, a few plates and half a dozen beautifully polished knives and forks that he kept in a box. The small sitting-room expressed its soul through a mass of books and candle-light.

Dorahy was ahead of them looking out the back door where he spoke to a darkness that moved.

"Who's there?" he inquired of a shifting twilight.

Standing by the water-tank, Kowaha showed up in the chiaroscuro of the oil-lamp, the pretty bluntness of her face shining in planes and

30

gentle arcs. She smiled merely and Dorahy, shoving his own face into lamp-light, asked, "Kowaha? What is it?"

Stuffed with shyness she could not speak. Stood staring up at him on the top of his steps, giggled a moment, staring at him and the two darker figures who had come in behind him. The solidity of them frightened her.

"You want tucker?" Dorahy asked then.

She shook her head and he was conscious that she was holding something.

"No tucker. Then what?"

She gestured with the bundle in her arms.

Swinging the lamp, he went down to the yard while the other two, breathing in dust and dark, stood waiting.

"What is it, Kowaha?" Dorahy asked, peering down at the coiled arms of her.

She held the bundle forward suddenly so that he could see the tiny child within, fuzzed and sleeping. She did nothing but smile, holding the child up for the three of them.

"Already?" Dorahy murmured. "Your baby already?" He had not seen her for several weeks.

She was pleased with herself.

Dorahy put out a careful finger to touch the sleeping face and breathed, "He's beautiful."

"Girl," she said. Laughing at his idiocy. "Girl."

"You've come for this?" he asked. He loved the world. "To show me your baby?"

"Show baby."

Lunt and young Jenner, male-abashed before the marvel of it, stood back in shadow.

"My friends," Dorahy said. "Tim and Charlie. But you know Mr Lunt, don't you?" She giggled at him again.

He was hesitating, searching for some commemorative thing that might be spelled out concretely.

"We must give your baby a present, eh? For luck. For lots and lots of it," he added, swinging round to the boy. "But I don't know what. I simply don't know what."

In the house Kowaha squatted on the floor above the child. It lay naked and kicking gently, frail, its skin a tender gold. Kowaha gurgled down at it.

31

"I have one thing," Dorahy mused, moving into the bedroom and shuffling through drawers. "Only one thing she might wear." He pulled out a little leather bag from which he drew a silver medal. "How about this, Kowaha?" And he handed her a small dulled disc with the arms of Trinity College, Dublin, insanely shimmering in the oil light.

"Classics," he said to young Jenner. "My final year it was. I knew there'd be a use for it."

Kowaha held the medal gingerly, lifting it up and smiling, then running her fingers over the embossing.

"For luck," Dorahy said. "It used to be my luck. In a way. I give it to you."

"Luck," she repeated.

He threaded it with a strip of leather thong. Then he bent down and placed the circlet over the baby's head.

"Little girl," he pronounced and he wasn't laughing about it. "Classical first."

M R SHERIDAN re-enters Dorahy's mind, which is boiling in this crowded hotel. He is sitting back as the others register. His gentleness is fraying.

Do you ever receive warrants against blackfellows guilty of offences? Sheridan asked.

Lieutenant Buckmaster shifted his weight from one foot to the other.

Very few. I have received two.

What do you do with them?

I try to execute the warrant and, if I am not able, I send it back again.

Where do you send it?

I send it back to the Inspector General of Police.

Would it not—Mr Sheridan's pencil began a slow tap—I repeat, would it not be much better that the warrants for this part of the country should remain in your possession so that you might be able to execute them as occasion offers?

I have got copies.

You have?

A copy is sufficient, Lieutenant Buckmaster replied sullenly.

Then, Mr Sheridan said leaning forward, do you know of a great many being in existence for various offenders? Copies, I mean, of course. What, if I may ask again, would you have?

Only two, Lieutenant Buckmaster said. The bouncing ball outside reached towards a window.

Sergeant, Mr Sheridan ordered, remove that child.

Two? he pursued. I thought perhaps there were three. What are the two you have, Lieutenant?

I know of one for Wilson. He paused.

Yes? said Mr Sheridan gently.

The bouncing stopped. Inside the court they could hear the gruffness of the sergeant. Mr Dorahy breathed ironically, Suffer, imperative, little children! It was all a question of a misplaced comma.

And one for Kuttabul Tommy.

For what?

Attempted rape.

And the third?

There was no third.

I think there was, Mr Sheridan suggested. You acted as if there was a third.

No, Lieutenant Buckmaster insisted.

Do you not know of one for Mr Lunt's blackfellows?

Mr Dorahy from the body of the court noted with interest Buckmaster ease his thick fingers about his collar.

There was no warrant.

But you acted as if there were one?

Perhaps.

For what? Mr Sheridan asked, softly, so that Dorahy in the thickening fetor of the little court had to strain to hear him.

The murder of a gin.

But, Mr Sheridan said irritably, the murder took place after you acted, not before. Is that not so?

I don't understand, Lieutenant Buckmaster said.

You will, Mr Sheridan assured him.

At this point the assistant magistrate intervened.

There was a coroner's report, he said. Was it that you heard of?

I'm not sure, Lieutenant Buckmaster replied sulkily.

Are you or have you been liable, Mr Sheridan went on, in the course of your patrol to meet any of Mr Lunt's blacks?

It is possible.

Of course they keep out of your way if they know you are after them; but if they came within your reach you might meet them?

There might be a chance—a very little chance.

34

But there was no actual warrant, was there? It had not been decided by whom this gin had been murdered?

Lieutenant Buckmaster declined to reply for a moment.

Mr Dorahy leant trembling against the hard arm of the wooden bench.

We will return to that, Mr Sheridan said. Tell me, he inquired, fixing his Bible-stained eyes on the sweating lieutenant, do these blacks not cross to the coast?

It is possible.

And make their way to the island?

It is possible.

I understood you to say earlier in your evidence that there had been one complaint by Mr Barnabas Sweetman and another from Mr John Watters with regard to depredations on their property?

Yes.

Then you were informed by Mr Sweetman what tribes had done these things?

Yes. He mentioned the tribe.

And are you going to tell us what tribe it was?

Lieutenant Buckmaster shifted his feet which felt larger than the world.

The Lindeman tribe.

Ah, said Mr Sheridan. And do you know, to change the subject a little, of other cases of rape besides that which you have mentioned? His interest was terrible to see.

Not exactly rape, Lieutenant Buckmaster replied. But assaults on little girls at Bingin and an attack on a woman at the Mulgrove station.

Their eyes met and held.

Do you think the crime of rape is common among the blacks? Is it on the increase among them?

It is on the increase as they become civilised.

As they become civilised? That is a strange answer, Lieutenant.

As they become civilised, the cases of rape become more frequent, Lieutenant Buckmaster repeated stubbornly.

You are suggesting that white customs lead to degradation in an observant other race?

I suppose so.

Mr Sheridan was feeling completely bemused. Idiotically he asked, Do you observe much mortality among the blacks?

35

Lieutenant Buckmaster blew his nose. There have been a number of cases since I came to the district.

Mr Dorahy began to laugh out loud. A great racking bawling sound escaped his throat.

Remove the witness, Mr Sheridan ordered without taking his eyes off Buckmaster.

S NOGGERS INTONED, interrupting some easy-chairmanship tralala at the end of the room, *Domine non sum dignus*, and there was an instant babble and quacking of agreement with him.

Bloody *thinks* himself, the chairman complained softly, unaware that Snoggers had publicly denied this. Order! he cried over his agenda sheet and unblotted papers. Order!

The council ripples petered out. The moment became a blemish.

Snoggers Boyd was the town's printer. He had found himself in this town more by accident than anything else, dedicated to bring out a struggling broadsheet weekly. Not one of the big men, but a necessary irritant. Not an active member of the Separation League, but a man who printed their agitations. He owned a pleasant home and a beautiful wife who had been in love, as far as he could judge such a private matter, for a few moments with old crumbling Lunt. During a crisis, his wife and Lunt had once held hands and at the moment, despite its brevity, Mr Boyd observed as well his wife's face full of unhappy movement. She had been nursing Lunt through a bout of pneumonia and the clasp of hands was permissible. She had never held his hand again, that he knew of, and he reverted to his cynical unwatchfulness.

"What we are here to decide," Mr Sweetman of the short dark curls and angelic playboy-manqué face said to his reordered henchmen, "is the punitive quality of our protests and the form they must take. Are we merely to restrain and hand over or are we to take action into our own hands?"

"Please!" he shouted above the dissonance then. "One at a time."

Mr Buckmaster rose. He had discovered the force of the eye which now he let move about the table, sifting the perhaps of those ten faces, each set in its own prejudice and bigotry. Man among men, he projected his strength into each watching face, even that of the town printer who had proclaimed his unworthiness. Bloody comic, thought Buckmaster. Aloud he said,

"This matter, gentlemen, is one that must hit deeply at the consciences of all of us." There were appreciating grunts. "A little girl—a baby, rather—removed from her mother's care"—he allowed a moist eye to rest for a moment on Benjy Wilson's face—"abandoned a week later in a state of filth and sick from lack of food. We are not interested in the whys of doing it. We are interested only in the fact that it was done. Fortunately she is all right now but that is not the main point, Mr Chairman. Not the main point at all. Are we to stand by while those things we cherish" (he thought briefly of son Fred and dismissed the thought) "are taken from us? And there is the matter of cattle, too. Part of our livelihood. The food for our children's mouths."

"Don't overdo it," said Snoggers, who hadn't learnt his lesson.

Swinging on him, Buckmaster cried, "By God you have a strange way of looking at things! We're here to determine fundamental attitudes."

Stubbornly Snoggers said, "I believe the blacks. They found Benjy Wilson's little girl about five miles from her home. They had no idea who it was. They did their best, damn it, to help and only left her out near Jenner's place when they found she wouldn't eat. Poor bastards," he said. "Give them credit. They tried."

Buckmaster was a bulging purple.

"We only have their word for that."

"And the Jenners'."

"Gentleman," Mr Sweetman interrupted, "it is the casualness of the whole affair. The irresponsibility. Are we to risk the continuance of this sort of thing? By our very softness allow it to get out of hand? This is"—he paused—"the thin edge of a very long wedge."

Snoggers's fat face swelled also. "They were being kind in their own way to that child," he repeated. "Kind. Are you going to take them to task for that?"

"There's the matter of six cows, some poultry and a horse," Buckmaster shouted. "My God! The horse alone demands reprisal!"

Snoggers said, "Count me out."

Buckmaster was still towering. This headless trunk of stone, the well-read Snoggers parodied to himself, stands in the desert. Jaysus!

"I move," Buckmaster continued, ignoring Snoggers as some kind of poltroon, "that we do not wait for a warrant from the south. It will take too long. I move that by next Monday at the latest we have prepared a punitive force, without sanction if you like—I repeat, without sanction—that will go straight to the scene of the trouble, sort out these blacks once and for all, taking whatever measures it thinks fit. Who's with me?"

Snoggers was almost trampled to death in the rush.

That's Lunt, dog-lonely after some brief supper of potatoes and beef boiled to rupture point over his vindictive stove. He's a front-step sitter and a reader of old papers that come by chance wrapped around his stores. He would be lonely but for his dog, the rusty strainings of his mills, and the hungry stirrings of his stringy cattle in the home paddock which translate him into a state of acquiescence. His lust for charity is eased by the gentle attentions he gives his animals, feeling guilt over his own supper when they low in hunger. He hand feeds them when he can afford it, waiting for the mills to tap their sources as he had waited for his girl. But that was another place, another time, and yet he seemed to bring ill-luck with him, for nothing thrives. All country has its black spots and he appears doomed to settle innocently on them.

But he read aloud to his dog and the great black shapes of the mill-monsters against the early evening. Vegetable prices in Brisbane are up. The recent drought has been responsible for over-priced greens in the Moreton Bay area. A terrible crime at Gatton. Women teachers seek equal salary rights. Man suicides from northern fishing-vessel, Gladstone, Thursday, a man whose identity is still unknown.

Like me, Lunt said, looking up from the month-old paper. He announced this to the dog and the nearest mill, which waved mechanically back in acknowledgment. My identity is still unknown.

He threw a stick for the dog who looked at it for a minute, wagged his gratitude, and remained by Lunt's feet watching it in case it moved again. Lunt clicked his fingers for him and lit his pipe, and that was how the sporting town councillors found him, grave with twilight amid the loneliness of sail-creak and grass-stir. The sky was one huge bruise of wider and darker air. Sitting there still, one arm dangling,

Lunt watched them through the home gate, their horses high-stepping through tussock. Then Mr Sweetman, who was leading, trotted smartly through the clearing and came up to sling his reins loosely over a veranda post. Buckmaster trotted after him and, totally at ease, the two of them made themselves at home on the veranda steps while Lunt expressed surprise or pleasure. The doubt was in him.

"It's a bit of a step up here, Charlie," Sweetman said. "You're pretty cut off."

"That's how I like it," Lunt said simply, straining at them with his tired eyes through thickening twilight.

His visitors' eyes were polished and active, saw night-fires a mile away by one of the water-holes, absorbed this and chewed at it while Lunt poked round his kitchen doing things with kettle and cups. These were firm on their saucers when he brought them out. His innocence was impregnable. He apologised once for not being much of a social cove and sat opposite them with his pipe going.

"You've got some company, I see," Sweetman observed, his eyes still on the patch of fire. "Down on the outer run."

"Just a few blacks down at one of the water-holes. Poor devils. You take sugar?"

Sweetman took sugar but his mind persisted sourly.

"You had them here before?"

"Sometimes. Off and on. They don't give any touble. Beg a bit of tucker now and then. I don't mind. Someone to share with."

Mr Sweetman shared Mr Buckmaster's eyes for a minute. Words were clogging their mouths and had to be spat out.

Finally Buckmaster said, "It's like this, Charlie. You can't be blamed. You don't know what's going on the way you're stuck out here, only coming into town for the odd day once a month, but these bastards have been behaving like animals. Beyond the law. Just like bloody animals."

Lunt decided not to enter a debate of such minimal invective. His eyes widened.

"Racing off with that kid, Benjy Wilson's little girl. Cropping off Ted Spiller's cattle. It's got to stop."

Sweetman kept making assenting sounds and movements that welded him, in a twinning of ideals, Lunt thought, to the other man. Lunt had slow eyes. A slow face. He looked up carefully over his tea.

"What actually happened to the child?" he asked slowly.

Buckmaster began an incoherent raving.

"Let's get this straight," Lunt suggested when the maniac paused. "The way I heard it in town, she was lost and they found her. Was she harmed in any way?"

This was not at all the way the conversation should be going. Buckmaster wanted unhinged loyalties.

"Half-starved, that's all!" he roared. "Isn't that enough?"

"No," Lunt decided after a long pause. "It's not enough. She wouldn't have eaten their sort of food. Perhaps that's why they were forced to steal."

"Oh, Jesus!" Buckmaster cried. "You'd excuse Judas."

"I might," Lunt agreed. "I might. Can I top up your cup?"

About them sudden dark. All the threatening black of the tenth station, a medieval obscurity for the town fathers who squatted like powers and principalities. Time for a Miltonic sweep of wings. Lunt watched them both with a half-smile they failed to decode and was conscious above their looming shoulders of restless light against the far sky.

"Polluted man," he said.

"I don't follow you," Sweetman said, "but I do know this. We want your help. You know these people. We're forming a party to round them up and move them out. If you'd join . . ." His voice held an especial note of pleading. "But we don't expect that. In respect to your niceties, that is. But you can help, you see, by saying nothing. Not preparing them."

"I won't do it," Lunt stated flatly. "These aren't the ones. You've got the wrong bunch altogether."

He was definite with his pipe. Refilled the kettle and stood it back on the stove, feeling the security of the banal matters of living crumble. Even the kettle rocked.

"We have proof," Buckmaster said through spittle.

"What proof?"

"Proof enough. I don't have to go into it, by God! They were seen."

"I see them also," the stubborn Lunt said. "I see them every now and then. If they'd had a child with them, a white child, in the last month, I'd have known."

"How?"

"By God, I don't have to go into it either! I simply know."

"Then you refuse?"

"Of course I refuse."

Sweetman tried placation. He said, "Think it over, old man. Don't make a sudden decision on a sentimental basis. We all do that."

Buckmaster, repressing, felt his face would split open.

"You're one of us," he was going on stupidly. "You have to see things like the rest of us."

"I don't think so." Lunt answered his kettle's summons. "I don't think so at all. I only have to see things the way I see them."

"Then you will warn them?"

"I'll do whatever I think proper."

"You'll regret this," Buckmaster threatened.

"No. You don't understand," Lunt said. "You never regret obeying conscience."

"Christ!" Buckmaster said. "You're mad. Mad mad mad."

In the heart of the next morning, under its early carnation sky, Lunt and his dog went round to the horse-yard. The mills were creaking, straining their guts to drag trickles of love from the red powdered earth. The land lay flat all round with its dusty scrubby shade trees making black dawn patches.

Lunt bent down and took a pinch of dust between his thumb and finger, sucked it and swallowed.

"Ah, you bitch country," he said. "I love you."

The dog trotted beside the horse across the mile stretch to the dried-out river where the camp lay. Lunt sang as he rocked in his saddle, out of tune and kindly towards sky: "This man comin', this man goin', earth stay flat and here. This man comin', that man goin', woman stay warm and here."

He laughed in his middle years at his craziness, and was still smiling when he rode into the camp and smelled the first of their fires. The dog shot away from him to bark at the blacks' dogs, circling them, then coming in for a snap and tussle. Three black men stood silent by the edge of the big water-hole watching him down the slope, watching his horse pick over the rock outcrop. The black faces shone as they saw him but it was only the sun striking up and over the coast range.

"Morning," Lunt said, and then greeted them in the few words he knew of their native dialect. They grinned at him and he rubbed his hands along his thighs, slid from the saddle and asked, "You fellers got tea?"

They nodded. Over their shoulders he could see two of the women squatting in front of the fire. A baby howled at their side. The morning was full of awakenings.

He dipped into their billy with his saddle mug, squatting also with the women who smiled and turned away. The men had not yet spoken, but he knew them both—old Bunyah and Kowaha's tribal husband, a splendid tall fellow called Koha.

He knew these things took time, so he sipped a little. The baby yowled again and was picked up to drag on a breast. Crooning sounds came over the fuzz of its skull. My God, he thought with reverence, they've grown from the earth. Straight from it.

Finally Lunt asked, "You have any trouble down here last night?" The tea left a bitter taste in his mouth. Or perhaps it was the dust still. His tongue felt troubled.

Bunyah came to squat beside him. He was fighting for the words. "Two feller. Horses. Dogs. Tell us move bloody quick time."

"We say," Koha added, "Mister Lunt leave us stay. He know us feller long time. Bin stay fish and things."

Lunt smiled. "They have a story," he said. "Think you took Benjy Wilson's little girl. Did you?"

"Gawd, no, boss!" Koha laughed. "Whaffor? One piccaninny here already."

"They mean business," Lunt said. "They're crazy men. They'll come again, with guns maybe, shoot you down, women and kids. What will you do, eh? What the hell will you do?"

Koha made a little dust-picture with his big toe.

"Can't move yet," he said. "Old man sick and still plenty fish this hole."

"But your women, your kids?" Lunt said. He felt hopeless.

"You help, boss?" Koha asked. He had his gods and was innocent about them.

All their faces were dark with waiting. Three other men had come up along the creek-bed. They had two more gins and a couple of half-grown children with them.

The carnation, meanwhile, had run out of the sky and the sun was up.

"Of course."

43

"What, boss?"

"Yes, I said, yes. I'm warning you now, aren't I?"

He felt desperate under the malice of the rising sun. One man, one rifle. They'd be back in the evening with guns and dogs. It would be a massacre.

"I think," he said slowly, "you ought to move back for a bit. Little way. Back towards the hills. There's more cover. By tonight, anyway. You can come back here when the chase is off." Koha was struggling with white-man talk.

"Move long time?" he asked hesitantly.

"No," Lunt said. "No. Move short time. Seven nights, maybe. But today. You can leave old Tiboobi with me. I'll look after him."

Koha stirred more dust with his reflective toe. He looked down at the patterns he was making.

Finally he said, "Gawd, boss, he no stay any time long you. He want come with us, his own people. He sicken more here."

"What's up with him?"

"He good-oh," Bunyah said. His age and dignity and curative powers were challenged. His old wrinkled skin shone brownly in the morning light.

Koha spoke rapidly to him in his own tongue, consonants straggly as eucalypts.

They're straight from the earth, Lunt thought once more, remembering how he had sucked that mother, tasting her on his tongue that very morning. For a flashing second another world was manifest, a lost and almost forgotten place of blue chairs and white mats and river-stirred curtains. Impossible. He wrenched himself away from the memory to follow the two men to a branch and bark humpy where Tiboobi hunched his illness under leaves.

The old man was gasping in his sleep and Lunt, bending over him, felt the roar of temperature from his body, heard the barriers within his lungs.

"He's got pneumonia," he said to the two black men with him. "You can't shift him. He'll die."

They stared blank.

"My God!" Lunt cried, raising his voice. "Devil disease. In here." He struck where he imagined his heart might be. He coughed for them. He gasped for air along with the man on the bed of leaves.

"Two days. Three. Unless I nurse him. Bring him up to the house."

They still stared. But Bunyah was beginning to frown.

"You heard me? You bright boy, Koha? You love this old man. You want him living long time?"

Koha nodded.

"You bring him to the house then, quick smart."

He backed out of the rough shelter which was made as much with love as with boughs and straightened up.

The old man groaned once more. "You bring him," he repeated, and did not look at the other two again.

It had taken him years to learn what the law had never learnt, that the best boomerang to use against them was the threat of silence.

Two of the younger men carried him there on a stretcher of stringy-bark. Half an hour had gone by before they capitulated to the threat of Lunt's sturdy back riding away without another word.

Lunt put the old man in his own bed, looking down at the black face against the torn white pillow. A bad anthropological joke. The tribesmen shuffled and were reluctant to go.

"Off now," Lunt commanded as gently as he could. "Off quick time. Look after your women."

Koha bent to lay his head against that of the sick man.

"I'll take care of him," Lunt reassured, "as if he were my own father."

Though there wasn't much he could do, he thought, as he watched the men, pigeon-toed and splay-footed, walk back through dust in the direction of the camp.

He sponged the old man down and rubbed in some chest embrocation he hadn't used for years. He fed him sips of cooled boiled water with aspirin mashed in it and sat by him and waited for the fever to go down.

At sundown the old man was worse, sitting up in the bed with his eyes turned in, the whites showing. Cries and moans of the fever-spirit were gabbled out, the congestion in his lungs thickening each sound. Lunt opened a tin of soup and heated it while the sick man babbled wildly. Having drunk it at a gulp he went back to fanning and sponging the dried skin and holding a blanket round the racked shoulders.

There were no smoke-lines by the river that evening, no cobber glow of fire. Somehow the camp had slipped away in the early darkness

45

and as the light turned blue and became star-scarred, he was glad that one thing at least had been secured, even as Tiboobi raved in the crisis.

Near ten he heard the horses go past. They were walking them, but he still heard the soft slurring of dust as they went round by the far paddock, the clink of a bridle, a snort from a horse. The dog stood braced by the veranda steps, his urge to bark stilled by his master's hand on his risen fur.

Not long, Lunt thought. Not long before they're back. He watched the hands on his alarm clock staggering round for ten mintues, fifteen, soothing the old man as he cried out, forcing more water between the thick lips. The frizz of Tiboobi's skull was grey. His heavily ridged hands clawed at blanket and tribe memories of the green coast.

Lunt was praying for him when the horses came back.

The men came in without ceremony, riding-boots heavy on the veranda boards.

Barney Sweetman's angel face loomed over Lunt where he sat beside the stretcher and five other faces glowed in the darkness beyond the lamp.

"You bastard," Sweetman said. "You rotten bastard."

Lunt said nothing. Buckmaster shoved through the door past a fringe of rifles.

"What's this then?" he demanded, staring at the old man on the stretcher. "What the bloody hell is this, eh?"

"Lower your voices," Lunt said quietly. "The old man's dying."

"By Jesus!" Buckmaster cried, whipping himself up for violence. "Then I'll help him on his way."

Suddenly and dreadfully he raised his rifle and blasted through the black man's chest.

Lunt sat there in the pathetic splatter of blood, still holding the old man's bony body against his. His hatred for the men in front of him filled the whole of his throat and banged in his skull.

"He would have died anyway," he said. "You swine."

He laid the body back on the bed. The stained sheets took on a brighter hue.

"Where are they?" Buckmaster asked. His mouth was still trickling the saliva of his excitement. He felt a tightening in his groin. He found himself levelling his rifle at Lunt who smiled now, and the smile was the thorn in the other man's skin.

46

"I have nothing to say," he said simply.

"You're the law!" screamed Buckmaster. "So you are the law! Where the bloody hell have they gone?"

"I'm not," Lunt said with finality, "saying a bloody word."

"Oh, Christ!" Buckmaster whimpered. "Do you want a massacre! Let's fix the bastard."

Sweetman uttered a Judas "Sorry, old man" and the rest of them seized him then. One of them went outside and brought in some saddle ropes and although Lunt fought them back a rifle butt knocked the sense out of him and they lashed him strongly with a lot of unnecessary rope to the dead man and then both of them to the bed. Face to face. Lunt lay with his lips shoved into flesh already cold.

DORAHY LIES on his narrow hotel bed and thinks of Charlie Lunt. Waiting round to register amid a bunch of old-timers in the lobby, he had stood apart from them when he could. Palsy-walsy, those others, clustering almost recognisable beside the pub's weary potted ferns with quick reminiscence, those tiny sparklers of recalled friendship cultivated for the seven-day stay with "We'll keep in touch" to keep them going.

How old would he be now? Dorahy wonders, remembering finding him, riding out there at the end of the week with the slaughters at Mandarana still a fresh stain. Afraid to enter because of the stench, and then seeing it, hearing the dead whimper as the dog snarled from the back of the room. A job more than he could stomach, but he had done it. Somehow. The ropes sunk deep in flesh by now, cut and falling away and Lunt dropping off the stretcher onto the floor with the terrible reek of his black companion stuck to his clothes and face.

Lugging him into the buggy, then, and saddling up, the dog as inert on the buggy floor as his master. Glancing back at the sunken face beside the dog's skeletal head and imagining—was it?—that once he heard the word "Thanks."

Young Jenner peers round the door of the bedroom, his face adolescent earnest, and says, "Sir, he's getting better. My mother says it's a miracle."

"Who did it, boy?" he asks.

"He won't say," young Jenner says. "Mr Buckmaster says it was the blacks did it."

"Desecrate their own?"

48

"He says it was a punishment for killing the old man."

"And what does Mr Lunt say?"

"He won't say anything."

"What a world!" Dorahy thinks. "What a world!"

He crosses to his window and looks out. Town looms out of rose. He marvels at the static quality of buildings he remembers, still there but nursing different memories for other eyes. He walks out to the veranda in front and looks down the road to see the school, extended and gardened, yet with a remembered window through which he had eased his mind while stumbling translation pocked the unreality of tropical summer. He can see the irony of it better now, the folly of discussing Hannibal's passage to power in this scraggy landscape that bore the frightful sores of its own history, scenes Suetonius would have regarded with horror—shattered black flesh, all the more horrible because of the country's negation—none of your soft olive groves and dove-blueness in the hills—heat, dust and the threat of scrub where trees grew like mutations.

Yet *Vivamus, mea Lesbia, atque amemus* put up alongside the scrabblings and the gropings, the arrowed hearts and linked initials behind the School of Arts, wasn't so different at that. Thinking of the slender boys bedewed with odours and remembering young Jenner in love with the slender ghost of the fat woman he had recognised in the lobby. Where, unable to rest, he feels that he must return. He unpacks his bag and hangs his other suit in the wardrobe. Womb-fluid is all nostalgia, he tells himself, walking back down the stairs, his puritan mouth keeled over towards disapproval.

At the foot of the stairs a man is waiting.

Dorahy looks uncertainly at a face whose features have been bashed by two decades of living since he last saw it. A name struggles to the surface and he knows who it is. There is nothing to this man now: a cipher once he had been washed up and let die.

"It is Tom Dorahy?" the lips ask.

"Yes."

"Remember me?"

"I'm terribly afraid . . ." He is battling to gain time. The lost shiftiness of the face disturbs him. He finds himself shrinking.

"Barney Sweetman," the old man says, confirming what Dorahy knows. "There isn't too much the same, but I'd know you."

Grudgingly Dorahy puts out a hand and has it pumped for a few seconds while Sweetman's down-and-out angel face crawls into his for deliverance.

"I remember," Dorahy says at last. "Things were different then. Are they any different now, I wonder?"

"A lot," the other says, and they both recall the high rock and the court and a certain hot noon. "Yes, a lot." Sweetman pushes his mouth into a smile. "I've cut right out of municipal politics altogether now. I'm still State member for this area. Gives me a wider interest. And there's no real retiring age, you know. A man has to do his work. You retire when the electors tell you and not a day before."

"And they haven't told you yet?"

"Still the same old Tom," Sweetman says, grinning. "You haven't changed, mate. No. They haven't sent me out yet."

"And Buckmaster?" Dorahy asks. "Buckmaster and his now middle-aged bull son?"

"Buckmaster's still here," he says. "But his boy pulled out of the police and runs a pub on the Palmer. A fine man he's turned out, so it happens."

"My God," Dorahy says. "My God!"

Sweetman places his arm around the thin shoulders for a moment. "You've come back, Tom," he says. "What's your reason then? You shouldn't have come back in a spirit of criticism. That's all over now. So long ago no one remembers."

"I remember."

"You won't forget, you mean. Are growing pains the only things you recall, eh?"

"Is that how you dismiss it? Growing pains!"

"Then why have you come back?"

"In the spirit of curiosity."

"I hope that's all," Sweetman says. "I've come along specially to meet you." ("Forestall," Dorahy thinks) "as part of the old place, to ask you round for a drink tonight before the official welcome next week. You'll be in that, won't you?"

Your lousy vote-catching manner, Dorahy thinks. "I'll be there," he says.

"Where's Charlie Lunt these days?" he asks.

Sweetman's face closes over. "Old Charlie," he muses. "Finally gave up that property of his. It was falling apart. He never did strike enough water."

"He lost heart?" Dorahy prompts.

"You could say that."

"He could have said more," Dorahy whispers. He feels very old suddenly. The girl behind the desk is watching them both. He is incapable of giving her a smile.

"Where is he then?" he persists.

"Somewhere up the coast," Sweetman answers at last. "A little mixed business. Better for him. Look after Mr Dorahy," he says swinging towards the girl behind the desk. Pulling rank. "He's one of our more important guests."

"Certainly, Sir Barnabas," she says. It sounds incredibly comic. She sighs too, Dorahy notices, and he thinks, "Ah by next election he'll know what it is to be told. He'll know all right."

"Have a bit of a kip, now, Tom." Sweetman uses a patting action on the other's shoulder. "You could do with a bit of a lie-down, eh? And we'll see you tonight about eight. We're still at the old place. Bit bigger, bit smarter, but much the same. You know me. Nothing grand."

Mr Dorahy has his lie-down.

How many men, Mr Sheridan asked Lieutenant Buckmaster, are there in your detachment?

Ten.

Ten official members?

The lieutenant squirmed. No.

Then how many?

Four official members only.

And were the men who accompanied you on this third expedition the same ones we were speaking of before, those same ten, official or not?

Lieutenant Buckmaster hesitated. Not all.

Who else, then, was with you on this expedition?

A few of the townsmen.

A few?

A few.

By what authority did they accompany you? I assumed they were armed.

I was sent for by Mr Romney.

Directly by Mr Romney?

Lieutenant Buckmaster shuffled something—his feet? his mind?

No, I acted on a letter received by one of the townsmen.

And who was that?

My father.

At the back of the court Mr Dorahy who had been readmitted to give evidence felt his lips in an unbearable twitch of a smile.

Mr Romney is a member of the Separation League, is he not? asked Mr Sheridan.

Yes.

Then he would know your father well—could be classed as a personal friend perhaps?

I suppose so.

What did you do, pursued Mr Sheridan, when you came to Romney's station?

I went first to the outlying properties and did not find any of the tribe there. Then I went towards the coast and followed it up to Tumbul. Finding no tracks there, I came back across the flats to Kuttabul where I discovered evidence that led us towards the Mandarana scrub. I found the blacks at the water-hole back from Mandarana.

What did you do then?

I dispersed them.

How did you know they were the blacks who had committed the thefts? Had you any direct evidence?

The boys at Mr Romney's told me these were the blacks. They said the tribe was in the habit of coming across their land to move south down the coast.

And that was the only evidence you had? Did you not, for example, recognise one of the gins who had been seen frequently about the town?

Come on, boy! Dorahy encouraged silently from the rear of the court.

The silence began to crackle.

Well, Lieutenant Buckmaster? Did you not recognise one of the gins?

The courtroom air was like a giant and fetid bubble of Freddie's blood.

No, he said.

For the moment, Mr Sheridan said, sipping at a glass of water beside him, let us leave that. Have you proper control over your troopers?

Yes.

But this group was not all native troopers?

No.

But you had proper control over the whole group?

Lieutenant Buckmaster began sweating again.

Well, Lieutenant Buckmaster? Had you control over the whole group?

53

I cannot really say.

Really *say*, Lieutenant? I put it to you that at one stage your troopers and the townsmen with you acted as separate entities.

That could be possible.

Had you given orders to the entire group?

Yes.

What was the nature of those orders?

I told them to go into the scrub and disperse the tribe.

Disperse? That is a strange word. What do you mean by dispersing?

Firing at them. I gave strict orders that no gins were to be touched.

And your orders were not obeyed?

To my knowledge they were.

But the group had split into two punitive forces, had it not?

Yes.

Then how would you know whether your orders were in fact obeyed?

Lieutenant Buckmaster offered silence.

Mr Sheridan's colour deepened. I must insist on an answer, Lieutenant Buckmaster, he said. If there are warrants issued then you are, I take it, acting correctly when you try to disperse or capture certain blacks. But in this case there was no warrant. I wish to know what induced you to give an order that could result in indiscriminate slaughter.

There was no—

Lieutenant Buckmaster, were your orders in fact obeyed?

I don't know.

I see. And do you think it proper to fire upon the blacks in this way in such circumstances?

They don't understand anything else.

How many bodies, Lieutenant Buckmaster, did you see when all—I repeat—all your forces rejoined?

I saw six.

Was there not a gin killed as well?

Dorahy leant forward against the rail in front of him, his face, his entire body, suffused with a kind of delighted anguish. He shouted, Yes yes yes yes yes, and for the second time that day Mr Sheridan had to ask for the witness to be removed.

*   *   *

54

Lunt lay on his bed listening to the dust settle. Or thought he could.

Not the same bed. He had burnt that, dragged it out into a rose of fire made by the first of the failed mills. Listening for the strain of rope and water being spewed up its pipes, he substituted the satiric fire instead, dragged on the putrid mattress where still he could see some of his own hairs and the old man's. Such a marriage. Consequently he uttered some sort of prayer during the sheet and the blanket. His girl had never. Not ever. He would have laughed if it hadn't seemed unkind at the best and blasphemous at the worst.

So he lay, returned and nursed back to some sort of health, for he had lost a leg, severed at a southern hospital, and he stumped round on his new wooden one. The only true separationist, he told himself, grimly smiling at the sick joke. Gangrene had got him, had entered silently a minor graze below the knee so that the old man's poison had done for it. So he lay, hearing the dust move, and knew that soon he would have to be about the simplicities of living—the horses, the dog, his few scraggy cattle whose rumps were leaner than his own. What day of the week it was he wondered, knowing he should have smelled out Saturday with his heart.

He put on his breakfast. The effort of it. Sat munching some bran mash in milk and sipping tea—the terrifying comforting monotony of it—and saw from the edge of his veranda, a long way off, a horseman who turned into Dorahy trotting across the outer paddock.

Dorahy was being rational and categoric that morning with the sun finally up and classes week-ended. He was full of dour logic.

"You must take action." He tapped the wooden leg. "The whole town is aware of who and when and why. Don't let it settle."

"There's no purpose," Lunt said, sad for the other bloke who was so righteous in his pettiness.

"There's every purpose. This stinking tiny town taking people by the nose and then ramming them in their own filth—or worse, the filth of others. By God!" he breathed.

"They've gone now," Lunt said. "My squatters. My dark campers."

"There was a massacre," Dorahy said, "the very next day while you were gasping it out. No one wanted to tell you." He couldn't resist ill-tidings for the life of him. "But there was a bloody massacre."

Here, Lunt recalled, was an explanation for averted eyes during his convalescence, the clipped-off utterance. Remembering the point of

55

light in a glass of water steady on a bedside table while truth somehow refracted around the steadiness of light. Lips became oblique as words.

But Dorahy was not oblique.

"Someone," he said, "Buckmaster, someone, lashed you to that bed leaving you to die."

"I'm unkillable." Lunt grinned for the folly of it while Dorahy stirred his tea angrily.

"The whole school is buzzing with it now that you've come back—like this." He gestured towards the wooden leg. "They're like blowflies buzzing over the dead meat of that week-end. The town. I'll stir things up, truly. There'll be a commission about this."

Lunt said, "That will only fatten their self-importance. They'll grow big with a commission. Let it rest."

"But it's not just you," Dorahy replied, wiping a trickle of tea from his long chin. "It's the old man as well. It's Kowaha. It's her husband. It's Kowaha's child."

"The child?"

"A miracle," Dorahy said. "I've been looking for one in this place. A blooming of Eden, as you say. They collected her, those vigilantes of justice. Some curiosity or oddity, they thought. The Boyds looked after her for a few weeks and now the Jenners have her. There's no one left, with the tribe scattered to buggery." The word sounded terrible on the teacher's tongue. He felt a vile taste and heard Buckmaster.

"I see," he remembered the other man saying, "the bloody kid came top in Latin! Some sort of prodigy, eh? You coach them younger and younger, Mr Dorahy?"

"She was more apt than the Lieutenant," he had countered.

Now he watched Lunt shift his good leg, rubbing at a stiff thigh.

"Please," he begged. "Please. Don't let them get away with it."

Lunt's clear blue eyes speculated on distance. The mills were unmoving, their arms dead wood. If only the water. It could be his salvation, that lost coolness.

"It could so easily have been us who did it," he said. "The luck of the draw. They carry their punishment inside. For ever."

"Ach!" Dorahy expostulated, mad with the need for retribution.

Young Jenner had fingered the silver medal on the baby's golden chest. It moved in tiny pulses. "She's a winner, sir," he had said. "You've given her your luck."

56

The timber house was full of heating air. Sun shafts became rapiers slashing the eastern rooms of the sagging building. Dorahy swung one like a cleaver. His arm parted motes.

"Whether you want or not," he cried, "there'll be an inquiry. Fred Buckmaster has to put in a report to fool justice. Oh, there'll be an inquiry all right and I'll speak if it's the last thing I do."

Yet at the time he gave only ironic yelps of laughter.

B ARNEY SWEETMAN'S house skulks behind a mess of
wattles.

Dorahy is unable to knock upon this door, for it lies open with a
frankness that is devastating. At the end of a lighted hall he can see
part of a big room filled with people and for a moment only is afraid
for himself and the folly of his tongue. His entry into light has the
manner of stage device, for the fifteen or so people who are there stop
talking as he stands hesitating before them all.

Sweetman swoops.

There is a glass in Dorahy's hand suddenly and he is sipping amid
cries of welcome that bring the bile acid to his mouth. He is clobbered
silly by their greetings as they all lie and tell him he's hardly changed.

"I'm much the same inside," he says awkwardly—but it is really a
threat—and this is a sardonic aid for those who talk only of externals.
Something makes him want to cackle at their absurdity, but he sips
again and the wine warms him. There'll be some kindness, he hopes.

"Part of the town," a fat man is saying about him with genuineness,
smiling. Where had he seen that smile? In what agonised situation
twenty years before?

"You remember the old Snoggers!" Sweetman cries, and Dorahy
is grateful to be helped, feels the trembling start in the hand that holds
the glass, and nods and says "Of course" as his eyes track beyond Mr
Boyd, town printer, to the bullishness of what can only be Buckmaster,
a ruined piece of flesh propped by the mantel.

"After all these years!" Buckmaster is crushing his hand. Dorahy
does not want to take communion but it is there, offered with fabled
obliviscence. "Why, it's like old times!"

58

All our eyes are smaller, Dorahy thinks. It reflects our nothingness. And he says, rather bitterly, "Not too much like old times, I hope," and watches for shadows.

"What's that suppose to imply, hey?" Buckmaster demands. But his smile is still in place. He is very lined and the wine that stained his cheeks once has now run its blemish all over his face.

"There were times," Dorahy says, resolving to be careful, "when we didn't see quite eye to eye."

"There were," Buckmaster agrees. "But that sort of thing isn't for an evening like this. Past is past, eh?"

Dorahy takes a larger sip at his drink and repressed anger. He wants to shout "Not ever" and whack the room apart with some claymore of accusation, but a certain smile on Boyd's face stops him. There will be other moments for that, the smile says, spelling out postponement—and he is puzzled.

"Where's Charlie Lunt these days?" he finally asks Buckmaster, to annoy him.

A knot seems to appear in the centre of Buckmaster's face.

"He moved up to the coast a bit," he replies. "Gave up his old holding."

"It would be pleasant to see him again," Dorahy says, remembering the room, the bed, the rope. "Is he well?"

Buckmaster shrugs and catches Sweetman's eye.

"He was invited," he lies. "He might turn up. Haven't seen him for years."

"But he should be here," Dorahy nags, forgetting his resolutions. He takes another gulp of his drink and feels a hugeness of just rage constrict his chest. "He's the most memorable part of the town."

"In what way?" Sweetman asks.

"A martyr. A saint."

"Oh, God, Tom!" Buckmaster says. "I thought you would be letting go by now."

"Saint Lunt," Dorahy intones, "appear and bless this meeting." His smile is lost in memories.

There are too many people in the room, even for its largeness. He is reintroduced to Romney and Armitage and Wilson and all the faces have a familiarity he is too tired to unmask, even that of Freddie Buckmaster who is lounging heavily against a window pane. He is confidently forty, now, and has a wife and two legal children.

59

Dorahy has another drink. And another. Mellowness or daring will set in. He corners Snoggers Boyd in an angle between living- and dining-room and asks again. "Where's Charlie Lunt?"

Boyd appears truly jovial, yet his mouth tightens and he says, "It wouldn't have done, I suppose, his coming."

"Why not, for Christ's sake?" Dorahy cries. "I'll fetch him. He can be fetched?"

Boyd sucks at his pipe, lips drawn back as he clenches his teeth.

"Come on now, Tom," he says.

"Is it possible?" Dorahy persists.

"It's possible he would be unwilling."

"Why?"

"Well, what good would it do? It's years too late."

"For justice to be done?"

Boyd frowns. "You're an impossible person," he says. "Lunt hasn't come near this place since he left. He obviously doesn't want to be reminded either. Who the hell do you think you are? Social conscience?"

"You're right, I suppose," Dorahy admits. "But I'd like to see him all the same. He was a truly good man."

"Let it rest a bit." Snoggers's eyes are sad. "If it's only seeing him you want, I might be able to arrange something. A run up the coast for you. I've been up there myself once or twice. How long are you here for?"

"Just the week."

"And why did you come?"

"You're the second person who has asked me that," Dorahy says. "Curiosity. That mainly. And a hope for delayed justice."

"That's the nub of it," Boyd says. "I feel as you do but I act differently. Have another drink."

He has another drink. And yet another. He allows his mouth to remain shut against anything bar social inanities, even to Fred, ex-lieutenant, who lounges across the room to examine him more closely. Buckmaster's soul grows bristles.

"You two yapping away here!" he accuses. "What is it? Conspiracy?"

Fred's crassness comes from the beer-pot belly-rumbles of secure middle age. He has a moustache horribly flecked with beer-scum. He grins at his former teacher and turns into a cartoon of himself.

"You haven't changed much," Dorahy says, referring to the soul.

60

"Nor you." It is as if young Buckmaster has caught on.

Boyd keeps smiling into his glass. He senses thunder on the left.

But someone in the room is calling for silence. Let's hear it for Sweetman who stands posed by a solid dresser holding out a toast glass like an Olympic runner's beacon. The conversation plays itself out in trickles.

"Old faces, old friends," Sweetman is throbbing as the party noises fade. "Welcome home. For it has been your home and will be as long as you remain." Cheers from some moron. "It is good to see so many of us reunited after all these years, though it is sad to remember those who cannot come. But here you are now seeing what the old town has turned into. Once, and you all remember that once, it was simply a village, a bit of a township. I mean no offence. But look around you over the next few days and you will see that what was once a township has turned into a thriving town of enormous economic importance for the southern States. Those of you who were with me in the Separation League know what this means. The implications."

He pauses to allow the implications to sink in. Boyd is again tempted to a liturgical *Domine non sum dignus,* but refrains and cocks a wink at Dorahy who is broodingly absorbed. He misses six platitudes and comes to to hear Sweetman, in a stage voice nicely broken between the kinetic properties of nostalgia and actual tears, talking about mutual love and respect, the necessity to pull together.

"Oh my God, the clichés," Snoggers whispers in an aside to Dorahy who frowns with his terrible righteousness and whispers "Twaddle!" back at him.

There are a few isolated bravos and an epidemic of clapping while Dorahy's hands remain firm around his glass. He is urged to shout down the fluff, the cobwebs of nonsense. It is not the time. He waits.

D ORAHY THAT Sunday was filled with Godtide. He had observed the vigilante grouping of the men as he rode through the township on his way to Jenner's. It was a horrible boil-up of masculinity, he thought, as he passed them by, resisting invitation with a cool wave and shake of the head. He sensed bloody trouble, the smell of it, all the way out of town.

Mr Jenner was hoeing vegetables in a patch at the rear of the house. The peace of it was almost comic. He was a tall man with a crop of receding red hair and a frightening calm. So slow appeared everything he touched one nearly missed the steady forwardness of it.

Dorahy said abruptly, "They're on their way. What can we do about it?"

Jenner put his hoe down carefully and straightened up amid the silver beet.

"Who?"

"The men of God. The town elders. They're out on a black hunt, as I predicted yesterday."

Jenner seemed to be staring into lost distances. "What do you want to do?" he asked at last.

Dorahy found his mouth full of angry saliva.

"Go after them. See that no harm is done."

Jenner sucked at this idea for a while. He could have bitten straight through to the centred seed but preferred rumination, if only for the look of the thing.

"Two of us only?"

"Your son, perhaps."

"Three! Two men and a boy! They'd laugh in our faces."

"Some protest must be made."

"It will do nothing."

Dorahy frowned. "It puts our case. I had thought Boyd—but he was with them."

Jenner smiled. "But so feebly," he said. He picked up the hoe and began walking back to the house. Dorahy followed. Day was beginning to blaze. In such sunlight, which could eat its way through sinew and bone towards the soul, both men felt exposed.

"Still," Jenner went on as they neared the back steps, "I do see your point. I'll come with you. The smallest protest force in history. My God! But we'll achieve nothing, you know."

Tim Jenner was painting railings. The wife and daughters were seated sewing on the long veranda. The contrast of it made Dorahy laugh sourly at the thought of that ten-strong band of yahoos bristling with guns.

He said, "It will express our point of view. Our conscience."

"They'll find us a joke," Jenner said.

"It will prick them."

"So?" Jenner said. "That isn't enough you know. Not nearly enough."

Dorahy said, "I'm wanting more than that, if it's possible."

"What, then?"

"I want them to know the town is divided. That other opinions have force and must be taken into account."

"What a hope!" Jenner said.

From the bottom of the veranda steps Dorahy smiled up at the three women on the veranda. Putting the case to them, he asked what they thought. He had never believed that to be female was to be incapable of judgment.

Young Jenner put down his paint brush and said, "May I come?"

"I should hope you would," his father replied.

"Then that's all there is to it," the boy said. He would lose his simplicity with time. His face shone. He believed Dorahy to be always infallible. "Are we taking guns?"

"No guns," his father said. "That's the whole point."

They rode out together, the three of them, trotting steadily north to Mandarana, aware both of folly and the older wisdom of justice.

The men were moving in a solid formation after the trees thinned out on the slopes west of the peak.

They were aware of, though at the moment they could not see, the dark shapes moving ahead of them towards the rock-crops and the scrub on the eastern face. Lieutenant Freddie Buckmaster, slicker than paint in a too-tight jacket with wicked silver buttons, pulled up his big bay and called a halt. Manoeuvres, he was explaining to them. Tactics.

There were ten men of God with him that sweating noon, well-mounted, well-set-up fellows, muscular as their horses and dangerous as their guns. Pillars of the town. Not even the flies troubled them as they sat loosely in their saddles, their thighs gripping lightly and easily at their edging mounts.

"We'll split into two groups," Lieutenant Buckmaster said. He was enthusiastic and sullenly young. "If Mr. Sweetman would take the northern side of the hill with four of you, the rest of us will go round by the south and pin them in." (After all, he hadn't read his Hannibal for nothing and momentarily, crazily, in the tea-tree scrub, Dorahy's face and sour snaggle-tooth smile blazed at him above a chalky desk.) "If they take to the slopes, as I think they will, we'll tether up and follow on foot. There's too much shale for the horses." His face was set in firm lines. "The dirty buggers," he said.

Trees were mnemonics for more and more trees.

In silent cheers and leaves the two parties cantered off, Buckmaster senior taking his burly form after Sweetman.

Sounds now of hoof-rattle and leather-squeak in a thickening air of tenseness and anger leaking out of their sweating flesh.

They had dogs with them, too, yelping and barking in a pack hunt as the leader scented and took off after the odour of black skin glimpsed briefly a hundred yards away.

On the eastern side of the mountain trees became denser than the logic of their movements.

"My God!" Roy Armitage panted, drawing in beside his leader, "this is too bloody thick. We'll have to leave the horses."

Young Buckmaster chewed on this advice for another hundred yards. His thighs took a bashing in the scrub.

"You're right," he admitted. A whip of tree cracked his face half open and there was blood apart from the pain. "Tell the rest."

They crowded each other in the one small space, clumping their horses together, and unslung their guns. Their irritated skins were demanding retribution.

64

Dismounted, they crackled through the trees on the lower slope that swept up to the beige and lilac shadows of the peak. Bracken dragged at their boots and argued with them. In the distance there was the sudden scream of a dog.

"There they go!" Benjy Wilson was yelling and pointing through thinner scrub at the rockier patches of the lower mountain where a score of clambering bodies glistening in light were scrambling fast and scattered up the steep slope. It was apparent from below that there was nowhere they could go but up.

Lieutenant Buckmaster paused, held up a masterly hand for attention, then tamped a leisurely pipe while his men fretted in check.

"The others will be here in a minute. The buggers can't get away now."

"I believe," Benjy Wilson volunteered eagerly—and there was saliva—"they've some sort of ritual ground up top. It flattens out near the summit. They'll head for that."

"Catching 'em at prayer, eh?" Buckmaster grinned and drew suckingly on his pipe. He was a lumpy lad with all the confidence of a very average intelligence. "Listen a minute. I think I can hear the other party."

The dogs were in first and then the men who held a confrontation under the disturbed trees, glancing up now and then at the distant diminishing figures still stolidly climbing up to the peak.

Snoggers Boyd, who had come, despite his protest, for a variety of subtle reasons the others did not know about, said over Buckmaster senior's shoulder, "Let the poor bastards be. We've given them a run for it."

"Are you mad?" Buckmaster questioned. "They've got to take a warning. They've got to be dispersed. We're going up that hill. Are all rifles ready?"

"Not mine," Boyd said.

"Jesus! Well, fix it."

"No." Boyd was mopping his fat sweating face.

"What?"

"God fuck Ireland," Boyd said simply. "I said, no. And no again. I've had enough."

"You'll do what you're bloody told."

Boyd smiled. His fat was of the genial kind, but his eyes were sharp. "I'm not going to watch you," he said flatly, "butcher those poor devils. I don't know why I came except to see fair play. And watch self-righteousness in action."

"Well, go to buggery!" Buckmaster roared.

"Thank you," Mr Boyd said, "I will"—turning his horse on the word to trot it away into the trees to the north.

"Oh, my God!" Buckmaster cried, appealing to Barney Sweetman. "Are we ready, then?"

The others were dismounted, their rifles cocked. Over all the faces was a sheen of appetite for something. They had a foxish look under the moving tree light.

"Fan out!" young Buckmaster cried. And the men worked themselves into a straggling line about the base to begin working their way up the slope, their feet constantly slipping and crunching on stone and gravel, their lumbering bodies bent forward with the effort of it, sixty degrees in spots once they had cleared the scrub; but their steady climb took them slowly upward towards the flattened altar of Mandarana.

Fred Buckmaster kept his glinting eyes on possibilities slipping brownly away at the crest, and once, stupidly, he aimed and fired at what he thought was a straggler while his impulse released something in all the men who began blasting away at tree and rock.

"Hold it!" canny Sweetman roared down the line. "Oh, hold it now!"

They crawled up another two hundred feet and it seemed they had the mountain to themselves under this hot sun. The light was dry and brilliant. Nothingness was scarred by crow-cry, distant and sad. Only rock, scrub and the long line of fox-faced men moving in towards a massacre. They were only ten yards apart now as the cone of the mountain narrowed and could hear one another's snorting breaths and the clink of boot on rock.

Just before the ground began to level out, there came a shower of spears and stones, a poor volley that would have had Mr Boyd in tears for the poverty of its protest. The men ducked, lay on the baking earth, and reloaded.

"Fire!" Freddie Buckmaster ordered his troops, and the useless shot whined up over the crest while the rattle of the rifles died away as they still lay there a minute before scrambling on.

When they came over the lip, the ground stretched flat for several hundred yards to end in a random-slung boulder heap guarding the

66

cliff edge on the western face. And nowhere was there any movement.

The men edged in towards one another, their eyes scanning the summit.

"They're in those rocks," Fred Buckmaster stated. He was categoric. "As sure as God made little apples. All we've got to do is flush them out."

They advanced slowly, still keeping to their line formation.

There were stupendous views out towards the sea behind them and in across the flats to far ranges. They ignored all these splendid airy spaces.

"Now!" Fred Buckmaster cried. And they broke into a run, whooping as they went towards a cleft in the boulders.

The world, the stupendous views, narrowed to a horror of shots and shouts and screams as they burst in upon the score of blacks herded into the inner circle of rocks. One spear caught Roy Armitage in the shoulder, but the others flew wide as the natives, awed by the bullet, became only a huddle of terrified flesh. They cringed against rocky shields. One old man made a break for the side of the rock circle, but Benjy Wilson brought him down with a bullet neatly placed in the centre of his spine. He lay moaning and twitching.

It was truly time to make arrests, but Buckmaster had lost control of his men who went forward and in, shooting steadily and reloading and shooting until the ground was littered with grunting men and there was blood-splash bright upon the rocks. Only five men confronted them now. The four or five women crouched wailing against the far barricade.

"Leave the gins!" Sweetman roared in a moment of sanity. "Leave them!"

There was a sudden silence and the five blacks still standing turned slow circles as they inspected the line of whites girdling the rocks. Words, at this point, failed. Freddie Buckmaster kept thinking, "Oh, my God! What now, what do I do now?" He really didn't know, having discovered blood and death. There was one gin he noticed, knew well by sight, having seen her on the outskirts of town. She was holding a baby closely against her breast and now and again it wailed.

"Make an arrest!" Barney Sweetman advised urgently. "For God's sake make an arrest!" He wanted things formalised. Already he interpreted the scene in terms of motions to be discussed and put, perhaps even as agenda.

Fred Buckmaster took a step forward. It was prize-giving day and the gauche fellow had never achieved such distinction before. His rifle was as limp as he. Some formal words seemed to be dripping from his mouth. The blacks moved back before him till they made a pitiful knot against his advance. He could see this pitifulness and the wretchedness of their defence so that some gland in him was disturbed to the point of his wanting to cry with shame.

And at that moment the gin whose face so moved him sprang with a tiny cry upon one of the rocks. Balanced there she looked in quick terror all about her and then, with no sound at all, hurled herself, still clutching the child, straight over the western scarp.

It was such a final gesture no one moved for a few seconds, numbed by the force of it. And then the white men rushed forward to peer down two hundred feet where they could see some shapeless lump lying still on the lower slope.

Only the crows kept going over with their lost cries. And the men, purged now and gazing emptily at the boulders and the dead, knew that no arrests would be made as the blacks, their faces drilled into nothing, stood motionless in this shock of tragedy.

Mr Boyd, rounding the base from the north and fighting clear of the straggly trees, saw a body hurtle from the cliff-top to the lower slope before the scarp. At first he thought it was some strange bird diving on prey, and he cantered his horse along easily to the spot where he discovered it was the prey itself he was looking at.

"My God," he breathed.

He dismounted and walked closer to bend over the crushed figure with its limbs stuck out at four grotesque angles. The skull had burst open and the rocks about were spattered with blood-flecked grey. And then, heaving at this, he saw the small body rolled to one side, howling at the end of a lifeless hand. His mind informed him it couldn't be as he bent over the unharmed child. Yet it was so. A miracle of salvation.

He picked it up and cradled it while it wailed thinly. It was naked save for a silver piece strung round its neck. The noon sun struck off the metal in small brilliant flashes and Boyd read Dorahy's name and puzzled. Puzzled for minutes, it seemed, when he became aware of figures at the top of the cliff looking down also and heard the rattle of hooves coming up behind him.

The three horsemen reined in. Dorahy's face was set in its usual sour and gentle lines, but there was an underlying tension of excitement. Jenner and his boy had an angry kind of bafflement about them.

They dismounted and joined him. Without words. The heat of the sun was full of speech. The baby wailed again as Dorahy came closer to examine the dead woman, the sadness of it, and then to look upward where the posse was outlined against searing cobalt.

Young Jenner, whose voice was choking, said something the others could not quite hear, but Dorahy spoke loudly for the boy and for all of them, his eyes fixed on the familiar and now disfigured body of the young woman.

"Lucretia," he said. "Lucretia lying naked."

BARNEY SWEETMAN is still the host of lush broad acres. He had owned most of the mill that crushed not only his cane crops but those of neighbouring farms. He had believed earnestly in Separation. He had implemented the policy of cheap black labour and in his minor hey-day had a barracks with thirty kanaka boys, the wide-veranda'd plantation house where he squired it around in white moleskins and blue oxford shirts. He had held many gracious drunken evenings on behalf of the Separation League for other planters in the district. Dorahy still recalls the night he had been invited for some crushing-season shenanigans, and on going to farewell his hosts had found the husband sprawled in the garden and the wife collapsed in the breeze-way. Tempted to recite a suitable fragment of Horace over their recumbent forms, he had been accosted by Snoggers Boyd who was still some drinks this side of sanity.

Dorahy has a sense of *déjà vu*. It is happening again as he edges towards the front door.

Snoggers says, "Not leaving are you? Don't leave. Spoil everything."

"I have to be sober to face tomorrow," Dorahy answers. At that other time he had added grimly, "I'm answerable to their sons."

Boyd had thought about this with some amusement patched at the corners of his mouth.

"But the parents aren't. To their sons, I mean. It's a strange world when outsiders have to set a better face on things." Now he says, "If you're leaving I can give you a lift."

"Well, perhaps," Dorahy says. "I wanted a chance to talk with you."

"Good," Boyd says. "I came with Buckmaster, but he seems to have passed out with jollity. Someone will get him home."

70

They look back in at the turmoil of upright but drink-flogged bodies. Buckmaster is snoring deeply from an easy chair.

"Yes," Boyd says sardonically. "Ah, yes."

They go back down the long hall and out onto the steps. The garden is sickly with frangipani and the overriding sweetness of cane. "In this small cloister," Dorahy wonders, "what vows are shattered daily?" And he asks abruptly, "Can you take me to Lunt?"

The crudity of the request startles Boyd.

"Well, now!" he says. There is a waiting pause. "When?"

"Tomorrow. At least as soon as possible. I have only the week."

"Why?"

"I think he should be here. For the official welcome."

"Why?"

"It pleases my sense of irony, I suppose. You think so, too."

"Do I? I don't know that I do. He'd probably refuse. It's twenty years, you know. Twenty."

They walk across to the side of the garden where Boyd's buggy is hitched to the fence. Despite the darkness, Boyd pauses before he puts one foot on the step and stares at the other man.

"Why won't you let go?" he asks.

"I can't," Dorahy says. "It's simply that I can't."

The ride back to the hotel is silent. But there is all the hushing surge of sea along the front. The streets, the disposition of them, haven't really changed; and consequently in the formless dark Dorahy feels tears prickling and taking shape behind his lids, so that when he gets out in front of the hotel with its sea-facing verandas and the long star-wash of the sky, he feels the merging of time then and time now.

"You don't really care for Lunt," Boyd accuses him over the hand-shake. "You're not a seeker after justice. You're just a trouble-maker." But he smiles.

"Perhaps you're right," Dorahy concedes. He feels unexpectedly humble. He is surprised into a silent admission of hatred greater than charity.

"You poor muddled bastard," Boyd says. "All right. I'll run you up there. My reasons are different. But I'll run you up. No persuasion though."

"What do you mean?"

"No trying to talk the old boy into coming if he doesn't want it. I'm very fond—or I used to be—of the old Charlie Lunt."

Dorahy leans against the buggy side a moment. He finds it hard to believe it has been so easy.

"Lunt's the only reason I came back," he says. And he is speaking the truth though it is a different truth for Boyd. "The only reason."

Boyd raises one hand before he takes the reins and shakes them. It is blessing and absolution in one.

O N THE veranda, post-breakfast, of the Sea Rip Hotel,
Gracie Tilburn, still with magnificent voice, is holding forth. She has gathered her band of acolytes from fried eggs and
bacon and a couple of anaemic cereals only. The veranda, open to
morning sun with its striped deck-chairs and rachitic tables, is boom-
ing with reminiscence and gossip. Gracie had married twice and on
neither occasion did her voice achieve the rich black quality she had
been told came with sexual fulfilment. Still, it is rich enough. Her
husbands' importance had petered away in direct ratio to her encores.
Manless, she realises how much she had needed each of them.

Her busy brown eyes take in the group: Benjy Wilson, widower;
old Miss Charlton who had run Sunday-school classes she had tried
to avoid—she is very old now and nods agreement to everything; Ted
Ellis and his wife, ex-groceries; Roy Armitage and Jack Romney, both
wifeless but still grubbing for money on a shared mixed dairy farm
down south. She smiles and it is radiant. The others could believe her
to be about to burst into song—which no one will prevent, at least
on the evening when the official speeches and welcomes have been
made.

There are other groups scattered in chairs along the veranda, but
they are younger or much older and have different references. Nostalgia has not united them all except in the accidents of greeting—
the casual wave, the nod, the cursory handshake.

"I'm cramming this in between engagements," Gracie is confessing,
"in Melbourne and Sydney. Simply squeezing it in. I very nearly
couldn't come."

They are all grateful. Some even say so. It wouldn't have been the same.

"But where *is* everybody?" she is asking the sea and the palms along the front. "Where's Tim Jenner? Where's Freddie Buckmaster?"

Her rhetoric does not really need an answer, but she gets it from Ted Ellis.

"They'll be in later," Ellis says. He thinks slowly, speaks slowly. "I've been back before. Seen them. The Jenners still have the same holding, only the boy does most of the work now. Not a boy. Middle-aged man. And Freddie Buckmaster is down from the Palmer."

Gracie Tilburn is all ears. "They were dear boys," she says graciously. "Dear, dear boys. I wonder will I know them?" To a chorus of assent, she sips her tea.

Dorahy is espied slipping by to have a walk along the front so that Gracie, who uses her tongue with the ease of a tapir, uncoils a sentence in his direction that sucks him back. Her face hasn't really begun to crumble yet and Dorahy, pulling up another chair, is wedged in between pure art and Old Testament.

"Isn't it wonderful, Mr Dorahy," old Miss Charlton croaks, "to be back?"

Dorahy would want to harp on his obsession, but their morning faces are too bland.

"As if we'd never been away," Benjy Wilson says. "The town's hardly altered except for the size. Shops in the same old places. Same people." He has another go at lighting his pipe.

"How's the family now?" Dorahy asks him, playing conventional visitors.

"Well, the kids are all grown up. Don't need me any more. They've moved out and away."

"What about that youngest girl of yours? The one who was lost that time. What's she doing?"

Benjy suspects no reference to the darkness of the past. "She's made me a grand-dad three times over. In Brissy now, happily married and all."

"That's good," Dorahy says musingly. He thinks of Kowaha. "That's good. I don't suppose . . . oh, nothing!" He cannot proceed with what chokes him.

"Suppose what?" Wilson is a big lumbering man, still primitive and slowly suspicious despite grandfatherdom. Or because of it.

74

"Nothing," Dorahy says. "I was just remembering."

A hundred feet away reef waters lick at the sand strip. The heat comes fiercely to life as the sun moves in square blocks along the hotel terrace, painting in yellow spaces the colonnades of wrought-iron stanchion. They are all seated in sun now. Nothing can be hidden.

Gracie Tilburn for one cannot hide. She presses Dorahy with questions. Has he heard from Tim Jenner in all these years?

A card or two. A longish letter one Christmas, so long ago now he forgets the substance.

He says, "Not really," and the sun clouts the side of his head for the lie.

Gracie is thinking at half her age level, smoothing the silk over fatter thighs, recalling lazy-daisied hats and the grass of a lost creek. Grief keeps pecking at her for the vanished past when even her voice had seemed purer. Sentimental, she senses tears washing behind her eyes and quickly sips more tea.

But Argus-eyed Dorahy has observed. He puts a hand over hers as she reaches out for the sugar.

He says, "It's the same for all of us you know. Just the same."

And then he remembers the swollen face of young Jenner entering the world of men, and the sun loses some of its sting. Dubiety about his role of avenging prophet nibbles, but there is not sufficient bite for him to alter his determination.

Ted Ellis, with unforced bonhomie, says, "Soon be time for that first drink of the day," and gets Romney and Armitage on side in a flash, rum being thicker than blood.

"Why don't I have that gift?" Dorahy asks himself. He has planned a solitary mooch along the front to bathe in a world of water and light. He is not and never will be a man among men, while Romney is saying meanwhile that it can never be too early and Armitage heads for the bar to fetch and carry.

He decides to drink with them, get on side. Buckmaster, he knows, would have no trouble achieving a nexus. "I must try to be," he decides, rejecting the idea even as he does so, "more like Buckmaster." But it is too late for his crabby morality, and when the rum comes he can only sip in silence.

Affronted, Miss Charlton recalls something she has to do in her room; Ted Ellis's wife does the same; but Gracie Tilburn, who is used to being a woman among men, stays put and orders a teeny piece of brandy.

"Not enough to ruin the voice," she explains, and her explanation is so coy Dorahy flinches.

He asks the others in a kind of cold rage, then, about Charlie Lunt. The other men make weak feints at vagueness and memory until Dorahy catches Romney grinning at Armitage, a rictus of prior and secret knowledge.

"He's doing all right," Romney says. "Very all right."

Romney is an ursine fellow, still tough at fifty, and nobody's subaltern. When Gracie asks what he means by "very" he gives another grin to his stooge and says it isn't for ladies.

"Are you a lady?" he asks insolently.

Gracie takes it well. Time has given her a wonderful callus. She says she hopes she is, but the insult has stopped her momentarily, for she takes refuge in brandy while her eyes beg Dorahy's like a dog.

"Will Mr Lunt be coming?" she asks them, ladylike.

"Now that," Romney says with a laugh, "I seriously doubt."

Dorahy loathes the manner of the man. "I intend doing something about that. He should be here. An integral part of the place."

"And what are you going to do?" Armitage challenges. He is a blond, devious man. "He wasn't invited."

A conspiracy, Dorahy thinks. He says, "As my guest. He can come as my guest."

"But he's close enough to have come back before this if he'd wanted to. He hasn't set foot in the town since the day he left."

"And when was that?"

"Close on eighteen years now. Just after you'd gone."

Only Lunt remembers the force of the wind that day, wind driving apocalyptically across his dusty paddocks for grass scourings. The sulky had groaned under his few belongings, for he had sold out at a pittance, hardly enough to buy the mixed business he took over. He said good-bye to no one except the Jenners and whipped his horse up for the trip north.

"Poor old devil!" Dorahy complains. "He was forced out. He had no option."

"Fair go!" Romney says, quietly warning. "You can leave us out of it."

But the other man pursues. "Were you not," he nags pedantically,

76

"part of the punitive force in those days, sidekicks to young Buck-master?"

"Where you should have been," Armitage answers flatly. "Christ! You're not going to muck-rake like this!" He slams his glass down in a mess of slop and spill. "We haven't come back to go chewing over the past."

"I thought that was why we had come."

"Witty bastard, eh?"

Gracie Tilburn is finally offended by this manifestation of maleness. She rises despite Dorahy's "Don't go."

The other three men are not even aware. Ted Ellis keeps grinning stupidly, but silk sweeps off and a lingering perfume plagues these perimeters of violence.

"We all have to dig dirt and eat dirt," Dorahy counters. He is sick at heart with their reactions but feels doomed to thrust and thrust at the matter even until someone might quieten him with a blow. "People should face up to what they have done. I only want repentance. For his sake. He was a good man."

Romney swallows the remainder of his drink in a huge gulp that hurts the muscles of his throat. Everything about him is powerful, even his steady and obtuse refusals that drive Dorahy into more prob-ing.

Dorahy keeps flicking the sore place until one of them tells him to shut up about Lunt and, manly, buys him a second pacifier rum. He drinks it gloomily, watching the few foolish swimmers who have appeared on the beach.

DORAHY IS fretting along the water-front on the second day, trying out the equation between blue water and blue air while he waits for Boyd. Words plague his mind. It is all words in angry buzzing debate, the most boneless of arguments, that sees no end of relief. He is sick with them, maddened by the circularity of theme that leaves him standing where he had begun. And it is on this point of noon hopelessness that Boyd's clopping buggy noses him out as he shelters below a tattered palm.

"Against my better judgment," Boyd says, leaning over the side. "Get in."

They sit in silence for a few moments while the horse snorts at flies. Dorahy removes his panama and flicks back the wet hair.

"I was despairing," he offers.

"A man must be mad," Boyd agrees. "But I'm keeping my word. My half-promise, that is."

Dorahy regards the sweating horse wonderingly.

"How far, then, is it?"

"Not far. About thirty. If we take it easy we'll make it by tea-time. She's pretty fresh."

"So he's as close as that! Well!" It is anti-climactic after all.

"Close enough for what you're trying to do," Boyd says. "But we'll have to stop the night to rest the horse. It could be quite pleasant— little fishing village north-east of The Leap." He looks hard at Dorahy. "You're sure you still want to go? You know what you're doing?"

"Quite sure." He looks at Boyd in return. Perhaps the maggot will stop gnawing when . . . "It's very good of you," he says.

"It is," Boyd agrees. "Something tells me it is the wrong thing."

78

He gives the reins a shake and the buggy pulls out smartly on the dirt road.

Jogging between the cane-field hedges from which heat and sweetness pour out, Dorahy confronts his demon with the pacifics of landscape, absorbing the scattered farmhouses, the kids waving from fence perches. He refuses to see himself as a trouble-maker. Wasn't that what Boyd had suggested? Already, in his dedication to seek reprisal or justice, he has involved himself so thoroughly in the politics of this small town it could be as if he had never left. When the cane-fields give out to the scrubbier landscape that looks as if it has only been pencilled in, the satisfaction of alienation comes back to him.

"This is good of you," Dorahy says once more, glancing at Boyd's stubby profile.

"We've agreed on that. But I'm still not sure why I—or even you, for that matter—am doing it."

"You're doing it for the same reason as me, I suppose. Or rather, I suspect."

"We'll see," Boyd answers.

He has slowed the horse down to a walk. The flies keep pestering beneath the brims of their hats. Dust puffs and filters and becomes a small cloud behind them. The last farmhouse has been left behind and the loneliness of trees reaches in to them on the narrow road. In the sultry air Dorahy finds himself nodding. Once or twice he jerks awake when Boyd flicks the horse into a trot and is aware of the other man sucking stolidly at his pipe, his face set like a compass needle on the twisting road ahead.

An hour trudges by. Mandarana looms up, its great hulk black on their right. Both men look and then ignore. Their thoughts are twinned for the moment and they each see the Sunday landscape, the body, the men on the peak.

"It's just past here, the turn-off," Boyd says. "There's a bit of a creek in a mile or so. I think we'll stop a while and give the old girl a breather. The road gets pretty rough after this. It's not much more than a track."

Boyd is strangely regretful now he has come so far, and he takes his eyes off the rutty road for a minute to inspect the map of Dorahy's face. The sour gentleness is implacable. "God help him," he prays humorously to himself. "He's obsessed and I am yielding to his vice." He guides the horse steadily and pessimistically on, but she is more skilled than he and picks her own way delicately between pot-holes. The road gives its own mandates.

On a grassy spit of the creek Boyd unharnesses the horse, hobbles her, and lets her crop the feed along the bank. The two men stretch out beneath a tree, smoking quietly, trying out their obsessions in silence. Above, the sky has become sulky with a huge boil-up of cloud from the sea, heavy cumulus dark with rain on its underside. Even in the hollow they are aware of a freshening in the air as small pre-storm winds rattle the trees.

"I'll make a cuppa," Boyd says. He fetches a billy and tea from the back of the buggy and in a few minutes has a small fire blazing between rocks by the water.

"How far now?" Dorahy asks. He is beginning to feel the mendicant.

"About the same distance again," Boyd says. He hands Dorahy a tin mug, fills his own from the billy, and sips, speculating on obsession and the places it takes one. "There are a couple of big cane farms out this way, two of the biggest in the district. I suppose old Charlie makes out with that and the few old fisherboys who live in his village. He never wanted much. Just to be let alone, I think."

"And I'm not doing that!" Dorahy sounds resentful.

"You said it," Boyd answers with a laugh. "I'm merely the guide."

Warm rain-splash falls on them suddenly. The fire hisses between the rocks.

"That's it!" Boyd says, looking up at the sky. "I'd better harness up or we'll get soaked."

Carefully he douses the fire with sand and, genial about Dorahy's uselessness, hitches his horse back between the shafts, and guides the buggy up the slope onto the track.

"Old girl!" he exclaims in sudden affection, slapping her fat rump, and momentarily preferring her to his bedevilled passenger. He hauls up the buggy hood and takes his seat, still clutching his unfinished mug of tea. Dorahy climbs in beside him, and the rain, bursting above them, drums hard on the canvas and bounces off the buggy steps.

"Shall we sit it out or go?" Boyd asks.

"Go," Dorahy replies. He is alive with fever, a spiritual temperature that flushes only the soul. He could be shaking, but he ignores this, setting his eyes on the last leg of the journey like a frantic pilgrim.

The horse is frisky after her rest, but the track, cutting through

80

mountain country to the sea, argues every foot of the way. It is not until they have come through the worst of it and the ruts widen into a dusty road leading to the east that the horse can sharpen into a trot, bowling them briskly into ploughed country black under the rain. Sheds stand on sky-lines. Three paddocks away a shuttered farmhouse turns its back. Three more hills and they can glimpse the sea below and to the north and east of them. Dorahy shifts restlessly on his seat. But it is another half-hour before the buggy rolls onto the wide sea-gazing clearing with its half-dozen shacks and the shanty of a store they have come to find.

In the easing rain, Boyd hitches his horse to the storepost and waits for Dorahy, who is sensing the full purpose of the journey at this moment, not merely the country ride they have come, and now the grey spread of sea. Boyd leads the way into the store, brushing heavily against the sacking drape that is hauled roughly to one side, and, in that inner twilight against which they can hear the steady comment of reef waters, rings a small handbell on the counter.

From the back of the shop there is a sound—cough? cry?—and someone is heard walking through.

Dorahy has his mouth ready to smile—the crisis of the dream—but it is a young woman who appears, a full-blood with crisp hair and a deeply pigmented skin. She looks at the two men standing there in front of the tinned goods, the grocery packets, puzzles for a moment, and then smiles at Boyd.

"Remember me, Mary?" he asks. "Willie Boyd. How are you?" Amusedly he catches onto Dorahy's surprised eyes. "This is Kowaha's little girl," he explains. "Grown up."

In this lost settlement washed up by the sea, the introductions are a banal joke.

"This is Mr Dorahy who knew you years ago."

But Dorahy is back at Mandarana's foot gazing down at the shattered body, the outrage of it, the baby in Boyd's arms. Something like tears is threatening. He cannot speak, only smile and stiffly take her hand into his. Shyly she draws back.

"Charlie around?" Boyd asks. "Tell him there's a couple of friends."

She smiles again, turning to go softly through the rear door of the shop and into the house. Within the minute they can hear his clumping irregular footsteps coming through.

Lunt has grown older. The seams on his face match those in Dorahy's soul as he takes Lunt's hand. Boyd watches them both curiously and sighs for the matter of it. But Lunt is full of astonishment.

"The surprise of it!" he keeps saying. "What a day! The surprise of it!" He is all smiles. "Come through," he invites them, opening the flap in the counter for them. "Come through."

His parlour is tiny. There are two chairs, a small table and some books. The room is jammed already. A small window looks out on a shaggy yard with a lemon-tree. "If this is the last-post nest," Dorahy thinks with pity—which is misplaced—"then the man is caged."

He wants to open something to let him out and it seems a pedantic shame merely to be going through how-are-you motions when inside him there is a voice shouting, "Remember when—?"

Lunt is slower, too; yet there is a deliberateness about him signalled by his face that has been hewn into a mask of forgiveness and tolerance despite those small lines of withdrawal. He says, Yes he had heard of the Back to The Taws week, and No he had not received any letter or invitation. Which amuses him. He supposes he could have gone up had he wanted. He laughs creakingly and listens with a smile to the simplicity of Dorahy's invitation while Boyd frowns with annoyance.

"Well, I was waiting to be asked," he admits. "But you don't want me back to please me," he accuses shrewdly. "Only to please yourself."

Boyd has to laugh with relief. "That's exactly what I say, Charlie. Don't listen to him."

Dorahy feels ashamed. But it is a temporary shame. He is mounted and away.

"It's justice I want done."

"You want exposure," Lunt says bluntly. "Fancy, after all this time!" He marvels at it. "I've grown like an oyster onto this bit of reef," he says, and looks past them at the backyard, needing no other solace. "Still," he adds, "it's nice to be asked—even for the wrong reasons. Very nice. I thought I'd been forgotten."

"Not that," says Boyd, who is guilty of neglect.

"That young woman," Lunt says looking at Dorahy. "Mary. Boyd's probably told you she's Kowaha's child. It's a long story. I won't bother you with it. But she came to me quite voluntarily about six years ago and asked if she could look after me. The Jenners had her till then. But I suppose you know all this. What I wanted to tell

82

you"—he smiles at the memory—"she still has that medal you gave her. Dorahy's luck. Remember?"

Dorahy remembers. He can only nod.

"No," Lunt goes on. "No. Not what you're thinking. She helps in the shop and cooks for me, but that's all. She has a husband now. Works on the cane." He thinks of the girl, years ago, who had never, not ever—and his face saddens.

Dorahy is silent. Something tells him he will win by waiting.

"Look," Lunt says and he chuckles, "I might come if I could bring her, too. That would make them sit up."

"They'd use her to rip you apart," Boyd warns. "They'd say you're a gin lover and grind your face in it."

"It has been ground before," Lunt says simply.

"Think about it," Dorahy pleads, sensing a weakening.

Lunt only smiles. "You two," he says, "you're not going back to-night. We'll have a yarn, eh? I can make you shakedowns on the veranda and we'll have a bite to eat. It's been a long time."

Boyd grimaces as if the pain has been transferred to him.

"We'd love to stay," he says. "Ignore this mad bastard who has his axe to grind. We've come to see you."

Lunt looks thoughtful. "It's nice to have been asked, anyway," he repeats. "Oh, I wouldn't be coming to please Tom. Just myself. Maybe a change away from here would do me good. I've only been away once in the last eighteen years. A man rots a bit."

Dorahy decides to press home. "Then you may come?" He is greedy as a child.

"Oh, my God, Tom," Boyd groans. "Leave it."

"We'll see," Lunt says. "I'll sleep on it."

Boyd sighs and shrugs. Is there some especial charisma in Dorahy, some magnetic tug that draws others like filings? Why, there's enough of the irritant in the fellow, he knows, to alienate people by scores. He understands this and yet still sees himself the willing courier drawn by some particular ascetic quality in the man. Fanaticism always has its disciples, he thinks bitterly. But why me?

THE SCHOOL OF ARTS is jammed with protestations of loyalty.

Someone has tacked bunting round the stage where a table and chairs have been set up for the welcoming committee. The whole room has a faded and worn-out look, but no one's complaining.

There are three hours yet before the committee begins its self-adulatory session of whoopee.

And perhaps three hours are enough for Buckmaster, who has heard of Dorahy's proposal to bring Lunt up for the opening hoo-ha. He rages inwardly and silently, a rage all the worse for its containment, and goes to Sweetman's house where he will renew his anger.

Sweetman's calm refuels Buckmaster.

"It won't matter," he says. "There's nothing now that can be done. They can stir up the past a little, I suppose, but everyone here will be beyond it. We're beyond it."

They are pacing about the front garden, monks of misrule, amid the sterile ambience of scentless gorgeous tropicana. The sky is crazy with stars.

"He must be stopped," mad Buckmaster says. "When are they due back?"

"Benjy Wilson says they set off up the coast some time yesterday. They should be back soon—if they're coming."

"Then we'll have to intercept them."

Sweetman snaps off an allamanda bloom and examines it so minutely he might be seeking his salvation in the flower's golden centre. Buckmaster's clenched fists whiten with the effort not to dash it from him—salvation and flower.

"My boy says to count him in," he continues. "He's willing to do something."

"What?"

Buckmaster lets the question pass. He'd let a lot of questions pass in his day, politically practising.

"Can I count on you?" he asks suddenly.

Sweetman worries this one. "To do anything now," he says, "might be a lot worse than simply letting him come, celebrate, if that's what he's here for, and go away again. In any case he might have refused. Tom Dorahy can't force him to come."

"But it's not Lunt I'm worried about," Buckmaster says. "It's that bloody schoolteacher. He always was a great nose-shover into other people's affairs."

"A stinking, righteous man," Sweetman says with a smile. "You hate them, don't you? Well, maybe Boyd's horse will lame or an axle break. Then your problem will be solved. But count me out of your plans. Do what you like. Only be warned, Jim, don't mess up things for the rest of us."

Yet Boyd's buggy is immune to bone-pointing. It comes back into town an hour after sunset and in the deeper dark takes Dorahy and Lunt home to Boyd's. And it is then, as they drag cramped limbs down and move into the shadow of trees, that Dorahy receives the first shattering blow and Lunt the second.

There is nothing Boyd can do: there is only the sound of the attackers' horses cantering away. He shouts for his wife and proceeds to lug Dorahy over to the steps. Then his wife appears and bends over Lunt, who has managed to sit up. Her stooped figure contains elements of tribal lament.

Dorahy comes to slowly. His head is an enormous throbbing pain which he holds in both hands.

"Well," Boyd says, unable to keep the satisfaction of being right from his voice, "that's the first of it. Don't say you weren't warned. A taste of stay-off, I wouldn't be surprised. Do you still want to go to the welcome-in?"

Boyd's wife has come down into the dewy garden with a bowl of water and bits of rag with which she is making wet plasters. She moves from Lunt to Dorahy, bathing and murmuring. At fifty the beauty of her bones is even more apparent, and the tenderness she has always

85

felt for Lunt springs like an act of contrition in the movements of tending. She recalls him as he was twenty years ago and is surprised how the moral rigidities of that time have moulded themselves into deeper statements.

"Of course they will be going," she says. "Especially because of this."

Seated in their living-room, the whirring in the skull subsiding: "Dearest Lucy," Dorahy muses, "have I ever argued with you yet?"

He watches her setting the table, serving dinner, and he absorbs the gentleness of her hands. He knows why he had never married before, that other time, and seeing her now reaffirms his reasons. The fire within her is rarely suspected by those who see only the skin of another, but Dorahy had years ago caught glimpses of flame that alone served to underscore her perfection for him.

"We'll be going," he says. "The four of us."

Boyd winces.

"What sort of confrontation are you after?" he demands. "Words or silence? Violence, is it? Something of what they have just done to you? Will you make a public accusation? It would harm you more, and you know it. Their tricky lawyers would see to that."

"I'm going to blast a way through the Alps with vinegar," he says. And then he laughs.

The protective warmth of the Boyds has an amniotic quality. Pain subsides. His soul is more swollen than the tenderness above his right eye; and amazement that the same bullish tactics are in vogue over-whelms him.

He eases himself upright on the sofa and, leaning over towards Lunt, says, "I brought this on you. I'm sorry." He is a man who finds it difficult to apologise. Squirming a way out, he berates himself, with the moist eye, the propitiatory throb in the voice! The insincerity of it! He cannot tolerate this self-revulsion, though it is a thing he feels more often as he grows older.

Lunt says, "I won't be turned into a martyr against my will. But the bastards have roused me this time. I'll go into that pompous ballyhoo with this whacking great headache and show I won't be forced out."

Boyd is pouring rums and there is immediate solace.

"This will cut through more than the Alps," he says.

86

And he is right, after all, Dorahy recognises, as the bite of it melts the inner rage.

Snoggers Boyd, entering into the spirit of it at last, has pinned sarcastic pieces of bunting, tie-shaped, to their collars. Lunt enjoys, but Dorahy merely tolerates. They make a pretty picture, he thinks, posed here preparatory to entering the old School of Arts from whose pediment sad streamers hang in reply.

People are moving up from either side, blocking the stairs as they revive memories in passageways too narrow for them or their inflated nostalgia. One quick glance and there, just inside the doorway, is Buckmaster shaking hands with visitors in an air loud with greetings and cries of recognition. The hall is too voluble.

While they pause before the crowd, a red-haired fellow with a wide smile comes up to Dorahy.

"How are you, sir?" he asks slipping automatically into the language pattern of his school days, and equally familiarly Dorahy slips back twenty years and says, "Well, thank you, young Jenner." They both laugh.

Time, thinks Dorahy, time! How it has gouged out the tenderness of youth, though there is still much that is innocent about the youngish man before him—the steadiness of eye, the firmness of mouth.

"I've come," Tim Jenner confesses, "to pave the way through Scylla and Charybdis. Barney Sweetman's up there, too. The wandering rocks. I'll release my father and we'll sail through in his wake."

Dorahy notices then the elderly man behind him. For the first flashing second he does not think "There go I" but "How he has aged!" Then he realises he is looking at a twin scarring of time. The paint has run on the masks, trickles that make the facsimile sour or disillusioned. Old Jenner looks frail now, but then so does Dorahy.

"Good to see you, Tom," old Jenner says. "And you, Charlie. What a marvellous surprise!" He takes both of Lunt's hands and holds them warmly. "Wonderful to have you here with us—for whatever we're celebrating. Maybe because we are at last a fading point on the map."

He is partly right, for the town has steadily drained out its people for ten years since the boom. There is no talk of Separation Leagues now, though this evening has brought about a quorum. Dorahy's head still throbs and he is giddy with yap and lights. He notices Lunt pass his hand wearily across his eyes and asks how he feels.

"Pretty terrible," Lunt replies. "I'm beginning to feel sorry I came. There seems to be some sort of brigade at the top of the stairs, too. Do you think they'll let us in?"

"We'll see," Dorahy says. "We'll see. I wish I wasn't feeling so foul."

Their party moves towards the congestion at the foot of the stairs where Gracie Tilburn is holding preliminary court. Momentarily Dorahy closes his eyes, reasoning falsely that she won't see him. He hopes blindness makes him invisible for the pounce, which comes, on the moment, with a richly pitched cry. She demands his recognition but her eyes are on Tim Jenner whose hands she seizes with palpable ardour. She is magnificent in puce, through the pink waves of which young Jenner is struggling towards a dream of pallid blue and lazy daisies. He cannot accept her at once, though her hands are demanding on his own.

He says, "Why, Gracie! Gracie!" but his voice is limp.

"When I sing," Gracie tells herself, "oh, when I sing it will be different."

She is not so unsubtle that she cannot notice his hesitancy; but bravely the slim girl, who is still present inside this plump woman, greets Boyd's little group with kisses all round, cheek after cheek. The grand gesture. "There," she reasons crazily, "I have put my mark on them." To her this means possession. Consequently she is all graciousness when they reach the small lobby in which Buckmaster and Sweetman are waiting.

They are overcome by puce.

Even their words, "I'm afraid this gentleman cannot—", are confused and drowned as she sweeps by. But they still bail Lunt up.

"Where's your invitation?" Buckmaster demands.

Lunt, still groggy from the head blow, looks up, recognises, and is silent.

"I'm afraid this won't do," Sweetman says, coming across. "It won't really do at all. We're sorry."

Jenner and Boyd shove their faces into the group.

"Nonsense," Snoggers says. "Of course it will do. They're all my guests."

Newcomers are impatient behind them.

88

"Would you mind standing to one side?" Sweetman asks. "Just till we get things sorted out. It won't take long."

"Bloody nonsense!" Dorahy cries. "We're going in."

The scuffle as Buckmaster and Sweetman converge on him and Lunt is a blunt parrying of arms at which more newcomers stare in delighted puzzlement. Buckmaster is almost bursting with the effort not to punch.

"Come along, come along!" Boyd says, edging his wife forward. And more softly, "You can't afford to be seen like this. It won't go well with the voters."

A minion is tapping Buckmaster's arm. It is almost time for the officials to go up on stage.

"God bugger you," Buckmaster whispers to Dorahy. "Get in then. Get bloody in before I kill you."

The hall is packed. As Dorahy fumbles his way along a row towards a group of empty chairs at the side, he is again amazed at the familiarity of faces like maps of countries he has once visited. The contours have subtly changed. The rivers have altered their flow. Hills are steeper. Yet they hold sufficient of their early selves to make recognition possible in the way one says, "And there was the corner store. There the newsagent. Once I ran along here where a hedge used to be." He takes his place beside Lunt who is managing his wooden leg awkwardly and observes Gracie Tilburn a row away twisting to catch his eye.

Gracie waves. She will be singing shortly and has no doubts about her magic. Like an empress, her bounds are infinite, and when Barney Sweetman spots her (he has glimpsed the wave) and invites her to join the official party, she concurs with statuesque magnificence.

Up here on stage, she decides, seated near the jug and the water glasses, is my true home. There are no corner stores in Gracie's vision, no newsagent with dog-stained hoardings, no hedges. There is only the blurred flow of faces and the noise made by hands.

A large lady arranges her behind at the piano. The queen is saved in a series of mundane chords. Everyone is standing for these moments, and when the anthem finishes Sweetman steps forward and waits like an old stager for all to be seated and all sound to subside. He's used to this, anyone can see, catching with his eye every trout in the stream.

"Dear old friends," he begins (and that's a smasher), "for I know I can call all of you that, on looking around this hall I am amazed and touched—yes, touched—by the number of people who have responded to my invitation to come home. For this is home for many of us still and was home once for those of you who have gone away to make your lives elsewhere. But even to them I say this is *still* home, the place in which you took first steps to manhood, uttered your first meaningful words, made your first plans, indulged your first dreams."

He pauses, having gauged the response to a nicety, as the applause breaks out.

"For many of you, rather I think for each and every one of you"—"Two," Dorahy murmurs to himself counting clichés—"those dreams were fulfilled. The point is that the memories and experiences you formulated here twenty years ago are still part of you and what you have become—part of this town. And the people who were in it when you were in it have become part of your blood."

"Hear hear!" shouts derisive Dorahy who is losing control.

People turn to stare and smile. But it doesn't rattle Sweetman.

"Now this is a good thing," he continues, not stalling for a moment, "for the town owes all of you something and all of you are indebted to the town. It is a marriage of place and person that cannot be ignored."

Strategy pause. The people watching him are subdued. This is not a moment for clapping. It is a tender moment made for silence, for seriousness. They all ache for his next words.

"Before I go further I have on stage with me someone who needs no introduction"—"Three," counts Dorahy—"to any of you. I refer of course to our own Miss Gracie Tilburn who has come all the way back from the south to be with us on this happy occasion." ("Four," he counts.) "She has graciously consented to sing for us once more, and those of you who remember her singing from twenty years back will know that is something for which we are indebted. It is moving to think that at the height of her fame and the peak of her career"—"Oh, my God!" says Dorahy, who has lost count—"she chooses to return here, to her birth-place, to sing for us. Ladies and gentlemen, I give you Miss Gracie Tilburn."

The racket of applause. Gracie stands modestly during it, and now moves over to the piano where the pianist is shuffling sheets of music. The opening notes of "Home, Sweet Home" are played and then Gracie, with ever so little trace of a throb, begins to sing. Her voice is richer, fuller, darker than in youth. The audience is emotionally stilled within its own darkness; but Dorahy whispers, "Say, eleven," so audibly his neighbours frown and shush him.

With an effort he constrains himself from leaping up and roaring, "It's nonsense! All nonsense!"

The applause is enormous at the end of the song. Hands are pulped. A huge and garish bouquet is rushed forward and Sweetman who is on his feet has taken the singer's hand. Smiles fly through the air like rockets.

Sweetman finally raises an arm for silence.

"Dear friends," he says again, "that response speaks for itself more than anything I can say. Thank you indeed, and thank you, Gracie— I may call you that?—for a wonderful opening of welcome. Those simple and unaffected words mean so much to us all. And now I'm going to call on James Buckmaster to say a few words. Ladies and gentlemen, James Buckmaster."

Tim Jenner has been affected. He is sixteen and gulping in great gobbets of Gracie's voice. He is down by the creek watching hat shadows alter the planes of her face. He is bashed outside the stock-and-station agent's. And he remembers the purity of his adolescent love with an ache that will not leave him free to hear Buckmaster's opening remarks. He only comes to during ". . . what we have done for this town is to build and strengthen it, to shape its future by the efforts of all who lived and worked here, some of us in small ways, perhaps; others in bigger ways—but all to the one purpose."

He pauses. Tim Jenner glances along the row at Dorahy, who is wrestling with an inner devil.

"This town has been built on sacrifice—self-sacrifice if you like— which is something that must take precedent when struggle and effort are required."

Suddenly Dorahy is on his feet shouting, "That's the word—sacrifice. How many? How many, eh, did you sacrifice?"

The hall is shocked. There are angry rumbles and two men come from the rear of the hall to seize the maniac by the arms. As they drag him out, he is still shouting, and when the porch is reached one of the bouncers whacks him hard across the side of the head.

"The world of men," he murmurs, looking up at his guards.

Boyd has forced his own way out to the porch. "Leave him," he says to the bouncers. "I'll get him home. He's not well. Come on, old chap," he says.

But Dorahy, dazed from this second blow, flaps like a bird, unable to stand. He argues pitifully, "I'm perfectly well. Get back in there. Get back in and show those sycophants!"

Boyd's hands and manner are firm. Somehow he steers him down the steps and across the road to where the buggy is hitched. The air is smelling of rain. "One blessing," thinks Boyd. Renewed hosannahs from the hall reach their ears and Dorahy frets again against Boyd's arms. "It's no use, Tom," Boyd says. "No use at all."

The hotel is like a shell cast up by the sea. Its only sound is the breathy echo of waves clamped against the listening ear. Boyd stumbles with him up the stairs and to his room, where Dorahy lies flopped on his bed and looks up vaguely.

"God!" is all he can say. "Oh, my God!"

Boyd uncaps a whisky flask. "Try this," he says. But it only strengthens Dorahy's tongue which lashes again and again, coiling like a whip round the same topic.

"I'll have to return soon," Boyd says at last. "Don't worry about Lunt. We'll put him up. Try to get some sleep."

Boyd is not a big man, but rising, finds himself towering over this rinsed-out fellow. Dorahy's cheek has swollen. The eye is already darkening.

LUNT IS NOT interested in retribution. He is a simple man and curious, with the inquisitiveness of the newly hatched. Yet there is no mischief in him.

After Dorahy has been hustled from the hall he continues sitting, stolidly listening to another three speeches, all kindred, and a final bracket of nostalgic songs from Gracie Tilburn. Ultimately the audience, an unintelligent monster, shoves its grotesque way to a room at the back of the hall where trestle tables support a sandwich supper. In the middle of this turmoil of recognition and reminiscence, the wave forming, breaking and petering out, the Jenners, Lucy Boyd and Lunt form a hard little knot which many of those present attempt to untie.

Sweetman pushes through the room to this boil lest it erupt. He cannot believe in the tolerance of others.

"Sorry we had to do that." He is referring to Dorahy. Old Jenner permits himself a smile while his son looks grave. "It could have been much worse. We have to think of the guests, the visitors. It's not pleasant to have someone going on like that at a reunion that should be friendly and warm. Not pleasant at all. We owe the others something."

Young Jenner says quietly, "A lot is owed to many people in this place."

"True. But we must live and let live."

"Especially with the elections coming up next month."

Sweetman replies with a poise that earns respect. "Right again. I won't pretend with you. When have I ever pretended? I feel I contribute something to the welfare of this place and I intend to go on contributing."

He is speaking more softly. All round them mouths are gobbling and gabbling. His back is slapped as he is hailed by wolfish passers and his smile of unutterable sweetness comes again and again between trivia utterances that for him have the utmost seriousness. He wears his geniality like a coat that he slips on and off with ease.

Tim Jenner is amused by such public-man antics and is still smiling at his own thoughts as Gracie Tilburn pushes to his side in the crush and slips an arm through his.

"Hullo," she carols. There is a faint whiff about her of lost summer days. Her face has plumped out and strengthened. "Remember?"

Too well, he thinks, twitching with the beginnings of a small pain that recaptures her voice and her throat, the sun-warmed hands of her by the creek. These subtleties are almost lost now as life has hardened the externals. He could weep for innocence, but says instead, "Of course. Your voice is still wonderful. Better, if anything."

"Tim," she says. "Oh, Tim." And she remembers one special day when she sang for him and Freddie Buckmaster in a summer-filled living-room and the voice, as if no longer part of her, made patterns like tapestry that she wove at exquisite will. Sad it is, thinks young middle-aged Jenner now, to hear that wistfulness from this stouter woman with a carapace of assurance. Losing as one grows. And the longing growing greater as one lives.

"I suppose you're married now?" she asks.

"Yes," he replies simply. "And you?"

"Was," she says. "Twice." And giggles like a girl. "The last is over now. Five years. A mistake."

Stagily she makes tiny mouths. Turns down the corners bravado style. Raises them. She is tempted to ask him if he is happy but senses his answer; and the heaviness of Sweetman's presence, and that of the father, the quiet confidence of Lucy Boyd—all oppress her. Deciding on gaiety, she tralas a little, asks after Fred Buckmaster and has him pointed out to her across the room. Her waves attract him.

"The gang's all here," Tim Jenner says. "God Almighty!" And Sweetman frowns at this and allows himself to be caught by another prodigal and drawn away.

Lunt is still chuckling as Freddie Buckmaster heaves his sweating bully-boy way towards them, stopping briefly every yard to pummel or shake other bully-boy paws.

"Well?" he asks, arriving on the tail-end of the chuckle and observing this limping stranger with an almost knowledge. "What's the joke, eh? Good night, isn't it? Wonderful night!" His enthusiasm is fake-right at this moment as he glares into Lunt's marvellously open eye. He shakes the firm hand of old Jenner, catches Gracie ("Gracie, I'd know you after a thousand years!") by the shoulders and gives her a smacking kiss on the cheek, says let bygones be bygones to young Jenner, and salutes his introduction to Lunt with the briefest nod. He is a practical man, and what cannot help him he refuses to acknowledge.

"How are you feeling, Mr Lunt?" he finally asks, driven by curiosity. "I heard you and Mr Dorahy had a spot of trouble earlier tonight."

"I'm getting too old for rough-house," Lunt says. "Does my presence alone incite?" He doesn't want an answer.

"We're a peaceable lot," Buckmaster says ambiguously. "We're not after trouble."

"Nor am I."

"It's not you. It's your mate. Why can't he keep his mouth shut, eh? What's he got to start stirring things up for?"

"We all have a destiny," Lunt says. He is feeling old and giddy and the stump of his leg throbs.

"Twaddle!" the ex-lieutenant says. "Where's Snoggers?"

"He's taken Mr Dorahy back to his hotel."

"Well, now, has he? What was the trouble? Too much grog?"

"Too much honesty," Lunt replies.

This sharp one goes home. A surly red shows on Fred Buckmaster's cheeks, exceeding the rouging that liquor and climate have given his skin. He says slowly, "I don't know about that."

On cue Boyd returns and sticks his head into the circle, one arm lightly slung about his wife's shoulders. He has a need to touch which no one has ever guessed at.

He says, "Know all about what?"

"Forget it!" Buckmaster says.

"You're not talking about old Tom Dorahy, are you? I've put him safely to bed feeling very frail." And continues thinking, "He's not the stuff of martyrs but of fanatics."

"I don't understand any of this," Gracie complains. Her coyness is being undermined by their intensity which she suspects but fails to digest. "Enough of this oblique talk! We're here to enjoy ourselves. Freddie, tell me all, I insist, all that's happened to you."

His confidences will liberate hers which are choking her in their urgency to be freed. Yet she plays the game and waits. Lucy Boyd has gone back for more tea. Someone is offering limp biscuits and sandwiches.

Freddie Buckmaster proffers the sort of information that he hopes will give him absolution. He tells her he has two boys. He tells her of the pub on the Palmer. And finally he swings on Lunt and asks him what he is doing back in the old place after all this time. Lunt regards him speculatively. Buckmaster is not a wise man, Lunt knows, and there is a brutality about him still that makes the older man cautious.

"Affection," he admits finally. "I liked the old place. I'm hoping for something. I don't know what. Now I'm getting on and feel gentler about things it seemed right to return. Just to see."

Freddie Buckmaster lets out a great guffaw, understanding nothing of what the old man has just said, but discovering some elusive effeminacy in the remarks.

"You must tell my old man that," he says between splutters. "You must tell my old man."

"He knows."

Young Buckmaster fails to understand this. He is obsessed with hard facts.

"But you only live thirty or so miles away. You could have come back before this. For affection!"

"No," Lunt says. "I was waiting to be asked. You see, I was driven out."

Right across the township people are yawning and dragging from beds. In the Sea Rip Hotel Freddie Buckmaster gives one final look at Gracie Tilburn, who is too bloody fat for his taste anyway, and heaves his own porky body into daytime.

As he dresses he marvels how he happened to get here. It was after the reception, he groggily recalls, and after the country women's supper, and after that his sulky to drive her home, a bit of spooning along the water-front—and then this. Well, he'd achieved it anyway after all these years. Beaten Tim Jenner to first base at last.

Gracie rolls heavily over and looks up. She feels all flesh. Her eyes widen vaguely as she looks at this man dragging on a tie four feet from her bed, and then she remembers. "Oh, my God," she thinks, and is filled with self-disgust. His gross thighs in shirt-tails appal. She wonders, if he obliterates them with trousers, whether she might be able to deny the whole thing.

"Darling," she lies, thinking of Tim Jenner, "what happened last night?"

He swings his coarse face on her and winks.

"Come off it," he says. "Come off it! We just had a bit of a get together." He finishes with his tie and proceeds to drag on his trousers.

Gracie thinks "Thank God" and smiles at him ravishingly. "I wish it hadn't been you," she tells herself. And she goes on smiling at him while thinking of Tim Jenner.

"Well," says this horror leaning over her, "I'll be toddling."

His reluctant kiss senses some of her own disgust.

"How long are you down for?" Gracie asks, feeling an insane need to make small talk.

"Just for the week," he replies, buttoning up. "The wife will hold the fort. She can hold anything. Great woman, that. Even toss out the drunks."

"Really!" Gracie yawns again and wishes he would go. "Then we'll see each other again. Maybe tomorrow."

"Count on that." He is lying also.

Closing the door behind him after blowing one last vulgar smacking kiss, he is jaunty as a dog let out. Almost he cocks one leg and makes such speed down the hotel staircase he misses the breakfast gong by seconds and is out on the front wrapped in innocuousness.

Gracie lies there and in a conglomerate of memories inspects husbands one and two. George becomes Frank in this melting process where she recalls George's blows and Frank's greed as one and the same thing. George had been handsome not only for her, and had finally sped absent-mindedly under a dray between one adultery and another. It still hurt to see him, even if only in the mind, alerting like a pointer at any woman who entered the room. But Frank she had simply left and almost forgotten. His monetary stinginess, his management of her funds had made it easy. He had lived off her voice like some huge parasite, and while she sang for both their suppers he had resigned from or lost one job after another, putting his idleness down to her need to have a manager. Gracie's mouth curls up in amusement at the thought of him on that last day when she had packed a smallish bag and left. He had been out buying himself a new suit and she had simply taken a boat south and stayed with friends. Oh, he had pestered her all right when he discovered her once after a concert; but she left for England, which was safer still since he didn't have the fare, and though he wrote long pleading letters and short terse ones he had finally given up. "There," she murmurs in a motherly fashion, burrowing under the sheet. "There, there."

At breakfast she is gay. Some weight has been lifted or curiosity sated. She talks rapidly and richly with Miss Charlton (relaxing morals) and Marge Ellis (rising food prices) and is conscious of a huge benignity as she hurls smiles and words, some of which are caught by Mr Armitage and Mr Romney at the next table. It's all cosy. All hunkydory. They chat across space informally in this over-big white dining-room.

Mr Dorahy is late coming down.

Constraint devils them when he appears, for by now all know what happened at the hall. But despite his blackened eye, his good-morning and his gentle smile are the same as ever as he unfolds his napkin and peers at the menu.

"Spot of bother last night?" asks crass Armitage. He is a pot-belly and large with nonsense.

"Only a spot." Dorahy smiles again directly into the other man's eyes.

"What were you on about, mate?"

Dorahy hesitates. He doesn't know whether to answer or not. Finally he says, "Something that happened here twenty years ago. You must remember."

"Bit long ago to rake up, isn't it?"

"No." He orders poached eggs.

Romney says, "It's too bloody long ago." He marmalades his toast savagely. And the savagery is detected.

Dorahy accuses, "Then you know to what I'm referring."

"If you mean that bloody nonsense down at Mandarana, then yes, I do."

98

"You call it nonsense! Seven people were killed."

"Blacks!" says Romney shortly. He takes a bite of his toast.

"There were other things. Lunt . . ." He stops himself. "Jesu Christe," he thinks. "Why go on?" He reaches for the butter and spreads himself a piece of toast too.

"Don't talk to me about Lunt," Romney blurts. He takes a swig of tea and it dribbles. "No one but a fool would have held on to that property of his as long as he did. Got out far too late. A mug, he was. Plain mug."

Dorahy is sick with the spasm of fury that takes him. He puts down his knife and grips hard at the seat of his chair. His fingers are digging wood. He swallows the leapt-up words one by one as he tries to gauge the truth of the two faces opposite him. This gristle is too much. He chokes and coughs and the eggs arrive.

The fabric of what passes for his discretion he has ripped apart himself in this cool white room ungeared to fractious debate. He sees other rooms, teaching rooms where he has always exercised a mastery of self, meeting rooms with the Separation League in angry spate and himself cool. Now, cutting brutally into his eggs and watching the yolk spurt out, he is conscious of his sixty-odd years and failure at the end after all. Projects unfinished, projects contemplated but not even begun, rise like iron men to deride. But he would complete this, he now decides. He would have the town recognise its martyr, relegating himself to a serving position without pain, for he has never been of the stuff from which saints are made.

"If there is one thing," he says, his innards constipatedly tight with tension, "that Lunt was not is mug. Not mug. He was unlucky from the start, but he never took his spleen out on others. He was generous, do you understand? Generous and forgiving. He could have given his life."

Armitage shoves his chair back impatiently. "You talk a lot of shit!" he retorts contemptuously. His belly swells with rage as well. Coming all this way to be preached at by some bloody unfrocked nun! A nancy. A bloodless man.

"Girlie," he calls to the waitress, "more toast, please."

"HANDS UP," Dorahy had said, "the boys who have not prepared this prose."

Eight hands were raised.

"All of you!" he marvelled. "Not one! Well," he said sadly, his snaggle teeth exposed in a disillusioned smile, "you will have to be punished. Line up!"

He rooted in the corner press and took out a cane which he wiped down with his right hand, lingeringly assessing the shape and the pliancy of it. It was all parody. All burlesque. The boys wore half-grins as comic Dorahy passed down the line of them giving the lightest of sarcastic taps to each outstretched palm.

When he reached young Buckmaster he did not even bother with the tap. Ironically, dismissively, he brushed him to one side with the most offensive of negligent plays of the stick. The boy turned scarlet as the master moved on flicking parodically at the next two outflung hands, and his hate, which had been till then a nebulous affair, crystallised into the stubborn matter that he would bear vengefully through to his middle age.

Dorahy was unaware. Perhaps. Their enmity, though tacit, had long been sensed mutually.

The boys returned to their places and Dorahy, wearily, despairingly, took up his chalk and began scribbling the work upon the board. The grains of it, the choking whiteness of it, saturated his whole being, and the phlegm he coughed anguishedly at the beginning of each day was a purging more of the spirit than the lungs. His hands dusty with it, he wiped drily along the seams of his trousers, slapped till small clouds arose. Looking through the classroom window for a moment

100

while the boys painfully took down his fair copy, he could feel that the whole landscape, right down to the seaward fence, was chalk. He sighed.

He remembers this now, standing uncertainly outside the building where once . . . He debates entry, overcome by the newness of the teaching block, the horrible assurance of small garden plots and shrubs. The room where he had taught is still standing, a warped agglomeration of white-anted timber by the far fence, and he aches and does not ache to enter it once more and taste the flavour of lost baking summer days. Chanting comes from the rooms nearest him. The deadly Gregorian of rote. He pushes half-heartedly at the school gate, wondering how he will introduce himself, and walks slowly, sobered, along the gravel path towards the first of the buildings.

The headmaster is young. He is a mathematician. He lacks humour and poetry. When Dorahy has introduced himself, has explained himself, his stiffness wavers above the mess of time-tables and lesson-notes that form the lyric of his days. He offers a few minutes from his grudging muse and goes out with Dorahy into the hot sun.

"We use it as a store-room now," he says looking at the tottering building towards which they are heading. "Old book stock, new supplies, craft material for the boys. But it's had its day, I'm afraid. The school council recommends that it be pulled down next summer to make way for a new primary room."

Dorahy wipes sweat from his forehead and gapes at his past. The headmaster unlocks the padlock and draws back the bolt and, as he pushes open the splintered door, a staleness of air and memory takes Dorahy by the throat. He walks past the dull young rules man at his side and stands, more or less, as packing-cases allow, in the approximate geography of the dream, gazing out the cobwebby window to the smartness of acalypha beds along the fence-line.

"It was here," he says, "just here. I taught them Livy. A little Wordsworth. It seems so long ago. None of them particularly apt, you know, but I hoped it might have given them something."

"Hardly practical," the brash young headmaster says with a laugh, "for boys in a place like this."

"The sentimental old fool," he is thinking. "Taking up my morning." He fidgets impatiently.

Dorahy does not hear him. He is disturbed to the point of tears by it all, by the deadly melancholy of fusty textbook piles, the worn bladders of footballs, the stacks of broken unusable desks.

"Just here," he repeats, recalling young Jenner's scrubbed morning face and the middle-aged sobriety of him now. And he says, smiling directly into the headmaster's eyes, *"Eheu fugaces, Postume, Postume, Labuntur anni . . ."*

"Of course, of course," the younger man mouths, not understanding. And "Well?" he says questioningly, giving a half-turn towards the door.

"Could you leave me here? Just a few minutes?" Dorahy asks. "I'd like to spend a little time. On my own," he adds.

The headmaster is appalled. He fears sentiment and mentally pig-roots like a nervous horse.

"I'm afraid not," he replies. He dangles his key meaningfully, giving the hint, and smiles. There is a boy he has to punish, he remembers.

Opening the door wide so that it cannot be ignored, he waits for the older man who is still trapped in the pity of the past. Those firm, eager or reluctant faces, he recalls, the marrow of my mornings.

Young Jenner grins at him fleetingly and says, "It's true, sir. You did add up," while Freddie Buckmaster scowls sulkily by the window. "Thank you, young Jenner," he says, and the mathematician, hearing his mumbles, squirms with shame for the old dodderer.

"There's nothing more you'd like to see?" he asks hopefully as they walk back once more to the main building.

"No. No. Thank you," Dorahy says.

The building has disowned him, he knows, the very ground that knew his feet. The whole of the morning is a plague of sunlight that threatens to beat him senseless.

"It's a mistake to come back," he admits and points ambiguously to his blackened eye about which the unimaginative other had not even wondered.

Their hands meet in the most counterfeit of gestures and Dorahy, turning his back on it all, goes, almost at a stumble, into the decorous, unfeeling street.

On that fourth day Snoggers Boyd calls round at the Sea Rip Hotel.

He finds Dorahy once again mooning along the water-front, a book in his hand. Some kind of tic obsesses his right eye as if it were a coefficient of anger. The blue of sky and water is violently peaceful and the island floating above the horizon looks like a close nirvana—except for the sun, which is a blistering outrage of heat.

They walk along the sandy front together to a seat under a couple of bunched palms.

"I have another favour to ask." Dorahy looks humble and his blackened eye makes his face a comic mask.

"Ah, yes," Boyd says, dreading. "What is it?"

"I've been doing some hard thinking. No. I haven't given up. Quite the reverse, in fact. I'd like you to publish an article for me."

Boyd takes quite a time filling his pipe. "What about?" he asks, then, "No. Don't tell me. I can guess."

Dorahy smiles. "The bile is low this morning. But only quiescent because of this—this idea. You could do it, you know. You're running that series called 'After Twenty Years' with all those low-keyed profiles of prominent figures. Fair enough, isn't it, to include one on Lunt? It could be the most exciting of the lot. 'Why I Left Town, by a victim.' " Dorahy finds bitterness has an actual taste.

"That's up to Lunt, surely."

"Not really. It's part of local history. You know it is."

Boyd draws hard on his pipe. He is no lover of the town's powers and, as a cool man, has always taken an onlooker's part. He has only to report, and he has always been canny enough to report without bias. He knows well which side his bread is buttered. Yet something about the suggestion—after all he is Dorahy's age—stirs unused wings. He sees headlines—A LITTLE INCIDENT AT THE LEAP, TOWN BORN IN VIOLENCE. All the trashy artifices of his employment could, with an almost amusing virulence, tear down the pretensions of Buckmaster and Sweetman. The interesting thing about it, he reflects, is that the whole town knew at the time but was never prepared to make outright challenges. It let things seep below the surface until they were finally covered with all the glosses of time.

To bring them up again now would—what?

Despite himself he starts to chuckle. "We could run pictures as well," he says. "Freddie Buckmaster with caption 'Vigilante Settles Down' or Barney Sweetman as the avenging power!"

Dorahy says quietly, "Why don't you?"

"Oh, my God, my dear Tom. It's impossible. The laws of libel for one thing. The election for another. You don't seem to realise the voters don't want to be jolted. They're happy with things as they are. Change is a threat, a worry. They'd resent me for it."

"Does that matter?"

"The laws of libel matter."

"You could get around that. Do it without names—except for Lunt's. After all, you were there with me. We came in on the end of things."

Boyd remembers the heat, the body, the high rock but can only protest, "In God's name what good will all this serve?"

"It will ease my itch."

"*Your* itch? What a bloody fake philanthropist are you! I suspect you don't really give tuppence for Lunt. It's a personal vendetta on Buckmaster and his mob."

Dorahy looks away from the other man across the water. He knows him to be right and admits, "You're partly correct, you know. I confess. *Mea culpa*. But I do give more than tuppence for Charlie. Truly. His name has been shut out of the town as though he were a public sinner. Is that fair? Is it fair to force a man to make himself a hermit just to save the faces of others? Because that is what has happened."

"I know. I know all this. And it might be interesting to rock the boat at that." He keeps toying with the idea.

"You've never rocked the boat."

"True. But if I were to—I say if—I wouldn't be doing it for you. I don't much like being—having been—a yes-man all these years. You grind my nose in it."

"Save your soul," Dorahy urges eagerly. "Go against the grain."

Boyd is pensive. He knocks out his pipe on the heel of his shoe.

"I'm on the point of retirement," he says, "after a blameless thirty years. There's nothing more they can do to me. We've thought of going south in another year or so." He is arguing aloud with himself with Dorahy straining for his predicate.

"Then you'll do it," he demands rather prematurely. The world is a giddy blue.

"I'll think about it," Boyd says. "That's all I promise you, but I promise you that."

LOST BETWEEN voyages in his own port, Snoggers sits, green eye-shaded, pencil at the ready, his inner man torn between doing and not-doing, between the validity of what Dorahy had demanded and the folly of it, the senselessness perhaps.

He'd kept a column and a half blank for the last of his series and wanted, insipidly, to do the right thing by everybody. Lucy with her calm and candour had urged him. "Do it," she had said. "Make it your final testament." Which is what it would be, he muses, with Buckmaster's re-election coming up.

Perhaps Lucy is still in love with Lunt. He wonders about this, staring idly at the calendar facing him on the far wall, and writes a line or two, transposes its high-pitched whinge down a third and re-reads. Balderdash! Slop! A minor irritant only unless he takes the bull by its ionic horns and slams home with all his power. Significance. That is the word. How tie in so that the significance of what he is doing with what he has already done has a total qualitative force like a battering ram's?

Ram all right, he recalls, grinning, thinking of Sweetman's amorous but tangential approaches to Lucy one long-forgotten Christmas when Sweetman had drunkenly seemed all hands and phallus. She had laughed at him with such genuine amusement it still hurt to envision Sweetman's crumpled foolish mask, the watery pathos of his myopic eyes.

Munching his morning-tea biscuit Boyd tries again. His thick tongue pursues crumbs in teeth inlets and something begins to ache sharply and persistently—soul? tooth? Glancing out the office window, he takes solace from the hachured sky beyond the palm. The evident blue seems infinite, is so; and as he writes again the words wrenched out of amusement and pain come more easily. Comfortably he has the sense of the world itself being unreal, and that makes what he is doing easier. And without venom, he jubilates, decoding fluidly and reasonably from memories he had thought long lost. Reasonably, he reassures himself. It must move reasonably. And he has another biscuit that he bites absent-mindedly without realising he is eating at all.

His mind keeps browsing among other pastures of the last two decades. That first ten years when he brought out the weekly broadsheet single-handed; the second when it became a daily and he had one man assist him with the press while he did all the reporting, writing, editing on his own. He has a backstop now and a cadet, but he is even more tired and is looking forward to the limbo of retirement.

Shaking himself into the present, he is, getting up restless from his chair, scratching around and coming back to re-read what he has written. Words come readily to Boyd—and that is his problem—to prevent that free flow from becoming merely the banal or the trite. He scores out a phrase or two and reads again, a little smile curling his mouth. It is difficult not to make Lunt look like the sacrificial lamb.

Mid-morning knocks on his sunny door bringing the head of Dorahy peering round. It is the fifth day and he is avoiding like the plague the hideous brouhaha of a grand picnic luncheon at the show-ground. Everyone seems to have gone while he is sticking it solitarily out for the week, enduring Romney and Armitage with their breakfast and dinner-time grunts. He is still a misfit and wears his blackened eye like a badge, while the town reinforces his Ishmael qualities after twenty years, stresses his unpalatability.

"Well then," he says to Boyd, "a good morning to you. Am I disturbing anything?"

"Nothing much." Boyd has decided not to tell Dorahy yet of his article. He slips the papers under a blotter. "Just routine stuff. Have a seat."

Dorahy pulls out the chair facing him. There are no *arrière-pensées* on the squarish face confronting him, no deviousness in the eye.

"It must be all in the heart," he says, concluding his thoughts aloud.

"What is?" Boyd is transparently curious.

"Nothing." Dorahy hesitates. "Have you given any more thought to what I asked?"

"I have," Boyd says.

106

"And are you going ahead?"

"I haven't decided."

"But there isn't much time, man!" Dorahy's heart suddenly plunges into a panic beating. "Half the week's over."

"Yes."

"Well?"

"I've given it thought, Tom. Quite a lot of thought. But let me do things my own way, will you?"

"It's always ultimately been the thinkers or the writers who get things done," Dorahy says petulantly. "Men of violence hardly ever score."

"True."

"And again well?"

"Look," Boyd cries impatiently, resenting his conversion, "leave it will you? I'm still thinking about it. And by the way, Lucy has asked you for dinner tonight. Just a few people, the Jenners, Gracie. Lunt is staying over till the end of the week."

"It will be pleasant," Dorahy says, "not to watch Romney slopping his mess of pottage. Thank you. And don't come for me. I'll walk over."

Outside the office of the *Gazette,* the streets are flush with visitors who can be recognised by their curiosity and a happiness that comes from living there no longer, Dorahy ponders cynically as he steps along the pavement with them. Here and there—the face on the coin—he recognises and waves or occasionally pauses to go through the same questions and greetings, explain away his eye and say in chorus How long for? Since when? Oh, marvellous, marvellous to see you, Hasn't changed much has she, the old town? and he cannot bear this Calvary.

He returns to the tea-room he first visited, hoping to find the girl there who at last smiled. She's still washing down the bar counter, but she knows him now and says, "Well, how's it going?"

Dorahy gives her his gappy smile and says, "I'm afraid not too well."

She is sympathetic. "That's the trouble, isn't it?" she says. "Things are never so good when you see them again."

There is a raw wisdom about her.

"You're so right," he says. "Nothing has changed really. I mean the people who were still here when I left so long ago. I had hoped for—

well, something. A gentleness perhaps. Or richer thinking. Or penitence."

He is almost talking to himself and the girl says, "It's tea you like, isn't it? I'll get you some."

This time there are no apparitions of the spirit. Young Jenner does not emerge to counsel. Perhaps, reasons Dorahy, the present reality submerges memory. He sees young Jenner now as the man he has become, much of the eagerness rubbed off him so that he appears in the garb of all his thirty-six years merely as sober and sensible. Dorahy sighs for it, and his sigh is interrupted by the arrival of tea.

Facing the door from one of the rickety tables, he sips and watches the street. The smallish palms down the centre of the road throw blue shadows and it is across one of these patches that he sees the older Buckmaster stride, ripping apart morning. Dorahy wishes himself invisible but the other has spotted him and comes to the doorway of the café.

Yes. He knows them all. Booms to the girl and pockets her goodmorning as his right. Exploding what little peace there was about Dorahy, he draws up an uninvited chair.

"I thought you might have gone by now," he offers tactlessly. "Seen all you wanted to."

"You're using the wrong verb," sour Dorahy says. "Done, not seen."

He regrets his spleen. It only serves to alert.

Buckmaster is chewing this over.

"Why don't you go back?" he asks, genuinely curious. "That or fall in with the spirit of it, eh? Why I've just left the happiest crowd I've seen in years out at the show-ground. Massive picnic. Ring events. Side shows. The lot. They love it and they're loving each other." He presents himself reasonably, his large wine-stained face seeking sense for the moment.

"You know why."

"But that's over, a long time ago. God, you make it all repetitious. Can't you see that? Not even Lunt wants it. You're trying to make him something he rejects, a figure of pity twenty years too late. No man wants that."

"I don't see him as a figure of pity. Nor myself. But I do see you and Sweetman as figures of violence."

Buckmaster's complexion deepens. "Girlie," he calls, "bring us some more tea, will you?

108

"Look," he says, turning a curiously worn countenance on Dorahy, "let's talk this out, man to man. There are things I regret. Naturally. Every man has those. But I—all of us—have been trying to live those moments down. No one's proud of them. They just happened in a natural course of events. It's part of history."

"History has two faces."

"What do you mean?"

"I mean your view may not necessarily be the right view. There's another side to it. I want the other side to be seen."

"After all this time you still believe that?"

"Yes."

Buckmaster gulps at his tea. "Then there's nothing I can say that will bring you to your senses."

"I'm very much in them."

Buckmaster says gently, "You're not, you know."

This seems to bring a temporary peace between them. Both of them smoke in silence; but it is a false peace and Dorahy is the one who cracks.

He says, "There's not much time left, is there? For living, I mean."

Buckmaster looks up at his fanatic face and there is a total weariness on his own.

"That's what I've been trying to say," he says.

YOUR FULL name is Thomas Wade Dorahy? the magistrate asked.

Yes.

And you are teacher in charge of the provisional school at The Taws?

Yes.

And how long have you held this position?

Three years.

Have you been, the magistrate asked, his face keen with the prospect of a new witness, a member of the so-called Separation League?

I have.

And for how long?

Two years.

Would you consider two years, Mr Sheridan pursued, a long enough period in which to know the other members of the league?

I thought we were here to discuss—

In good time, Mr Dorahy, the magistrate said. I am asking you questions that may have pertinence. Please answer the question.

Yes, I would, Mr Dorahy said. He was inclined to truculence.

And did you consider that your membership of this group required certain loyalties from you?

Mr Dorahy hesitated. It would depend on the nature of the matter.

The nature?

Yes. Whether the pursuits on which the league was engaged were likely to conflict with conscience.

I see. Mr Sheridan took a long look at the dour string of a fellow.

And was there ever such an occasion—where there was a conflict of conscience?

Yes.

I take it you are referring to incidents on the twenty-fourth of June at Mount Mandarana?

I am.

Were you in fact a member of the reprisal team?

No.

Then you admit you would not have complete knowledge of the actual events of that day?

Mr Dorahy squeezed his hands tightly together. I saw enough.

That is not quite the same thing, you agree?

Mr Dorahy was silent.

Well, Mr Sheridan asked more loudly, do you agree?

I suppose so.

What actual events did you witness on that day, Mr Dorahy? Tell us in your own words.

Mr Dorahy cleared his throat. He could feel a trembling beginning.

On that morning on which I suspected there might be some active reprisal against the Lindeman tribe, we rode north to Mandarana to see if we could prevent what we imagined might happen.

We?

Mr Jenner, his son and myself.

Go on.

We came round by the western base of the mountain in time to see Mr Boyd who had been a member of the party bending over a dead lubra.

And who was this?

A young woman called Kowaha.

You knew her? Mr Sheridan asked with horrible interest.

Yes. I had given her food on a number of occasions.

And for what reason?

None—except that she asked. Mr Dorahy went red with indignation at the implication.

And how had this lubra come to die, do you think?

She appeared to have fallen from the cliff. She had her baby with her.

And was the baby alive?

111

It was.

Would you imagine, Mr Dorahy, Mr Sheridan asked playing a small five-finger exercise on the edge of his desk, that the gin might have been helped to her death? Pushed say?

I don't know.

But you must have some idea. You say you know these men well enough after two years to assess a situation.

You are leading me, Dorahy protested. She was morally pushed, that's all I can say.

Ah! Then you admit you have no grounds for accusation of any violence at all against the members of the Separation League?

No. That's not true.

In that case how many dead did you see?

Only one.

The woman?

Yes.

Then you had no knowledge of what had actually occurred on the peak of Mandarana?

No. Yes. What I heard. Mr Dorahy was beginning to babble. You forget I found Lunt. Found him a week after these events. There was that as well. Violence like that. Oh, my God!

You must control yourself, Mr Dorahy, the magistrate said. He took a slow and careful sip from a glass of water. Mr Lunt has declined to give evidence. Suspicions, opinions are not facts and must not be brought forward in this court.

This is rubbish, nonsense! Dorahy cried out. You cannot allow justice to miscarry like this.

Mr Dorahy, the magistrate intervened, his face bright with anger, the court must not be addressed in this way. Unless you can control yourself I must ask you to stand down.

Control myself! Dorahy cried. Oh, my God! Control! His face began to stream with tears.

Through the glaze of them he observed young Buckmaster smiling at his father.

Mr Sheridan was enormously embarrassed. I must ask the witness to stand down, he said.

112

BOYD HAS put his press to sleep. "It's done," he thinks and looks at a pull of his main story. Read in cold blood, it is far more drastic than he had imagined it would be. "Oh God," he thinks, "but it's done now! The wolves will be onto my sled while Lucy and I brave it out." Sweetman smilingly benign before election time will have his face changed for him. But how will the public react, he wonders. Put their money on the old favourite? Sweetman is out there wearing Buckmaster's colours and riding hard to win.

He rubs his palms together a little at this, feels the sweat skate between them, mops his neck and face with his handkerchief and gives a tuneless little whistle. His backstop, Madden, is putting the next day's issue together in the back room. Nothing can go back now. Only forward. Trumpets blaring, the troops on the move and Lunt, Dorahy and himself facing the blast of them alone on a high hill. Or valley, is it? Gully? Not even the dignity of height.

"I've wanted," he thinks, "to do something like this for years."

He slips the pull into an envelope and shoves it in his coat pocket. He roars, "Madden!" and the young rabbit face of his assistant peers gap-mouth round the door.

"I'll be out for about an hour. When McKay comes back tell him to hold the fort, will you? I'll be back soon."

The street is blistering but it is only a short distance to the Sea Rip. Glare and sun work away at him and even panama'd he feels the bite of northern light. His eyes squint. The heat does not lick but rasp. Excited, nervous at what he has done, looking forward to seeing the last of the town with his gesture so firmly behind him: he will be able to do nothing but leave.

He passes Buckmaster who is leaving some café on the main street and they wave cheerios that will never be waved again. Already he has a sense of homesickness and observes with the eyes of the newly arrived or the about to leave. There's sadness in the docks at the end of the street, the boats pulled in from journeys on blue water, masts somehow thin.

Dorahy is only fifty yards ahead of him.

He saunters, then, to let him get back to the hotel. No point in having the day pronounce them to the roaring world. He wanders down to the water-front where peelings and papers wash round the piles and, watching the thick syrup of water slap and pull at the wharf, he has a slow smoke.

Dorahy, his glasses making him older and more benign, is lying on his bed reading when Boyd finally gets there. There was a gay party on the front terrace of the pub with Gracie Tilburn queening it over a bevy of drones. Waves. Cries. The party envisioned now as he gazes down on the solitary Dorahy who has uttered nothing but a little grunt since he said, "Come in."

"I've got something here you might like to read," Boyd says, pulling the envelope from his coat pocket, and tossing it, an unconsidered trifle, onto the counterpane.

Dorahy slings his long skinny legs over the side of the bed and sits up. "You've done it?" he hopes aloud. Unfolding and then reading, his face changing with each line. The shock of it! Even the forgivable journalese! He reads the last few lines aloud and gives a great cry:

"At last! And no one named. It's a miracle of circumlocution. No. Hardly that. Of discretion. Oh, my God, Snoggers, it's more than I wanted! More!"

There are tears somewhere. Each man looks away from the weakness in Dorahy, struck to the pith of him, and Dorahy gets up and goes to stand at the veranda door of his room. He is gazing across the water to the island. The dozens of blues. The island sky-floating above its own shadow. Isolated laughter from the terrace below. It is as if he is prepared to drown now in blue, the end being here at last.

"You've done it for me," he says turning to look at Boyd, with the weakness safely out of sight.

"No. Not for you, Tom. It's my own gesture. Sorry to take the

114

credit from you. But truly I have done it for me. Some rash beneath the skin. It is dying now, with this."

"What do you think will happen?" Dorahy is eager as a child.

"Who knows? There's a final get-together in the hall tomorrow. Last night and all that. You and Lunt would be crazy to go. Buckmaster will have all the speeches organised. Stay out of it. You've made your point already."

"You've made it," Dorahy says. "I was only reporting. It will finish you, I suppose," he adds reflectively.

But Snoggers will be carrying a swag of victims with him.

"Do you mind? Really mind?"

"At the moment I'm too exalted with the excitement of it. Later, well, I don't know about that. Can't say. Already I feel the griefs of farewell."

Dorahy is silent, then he says, "I feel guilty about that. Truly. But settled with God, somehow."

"Or the devil," Boyd suggests. "You are a real *agent provocateur.*"

"Maybe. Who knows? Who really knows? . . . Would you like a drink? Have you time or isn't it wise?"

"It's unwise, but I'll have one."

The darkness of the bar-room, its docile shadows, peels some of the age from their faces. They talk of nothings—the heat, the landscape, the last few days—and are halfway through their drinks when Sweetman and young Buckmaster walk in. They are the eclipse of the soul.

The noon door of Boyd's office has, with its closed-for-lunch sign, a vulnerable innocence that persists even after he has let himself in. The street outside is practically empty except for a dog lifting its leg against one of the *Gazette* hoardings. A passing comment, thinks Boyd. Just wait till tomorrow. Madden is still folding in the back room and is halfway through the issue, perspiring languidly with his shifty rabbit face bent in a whitened concentration over his work.

Boyd takes the completed papers and piles them on a trestle slide against the back window, thinks better of it and locks them in a press.

"When you've finished," he advises the crouching Madden, "lock the rest in as well, will you?"

He goes back to the front room and looks out the door at the dusty, decent street with its knobs of palms. Nothing moves. Is he imagining the lull? Then around the corner a dray rumbles and creaks past as he stands there watching and blinking. Just outside the horse drops its sweet-smelling dung. If he were a man searching for omens then he could find this lucky and could even grin. Chickens' innards, the movement of wild stars, the way counters fall. But he recalls unexpectedly the whiteness of Madden's down-bent face prosily withdrawn as he folds and stacks, folds and stacks, and on some uncrystallised impulse goes down the passage to the back room and stands regarding him for a few speculative moments. He does not look up. Why? Boyd wonders, with an unreasonable spurt of irritation.

"Here," he says, testily, "I'll give you a hand. We should get them finished by three." He curses McKay for being still out at the town picnic reporting the follies.

They work in the heat and the silence into which the clock drops its seconds like blows. The tap over the basin drips unrhythmically. Irritable, after fifteen minutes, with a kind of abrading curiosity, Boyd stops his automaton hands and regards his backstop, notes the indifferent pallor, the sparse stringy hair, the unhealthy flush of some skin disorder erupting on the starved-looking angles of the jaw.

"Have you had a look through it?" he asks.

Madden's spidery hands hesitate in their work, but he refuses to look up. He knows the reason behind the question and has not yet discovered his own true reaction in the matter. Stalling, he says carefully, "Had a glance." The hands have not once disrupted the rhymes of work—fold, press, fold, press, stack.

Boyd is cautious, too. This will test his loyalty, he decides, about which he has long had his doubts. The boy on the burning deck, Horatio at the bridge. All the troubadours of fealty singing together.

"Tell me, Joe," he persists, "what did you think of my centre-page story? The one on Mandarana?"

At this moment, Madden is not anybody's man, though he is a white-corpuscled fellow with the seeds of treachery bred into him. His pay is low enough for him to be suborned by anyone at all. Wageless and gutless. There have been past occasions when money has produced bogus red cells of a meretricious attachment. He grins uneasily, remembering.

"Fair enough."

"Dangerous?"

"I wouldn't know."

116

Boyd places another folded paper very delicately on the pile: he is a man in whom the most vast of angers produces only the most antithetic response.

"But you must have some idea," he argues softly. "Do you think I am pushing it too far?"

"Maybe."

"Then you know the background of all this? The things I've left unstated?"

Madden's pimples appear to flare. He says, "I've heard a thing or two."

"So."

The hands resume their work while clock and tap wrestle it out and in the superficial air of truce Boyd gradually decides that he doesn't trust Madden although they have worked five years together. "Printer's devil!" he decides.

He is right not to trust. At some unspecified hour of concealing dusk Madden, with a discarded copy of the next day's *Gazette* folded small inside his shirt, seeks out Buckmaster to satisfy unformulated notions of preferment that he bears like an inner rash. If he wanted outrage, then he has it, observing the passionate explosions on the face of the reading man. Foolishly, Buckmaster cannot control his rantings and Madden grows small with fear and satisfaction.

"I won't forget . . . will make amends . . . take my word . . . a promise a promise . . . very shortly you will be . . ." he raves to his shrinking stooge. While despising.

Madden can only smile and tremble with the excitement of disloyalty that has never bought him anything really yet. As he returns to dusk, his devious compulsions satisfied, he is perplexed by the inner emptiness that overtakes him.

B ETWEEN THE steak and the orange mousse, the flirta-
tious warblings of Gracie Tilburn and the more sombre
conversation of the Jenners, Boyd becomes so conscious of an oppressive, almost sonorous quality of evil that he feels he cannot com-
municate, even on the flattest levels, with his guests. He pushes his
chair back under his wife's anxious eye and says, "You'll have to excuse
me for a little. I have this persistent feeling that things are not all
right at the office. Don't ask me to explain right now, but I'll have to
go back there to check up." His fat-creased eyes are unhappy.

"Take me with you," Dorahy suggests. There is a moment's silence.
Lunt questions with raised eyebrows, and finally, "No," says Boyd.
"No. Not for this."

He leaves them while the pudding wilts. Outside, beyond the curiosity of their eyes, his own tension runs wild for a few seconds. Only
a mile from town, he decides quickly that saddling the horse will not
be worth it and sets off at a fat man's jog-trot, his heart knocking and
his lungs soon announcing the pain. Gasping, he slows down to a
walk and as he comes to the last straight stretch before the stores
begin, he sees that which he has dreaded.

Fire is all rose and gold, excitement and orange joy, leaping and
threatening, with blacker centres to flames than the heart could imagine. Its appetite increases with the reds and yellows, a hunger to paint
colour all over a street's canvas. Its sound is animal and high-pitched
and Boyd, who has seen its menacing light long before he hears its
voice, knows exactly where it is and why. There are ghoul watchers
already by the time he arrives and he can see, even from across the

118

road, that someone has bashed in the front door to his office and that the room at the back is fully ablaze. He races ahead of his throbbing shadow across to the pulse of it, but the heat is too strong and strikes him back again and again. The smell of spirits is still in the air.

He retreats to the knot of watchers and someone—friend?—says, "They've sent for the fire boys, Snoggers. The hoses should be here in a minute."

Helpless he is, standing watching the work of a life-time gobbled in moments. They are all agape with it, and by now there are children in night-wear yelping with festival. Flames throw wild light on the faces of the crowd, and Boyd, illuminated like a saint, prays, "Christ, oh, Christ, let them hurry!"

Time crawls in deliberate collusion with the speed of the flames now mounting in spiralling peaks above the shop's eaves. Boyd, who is insane with suspicion, wonders have the firemen been suborned, when suddenly the dray lurches round a bend of the street. When the water starts to pour the crowd gives out its bestial sigh. Of regret? Boyd wonders viciously, for the shop next to his had been starting to catch and the crowd was being denied its bread and circuses with every conquering hiss of water-play. The two hoses are turned against the scarlet heart of it all which burns and slows, burns and slows. It is controlled within minutes, but the hoses have come too late, Boyd knows. Slushing through puddles to his burnt-out front office, he is conscious only of black ash and water, the rubble of twenty-five years accumulating behind his rage and hopelessness. He would weep but for the watchers, and defiantly pushes his coughing way through smoke denser in the outer room, where he can still make out the ruined press and near it the clotted, reeking pile of the next day's issue.

He gives the smouldering heap a kick and sparks and smoke fly out.

"That's all it would have been, anyway," he thinks sourly. "Sparks and smoke." A miserable fireworks at that, a fizzer, followed by a lot of political obscurantism.

He walks more slowly through the wreckage back to the front of the office and it is not amusing, not even faintly and hysterically funny, when a renewed blast from the hose hits him with such a wallop he is knocked to the ground.

Through this sour comedy he hears Buckmaster's voice giving directions. "Hold it, you fellows," he is saying kindly. "You've hit Boyd. There now, spin it over this way."

Boyd scrambles to his feet, his clothing a mush, and he walks to the sound of the voice on the edge of the crowd and his eyes catch Buckmaster's and hold them.

"Administering the sacraments, too," he says.

"We should have insisted on going with him," Dorahy says, addressing himself to the Jenners and Lunt.

Dinner is over and he is standing in the long living-room facing the others who are seated near the window. They are all conscious of the revival of a long-lost warmth that both soothes and disturbs. Gracie has ceased examining young Jenner's wife for flaws, and loves both of them, while Lucy for the second time in their lives takes Lunt's hand and extends the other to Dorahy, embracing him as well. Her anxiety reaches out for the significance of hand-clasps, the touch of eyes.

Lunt says tiredly, "Will someone tell me exactly what is going on? I feel you others know."

Lucy releases his hand and swings in her chair to face him, to disturb his resignation.

"Only Tom knows," she says. "It's the paper. Tomorrow's. There's an article about you and the trouble at Mandarana."

Lunt laughs harshly. "So long ago!" he cries. "He didn't ask me. Didn't ask whether I'd mind."

"Should he have?" someone asks.

"I think so," Lunt says. "I do think so. I haven't come back here to make trouble. Tom talked me into coming back, God knows how. I don't want the mess it's turned out to be."

Dorahy says pacifically, "It's no good going over all that. It's done now and there's nothing we can do about it. It's my fault. Was my suggestion. Blame me if you like."

"You've made a lot of trouble," Lunt agrees. "Who's it going to help?"

For the first time in a week Dorahy is stringently honest.

"It's going to destroy," he admits. "Buckmaster. Sweetman. They'll be exposed for what they are."

120

"Do you think anyone really cares at this stage?" asks the older Jenner. "Do you?" He is as persistent as Dorahy.

"I hope so," Dorahy replies. "Oh, I hope so."

"An avenging angel," Lunt remarks. "You're mad, Tom. I mean that. Crazed for a wrong cause." He frowns. "And now Boyd thinks they've got wind of it, eh? Can't any of you realise that I've come back through love, not hate! Love!"

Dorahy's explanation is pithy. Lamp-light makes anything possible with its antiphon and response of flicker and flow. The clear glass mantles give definite truths—which subdue. They sit in silence after his words, listening to the night outside where there is nothing but the noises of insects in the viscous air and the looming authority of trees whose branches reach out and touch the three wide verandas of the house.

Restless, Dorahy walks out to the head of the garden steps that plunge into night-dark with the assurance of a swimmer. Like everything about this house, the steps are firm and resolute. The township is a mile away on the northern road and, examining the sky for portents, Dorahy could swear to orange light. He ponders fire, dismisses and reponders. The glow swells and fades. He goes down into the steady dark of the trees and walks though the scent of cane and frangipani to the road that runs with few curves back to the hub of it all. He can see nothing.

Yet returning to the veranda and looking back into the lighted room he does see something after all.

Gracie Tilburn is seated at the piano and is playing and singing "Auld Lang Syne." Her voice floats like a miracle on the waiting air. Young Jenner is absorbed in her. He might be sixteen again. And in the corner of the window bay Lucy and Lunt are sitting with hands clasped. They look at each other and no words come.

GRACIE TILBURN is soggy with tears.

Lonely in her hotel room, unassuaged by the banalities of small talk that have sustained her throughout the week, she gives way to an urge to weep that has been pressing at the back of her heart all day. Once yielded to, its luxury becomes addictive and she weeps for having wept, groping through oceans of regret, a baffled swimmer who has lost track of the life-line. There has been a concert (successful), several women's afternoon teas (tepid), and three private dinners at homes where the male guests were reluctant to flirt under their wives' noses.

She is weeping for Tim Jenner and the loss of him—that is, the loss of the sensitivity of him. She won't credit him with having aged and sees him devoured by family cares—though at the concert she could have sworn that he was regarding her as he had once regarded her while she sang. Blinkered, he is. Like some dray horse that looks neither right nor left, strains on the load, and pulls and pulls and goes forward between worlds of happening without a sideways glance. The fool!

But is she any happier for having glanced sideways too often? She gulps noisily at this thought and hears an unexpected knock on her bedroom door with rage. How terrible she must be looking with the practical ravages of grief all over her person registering a kind of monochrome complaint!

She does quick things to her face and hair before the spotty mirror, straightens skirt and blouse, dabs powder wherever, and re-thinks herself as she opens the door on Boyd, who is standing in an attitude of submission. To what? she wonders.

122

He is surprised by her puff-ball face, usually so elegantly clad in clichés. Flesh is making its own admissions and he drops his eyes to conceal their first flash of curiosity before inspecting her frankly.

"Hullo," he says. "I'm lucky to find you."

"Home-sick." She explains her face away. "For here and there."

"Coming back's the devil, isn't it?" he comments, aware of her lie, and hesitates before he says, "Lucy and I won't be able to join you here for dinner this evening after all." It seems like a blow to her already punched-silly face. "I'm sorry," he says. "Lucy sends her love."

Gracie can feel the moulding of her face gradually return to its normal shape. She puts out both her hands. Words are never enough. Boyd catches them, though he had thought of giving them a miss— and begins to smile at the idea. Friendship is like trapeze artistry for gods of the high wire, he muses: one swings and the other, trusting in the first and in God, wheels over all sorts of abysses of mistrust to be caught firmly by welcoming hands. Or words. He would hate to let her drop, really. She is more vulnerable than ever with the lineal registrations of time upon her face.

"Never mind!" Gracie cries. "How kind of you to call! Would you care to have tea with me on the terrace before you go back?"

He doesn't care to, but he will. He says so. Her eyes widen with pleasure. She had not believed he would. Some piece of male, she thinks thankfully, any piece, in dutiful attendance. She gathers her bag and goes out with him into the hall which is full of gothic gloom, green light and polished cedar. The stair-case is almost baronial. Its curves meet their obliquity, there is a momentary clash and they descend side by side.

Gracie's face is fully remoulded. She will be able to be coy soon, and by the time they arrive at the antithesis of all this—wide green front, palms, blue water—she is recovered in full. In white, she thinks with non-sequitur vanity. I'm at my best in white. Women should wear lots of it. Hers, though crumpled from a passionate hurling of herself upon the bed, is frail and lovely. The creases are natural enough. She steers him to a table beyond the others who are having pre-luncheon drinks. Leaves grow over this end of the terrace, broad, green and sharp with light where Boyd seats her absent-mindedly and drags over a cane chair for himself. All the morning he has been supervising the clean-up of the wreckage in his office and is still numb. Dorahy and Lunt proceed endlessly past him, the fiasco of them both.

They amble through pleasantries for ten minutes, Gracie pouring his tea with what she believes to be old-world charm, and they gaze at each other less stiffly above the cups.

"Tell me, Gracie," he says, "do you remember the affair at Mandarana? I know you were only a girl then, but I thought perhaps you might."

She is astonished at the change in him during the very utterance. The roly-poly cheeks lose their bluntness. The eyes narrow.

"Of course. But it is twenty years ago now."

"That's what everyone says. Did you know Charlie Lunt at all in those days?"

"No. Not really. I knew who he was but that's all."

"Did you ever hear any talk about what happened to him?"

"Some. Some. But it's so long ago," she repeats. "It's hard to remember."

"What do you think really happened? I'm curious because my life's work here was destroyed last night as a kind of bitter result." He takes a sip of tea and it too is bitter on his tongue. He has no use for sugar.

"I only heard what you others heard. What Tim Jenner told me. How they cared for him. That sort of thing."

"Did he ever accuse anyone?" Boyd muses aloud.

Gracie shifts her chair into a bigger shade patch. "No," she says. "Never. Tim told me he wouldn't talk about it right from the very first."

Useless, Boyd thinks. Hopeless. Why do I care? Have I caught the itch from Dorahy? Certainly he is mad with anger over last night's disaster and now is beginning to assume the cloak of avenger as well. Is there no end to it?

Take this hotel. Any hotel. Place in it artificial scenes of welcome and farewell. Match the stain of easily wrung tears with the green wall-paint, and the laughter with glimpses of starched table linen, and still you have nothing. The impersonality is truly miraculous and you hate this for ever and all places like it. Against this backdrop Boyd prepares for a plunge.

He enlists Gracie's moral aid. Can he count on her? Does she believe in the essential evil of men like Buckmaster? She nods, only half-willingly, but she nods. Is that all? The nodding head? The acquiescent shoulders? On the last evening of all these false evenings will she plead for Lunt through actions however indirect?

124

Gracie is accustomed to deviousness of a more polished kind with only herself at stake. She is ignorant of how to act for others.

"How?" she asks. Boyd tells her. By refusing to sing. By giving reasons.

But the programme has been prepared, she counters. She can't do this. But she can, Boyd insists. Not only can. Must. For Lunt. For Dorahy. For himself.

It's male logic, she thinks. Totally self-involved.

"You know, I don't really like Tom Dorahy."

"You're not doing it for him alone. It's Lunt, Lunt."

"But I scarcely know Mr Lunt. And he doesn't want it done for him—twenty years too late."

"There's me," he says. "And the Jenners—Tim and his father believe in Lunt and the wrong done him. They were people you loved."

She is silent. The tea has grown cold and is still undrunk. Her relationship with Tim was once the slowly unfolded rose of her. Now it's the worm in the bud.

"If I could talk it over with him—Tim, that is." She hopes and Boyd understands more than he displays.

"I'll arrange it."

"It's too late now," she replies, meaning something else.

"It's never too late."

She comes suddenly to her senses. The gut of her is disturbed, but there is a coherence about this man speaking with her that makes her loves and fears seem paltry. She understands that he is seeking now more than vengeance for last night's blow, that he sees the town as seeded in disaster and brought forth as bitter fruit.

"Forgive me," she says with honesty this one time at least, coyness put away and the trumpery of it. "I'm thinking too much of me. I'll do whatever you wish."

Boyd leans across the table and takes her hand. The table rocks and tea slops in both saucers. It is comic at this moment. Boyd is fat, shapeless and unheroic to look at. His virtue is in his voice or his smile. He gives her both.

The treacle of summer. It filled the courtroom in glutinous waves. Mr Sheridan had gone so far as to remove his coat—and that without diffidence. He did some paper-shuffling, refilled his water glass from the jug.

So far as can be ascertained, he said, peering hard through his spectacles at the packed room, there is no certain evidence that Lieutenant Frederick Buckmaster acted altogether improperly in the affair at Mandarana on the twenty-fourth of June.

He paused to glare at Dorahy who had let out a snort of rage. No certain evidence, I said, and that I mean. My colleagues and I have sifted all the evidence brought before this select committee and our findings are that, while there were certain irregularities in the proceedings of that day, the entire unhappy events were the result of wrongly placed enthusiasm, a perhaps too nice sense of injustice and the understandable grievance of men who found the difficulties of living—and I mean pioneer living—aggravated to an unbearable pitch by the extra annoyance the blacks posed to their efforts.

Annoyances! hissed Dorahy. His hands were clasped so hard the knuckles ached, and the ache spread up his arms till it touched the acute perimeters of his mind. Unheeded, sweat dribbled its way down the nape of his neck. From outside the fragmented words of passers-by floated improperly in, to the annoyance of the magistrate who frowned and cleared his throat.

Hideously, Dorahy became aware that Lieutenant Buckmaster, seated down from him two rows and to the right, was beginning to grin. A twitch, like some frightful tic, attacked the schoolmaster's knee. He leant forward as Sheridan continued speaking.

While our findings tend to absolve Lieutenant Buckmaster from deliberate malice in the matter, nevertheless the court feels it must warn him against acting uncircumspectly or with undue haste in other matters of this kind. Distance, and consequent delay with the arrival of official advice, have had an adverse effect in the whole unfortunate business. However, Lieutenant Buckmaster is warned that in future he must not act without due consultation with his superiors, even if the delay seems impossibly difficult in the circumstances.

Warned! cried Dorahy over the shocked and packed room. Warned! He was on his feet babbling.

Mr Sheridan glanced at the assisting constable, who shoved his way along the rows until he could reach Dorahy.

A travesty! A farce! Dorahy kept shouting. Strong arms were propelling him to the aisle. Within the blur of faces round him only Buckmaster's shone with the greasy clarity of success. You! he cried incoherently. You you you!

126

As they got him outside into the brighter day, he could hear the magistrate resume his monotone summation.

You must try to keep calm, sir, the constable kept saying. He felt sorry for the silly coot. Try having a bit of a sitdown in the shade.

Dorahy was weeping hopelessly, the tears and the sweat griming his fanatic face. Let me back in there, he kept begging over and over, pushing beyond the constable's barrier arm at the closed courthouse door. Let me back.

Sorry, sir, said the constable, who was firm and kind as well. If you don't stop it, I'll have to take you in charge. He steered him to a bench alongside the hall. Just sit there, like, for a bit, he said. It's the bloody heat getting at us. That's what it is.

He stepped back and took up a guard's stance by the doorway.

Dorahy came to his senses slowly. He wiped his face off with the arm of his sleeve and sat there till the heart quietened. From the courthouse came the shuffling sounds of the assembly rising, but he didn't move. He sat his shame stubbornly there and watched as they came out, watched and watched and found no words for it.

I T IS the last night.

Take time over this, over the pathos engendered by the lamps, the slow rain on the iron roof of the hall, the wistfulness of streamers coming loose. There are too many people and by now some of them have lost the crack-hearty jauntiness of that first evening and have their faces settled into the lines that betray their age and a grief for it which they attribute to this last act of farewell.

They are wrong. They have simply regained themselves as they are, not as they used to be. They are simply a crowd of elderly people, disappointed by time, who are longing to get home. And this common denominator, home, is not what they have come to visit after all but that which they have left.

They are more critical of the place, too. Its shortcomings are beginning to be listed on their tongues. They know they could never settle here again. They are glad they got away. They are disappointed in each other: the fabled jokester, the hero of other years, is disguised by fat and wrinkles, is a feeble punster at that, who worries about his audience more than his words, is become a bore with ill-polished shoes and a suit that sags. The beauties have turned shrewish. God bless the lot of them, for the unpleasantnesses that once irritated are beginning to reassert themselves. Skins are peeled from eyes.

Barney Sweetman is chairing again. Buckmaster is by his side. Their wives are on stage as well, dried-out ladies who are over-powered by Gracie Tilburn, guest artist in lavender silk. The flowers in vases are all lies, and they are limp from strategy. The bunting is conscious of hypocrisy.

In this hall, noisy with conversation, last-minute recognitions and

128

bogus promises to keep in touch are made. It is sizzling with an amity in the centre of which Boyd's party is seated halfway from the door. Dorahy, pale with anticipation, can barely speak. Boyd, stocky as a bull, has his intransigent jaw set and jutting. He has the manic fanaticism of the recently converted.

When Sweetman stands and raises his hand for silence, the buzzing roar of the hall subsides as eyes focus on the big fellow who is more or less king of the kids, of the town, an infallible potentate. Up there he is speaking *ex cathedra,* and they prepare to hang on his lips.

"Dear old friends," he begins and his audience, strangely enough, instead of melting, hardens. They are not aware of it themselves, but they have fought forward to a sort of self-truth which sees themselves as less than friends. There have been too many petty arguments, too many misplaced remarks, a lack of delicacy in reminiscence; too much has been forgotten and too much remembered. "You are probably feeling tonight as I feel, tremendously sad on looking about this room and seeing faces familiar and meaning so much."

The crowd generously goes with him. After all it's a bugger of a job, this speech-making. But they go only a little way.

"We have had a week of recollections and memories, but more than that we have had a resurgence of the spirit—yes, the very spirit—that helped create this town. I find this moving, indeed." He pauses—it is a moment when he could have wiped his eyes but doubts the wisdom of the gesture coming too early. He goes on in a voice calculated to wring.

"The soul, or rather the life-blood of this town is its people. Yes. I say it again—those people who gave all they had to the building of it." A more weak-minded claque cheers. Some women dab hankies. "All we have built here," Sweetman continues, seizing the moment by its straggly forelock, "comes more or less from nothing. What you see now is the result of our work, our work and all we put into making this town what it is. I could name those people who are sitting before me with us tonight. But that would mean naming every one of you"—That's clever!—"and looking around at one another as you are now you see there, in the faces on each side of you, in front and behind, those who were the builders of the future."

Dorahy thinks he might vomit.

"In those days," Sweetman says, "you might remember the struggles we had with the south. You might recall the Separation League. The struggles to get coloured labour. The opposition from those who understood little and felt less about those problems peculiar to this part of the world. And all the time—I repeat, all the time—in the face of these difficulties, we pushed ahead doing what we believed to be right, sacrificing all for the sake of those who would come after."

Prolonged cheers. They are melting again.

"Yes," he continues when the blast subsides, "we were unpopular boys in the Separation League." He allows himself a roguish grin, but it comes out crooked. "We were firebrands then. Younger, of course. But firebrands. And I choose that word especially because we were burning with zeal to promote the interests of this town."

His choice of word stuns Boyd and Dorahy. The monstrous cheek of it, and Sweetman, legs apart, braced before his world!

"We were interested only in what concerned the good of us all. Dear friends, tonight, as you are on the eve of departure, I want you to take away memories of those times and remember how we fought together. No battle against the nation's enemies has more sincerity and strength than the battles we fought. There is no greater comradeship than that which we had." He stops to allow them all to dry their eyes. "Now that we are all of us nearing the twilight of our years, there is this we can remember—what I have said tonight will shine as youngly for you now as it did then."

The applause is sickeningly tremendous. People can drown in shallows. Dorahy is coughing into his wet hands while Sweetman smiles like a Messiah.

"And now," he says, "once again I have pleasure in asking your own Miss Gracie Tilburn to sing for you—as she sang earlier in the week—directly to your hearts."

There is another storm of clapping and the pianist comes on stage to the worn upright. Gracie, splendid in that fluid silk, moves to the front of the rostrum, inwardly hesitant despite that outer assurance, and Dorahy and Boyd hold their breaths. She is torn between what she has been asked to do and what the crowd expects—and it is a wink that does it.

Centre front, Freddie Buckmaster catches her eye and closes one of his in a huge and vulgar implication. Her disgust rejects him afresh, and she hears her own voice saying firmly and richly through the pianist's opening chords, "Ladies and gentlemen, before I sing to you

130

tonight, I ask you to give up a few minutes of your time to listen to Mr William Boyd. He has something to say to you all."

The audience is rattled. The pianist half turns. Sweetman, who has regained his seat in showers of light, starts up, but not before he sees in the heart of the hall Snoggers Boyd standing on his chair and circling so that he takes the entire gathering into his compelling eye.

There is some uncertain clapping and a lot of murmuring. As Gracie resumes her seat, an isolated cry of "Shame!" rings out.

Boyd is standing perched there above the goggling crowd, an unimpressive man except for his voice, which will have profound and resonant convictions. Carefully he waits until the silence of speculation has deepened and then he begins, speaking quietly.

"Ladies and gentlemen, I will not take up much of your time." He knows there isn't much. From the corner of his eye he can see Buckmaster père on stage gesturing to his son. "As you know I have been writing a series of articles for you each day on the very people who have loomed large in the progress of this town." The silence has a trembling quality. The air quivers. "You are all aware," Boyd continues, "of the misadventure that overtook the *Gazette* last Wednesday evening, when not only the next day's issue was destroyed but also the plates to set it up. When Mr Sweetman chose to speak of firebrands he couldn't have chosen a more apposite word, for the firebrands are still with us."

He lets his allegation rest in half a minute's tension. The hall rustles. They get it. There are shouts of "Sit down, old man!" from the Buckmaster claque, and Barney Sweetman is observed leaving the stage. But Boyd merely pitches his voice above the beginning din.

"My offices were destroyed, there is no doubt about this, deliberately"—he emphasises the word—"and perhaps by the very spirit which Mr Sweetman said animated some of us in past years. Who would do this, I do not know for certain. But I do suspect. What I do know is that I was going to tell you all of a humbler soul than those who waged battle in the Separation League, a humbler spirit than those who fought to use coloured labour cheap, a meeker spirit than those who waged unceasing war against the blacks. I am referring to Charles Lunt who is with us in the hall this evening."

The stillness is fragile. Boyd's wandering eye observes Sweetman in consultation with two bruisers of young men by the rear door.

131

"Perhaps," he goes on more loudly and strongly, "many of you did not know him. He was not a pushing man. It's more than likely you were unaware of him, for he practised his charity without airing it. But tragedy attended him. In his efforts to befriend those blacks who camped near his lonely farm, in his efforts to protect them, he lost a limb and almost lost his life."

On stage Buckmaster is going mad. His insanity boils blood, thickens features, clogs the shouts and gabbled directions he is trying to give his bully boys who have come up the aisle and are struggling to haul Boyd from his chair. As Boyd wobbles with the dragging arms, and as Lunt is seen to rise beside him stumped by his wooden leg, other shouts of "Fair go!" and "Give him a go!" rattle from all over the room. The audience has been split in half.

Gracie Tilburn, her red hair ablaze, rushes to the very footlights and pleads for silence. It is so outrageous for a woman to assert herself among men, the hall is temporarily shocked and muted. Fred Buckmaster, shoving his way along the side to get at Boyd, is so appalled he stops to screech at her, "Sit down you crazy bitch!" Some devotee clips his mouth for that, and another tussle starts.

Finally it is Barney Sweetman who shows reason. Politically. His angel face torn, his age humped all over his thinning shoulders, he cries high-pitchedly from the very back of the hall, "Stop this, everyone. Stop spoiling the week." His voice cracks suddenly with the effort of it. "Stop negating," he croaks, "those very qualities I spoke of. Stop!"

The crowd looks from Boyd to Sweetman, who cannily takes a punt on reasonableness. Shrewdly he guesses at the course the crowd, this mindless animal, will take. Boyd is a village innocent after all. Sweetman knows all about crowds.

"Let Boyd be heard," he pleads, giving his failed-playboy smile. He'll go down as a fair player if nothing else. "Everyone has a right to be heard."

The factions subside into murmurous dissidence while Boyd, flinging off the restraining arms, regains his balance. He gazes all about him and senses the split.

"As I was saying," he continues, "there was a certain night that year, twenty years ago, when Charles Lunt paid dearly for what he believed, when he paid for the very respect he gave humanity." Boyd goes on speaking more quietly and persuasively now. The awakened crowd, scandal-hungry, ravenously wants every word. ". . . and it was there that someone from the town, Tom Dorahy, in fact, found him, lashed to the dead body of his native friend." Boyd pauses and looks about the hall, but his eyes finally come to rest on the stage. Who would do a thing like this?" he asks. The crowd is stirring and whispering, but the whispers hiss. "And two days after this, as many of you remember, a trumped up vigilante force rode out to Mandarana and in cold blood dispatched six of the natives from Lunt's tribe. I call it Lunt's tribe, for they were dear to him. But more—one of the terrified gins flung herself over The Leap, her baby in her arms." The crowd is dumb with it. "It lived, that baby," Boyd says into the expecting silence. "It was cared for by my wife and me and then by the Jenners. You all remember her. And then, somehow, whether it was an instinctive turn towards the protector of her people we will never know, but that young woman sought out Charles Lunt and has cared for him these last few years."

Everywhere there are eyes, Boyd observes, polished and gleaming. They are watching his mouth, clutching at what it has to spill.

He says, "That was the story I intended telling you. It is nothing worth burning a building down for, as you can see, but it is worth the telling for it is simply another sample such as Mr Sweetman gave you of the martyrdoms this town exacted. Why anyone should want the story not told, you and I can only guess. It is a matter I leave to the consciences of those who tried to stop me. I make no accusations. The matter can stand there—but at least I have spoken out."

Sweetman has guessed aright.

The crowd is embarrassed now. It has been told things it did not wish to hear—not now, not when it has been softened into a spurious amity once again. The champion of their mediocrity is twitching on stage before their astounded eyes, and even their mediocrity by this turn of events has been belittled. Sweetman had given them an image of themselves to treasure, and now it has been scrawled upon by this other man. Some resent, even hate him for it. Others, believing in the imperial order of things, have their loyalties to the town powers cemented. And many, teased by Boyd's story, are filled with a grieving quality of love. Arguing and shouting break out. The crowd is two-headed. Everywhere people are standing and pushing out from their seats in an animal perplexity, and it is in vain that Sweetman shrills for order over the chaos.

133

As Boyd resumes his seat, the tension leaving him, he is suddenly aware of Lunt's face, an aged and dreadful white, bending towards him.

"Damn you," he is saying softly and penetratingly. "Damn you both. Damn you, damn you!"

He struggles upright, his wooden leg catching for a moment on that of a chair, and then he has shoved past the two of them to the aisle and is wrestling his way out through the crowd.

Shocked but immediately aware, Boyd is on his feet after him in silent pleading for understanding. Dorahy, stunned by this condemnation that has rammed the truth home at last, sits on for a few seconds, then, driven by an ego-wild need for absolution, fights his way up the aisle after them.

Through the sweet and the sour of it Lunt, Boyd and Dorahy push their way to the rear door. There is an acrid taste in the mouth. Arms seek to restrain them, either through love or hate. Hands clutch. Voices hail or accuse. But they can only shove sweatily through the praise and the blame towards the cooler rational night outside.

Buckmaster towering, blood-pressure up, is now screaming hoarsely for silence in the stifling room. He signals to the pianist and while she hits some expectant chords and while the audience, grudgingly accepting this signal at last, fights its way back to seats, the three squeezing through the doorway are conscious of having taken most of the hatred with them. And it is when they reach the top of the steps that some unknown, sour with self-disillusion, lurches out from the shadowed avengers who have been waiting for them and hurls Lunt brutally down the stairs.

From on stage Gracie Tilburn watches with horror, even as she takes up her position beside the piano, a small hate-pack headed by young Buckmaster, Romney and Armitage, surge out the double doors after them. She sees the Jenners jostled carelessly to one side; she glimpses Lunt being hurled and sees Boyd and Dorahy taking themselves after him.

Mechanically, she starts to sing.

Outside, Lunt is lying on the ground, his wooden leg hideously askew, his body sprawled face down. In his forced descent he has whacked his skull against a corner post and lies there utterly still. There is a small trickle of blood already blurred by rain.

Boyd bends over him, and then looks up at Dorahy.

134

"Well," he says bitterly, "you've had your martyr."

Then the pack is upon them, silent, and deadly because of this. The two men find themselves hauled by enemies who seem all clenched fist and boot to the private darknesses at the side of the hall where the gristle of their argument is stretched and torn.

While they endure the splitting punches and the duller agony of kicks, from inside the hall Gracie's voice rises liquidly in song. She is telling of old acquaintance as Dorahy goes down at last, seeing Boyd, his face dark with blood, leaning sideways in slow motion. Dorahy is so tired he accepts the fleshly damage of his enemies like some peculiar blessing, lying on the rain-wet grass, his lips curled in the smile of pain. Somewhere close beside him Boyd is groaning into the air as Gracie's voice soars and falls in nostalgic untruth.

The hate-pack is gone now, leaving them alone in the dark with the singing voice going on and on, endlessly it seems, through their battered ears. Full-throatedly, the audience joins in the singing and roars chorus after chorus.

It has almost forgotten the victims already.

THE ACOLYTE

FOR AMY WITTING

who also knows
"how the work goes naked to the weather"

"There's been an accident!" they said,
"Your servant's cut in half; he's dead!"
"Indeed!" said Mr. Jones, "and please
Send me the half that's got my keys."

HARRY GRAHAM,
Ruthless Rhymes

I

"CREDIBLE?" HE ASKED, swivelling his dark glasses round on the chair where he had supposed Neilsen to be sitting. But the chair was empty and Neilsen, shoving his sticky proboscis critically over a port, had ambled across the room to the piano and spoke his mercantile rubbish straight into the back of the questioner's head.

"It's a splendidly crafted little score," he conceded. "Splendidly. Bubbling. Active. Mildly sardonic at times, I think you'd agree, Holberg, but only mildly. And always utterly credible."

He paused for a connoisseur's sip—it might have been a wine he was discussing with his mush-phrases—and swivelled on me for the confirmatory clauses I'd been in the habit of giving for years. But my tongue was in clamps. Through the glass wall at the end of the long room doric trunks of trees sleeted with green tottered all along the edge of the valley like some massive breakwater heading into the distant scrolls of sea. And there was rain, the continuous speaking drizzle of it spitting on glass, on terrace, on the bird-stained statuary among the bushes and the banana clumps. Wherever I looked there was a kind of subtropical smudginess, the reduced emotions blunted by heat and wet that induced mould not only on the contents of the room—shapes which Holberg needed to apprehend by touch—but the tactility, too, of my responses. I shrugged and said nothing, observing Holberg's frown above his glasses. Certain captive objects were practising their own form of insubordination—bamboo blinds flapped

141

in air stir and Hilda's kitchen voice—effect off-stage—careened from a crash of crockery and the sudden stench of sauerkraut.

I want to assure you from the beginning, now that I am absorbed by my revolutionary climacteric, that I had all the properties of a suitably structured childhood. Fruit-juiced, three-mealed, educationally toyed, disciplined with all the footballer logic (tempered by a scatter-brained phoney intellectualism in my mother) that a middle-class dad with a company car and conservative expense account could display. It was intensive gardening and my tiny shrub grew into the sort of sapling they felt they deserved, just a touch of thrips on the leaves at the right time, a non-dangerous performance at examinations and two cups for running. Poking my fifteen-year-old snout into the diffident houses of the underprivileged who lived on the perimeter of our country town, I caught exciting whiffs of a different sort of privilege, a plosive bumalongerie of hanging about, just—hanging about; to lounge, absorbed in nothing but the physicality of each other's adolescent flesh while we batted back and forth the sort of jargon talk that excluded every age group but our own. I suppose it was a class of sub-male vitalism, harmless but exciting to me because it explored part of the world so unlike my tepid and non-worldly term-time existence. Since I didn't altogether fit in with the beady-eyed milk-bar boys, I was soaked in a kind of envy, fighting every inch of the cussing way for recognition. I had to settle for an insipid watered-down toleration.

It was with half a dozen of them that I would bum truck rides to other towns, learning to drink where no one questioned my tall-for-it age, or, waiting until the sun bled itself over the grass plains, lug off to stand our attentive pimples at the greasy doors of dance-halls, the epicentre of the up-swelling brawls in which we were sometimes involved. "Where have you been, son?" rotarian dad would ask. And I would fob him off with some long-winded lie that we both knew he did not believe: the mirror-world of between-terms where I saw myself from the left as it were, a lanky reverse of what my more reputable rackabout acquaintances supposed me to be. If my wealthier pals—Judge Traill! Dr Sibley!—asked me home for a holiday week, my mother would become quite faint with pleasure. I was too kind a boy to let her know how it bored me.

You want to know how I got where I am? How the sauerkraut, the long glass room, the port-bibbing sycophant, the great man crabbing his way along the fly-walk score of a negligible quartet? None of your big author pretence, mind you, that this is the couch serial rendered coherent to my alienist. None of that fake hogwash at all. This rain has an insistent nostalgia that accretes recollections like its own continuing droplets, and I am reminded thereby of my appalling normalcy, the copious banalities of the day to day to day over the last twelve years of discipleship.

Which began, minuscule, at Grogbusters, a border town of rangy street sprawl in the southern part of the State with apple and grape farms plotting its granite ridges and sheep on random story-book squares. Far enough from home to blanket our indiscretions. Close enough for flight. One frosted evening of spiny planes of cold we trundled our holiday restlessness into a school of arts fifty-fifty (Of what? Loomer asked, heaving a phlegmy cough) and propped languidly along the side-wall to snigger and envy. A three-piece band was working prosily over the latest crotch-boiler and the dancers were bent into agonies of intimacy. After a while my eyes sheered off and were absorbed by the players: man on sax, butter-fat; thumper-drummer; pianist. Yes. The pianist. A curly fellow built like a full-back but with a manual finesse that even to me was apparent, perhaps in the sensitivity with which he conceded the rights of the rest of the group.

He was what you might call a folk-figure in that town. A kind of off-beat conservative who made out financially on a pension and jobs around the clubs. None of this I knew then, gawping with Loomer in the blaze and beat, but I sifted through a lot of persuasive half-truths later to discover a more-or-less about him, that he roomed in a boarding-house, played serious music, drank at every pub in town and was a small lion for almost every inaccessible socialite Grogbusters could boast: the sort of women who collected amusing oddities to stave off boredom—shrunken heads, the preserved genitals of native hillsmen, shark-tooth cigarette holders, freak carrots shaped into the hustings features of your favourite legislator—oh, anything that might provide pseudo-artistic talking-point at Grogbusters folk evenings. With that inexplicable mixture of charity and curiosity that surrounds the afflicted and satisfies some cannibal hunger in their patrons, he became a recognizable figure in better homes who greeted his Liszt and his Ravel with an almost offensive astonishment that seemed to marvel that blindness had not removed every other faculty as well.

They enjoyed guiding his uncertain feet around homestead verandas until it bored them or watching him eat with his fingers more difficult chops, repulsed and fascinated, and tolerated his drunken jazz assaults on their untuned pianos because his affliction was so outrageous and so total. Not that I discovered all this till much later when it began to be realized that he exaggereated his genius and his helplessness and took advantage of the nongs to put on ballerina turns of temperament: tiddling blues'd Bach at the R.S.L. and turning in sonata versions of "Cheek to Cheek" at soirées. It was ages before they knew they were being had.

Only twice in those last two years of school did I ever talk to him although I saw him often enough persuading some rachitic bar-room piano to applaud our libations. My thrips increased. I was growing away from Loomer and Sack who had first liberated me, and growing away too from Rotary dad and C.W.A. mum whose importance for me was now limited to my financial needs. *Eheu,* for that. *Eheu.* You see: my expensive boarding-school had given me something, if only the sensitivity to regret the need to use other people, assimilated along with the school song. Just after I had croaked its rousing choruses for the last time, war broke out and I returned home to a febrility of recruitment agitation fostered by my father's contemporaries who'd done their bit twenty odd years before. Loomer and Sack had already gone and I sat around heavily at home brooding over my future, playing records and irritating my father, who kept demanding of space, "The boy must have some idea what he wants to do. I knew at his age. My God, I did!"

A rictus grin concealed my terrible, my real despair.

How the sauerkraut?

The first of that twice. It was a year ago: beyond the age when I could cutely hand round my mother's cakes at her afternoons, I had been raised to the status of accompanying ("This is my boy!"—dad) adolescent who might be allowed a sherry while all round him the adults swapped crops and town politics and sporting fixtures. A little evening at the McEvoys. Not any evening, mind you, but a pre-Yuletide whacker to celebrate their apple orchard, the largest in Grogbusters, becoming engaged to a sheep property farther west. I was a shy boy, and after congratulating the merging couple huddled myself near a food table and sipped my sherry and watched and listened.

I didn't know about love, but it seemed to me that the happy pair

144

were doing the right amount of social canoodling and I became bored with watching their performance and concentrated on a little knot not far from me. Their names? Well, it doesn't matter now—Reg, Ted, Joe—that sort of name; but at the heart of their circle was the pianist character I had seen on my sorties with Loomer and Sack. He must have said something funny, for they all roared and after a while one of the men said, "How about giving us a tune, Jack?" He swung round obligingly and I saw he was wearing dark glasses, just as before, though I hadn't been curious about them, merely put them down to gimmick, fad. Mrs McEvoy had him at the piano in a flash (determined to get full value) and Mr McEvoy roared, "Silence, everybody!"—grinning like a goat!—"Jack's going to give us a bit of a tune."

Everybody held a glass at attention, the sheep property slipped an arm round the apple orchard, one or two ladies gave hasty whispered explanations to neighbours (what? what?) and the man at the piano, giving a little smile, began playing a Bach transcription of an organ fantasia and fugue. I knew. I'd heard it in chapel. Some rub-off from those expensive fees. He played magnificently, even I knew that, sixteen and thripped, sipping my sherry and watching his powerful shoulders driving that piano into massive statements. They all sat or stood around, a little uncomfortable, and they waited a long time for him to finish, and when he got somewhere near the last variation in the fugue I became aware he was fiddling around with it, cheeking it up with some crazy Fats Waller stuff, but everyone, reverent as hell, nodded and watched and nodded and when he had finished clapped a lot and said that was wonderful and Mr McEvoy offered him a beer and said, "Great playing, Jack, but how about something with a little more tune to it, eh? Something sentimental for the kids." And I began to giggle and father spotted me and asked, "What's up, son? I'd go easy on that sherry if I were you."

After that, I spent the rest of the evening by the piano. He slipped into the sort of easy stuff they wanted and could talk through and I dragged a chair over to one side of him and watched his hands turn melody inside out.

Dancing had started. My parents had forgotten me. During a break between numbers the pianist turned in my direction and said, "Get us a beer, matey." He smiled widely below those dark glasses and I was off in a flash. "Thanks," he said when I put it into his hand; and I noticed his unsureness in taking it.

145

"I like your playing," I said. "It's great!"

"You do, eh? Well, I can't do much else." He took a long drink and put the glass back on the piano. "Except that. I'm quite good at that."

I giggled and he swung on me again.

"That funny, is it? You're only a kid, aren't you?"

"Sixteen."

"Well," he said. "Well."

"I've heard you before," I offered, wanting to extend the conversation. "Round the pubs and places."

"My meat and drink," he said, letting his hands drift into nonsense.

"What was that?" I asked when he'd finished.

"That? Oh just something I wrote. 'Sober Gentleman' I call it. The evening is full of them. Hand me my beer will you, matey?" I reached it down and he fumbled it, splashing his trousers, but he didn't seem to notice. Something was stirring in my mind. You find me slow, I suppose, but my experience was a small pond. He was digging about for cigarettes, having trouble with the match, lighting it.

I said (oh, I blush now!), "Why don't you take off your glasses?"

"That's why," he said, removing them.

His outdoor handsomeness was dissipated for a horrible couple of minutes: one eye entirely closed—no eyeball? I wondered—and the other permanently opened on a yellow clotted muscle with a faint smear of blue where the iris had once been.

I buried my outrage in sherry. "I'm sorry," I mumbled. "I'm sorry."

"That's right, matey," he said, slipping his glasses on again before I had time to make a greater fool of myself. "It doesn't worry me m'self."

My shame swamped me. He went on playing as if nothing had happened and after a while I managed to slide away under the cover of a group of other urging guests who were demanding this and that and this and I stood across the room from him watching him in his darkness obliging through his growing drunkenness and I marvelled and I wondered.

And the second of that twice?

Moments have a method of impingement that clarify their later importance by a variety of hey-nonny props that fix that time, that place for ever within the wavering fringe of atmospherics—a saloon bar just on the crash-point of closing time, my fifth illegal schooner

146

slopping across the downlands of waxed wood and three old drunk-bums whose conversation reticulated coursing topics (Fancy Boy, Currency, Fancy Boy, Royal Sound) on and on and on. *Eheu* again. But it was festival for me, my final examinations over and an emptiness ahead. The boy had no idea what he wanted to do.

The street door opened and let in the heat and dust of muggy December and there he was, steered like a broken-down toy.

There was not much of her to steer him and I noticed only a fragility of bone and diffident flesh, a crop of flax-coloured hair that adjusted itself brilliantly to electric light. She berthed him at the table next to mine while I watched his big hands flap about for perch, settle on a chair-back, and then the smile of vacant trust on his face affirm itself in a confidence of recognition as he sat.

A year had aged me. I'd learnt to bridge distances, observe more coolly. There was a disappointing flabbiness about him now and I could see there were not more than ten years between us. She deferred to him with peculiar patience, fetching the drinks, skewering a cigarette into his "thanks, matey" mouth and lighting it for him. It might have been one of those votive candles lit for desperate requests. And then she caught me watching them. Her eyes slid in their neat triangles of lash, hiding with a skulking resentment at first until I nodded, and she nodded, turning quickly away to splash round in the shallows of whatever he was saying. I should have got up and left instead of watching in on what appeared to be the first steps in ice-skating. This rink of personal relations had them skittering like mercury. Poor bastards, I was musing with newly acquired adult sympathy, and I was curious too; and then it was time please pullease and the three of us sidled into aniseed night. It was outside the doors that I spoke to them, hoping that he would and would not remember. How, *how* the sauerkraut? First words should have *brio,* and memory, unmuzzled, bay them back across the grassplains of years with all their former expedience. I don't know. Perhaps I bleated adulatory words about his playing. Said I was looking forward to hearing him again. Said we'd met once before. Suggested coffee like a better-class pro. Wise before the event said, "What a boring bastard you turned out to be!" No. I couldn't have said that. Could never have said that. And definitely alas again.

The striped bull's-eye of the night. Hot spots of street-lamp acid dropped along main street outside the fug of the Greek's where we eventually found ourselves, the most refined of pickups, tentative as Bass and Flinders doing a *Tom Thumb* along the coasts of each other's experience. I recall that. And the sad rubbish accumulated at the outer corners of the spread glass doors, chucked-away wrappers from the theatre crowd littering their chocolate and chewy rapports with gilded marcelled cow-girls. Nor can I remember what we talked about in any detail, only the kinetic gestures of the beginnings of friendship (Careful with that word, I warn myself. Care—*ful!*) that was mumbling its way into being over the coffee that night.

When I knew them better—and it was easy enough to track him on the job—Ilse's shyness thawed. Memories here of a bubbling chromatic laugh, her pinched features anxious over raisin toast, small thin hands plucking at his sleeve. Or was it mine? She had a younger sister called Hilda whose features repeated hers, only with a startling variation that brought them an absolute beauty. Hilda and I formed the lunatic fringe round Holberg's helplessness. But of course all this happened gradually, gradually.

"Was he born blind?" I ventured to ask Ilse at a stage in our jaggedy relationship that I thought might sustain such ghoulishness.

Ilse fixed me with her blue-chip eyes. As his landlady's daughter she could speak *ex cathedra*.

"Jack," she said—he had been christened Rowley—"was born with normal sight. It was a disease, fly-strike, when he was a baby."

"But God, how?"

"Parental neglect. His eyes got an infection. Then they got fly-blown."

"My God!" I said.

"He sees them sometimes, his parents, I mean," she went on, pleating bits of table-cloth as she spoke. "His aunt took him over when he was little and his folks were itinerants, anyway. Fruit-pickers. I think he visits them now just to remind them. Of what they did."

She smiled quite deliberately and I saw the other face of evil. It hadn't occurred before.

"How do they get on?"

"He's a patron, like God," she said.

We solved the enlistment problem by enrolling me at university in one of those secure faculties like engineering (essential service for the country's ultimate good) and for five years I learnt about building

148

bridges and dams and roads, took up an overt rooms-man's culture by garnering a scraggy collection of records and started serious concert-going. I've always liked music, but I think I might safely describe myself as a non-achiever. Intelligent enough, I suppose, but a flop in the crunch. My school reports bore home regularly the euphemisms of kindly teachers frightened of losing their jobs: must make more effort, they wrote; capable of better work, they wrote; does not perform to capacity. The choir-master stepped out of line and said, A dreamer, but he does seem to have some feeling for music even though he *talks* his way through lessons. He taught me piano for twelve terms, but I disappointed both of us.

It was while I was listening one Sunday morning of dreary winter rain to a radio orchestral hour that I found myself in tears during the *tempo alla marcia* from a serenade by Dag Wiren. They were, I imagine, the tears of supreme identification with some sort of witty gingerbread landscape beyond this college room, the slow vision of the river, goose-stepping parodies of all that khaki effloration that cantered round town.

Tears were, for that matter, only tears, and I took a couple of headache powders before I went down to college dinner with all its cafeteria nuances. As I gloomily poked among the dead vegetables I asked myself why here? why doing this? My mid-term assignment, half-completed, was never to be finished, not in this mood which suddenly rejected all the rhythmic variations of steel and concrete. And no again. Not the birth of musicianship in novelettish manner. Birth of bum, if you like, no-hoper, bludger, drop-out, failure, slap in the face to parental care and so on and so on. Truly, I did think about it all most of that night, yet still in the Brisbane morning of *consommé* grey, I packed a small bag, told some nonsense tale to the warden and took the morning train up to the downlands through the slow and chugging hills.

"This, of course, is absolute imbecility," rotarian dad said man to man over a beer that night. My mother was inclined to tiny screams of outrage. "You simply have to finish the course now. Quite apart from the sheer economic fact that we have supported you for four solid years and the ethical fact that you do owe us some sort of moral gratitude, what the bloody hell else is there for you to do?"

Why, my mother kept crying piteously, why why why?

I went out into the non-nagging night and drove the parental car

149

into Grogbusters where by the grace of God I ran into Loomer, who had been out of the army for six months with a shattered foot and had only reached the hobbling stage. Things were no longer the same, he told me. Jack had left town under the patronage of his aunt and was studying composition at a southern conservatorium. He didn't put it quite that way, but I am a born extractor.

"When?" I asked, lumbering vainly after Holberg's effortless trajectory, after those holiday sessions in country bars, those jazz sessions in clubs, funk-hole that had kept me going through the last four years.

"Last month. He said he'd write."

I hadn't heard (hurt, hurt!) although there had been rare ill-typed messages that contained little personal news ever, only rather diluted philosophic trivia on weather and scenery which he always pretended to experience to the full. Is that cruel? I don't mean it to be. But somehow I was always upset by his "the country is looking beautiful at the moment. I wish you could see it." Although I realize now that he could know even though I failed to understand how, then I refused to accept that it were possible. I know he felt leaves, flowers, grass, small animals and the motionless objects of his home with those interpreting fingers until he had built up a babylonian library of shape memories. And once, but only once, after he had known me some months, he asked could he run his hands over my face. Feeling his fingers track down my profile and then sweep round from centre forehead until they met at the point of my chin, I was conscious of unexplainable personal loss as if I had given myself away for ever.

"I'd know you in the dark!" he had said, laughing.

We were friends after that, the best of friends, the four of us, but he never did talk much about his early years, only about his aunt who loved him so much she would refuse him dependence in case it ruined him.

"What about Ilse and Hilda?" I asked Loomer.

"They're still here. Glumbums. Absolute glumbums! Ilse was all broken up when he went away. I think she had ideas about him. You know what a great damned martyr she was. Hilda's still working for her mum, making the beds, sweeping the joint. Take her out sometimes but she's got these uppity notions."

Like what? I was tempted to ask, but, looking at Loomer's mouldering mug, decided to wait.

This probationary weather.

I stayed home the rest of that week listless between my father's anger and my mother's meal-time sulks, then took refuge one late Thursday afternoon with Ilse and Hilda. Absence had made them even more palatable with their blondeness, their interrogatory German accents, their cottage-cheese skin. We sat in the dark back kitchen of the boarding-house which smelt of sandsoap and onion, drank black coffee and became accustomed to each other again. It was only when I mentioned Jack that the tautness between us relaxed and Ilse burst into tears and puppy-whimpers, her straight feathery hair dropping its distress all over her face.

I sat there in my male awkwardness, appalled.

"She loved him," Hilda said, challenging my embarrassment straight over the coffee, over the sliced sausage. "She wanted to marry him."

I wriggled about on a chair suddenly too hard. "How did he feel?"

"You know how he was," Hilda said as if the explanation made her infinitely tired. "Gentle. All the time gentle. To everybody. So you do not notice he is brutal, too."

"Brutal?"

"In his selfishness. His complete involvement in his own darkness, as if he loved the cage with the cover. A swing, you know, regular bird-seed and lots of people poking their fingers under that cover through the bars and making clucking sounds. I loved him, too."

It was like being in a slowly filling gas chamber under the clouds of their double grief.

Naive for my years. Why had I never noticed?

"I'll take you out for a good stiff drink," I said. "Over the border and out of this town for a bit." Straight through Ilse's pitiful blubbering.

I think their mother was relieved to see them go. Her phlegmatic twelve stone differed so from her daughters who had been born here and retained only the cuckoo-clock vestiges of their fatherland. They put on scarves and dark glasses and we drove south. The drizzle had started again, endlessly, endlessly, and two remembered themes from Sunday's music kept muddling themselves in my head while I picked my way through the bony apple orchards into the hills. I didn't mention Jack again, biting his name off the tip of my tongue like a poisonous bud every time I sensed it sprout, so that after a while they cheered up and clashed their youngness against the climate—of everything, I mean—and by the end of the day I was in love with Hilda.

151

Indoctrination prevailed. The cheque-thickened voice of paterfamilias managed, by a simple and irrefutable sorites that took moolah as its major premise, to persuade me back to second and third terms, an undistinguished degree in civil engineering and a minor position with a firm of bridge-builders. And what sort of a life is that? Remission periods I spent at week-ends in Grogbusters, courting Hilda in my diffident way and mollifying Ilse. Sometimes Hilda escaped and joined me in town. I took up in turn the clarinet, the French horn and the oboe, and when it was apparent that I had little practical facility I concentrated on the dynamics of composition, which had a mathematical sweetness for me like knitting for old ladies and filled in those hours that could have been more healthily employed poring (pawing?) over girlie magazines or clashing my tonsils at the footie. There's sadness for you. I understood a great deal about musical construction but couldn't play three bars together without causing anguish.

Meeting Hilda for quick snacks on the Terrace or down the Valley and oh the sadness, the intolerable sadness of the trams jerking like cripples to predestined ends at river ferry-sheds or the aimlessness of outer suburbs sunbaking under the range. One week-end that she came to visit me, banging her way in with her cheeky sports car, we made no bones about this but shot off for the coast with its canvas ghettos pocking the blue curves.

In a rococo restaurant crouched behind traveller palms we nibbled away at prawns. I held one delicate peeled shell to the light. It was a match for Hilda's lower lip which at that moment she was licking with a sharp point of tongue.

"I ran into Jack last week," I told her, watching hawkishly for response.

She gave me one of her glass-angled glances. "Jack?" she repeated softly through pink prawn. "Where?"

"In town. He was up for some cultural junket where they were putting on a little number he'd written for bar-room piano, cuspidor and schooner glasses. There he was grappling his way down Queen Street like a man who knew exactly where he was going, the great handsome hunk, and heading for a bar as if he were electronically guided."

"You're an unfeeling man."

"But I'm not. I'm very feeling. I feel about you."

"I want to hear more about Jack," she said, dipping for another prawn.

What I had always liked about her was the differential that governed her response, tuned in as I was to the responses of my mother's blue-rinsed pals. She irritated me now and I said tartly, "You're still arrested at the he-said she-said stage of any story, aren't you? The true graduate from Grogbusters! Well, I took his arm and said something muffled and he swung round to me with a great cry and roared my name to the lunch-hour crowds. So we drank and we talked and we drank some more and we talked some more. He's doing very nicely, thank you. Scholarship for Paris next month." I watched her face drop. "Two years."

"Did he ask after us?" Hilda said sulkily and selfishly.

Between interstices of traveller palm an oiled wonder-boy was hoicking his board to the water. I stared after his flesh-gleam until he was sun-lick only against a violence of blue and white, hearing Jack's voice mild as silk saying, "And how are my goose-girls, eh?"

"He did," I replied. "But as one asks after the weather."

The moment I said it, I was sorry, quite apart from the fact that it was a lie, for Hilda's face became small and rocky, some piece of beautifully polished quartz. Inexplicably I didn't want to retract even though the quartz now was beginning to crack and crumble. The truth of it was, I resented sharing our monster.

Moronically and ill-timed I leant across the unsteady table and took one of Hilda's tiny feelers.

"Let me make love to you," I almost pleaded.

The rock melted. The mouth curved into the most heartbreaking of arcs.

"Of course," she said without any hesitation at all. And that should have warned me. But I didn't know for a long time that she was punishing me.

Love as a punitive process? I ask now, along with the sauerkraut.

I took her back to a sea-anted hotel down the coast; and that night listening to the water-muscles strain along the sandy plaza we made our own fumbling interpretations on a rented bed, our emotions diametrics, though I wasn't aware of it then. And in the early salt-light looking at Hilda's lank blonde hair and features smudged out of recognition by the pressure of my own I was betrayed into over-confidence.

"We could live together," I suggested, but she didn't answer and swung her naked body straight from the bed and began to dress, without haste, I may add now, and with the confidence of one who has achieved a desired and secret end. That nagging gloomy sea, freighting legends on every wave, although it was sparkling like plums under sunlight. Pulling on my clothes was like robing for tenebrae. There was a death, somewhere, and no communion.

"Your trouble," Hilda suggested pensively as she drove back, "is the fact that you're so old. I mean you're not young."

My twenty-two years howled fog warnings. "Oh," she continued, speeding up the divided highway, "not in years, of course."

And she left me with that. To brood and resent and then reject all the way back. The car was doused with a nauseating spearmint that she chewed and chewed. Sun. Leaf scribble. Marauding trucks. Scabby settlements. Town. Fighting all the time to keep my head above spearmint, noting the ankles, calves, thighs, arms, oh everything that last night I had tried to possess. Some second mortgage needed for ownership?

When she dropped me at my room, trying to make amends, I leant back through the car window.

"Jack's still here till the end of the week. Would you like his address?" A coaxing dreading smile. My crocodile jaws ached.

"I don't think you should mention him again," she said. Leaning her head to nuzzle against me so that I was unable to see her face, only the hair flowing down like sun. "It's you I want to see."

Oh bitch bitch bitch.

Twenty-three. Hilda. Still Hilda.

Twenty-four. Time to do something. Hilda sporadic.

Harbour construction in the far north. Too many, far too many pineapples mangoes papaws avocados. A bright freckled girl at a company dance with a shiny smile and compact kisses, toppled by sandhills more than ourselves. And at Christmas with rotarian dad and Country Women's mum both a shade less volatile, Hilda snapping family crackers with us and plucking at a piece or two of glacé fruit on the verge of an engagement. On the verge! Oh you punster, Vesper!

My father was given to pop phrases like "too much on your plate" or "never explain, never apologize."

"The trouble with you, Paul," he stated ponderously, filling his glass again, "is that you don't have enough on your plate."

My mother flashed a coy look of possible enmity at Hilda, who took it like the Teuton she was, cracking an almond between her beautiful white teeth. "Explain," she said between shell fragments and offering more cheese.

Dad gave the hearty tolerant roar that he reserved for New Australian gaffes and proceeded boringly to explain while Hilda kept a learning face turned to his, the frightening logic of her beauty and the perceptiveness, the amused perceptiveness, of her eyes failing to floor him. He ground along through twenty excess clauses.

"Nothing is definite," Hilda offered after this long time with understated modesty. "We thought in another year, perhaps."

"Of course, of course," my father said. "Take your time about it. Take your time. It's a very important decision, one for a whole life, in fact." He twinkled at cringing mum. "Look at us! Never regretted a day of it, have we, dear?"

She made sop-snicker sounds over the sparkling hock. Fiddled with his Christmas brooch.

"Above all, we want our Paul to be happy," she said. "And you too, dear," she added unfortunately. "Both of you to be very very happy."

"Mother," I said, patting her thinning arm, "I love you with every oedipal pore of my entire body. Having been moulded into what I am, a colourless mechanic, I feel the least I can do is make you two happy. I feel that's all I'm expected to do. *I* don't come into it."

"What's this? What's this?" Dad with a drunk-flush. "What's that you're saying, son?"

I began to laugh, spluttering, baptizing them with hock. Hilda had to clap me between my elderly shoulder-blades.

"It's because," I managed, "because I'm so bloody old."

"You've drunk too much, dear," mother said. She really did look sad with her fibro-mould hair-do and her kind and tentative face. I was whacking away towards Canossa in an instant, putting genuine arms round her this time and sensing Hilda's curious eyes. The old Christmas tree in the corner was going bald. Curtains faded. Golf trophies in need of a polish.

"That's it," I soothed. "That's absolutely it. I'm sloshed." And not only a polish. They'd been there too long with the dreary Wedgwood mother had collected at bridge drives and the first present I'd ever bought them both, a tea-tray with a faded parrot bestilled on a fruit bough. Tin. (You have to remember I was only seven.)

"Being only seven," I went on, "I can't take this hard stuff."

The room was suspicious of me. All those well-known pieces of walnut veneer backed away like thoroughbred horses. I dreaded hearing them whinny. Went back to my chair. Rode it like a gentleman. Took Hilda's hand in one of mine and mother's in the other (Look! No reins!) and swung them kiddingly back and forth. No one spoke for a minute and I felt those two familiar but stranger hands tighten, though for different reasons, round my own.

"Skål!" said international dad, toasting the three of us with his glass. "And lots more Christmases together."

It was a betrothal of sorts.

II

YOU WENT IN past executive-type pebble gardens, a filtered fishpond and some free-form concrete shapes to a lobby of glass brickery and tilery and original paintery. It would reassure the bowels of anyone's cheque-book, firming them at once. The drawing-room where I worked with a university-type Loomer called Slocombe was tucked well away from this mind-spinning floss three floors above. But it did look over the harbour past the alumina works and the dust cumulus to the tearing dazzle of the floating islands. Sometimes we were forced to work against the pulse of summer in dark glasses to cut the glare and perhaps the slowness of the breakwater growth we were busy flinging out from the southern scarp of the harbour—a dadda arm to protect the wharf complex we were contracted to erect for the alumina works. Their massive silver colons were being diverted already towards our temporary loading bays. I was missing the magic of it.

Slopping down iced water from the dispenser, Slocombe squatted his animal rump on the corner of my table. His eye skittered across the abstracts on my board, everything clean, every product of my horrible clockwork mind. Through glass I could see the workmen, slower than November, anting around on the dredge, and a yellow post-historic dinosaur lurching and munching and chucking into a waiting truck.

. . . he was saying. "The whole bloody thing might. Us gods of the paper wall sitting here fat-arsed, opting for the fantasy while those blokes down there are all for the reality."

"Might what?"

"Pack in. You don't listen, Vesper. The survey boats reported two miles of reef damage and several sand-spit changes on the outer island fringe. It's altered the whole of the northern current course. In another couple of seasons we'll have a channel sweeping in towards the break-water tip like a tidal river."

"It will be in the reports," I said. Too many avocados papaws mangoes. I yawned. "Hand me a drink, Nev. Ours not to reason. Just to do and do and do, dying in millimetres."

"The whole structure," he went on, ignoring me, "will need treble reinforcing or maybe some kind of added divergent breakwater rather like this." Beginning to sketch on my scribble pad, his bullishness suddenly delicate, half an arrowhead jutting back, the barb deflecting to the north-east. I said yes and yes and I supposed it would work until the next cyclone removed more reef and more sand formations and I wouldn't bloody do it.

"The trouble with you," he said bulging at me, "is you have no social conscience."

"I've been told a few things the trouble with me," I said, "and don't give me that social conscience rubbish. You're a bosses' man, Slum, and ultimately interested in capital enterprise and protecting the goodies."

He rolled off my desk taking my scribbler with him.

"I'm seeing Taurus this morning. He's getting a panel of beauty consultants in from the south. They'll have the final say. And don't forget, Vesper, you are *my assistant*."

Those sand-flies of italics. "I am a natural assistant," I agreed. The dinosaur had lurched across to another. They were nodding their necks together. Slocombe hadn't even heard me. I was tempted to emit a gigantic lewd howl at my condition that would paint its own enormous abstract of pineapple salads and orange dust, of week-ends skulking for coolness on the island, of segmented avocados and banana prawns eaten with inconsequential natter from departmental heads whose soft hands became rock-like round vermouths and the bright freckled girl whose compact kisses eased me less and less, now bearing a tray of in-mail.

Dear matey, said the second letter I opened. (Oh, I had waited for this one. Let me give it to you straight without its atrocious typing errors.)

158

It's been a long time, a long time without you and the goose-girls. Motivated by the Austrian landscape which is absolutely breathtaking [did it really take yours? I pondered sourly] and the beer—you should see some of these smaller towns!—and the music, yes of course the music, matey, I am filled with a dreadful longing to be back. My scholarship ran out last December and I have been simply nosing around for a while, filling the pocket with a bit of small-time concert work—the equivalent, I suppose over here, of playing for the Grogbusters croquet club—but mainly sorting out my ideas. More of that when I see you. I've decided—perhaps it was decided for me—that I'm not really performer stuff—not the mind-shattering big-time, anyway, and there's been a great deal more interest in what I've written than in how I've played it. That little trio I wrote which you came to hear in Brisbane went over well at a small influential concert-hall in Munich last year and I worked like a bastard, matey, on a beer-stein quartet all through the summer which some nostalgic bug made me dedicate to you. Why? For God's sake why? It's a pastiche of beer-halls and Grogbusters evenings with the goose-girls plaintive in the larghetto. Do I whet your intellectual taste-buds?

You'll see me in a month or so. Well, the old place will see me. No one has told me your exact address—how the goose-girls hate specifics!—so I'm posting this home, along with the threat of my imminent presence.

Yrs, Holberg.

Once, yrs Jack. Once. I turned the envelope over and inspected the readdressing of rotarian dad. Something to see me through the longueurs of this week at least. There was a letter from Hilda as well, but she has heard nothing from him, my father practising a long-due discretion. Heat prickly as lantana scratching at the air-conditioned windows to get in. Down on the waterfront the shadows had dwarf-shortened beside a sea without scales, and a bunch of workmen were squatting under the orange neck of one of the dinosaurs, swilling tea. Far out some irritant boat speck lay unmoving on this world's eye.

One two three four—I could count right through the last fourteen months and evaluate nothing, nix, matey, but sweat charts, a creeping length of harbour wall, a town decorated with the five-second sparklers of small snob drink sessions, prole lobster raffles, some terminal scuffles of unemotional yoga with the company secretary that left her freckles more prominent. She scuffled around quite a bit and it was half a summer before I discovered that I was sharing her with Slocombe. Rebaptized Slum Chum by Vesper, master of syncope:

159

A girl with a fashionable bocombe
Once seduced an old buffer called Slocombe.
To all accusations
Of tarty relations
She replied, "He is just a good Chocombe."

Though I offered him this gift in copperplate he crumpled it into the lavatory bowl and flushed it away.

This morning, that morning, was honeycombed with personal restlessness. Evening swells up in lavender, blue, black in these parts, the twenty-thousand-fathom sea of acceptance and a sort of timeless soothing, only to be worried out of its mind by a scratch-rash epidemic of star-white. That's how it was that noon time. I pinned fresh draughting paper on my board, thought intermittently about Slum's suggestion, nosed, dying, through harbour board reports for the last ten years, fed some lack-lustre data about current pressures, changing tidal depths and land resistance into the computer downstairs, and kept my paper blank. The dinosaurs were munching again. I made tea. Freckles came up with a loud-mouthed statement from the computer and examined me carelessly as she handed it over.

"You look"—struggling with her basic English vocabulary for a word—"fagged," she brought out with a mighty semantic effort.

"Fetch me my portable," I said. Crocodile smirk of reassurance. I watched her lug it out of the locker and set it down on my side desk. She had North Queensland peasant legs and my present revulsion was largely sympathy, I swear.

"Oh God!" she said through well-known tracks. "Not that again!" For I had begun playing the Dag Wiren as loudly as my strained machine and the harassed surface of the record would allow. A secret vice. They'd been on to me a long time.

She sat there with the stoicism of her legs, drinking tea with me and trying not to listen. So I turned it up.

"Jesus!" cried Slum bounding into the office during the final blasting bars. "Is this a place of work or a bloody prom?"

I allowed the needle to scratch on for a minute and watched his hands itch. "Have a cuppa," I said.

Slum wore horn-rims over his innocent eyes and taffy curls to match and was lovable except when he bent for bosses. Moving in the shadow of Taurus, he ordered Freckles to bring him coffee and to sit in. I thought how intimate it all was, the three of us, proxily related through

160

the stenog, and began to giggle at the fiction that everything, everything was peachy-keen. Working in trios and quartets, I was beginning to think, was becoming a habit of slow destruction for the natural soloist. But then I wasn't that. Manipulative? In the long view of it all ah yes; but now resistant to the whole ambience as I toddled along my shaky proscenium that could only terminate in a fall into the pit.

"I'll just put you in the picture," Slum said, sounding more like my dad's son than ever I could. His pencil, with a life of its own, tapped paper sheaves.

I couldn't now reproduce one word of that technico-business schmaltz he was peddling, but I heard him through, watching but not seeing Freckles taking efficiency notes on her crossed knees. The outer world's antithesis suddenly jazzed into its truly explicable blue and yellow, an epiphany that brought me to a self-sense for the minute, the country boy at home with earth smells and rain smells and the parables of trees.

"Now what do you think about that?" he was asking with a sated grin. His vaguely blue eyes and Freckles's walnut-coloured ones riveted on me.

"I was thinking of going on leave next month," I said. "The firm owes me four weeks."

Slum gave a half-choke. "Leave me to carry the pack, Vesper? My God, you are selfish!" Perhaps he *was* dad, hideously ubiquitous. "You'll have to pull a bit of weight round here for a while. As a matter of fact, son, the works inspector wasn't too pleased with the structural supervision on number three and I'm telling you now, though if you want to know I refrained before because I thought he was simply a picker and you needed a break. But I'm telling you *now*."

"I'm all gratitude. Every part of me, gratitude."

Freckles began to snigger in a shocked way.

"The thing to do," Slum went on, ignoring me, "is to get down and have a yarn with McCoy, who's a rational being if ever there were one, and get his opinion set up for Taurus. You can spend the afternoon doing that while Jenny and I sort out these notes."

Freckles offered a smile of genuine communism.

There was a chess end-game factor about all this I concede, but should I bore you with details that bored me? Parapet-poised I was about everything that day, with an unexplainable anxiety sending a mainspring whirr through my stomach nerves as the sweating afternoon and McCoy, foreman of works, wore me down. Standing in the shadow of number three, hand caressing a sleeping dinosaur. Its golden flanks. Its working thrust of a neck. McCoy's was stringy with tendons of Presbyterian earnestness as he enlarged a practical man's logic. I nodded at strategic places and walked back, pushing against sun, to write a report of what he had said, a report that was entirely congruent with Slum's earlier suggestions. Freckles worked back that night typing it up into hierarchic elegance while I fiddled about with preliminary drawings. Here was the total I could do; and that night round eleven, after Freckles had taken her stoic legs home, I drafted an application for leave.

I was like a dog in many of my responses. Beg! I begged. Sit! There I was slavering and grinning with my front paws paddling. Heel! I wheeled back to the sniff-rear of ankle in a second. Play dead! Down on my back in a flash, eyes checking, rolling in their whites, to gather the response.

Holberg had sent a last-minute cable and there we were, Hilda and I, slumped in her car outside the airport, lictors in attendance to take him back to Grogbusters. Fifteen minutes, thirty, forty-five.

My hand rested its exhaustion on Hilda's knee.

"Servants of the lord," I commented, bitter for the wait.

"We are, rather. I said so once, remember?"

"Perhaps you shouldn't have come."

"Why?"

"A pricking in the thumb. A malaise since we left this morning, despite the downlands and the weather."

"It's nearly four years."

"My malaise?"

"Since I've seen him. Perhaps that, too." She didn't try to spare feelings, that cream-cheese Teuton. "My malaise, I mean."

"He'll have changed. Be unrecognizable. We'll be overcome with word-lack and embarrassment and it will all be bloody frightful."

"You'll be able to judge in a minute," Hilda said tensing suddenly beside me, her eyes gummed, by God, to the far sky. "Here it comes!"

I could have believed in flying dragons once and did so then, seeing this pregnant roc swoop in, circle, taxi and pause. Our ears flattened by sound, we watched it give birth in scores until finally Hilda's fingers bit into my arm and I knew she had spotted him.

162

"There!" she was crying, half-risen in the cramped seat. "Over there!"

No fanfare. Only papers tearing along the Cyclone fence in the after-draught. The flat heat of Eagle Farm. A boiling of waiting families onto the welcome strip outside the terminal. A luggage trolley racing across bitumen. And Holberg coming unsurely-surely across the tarmac helped by the prettiest of the hostesses.

We looked at each other. I inspected Hilda closely for tears.

"It'll be a fair while with customs," I said. "Let's stroll over."

When I look back, when I care to, that is, I see, three-dimensionally, the two of us electrically separate standing between paper-stalls and the bar, watching the overseas door like pointers. Something had stripped our tongues. Hilda's hair—I touch it in memory only— dripped like silver wire—I say wire—across her cheek, an infinity of parallel chords onto the pale sectors of skin. Her body was a still and final statement.

He had changed. As he paced tentatively along the cattle-run bringing them out, tapping with his stick, I observed that a thickening had barked about his entire body now swaddled in tropic carapace: the noisiest of shirts (it could only have been chosen by an enemy), wrinkled white strides, and a rakish panama. But it was a muscular thickening of assurance as if he sweated confidence even while the face was unaltered. Could it be right to suspect that, protected by his blindness from visual shock and suffering less emotion, oh quantitatively less emotion, there was, too, less lineal registration of complaint, petulance, envy? Cushioned in dark. Eiderdowned by his own disability. For everything I saw affected me, now I consider, more than those things I heard. Words are only words. The thinness of the mouth that utters them is the shot in the sling. I've been more wounded by muscle twitch than flash phrase. And more rejoiced. You see? At that moment my sympathy, my traditional conventional sympathy, changed to envy. He was spared such a lot.

"You're a twisted character, Vesper," my drybones Latin master once pronounced as he lingeringly explored a private note-book where I roughly (Lead Age Latin) translated our filthy fifth-form jokes. *Quod meretrici dixit episcopus?* I see the North and Hillard prose composition propped open at its ink-blotted section on *oratio obliqua!* I see other things. Everything I do see and have seen produces on my mild choirboy face microscopic scribbles of reaction. I see the rowing-crew scullgullers shooting along the Nerang in terrible refractions of light

163

(skuh-hool! skuh-hool!). I see lecture rooms and the student next to me covering his notes with doodled breasts and thighs. I see Sunday-morning children in church-time gladrags tittuping along Sunday-morning streets. Have you noticed, Holberg, how little girls dressed in their best strut self-consciously, the heels brought down firmly, thump thump, the rest of the foot raised over-high before it swings down? I see a butterfly skimming with drunken misdirection. I see Holberg, and the shock of the unexpected, upright, copulating animal fashion from behind with one of the statues along the terrace, his hands clasped firmly round the plaster breasts. I see and I see and my face changes accordingly. If only I might simply have listened.

"Don't speak," Hilda advised as he came through.

We moved forward, taking an arm each, and his dark glasses swung right, swung left, his face broke into a grin and freeing one arm he felt for and found my face while I waited as his fingers spelled me out.

"Paul, God save us!" he cried. "How are you, matey?"

"There's someone else," I said.

Holberg turned away from me and I watched watched watched *watched*—the inaudible orgastic scream—perhaps then I should have been placed under restraint—his white ginger-haired paw pause along her forehead, the shallow basin of her eye. His hand dropped back by his side and ten seconds were screwed to high pitch on the nut of our silence.

"Hello, Hilda," he said. "Dear Hilda."

This time when I inspected, the tears were there.

He gave a public recital the second week he was back. It was a fearsome programme (Webern, Schönberg, Milhaud) for Grogbusters and plumped out by a suite he'd written in Europe. No one liked it or understood; what they wanted was wuh-hun enchanted heavening; but they all pretended in their stiff serge and their gathered crepe, for this is a country where there is simply nothing like the home product. Nothing. And when, with that kid quality of his, he played as a giggle encore one of the honky-tonk numbers he had first popularized in the pubs round Grogbusters, the audience went mad. He was their boy made good. Yum yummy! And if you think that's a sour note, let me insist that I, too, sitting there wedged in between the goose-girls two rows away from my parents and their *Oklahoma* pals, was delighted by his joke, the sheer good-natured fun of it, following as it did on such an exhaustive display of technique. We shouted up to him under the shelter of the smacking palms as he stood there with his limp curls, bowing ever so slightly this way and that. His life wound was smiting us, I see now, I see now, but we thumped our feet and walloped our hands into painful redness. We thought we were doing it for him, but I know now we were doing it to ourselves.

"My God, he's marvellous, marvellous!" Hilda gasped like any teen-age fan, and the three of us aching on masonic chairs were gummed by a sense of ownership.

We didn't see him directly afterwards, nudging our slow way into the car-jammed main street, into the dust velvet, into the brittle down-lands air, for he was devoured by a welcome committee of thick bosoms and chests desperate to claim suckledom. But he joined us later where we were waiting for him beneath the golf trophies and the tin parrot. Ilse went white when we heard the taxi draw up and his slow groping stick tapping its way like a feeler into the yellow welcome of the hall. But Hilda went red.

He was festooned with dying congratulations and ours hung round him like fresher myrtles as he kissed each of us in turn, a music-hall trick that made father choke on his whisky.

"Now I feel I'm back at last," he announced, spreading himself along mother's new perplexed covers. His handsome even face glistened, a stretch of brick pink too vitally healthy. "It even smelled the same, the town, I mean, the hall. God, it's good. It's good. I can't tell you how damned good." His enthusiasm hurt. Us. He breathed deeply, his head focused nowhere, but his hands drumming on the arm-rest so that for a moment I felt what it really was like to be lost in the dark. He was always lost himself without something to hold—a glass, a cigarette, a trinket that he examined more minutely with those fingers than I could with eyes. Ilse patted his hand and placed a drink in it and I watched the physical tension melt away along the wrist, the arm, the shoulders, taking his mouth into a known place.

My parents were coping very nicely with a social situation out of their experience. Jack had never been invited there before but father's presidency of Rotary plus his frequently uttered philosophy that it took all kinds would tide him over meetings with millionaires and strippers. He was, truly, an amiable man, a bit florid, a bit bonhomous, but under the pomposity, kind; and he loved me.

Mother was flirting with a sherry. I see now its clear amber spot as she said, pushing the conversation along its hideous macadamized clearway, "You know Paul and Hilda are getting married at the end of the year?"

I'll say this for rotarian dad—I didn't know till then how perceptive he was—he winced.

Jack panned his face round to where he knew me to be sitting and then on to the direction of my mother's sixteen-hoarse-power voice.

"Well," he remarked after a perceptible pause, "that's great news, matey. How did you keep it so dark?"

"You didn't write much, you know. It happened during the silences."

"Guilty. But then there was only place-dropping shop talk."

Hilda interrupted rather sharply. "That's all this is. Shop talk."

"Oh," Jack said, "this is more boutique stuff, isn't it?" I got the impression he was laughing at me. "Nothing off the rack about this."

"Nothing's settled, you know," dad began to boom, topping up glasses as if my life depended on it. "Paul's still stuck up in the north and he's not sure what will be happening there." God bless, dad, your penchant for the vague euphemism. For once I didn't resent the paternal hand momentarily on my head—he became immediately the man who had spent whole afternoons punting balls with me, showing me how to handle a googly, watching me plough across the local pool. I sat there in my school shorts, socks wrinkled with anxiety round my sandshoes and picked at a scab on my knee. Self-consciously. "Twelfth man again?" dad had said to my gaga disappointment. "Thought you'd make it this time."

"That's right," I agreed a mile too cheerily. "We are young, strong and healthy. But who's sure of what?"

"That's true," Jack said, and his spare hand stroked the belly of his glass. "Though I'm as sure as can be that I have some sort of job lined up for the next twelve months. Composition classes at the Con, mainly on the demonstration side, though, because there are a few practical difficulties with the theory classes. But it's all laid down on the line, matey. I won't have to play quite so hard for my supper."

Speak, Ilse. For God's sake speak! She had slumped there in a curdled jelly of pleasure and grief which I could feel across the room, quite apart from seeing, her thin and anxious face turned all too seeingly upon Holberg's. Perhaps he sensed it, too, for at that moment

166

he asked what she had been doing with herself in such a matter-of-fact tone I wondered whether she would be capable of answering.

To our total horror she said quietly, "I think I've been waiting for you."

Mother started to rattle savouries around. Dad said what about drinks anybody?

Jack said, "Dear old Ilse, I don't think you should have done that. An old crock like me isn't worth anyone's trouble. It simply isn't worth it. We'll have to find her a nice juicy grazier, Mr. Vesper, who's mortgaged to you up to the hilt."

Perhaps when one has never seen the results of words their uttered importance seems less, though I am baffled as to how a man attuned to the subtlest of intervals could fail to register the implications of deliberate dissonance. He should have had perfect social pitch. For years I have been incapable of using the telephone except for the most banal of services. It must have been like this with him—speaking endlessly into a black Bakelite cup when he addressed anyone at all, unable to gauge the force of what he said or what was replied. Frankly I don't believe it. Not now. Not now.

"You wouldn't know, Jack," Ilse gasped angrily and viciously, "you couldn't know, but I am not so unattractive that someone would have to be paid to take me." And then she began to sob, not a polite gauzy sniffle into her handkerchief that we might have glossed over but a gulping collapse of stored-up resentment and pain. Holberg sat uselessly in his chair, his hands clasped round his whisky, his mouth closed against everything. He would not, I estimated, even inhale her grief. And what could I do? I loved them both.

"It was only a joke, Ilse love," Jack said after a hideous lacuna which not even my crazy mother ventured to fill. "Look. I'll prove it." He stood up, a doom figure, and began feeling his way cautiously across the room. The piano? he kept asking. The piano? Pieces of Wedgwood fell. A chair scuttled back. My mother got him in front of it—sometimes it was like steering a Sherman—only his hands moved with grace—and he stroked a few introductory chords, stopped, half-turned and said, looking by mistake in dad's direction, "I wrote this for you, Ilse, late last year. I'd been staying on the outskirts of Berne, a funny little place packed with tiny stone houses, and a gurgle of a river as well and simply dozens, dozens and dozens of small girls running to and from school. Would you like to hear it?"

167

She could not answer so we did it for her although he hadn't bothered to wait, filling the stuffy country drawing-room with lime-fragrance and shallow waters and the flag-flutter of diminutive skirts. The untuned Lipp was only a means to an end, Holberg's end of modal cadences structured round a tune taut with impudence and youth.

"There," he said when he had finished, "and what did you think of that, eh?"

"Tell me," Ilse said, "were the skies blue, too?"

In all the time I had known him, I had never once heard him make use of a colour.

He sat very still for a long time suffering the boomeranged blow of his own brutality.

"Yes," he said at last, "the very deepest."

III

TIME, OF COURSE, is static. I've always believed this. It is we who go. I'll trot out some Martial for you in a minute.

Time: Vesper moving through the stills of June, July, August. I have just finished reading a letter from Hilda telling me she married Holberg a fortnight before. (She calls him Holberg.) It is eighty-seven degrees on the veranda of my flat, humidity ninety, and I receive a wave of such cold the surprised eyes of my heart widen. They widen and flutter.

I am the gauche butler when the curtain rises, the dusting maid, the harem eunuch. I sit unmoving for one minute, two. The shadow of the mandevillea planes the side of my numbed face. The audience is holding its breath, bored, for action. No action. The eye gluts on detail. Each floor-board in this sagging veranda presents its individuality of splintered being. Leaves stir their own colours, expose veins and ribbings, grow logically from twigs whose pigmentations, I observe, are no one colour as I had supposed but a stew of sienna and pink. Holberg, you will never see Hilda. You will touch her expressive arms but you will never take note of the blends within the skin. You might devour the mouth but never once see the colour of prawn, the glister on the lower lip. You might be able as sexual sculptor to reproduce her, sensual inch by inch, but never, Holberg, never will you know just how her eyes or mouth widen or narrow in love and disgust. Holberg, I wish you could see.

Since there is, in all these moments of high tragedy, the lout hoot

169

from the stalls, I find I have left my lunch chops burn. I waggle one cindered short-loin beside me in the mirror and make favourable comparison. Observe this fulsome flesh, the face firm, pulled down a little by shock, but built for endurance. I am, I tell myself, of the stuff of martyrs, waving this failed St Lawrence of a chop beside my steadily pained eyes. Nothing but bone. It isn't in the race with me when it comes to looks.

Knowing this is only balm and that the sting will return I stuff myself with anodynes. There is drink. There is Freckles.

She says wisely stoic from the neck up as well: "But you could see it coming, couldn't you? There's something about you makes these things happen."

"Like Slum?"

"Well, yes, like Slum. I'm unoffendable on that score. Why don't you take a point, be ruthless, put number one first? Everyone else does."

"It's not in me."

"There's a little of it," she said, but smiling nicely. "I mean the way you've used me."

"We've used each other, haven't we?"

But I wouldn't allow an answer.

Holberg wrote at last a farrago of victory and apology . . . utterly without collusion, matey. It simply happened. Hilda is *devoted* to me and I suppose that's what a man in my condition needs. Not that I want to enslave her, we both understand, but she makes my music possible. More possible. You've got to realize if you can that this is my greatest need. Write to us . . . He didn't mention Ilse and I didn't reply, couldn't reply, though by the next Christmas I was sufficiently liberated to hear him through patiently in a radio recital and inspect a newspaper photograph and clipping. A marriage of apposites! Hilda, staring back calmly from the pointillism of print and wearing what can only be described, folk demure, as a sort of rural dirndl and peasant blouse. The longer I ravaged this likeness with my eyes, the worse my condition. I folded the clipping smaller and smaller till it became a square inch of paper only to be rammed in an unused pocket of my wallet where I found it yesterday, absolutely yesterday.

The breakwater with Slum's extra arm was almost complete, the wharf loading complex uglily perfect for four hundred yards. Taurus held celebratory drinks in his office with four of the draughtsmen, the works manager, Slum and me. As a concession to social sexual needs the stenographers handed round drinks and savouries.

We all held sherry glasses and watched the green sinews of the harbour pitting themselves against the wall. Taurus was fat with satisfaction and stared longer than any of us through his managerial plate-glass at the five o'clock dinosaurs, the emptying waterfront. I suppose he felt the manic satisfaction of a poet, gazing down on the dactylled roofs of the wharf, the caesura point in the massive concrete wall.

"Well and well," he said at last, turning, his mouth greasy with Chestnut Teal and ignoring us, "I think we can congratulate ourselves on a job satisfactorily done." His eyes meshed with Haggerty's, the works manager. They did a two-part invention of self-esteem. I pinched Freckles as she wandered past with some limp anchovies. "Another month or two should see us through."

Haggerty was smiling as if he'd poured each cubic foot of concrete himself, as if he had sweated over the work-boards as Slum and I had sweated. "There won't be much trouble with this one," he said, "short of a disaster that might rip up the whole coast, eh?"

"That's what we want!" Taurus swallowed a stuffed olive. "I'm giving the go-ahead to the bauxite boys the week after next. They can start a bit of preliminary storage." He patted Freckles absent-mindedly as she offered bread and wine. "We'll run a trial loading after that and see how the process handles."

Fuh-hirm, fuh-hirm!

Out of the corner of my wary eye I spotted Slum making giggle-eliciting propositions to Freckles. Nothing moved. Only Hilda could move me, yet all the same I lumbered across the room in time to hear the unequivocal Slummatum—it's my turn! The hey-nonny of it bleated mournfully across the steppes of my emotional desolation so that I pined at that instant even to play gooseberry at Grogbusters, warming up before the candle-flicker of their residual interest in me. It was genuinely time to move on.

"I think you'll be having all the turns, Nev old man," I said, intruding on his suddenly red face. "When that first load of bauxite goes down the chute, I'm off."

Freckles's bright dotty face dropped for the merest time. Secure on those stoic pins she edged a foot closer to the security of Slum's leather-patched tweeds. I see you, Freckles, resting your lucid non-give-away smile on your plaited hands; naked beside me in cars, beds, on beaches—the legs are mercifully hidden by perspective—shaking your neat rump before juke-boxes with problems of their own; swimming, moronically carefree, through sharky waters.

"Leaving?" they ask in idiotic chorus. They eliminate the baldness of my statement with unbelieving guffaws. And Taurus comes up at that point, bull-elate, and says to Freckles—it is theatre of the absurd: "You tart around a bit, Miss Lehmann? How about dinner tonight to celebrate?"

"Tart around!"

"I'm sure"—rhinoceros eye, cusped upper lip—"you know what I mean."

"Know? I'm independent at that. I lead my own life."

"Then lead a little with me."

A sporting girl, she swivelled to pat one of Slum's agreeable leather patches. "I'll be right back," she assured him. "Right back." And went straight off with Taurus to collect her jacket and vanish down the lift-well.

A celestial props boy was painting green across the backdrop, divine luminosity. Slum strode to the makeshift bar and recorked one of the sherries, which he plunged proleishly into his jacket pocket right under the noting eye of the works manager. Slum's face looked as if it had been worked on by a grader.

"Let's get pissed," he said glumly to me.

"Where?"

"Any bloody where."

"I'll tell you something, Slum. While I like your suggestion—it's admirable to say the least—I can't stand these views. Not even from your hillside flat. Not even obscured by night and alumina fumes. Let's drive into Dingo and tear the place apart." And I gave a stage laugh for my own irony.

Dingo was and still is a hideous little outcrop of houses poised between hills of that peculiarly gaunt Aussie raggedness so ugly its demands for love eat out the observing heart. The pub totters on the brink of every known disaster and smells permanently of beer and mangoes. We slumped our failure at a crippled table on the veranda in the moist dark and steadily drank our way through commiseration (false), friendship (temporary) and a distanced state where each of us observed two of the other with disgusted appraisal. At one stage Slum removed his glasses and his eyes vanished. I wonder what Freckles had seen in him. A horse whickered under dew. Mangoes rotted. At midnight when the local constable went home the pubkeeper began sorting kith from stranger and Slum and I fell into the car where he remembered the sherry and emptied an inch or so into his hopeless mouth. Gulping like a drain. I leant my nausea against the side of the car and the grass exploded in a soft bomb against my nostrils.

"At this precise moment," Slum was whingeing.

This was no *non sequitur*. "She'll get a rise."

"I didn't mind you, old man. Knew about you. Taurus has an unfair advantage."

"Ah, shut up!" I said driving straight over a heap of rusted beer cans and crushing Holberg's glasses into his amiable face. Music and blood glittered off the tops of mangoes. Wheels trailed fragments of him all down the wobbling hills while Slum snivelled beside me in the reek of sherry. He removed his shirt and kept tipping and missing with the bottle until his chest was soon matted and gluey and stinking and neither of us cared, not much, for I was varnished by my secret hate as much as he was with wine.

"You keep missing the bloody trees," he kept complaining. "Pile her up, why don't you?"

Death wants to miss me. It's sheer viciousness. I am filled with a drunken self-pity that widens into a charity sufficient to take Slum home with me where, pensive on a travelling case outside my locked door, sits Ilse under the lemon-drip of her hair.

Symbolically Slum crashes at her feet.

No no no no no. To be uttered with a slight well-bred nasal intonation. Ilse, poor abandoned handmaid of the lord, had simply nowhere else to turn. It surprised me she had not come before and the sight of her water-nymph forlornness—the rushes crackling, the stream drying up—seemed a natural culmination of a grief that time had done nothing about.

She had, she confessed, tried everything. Another job, another town. Two bum lovers who travelled in wines and softgoods, a last desperate move to the city where, pawn's gambit and household for three, she played a mini-Greek tragedy of devoted sister ministering, ministering. They devoured her *Schmorbraten*, her *Spätzle*, her *Torten,* until their uncalculated and killing kindness—the matey pat from Holberg, the sisterly peck on the cheek—evoked the long scream. Bitterly she nailed a whole tray of failed *Plätzchen* to the wall above their bed forming the word good-bye. It took her three dozen, she confessed with un-amused domestically tight lips, and I sat there with her, holding her aggrieved little paw and envisaging Holberg feeling out the message with his fingers. It was only last month that he confessed to me they had squatted there and eaten the lot.

My inertia accepted her into a randomly patterned domesticity where I would find Ilse, white-faced, sliding unobtrusively out of the shower, a meagre towel clutched forlornly round her humid skin or, lost behind hair, turning steaks pensively in the rudimentary kitchen behind the living-room. She slept on a shakedown near the veranda doors, and at night as we both lay separately and tossed with our useless predispositions it occurred to me that instead of effecting a cure we acted as constant irritant reminder. After a week or so she found herself work as a shop assistant in one of the tatty department stores uptown and opposite a hotel where we would meet after work to suck our gloomy gins directly in the blast of some revolving plastic daisy. Ilse's own petals kept drooping and closing.

It must have been a month before Hilda became curious about her sister. I opened the letter out on the bar-room table and read its contents impassively to Ilse's bitterness.

She shrugged. "They care!"

"Well, they are trying." I decided against reading Holberg's post-script—give Ilse my love.

"Don't answer," she said. "Just don't reply."

"Oh, come on," I said. "We've simply got to pull ourselves together some time, why not now? I like them both. I love them, Ilse. And you. This sun and heat are burning me back to my senses. I've even written them a little wedding present."

"You what?"

"Oh, just a parody. The Loan March from Weddingrin." She didn't even smile, the bloody-minded Goth. "I'll tell them you're well and with me when I post it off."

She had some Russian gestures, too, picked up from her maternal grandmother, an attractive genetic fall-out that would make her prop her hands in the acceptance palms position. She flapped them now just as Slum, lurching through the door punched silly by heat, fell straight into them. If you have one of those black brooding minds that follow through like railway tracks to the empty station, the locked waiting-room, the failed bulb, then you're a sucker for switched points, a log on the rails, the maniac guard with the warning flash-lamp which will wobble new disasters in your face like a cheer. Slum didn't beat about the bush.

Wedging another chair into the table and leaning forward, his inky fingers tapping in the slops of our conversation, he accused: "Taurus tells me you've made formal application for a transfer."

I watched Ilse's mouth open briefly and close. Softer than Hilda's. Smaller. It was stuffed with protest. Who would have thought? And how is Vesper at his vespers now in the long blue latinate evening? The menace is only peripheral I assure myself, sorting quickly through a dozen snaps that display me as the solid citizen arriving at the job on time, reading my books, wiping down the draining-board, pruning the mandevillea, camouflaged with stratagems that can only reaffirm my essential dullness.

"You knew about it." I take a casual sip. "You knew I was going to. What's the difficulty?"

Theories were stalking round his baffled eyes.

"Anything lined up?" he asks.

I got up to buy him a drink and while I waited at the bar believing I heard the enemy retreat, the last throb of retreating trumpets burring the last hills, turned to observe Ilse suddenly granted the gift of speech, an outbreak of epidemic words that whistled about his cringing ears. She was bombarding him with questions and his eye in recoil blinked its confusion then moulded it to a slow wink. These are the things you miss, Holberg, I cannot insist too much. I have watched your face registering the effects of those racy diminished sevenths that you ram, bomb-crude, into a knees-together prissiness of formal composition, but you never register the pleasure on our faces as you do it. We chuckle to convey and then you respond. Hearing touch taste smell. Oh my God!

"I'm going back south," I announced as I put Slum's beer into his strangely beseeching hands. "Administration at the lowest level for the Department of Roads."

"Christ Almighty!" Slum cried through a white scum moustache. "You're a harbour man."

When he presented me with that word, my past crystallized all its impossible non-happenings as dreary as gateless fences along which I

175

had trudged my conceits and modesties, my ironies and honesties like some bob-a-head-flock that had left for me only the delicate rasping flavour of the dust.

"I'm not any sort of man," I admitted. "Not any. I'm content to sit in your shadow, Nev, or anybody's shadow for that matter. And as long as I get two meals a day and a roof I'm happy. I'm that much of a man, see? Still, I always like it to be a shadow of substance, pal. The light thins everything out up here. The shade falls patchy."

He took that, rolling his eyes at Ilse in a the-poor-bastard's-crazy absolutionary fashion.

Ilse said, "I can't go back."

Here's a complication of the plot as the reviewers say, a curt spot of prose that will not stand amplification.

Escaping between the horns they call it, those matadors of the dilemma. I straighten my suit of lights, give it a twitch or two. "Why not stay on up here for a bit?"

"You *are* a swine," Slum said, patting Ilse's lonely hand. "Just when she's settling into the place."

"She'll have you." If only Ilse could have laughed at it all, but she still suffered from the blunted humour of a woman not yet out of love.

"She most certainly will," replied Slum, already occupied by wistfulness and the very little-girl-lost quality that was starting to become the mite under my skin. Her flesh ignored his.

She stated, her eyes coldly on me, "You're very like Jack."

"Explain, please."

"No. Not for a minute. You know exactly what I mean."

Sometimes I have thought in azurous moments of divination that perhaps I am Holberg's other self, his seeing self, and while I store up, programming into my giant Cyclops eye like a slave computer, he expends all his heart-pulse on interpretation. It could explain my bondage, which has all the transparency of cellophane but is a thousand times tougher.

I watched Slum grow uncomfortable. I watched, you see. But uncomfortable myself? Oh, there was this and that tenderness within me—tested, accepted: dad fumbling a drive onto the cool non-fool plain of the thirteenth; mother wrecking flower arrangements at a masonic luncheon; a twist of the skin on Ilse's bowed neck; Freckles's impudence. I've made faces my trade and see whole landscapes in people. May I crampon up the rocks of your indifference? I may? Pitch camp on the shallow ledges of your eyes and sit out the blizzard? There I am, Slum growing uncomfortable and self so packed with the huge non-committal un-huh, I am filled also with self-loathing. The ironist in me at this point always makes me want to pick up the telephone and dial Bible Gems with Melody or Boating Weather or Gospel Good News. That's what the directory says, fellers.

"Let's have anotheree," I say. What else is there to say? Slum keeps nervously rubbing the corner of his mouth as if he is weighing an utterance. In one corner of the lounge the barman is raffling a lobster. On my way to the lavatory I buy Ilse a ticket. She wins it. Jesus! There we are with this large crustacean in a bag on the floor beside us, listening to its pitiful assays to escape as it feels round and round the wet sacking. Slow, blind, unending, it fumbles and fumbles, and as the same image racks Ilse she says sharply, "I'm sorry. But I can't go on drinking at the moment, not at the moment."

Slum blinks innocently and rapidly. "What's the matter with you two? Eh?"

We cannot answer.

"Let's go back to my place," Slum suggests desperately, "and cook it."

Somewhere along the waterfront Ilse and I released the lobster into the secret harbour tides.

"Not even a thank-you wave of the flipper," I commented unfortunately as it slid from view.

"Don't!" Ilse pleaded. "Don't!" She was crying, her eyes screwed up like a baby's, her face stained pink with the congested effort to repress her howls. My own soother flipper did nothing for her, but I kept it about her none the less all the way back in the car, past the swamp-reclamation area with its Kiddicraft construction houses, the sub-station, an exhausted timber-yard (sawdust fires in the dark), up the long curl of hill that parodied the long curl of sea beneath it, right round the posh houses on the heights to Slum's front door.

He never locked up, and after doing courtesy peers up and down the road for his beautiful beat-up car, we went in and sat in the soft dark waiting, listening to the refrigerator switch itself on and hum with boredom. I switched lights on, made drinks, wandered into the

177

bedroom to check on my choir-boy face—was I *that* unfeeling?—and opening the wardrobe door in search of a hairbrush found Taurus crouched preposterously under the clothes-racks.

He uncurled and stepped out like a fool and we both stood in a goggling silence.

My tongue swelled round several conversational openings. Nothing came.

"Where's Slocombe?" he managed finally with what I regarded as monstrous recovery. "I could do with a drink."

I agreed that it must have been stuffy in there. (The tiny spy had been checking on Freckles!) I dangled a hangman's smile. "Come through and join us. Would you believe I've just made some?"

In the selfish involvement with her pain Ilse was surprised by nothing. She stirred the knowledge of his presence casually in with the ice in her glass, one long pointed swizzle-stick of a finger forcing one cube under and then the other. Flexing banalities I made introductions to which neither of them listened, drowned glumly in grog until resuscitator Slum burst in the front door with bouquets of supper vegetables.

"Just a social call," Taurus was obliged to explain under a cascade of lettuce and tomato. "I ran into Vesper," he kept lying, "and he coaxed me along."

Slum examined the quality of this statement over a truculent lower lip while his hands dangled their useless digits at his tweedy thighs. Fumble-bum, in his stained shirt and the twisted token of a tie dragged sideways from the point of strangulation, every scrubby inch of him was resenting and resenting. Taurus, practising sartorial one-up-manship, flicked pansily at some of Slum's wardrobe fluff that had lodged on one starched shoulder and took a calculating mouse-sip. Then he pecked his way through a few platitudes while Slum crumbled into an easy chair and observed him while I observed Slum.

"Where's the lobster?" he asked after three failed jocularities from his bull of a boss.

Ilse put her drink carefully on a side table and locked her fingers. "We took it home."

"Home?"

"Back to the harbour."

"You're crazy!" Slum roared through his grubby irritation. "What will we eat?"

178

"Have you ever seen crabs eating each other?" something made me ask. "Alive. If one has the bad luck to fall on its back, the rest pounce in a flash. Nibble nibble. With the utmost delicacy, of course, getting their proteins live. On the claw, as it were. Let's eat each other. Everyone does."

Their mouths all curved into disgusted crescents, then they ignored me. Rightly. We listen to it nightly on the news—political state smorgasbord, racial dinings, organized meatcubing called the glory of war, small private enterprise attacks on old ladies, petrolled and fired gentlemen in bus-sheds, children dawdlers on the way to school. They're all at it everywhere, and we ignore it and go on munching our own vegetarian servings while outside the carnivores pause for a minute and smack their lips. I said all this and they still ignored me. Perennially ground-down Ilse took refuge in the kitchen and began to tear lettuce angrily under the racing tap. I heard her whimper once when she cut her thumb on the tomato slicer and after that there was only the steady sea-grumble of Taurus as he talked desperately on and on about the possibilities of the fourth loading bay. It didn't delude me. I know my bosses and my butterflies and this specimen was jerking hopefully on the pin of my discretion. I've never been a winner, you understand. Not ever. This was the only time. Can you believe that my mind crossed its lank legs, settling back to savour the repay of social interest on four years of biting office littlenesses?

Slum had papered his flat with succulent travel posters. Behind Taurus's balding cranium a pair of Thai breasts formed an audacious colon for his every thinning utterance. He was confronted above the stereo by the parenthetic statements of Balinese thighs. Trying not to rivet, poor old sod, and with Freckles's unsatisfactory limbs an unsure prop at the back of his mind. Their absence failed to reassure or relax.

"Excuse me?" I asked because my inner smile was threatening to collapse my poised outer man. "Excuse me, please?"

And I joined Ilse in the kitchen where, to her vast and furious amazement, I kissed her savagely above the saddest of salads.

"You can't repeat a success!"

Ilse was lacquering a burnt pie-shell and filling it with a meretricious arrangement of everlastings.

"But you can repeat failures," she replied with her juggernaut logic. Then she smiled. Oh Ilse, it does nothing to me, do you hear, nothing, despite its impish crescent, its sudden and breathtaking whiteflash.

The wardrobes were stripped of me, bags packed and stacked, steps for Fingal (his face shiny with unassuaged departures) in one corner of the tiny living-room whose minutiae of four years' wedlock (the water-stain on the plaster, a certain warp in the wood of the skirting-board) released the same womby cry as the cave for the cave-dweller (fire-burns on the roof, the midden-heap of shells). Hearing it, hearing it, I walked out on the balcony to examine for the last time the sensible and indifferent leaves of the mandevillea, the houses opposite, the weather-stricken infirmity of my car parked in the road below on whose dulled Duco I dropped, I confess, one solitary benedictus of a leaf.

Taurus, for reasons neither of us found necessary to mention, had made the crooked ways straight and the rough places plain in my search for job redemption. His references glowed with the danger-ousness of phosphorescent paint—which is all they were—and reju-venated by a resurgence of Freckles's interest, he extended himself in social niceties. To expressions of grief and pain at my departure over which the silent cheer of Taurus was audible to my doggy ears, the staff presented me with a plastic wallet. Snap-frozen hullabaloo. My impact had been less than that leaf at which I now stared with all the bitterness and jubilation of farewells nostalgic in my blood. Ilse was staying on, indefinitely. Slum had seen to that, being then and for ever a man of the moment, anybody's moment.

"I'll just have a bite of lunch and push off," I called back through the undusted louvres.

The flat was suffocating with Saturday morning, smells of beach days and ruined barbecues, of shopping bodies trudging more slowly on the holiday hills, the twang of late bacon breakfasts.

"I suppose you're happy," she said, private-eyeing me under her white lashes.

"To be going?"

"Yes."

"Relieved"—cautious Vesper!—"would be more accurate. Oh God, Ilse, don't take on, there's a dear! I mean the job, the town, the heat, the rotten rotting climate. The moment's too late for last-minute heart-feltness. I'm emotionally broke."

She shovelled some cake onto a plate. Its thick yellow wedge made me want to gag.

"It's like those collection days," I went on. "Those button days. There's always the worst of the spastics wobbling in his chair on the hottest part of the pavement, the day I haven't a cent to spare. And he goes urggh brarck at me with his head lolling and I can only smile stiffly because I haven't a bean and my compassion makes me want to shove him over the railway bridge."

"Don't you pity me!"

"Oh, I don't. Rest assured. But I pity me! It's all taken up for me at the moment."

"Drink your tea," she said, the mothering bitch. And I felt my eyes swim then, reaching over to take her food-wrecking paws in mine and give them a squeeze. Slum was to squeeze them for a long time after this, settled-into-yobbery Slum, to whom Ilse painfully assimilated through the knuckle-cracking kindnesses that finally made her believe in his charity. Not that she was born to be happy, but, no diva, she was unable to make grand tragedy from her failures. Now *that* I do understand. *Prosit*, Ilse! *Prosit!*

The way she held her cake slab and bit with those white seed teeth, she might have been picking at the most exquisite of *petits fours*. I tried to see her as I might looking through the dirtied cellophane of Slum's intentions and there she was, slender-boned, peach-kernel pale, the kernel that if one nibbled would give its own slightly bitter flavour. Nibble away, old boy! This is my last morning.

But he was there, all whoopee and wallop, lugging my busting bags down to the boot with Freckles in attendance, her smile compact as ever, her speckled eyes wistful behind their shaggy lashes. They had no rapport, those girls, although Freckles had a sunny candour about her that this blonde mini-Wagnerian had deliberately to resist.

This is a snapshot party in sepia. Only three have come out. We stand by the car having ploughed through the ankle-deep sand of farewells. Ilse is brave with Slum's arm about the admitting droop of her shoulders. Freckles is shiny with tears. "Write," they are all ordering. "Drop us a line. Let's know how it's going." "Rest assured," I say. "Rest assured." Freckles hands me a parcel pansied with rosettes. I am the prize stallion of the north. The purple unhinges me. "Don't open it now," she urges, and I'm glad because Ilse has handed me something, too, and from its shape and weight I fear a culinary *abschied*. Despite the sepia, the monochrome, the days here have never been plummier with the heat mist rising from the sea to dab bloom everywhere on the crackling green. Slum is stacking a carton of beer on the back seat as I climb in. I take one last look at the mandevillea whose favour I bear on my flyaway roof and let in the clutch.

Making my face, my body abject, I drive slowly into the dust.

The driving mirror gives me them still, right to the end of the periodic road, three diminishing figures waving, waving. I see, as in a pier-end peep-show, Ilse unexpectedly slap Freckles on the arm, but the sting of it is lost to me as distance makes movement fluid and vague when Slum turns his public-service remonstrating face to them both. They vanish.

And now I'm Holberg casting back with my no-eyes as I drive, to observe them enter the stripped flat, numbed by this tiny operation of departure, yet as the anaesthetic wears off sitting decorously under the trumpery drypoint I have bequeathed to Ilse. The holland blinds stir in reef breeze, the kettle screams them to attention, my uneaten cake, bitten once for politeness, lies on my plate, and it is at this moonshaped evidence that they stare and one of them—which one?—says, "A funny bloke, wasn't he?"

Already they have forgotten me.

IV

I HAVE outlasted the barrage of forty-eight months and am, in my own unambitious way, a tame Taurus with a slave-yard of ten juniors, a secretary the antithesis of Freckles, membership of the Schubert Society and a bad case of celibacy. Bathgate reassures me. Married thirty years ("The worst is now over!" he exults, playing a tiddly-tum Bachlet on his farouche Bluthner), he drinks furtively with me in fester-spots at Valley Junction where, despairingly six days a week, he gives piano lessons to older students in an upstairs studio white-anted with trombonists and cor anglais players. Our concert season tickets have brought us together again after those few long-gone terms when I flirted with pianistics, side by critical side on the Town Hall leather-bottoms, stunned by organ-pipe glitter and smoking our relief at interval. His pudginess, his ebullience, his over-spiced gratitude—"A thousand thanks, dear boy, a thousand thousand thanks"—when I drive him home after concerts, his limping gallantry as he waves a farewelling stick, all delight me. My celibacy probes: where is Mrs Bathgate? I discover after a few months. Emmie, a chrysalis-frail woman whose limbs are gradually turning to chalk, is bedridden. Bathgate is now an expert on washing powders and the cheaper cuts of meat, turning his domestic expertise into a joke. I have seen him leave the Telemann record he is playing for me to serve a faint and distant cry for succour; absent four bands he returns to the music-thick living-room to explain she has spilled *her* soup ("the widespread effects of multiple baptism") and the bed linen has had to be changed. Testy pouches in his cheeks and the blood pressure up. Then the record is restarted and he's away. "Tum tee tah tum tah tah!" he manages to sing and grin. All his days are Maundys of forbearance and recovery.

"Why change the *status quo?*" he inquires, cocking a twinkle over his imported Scotch. "Why bother to marry, eh?"

"I'm a born limpet," I explain. "I need a rock. The years wash higher. I want a high dry place."

"You poetic bastard, you!" he cries delighted. "But you're absolutely crazy. I haven't seen a marriage yet. . . ." Trailing off into magnification of failures.

We sat one Sunday afternoon in the rose-sodden park near his flat watching the lawns slip away from us to the riverflat where a pack of wolfish small boys with a soccer ball were punting it up and down the tar path by the water. The faintest harmonics—tuh-heem! tuh-heem! He had put his wife into hospital just a week ago for the treatment she had to receive every six months and in some sort of despairing viaticum two nights before had managed to overdose herself with sleeping pills.

"She's all right now," he confided, staring helplessly at the convent on the far side of the river. "But I don't really know how she came to do it. My God! Look! Nuns playing tennis!" We looked while he became pensive. "You know, you won't believe this, but the silly old girl's jealous of me. All those lady pupils worry her to death. If they drop in to return a record or borrow a bit of music, she bungs on a turn as if I were the Casanova of their lives. Me!" Flummoxed, he gawped from the crater of his mountainous tweeds. "They're all the damn same. You stay well out of it."

"I don't have much choice."

"Piffle! But stay out all the same. Last year one of my dearest friends—you'd have loved her, you know, absolutely loved her—hanged herself on the rotary clothes-hoist among eight of her husband's drip-dry shirts."

I began to laugh. "Why?"

"A foreign lipstick on three of them, dear fellow. He found her hanging there when he went to get the washing in."

"Sheer malice!" I cried indignantly. Nuns' cries clearer than gulls floated across the slow coil of the water.

"But she had washed them first. Wifely to the end."

184

"You're a terrible liar, Fred," I said, refusing, absolutely refusing, the effect of his ambiguous smile. Later I discovered it was true.

So many roses, thousands of them, their chorus-girl vulgarity and cream-puff splits of saffron and madder mazed us in as we ambled back past the kiosk, the old men at the concrete draught-board under the trees. We paused a while to watch as they moved the great flat pieces with metal hooks, but their rheumy eyes never flickered once in our direction and we pulled the evening down at the park gates and the trams whose jolley poles were giving off their first blue cracklings of dust.

When we were crossing the metals to his flat (oh that reduplicating slapdash senility of pensioner garden shrubs!) he asked after Holberg. Was he well? How was the lovely Hilda? He hadn't seen them for months.

But I had.

My hurt hadn't been able to survive. I might have lost Hilda, but it was more than that: I felt as if I had lost some vital part of my early manhood.

Deliberately, one evening after a recital, I hunted them down, both backstage at bay with newsmen. Hilda's weariness hesitated the moment she saw me, then her face slackened with relief as she smiled a year away, erased it in an instant.

"It's Paul," she said, one finger (respectful?) on her husband's arm. Who was it I'd really wanted to see, I ask myself now? Who?

He let out a great roar and swung about, ruining a photograph, and felt for my hands. "About time!" he cried. "You bloody awful loser! About time! Oh my God, this calls for a drink, matey. A drink! Hilda get me out of this place and find me a drink."

Do you want all of it, then, how we renewed ourselves until two or maybe three in that morning, skipping the sore places and stroking only the good? I watched Hilda watching Holberg and suddenly it didn't matter any more, not as much as I'd thought, respecting her obsession and finding mine still there, but shrunken like a growth that had received treatment. The radium of distance. Until she said, "We've missed you, you know," the prawn-sheen still on the lower lip, the eye dimly blue.

So I let my battered self be drawn in again, but circumspect, watchful, starving my need.

"Not since he resigned, anyway," Bathgate stated flatly, crashing open the Cyclone gate on an importunate hydrangea.

"I don't see them that much myself." (Where are your old school friends these days? asks mother. All those nice young men you went to school with?) "Sometimes at a concert. Once or twice they've come down for lunch. He's too much of the great man. Well, the incipient great man."

Bathgate became rueful at this. "What a pity, eh? What a pity! As a student, you know, oh, years ago when he first came to me, he always had the common touch. A pleasing diffidence. That's what I liked about him, despite his talent. And it was only talent, then, not being unfair at all. But a largeish talent. Never thought he'd blossom like this. Has he taken vows of intellectualism, then?"

"He's over forty now," I offered, as if that might explain. Hilda, that makes you the same age as me, give or take a little, but it has mainly been take, hasn't it? Though you see me better now as the three of us face each other over one of those expensive lobster lunches Holberg always insists upon. We inspect each other beneath the blank lenses of the husband and I see you seeing me seeing your naked body against early window light in a dim lost room along the coast. Your eyes flutter slightly, the merest shadowing across cheek bone before you look directly and say directly, "More sauce?"

"And he has two symphonies behind him, one of them good." I add that to convince myself of my own generosity. The mendicant who begs of himself.

"What's he doing now?"

"Musically?"

"Any way at all."

We were drinking Scotch on the pre-war lounge suite (fractured springs and sudden tumours) under some terrible dark-brown Burne-Jones prints.

"He's constructing his own monument, a giant mausoleum of a house on the edge of a plateau somewhere near Tamborine. Monastic seclusion to court the muse. I don't know where he's getting the money from. Maybe a rich patron. Maybe his aunt."

Bathgate glanced round his twelve-by-twelve sitter and pulled a circus face of rich disgusted envy. "The battery hens!" he groaned. "Laying little intellectual bantam eggs. Here we are, Vesper, you and me, and nothing to show. Well, nothing for me, anyway, except a

186

gaggle of lady fowls pecking away at sonatinas and scattering notes like bird-seed. Cultural Onans."

We sit in the companionable silence of mutual failure. I'm lonely, have I mentioned? Searching for the other half of my equation, some pure and lucid statement of equality. Four years in this carbuncle of a town have poisoned my social glands although once, earlier, I used to try. Ringing Cushway . . . "How about a drink?" "I've had one." Ringing Delandro, senior prefect, shared study with, now nuts and bolts (de luxe): "How about a drink?" "A what?" Ringing Kotsifas. Ringing Mensch. Ringing Sibley. Ringing Traill, Willis, Yuill, Zacka. I plot a track down class roll of '39 and come up with domestic commitments and sudden trips interstate and personal acceptances followed by secretarial cancellations. Was I that odd?

"All I want"—Bathgate was being expansive and it was sad—"absolutely all I want now is a trip back to the southern counties and maybe a concert or two in London and a couple of evenings with old George Yorke. That's all. Last wish of the dying. I've told you about old George, haven't I?" The comic query and protest in the bleached eyes. "And I can't make it. Won't make it now."

He adds that it must be good to be young and I ignore him.

"You could put Emmie in a convalescent home for a while."

"But I can't, you see? That's it." For a minute I thought he was going to cry. "I've got these old-fashioned morals about responsibility and all that. A stinking High Anglican conscience. She'd go and die on me and then where would I be?"

"Free?"

"It's bathing her," he said irrelevantly, "that really gets me down. Once it would have been a pleasure." The old priap gave a jaunty grin. "Now. . . ."

Genuine mourners for the inability of flesh to sustain its illusion, we inspected the wasted body and I couldn't prevent myself as well from totting up Fred's aggregate: the grog flush, the paunch, the white fluffed skull that was all that remained of him.

"I know," he said, anticipating me, "I know I run to seed, too. But inside, dear fellow, I am as spry and crackerjack as I was at twenty. The pity of it!" And he shoved out his hand-crafted shoes, inspecting their dapper points with all his courageous aplomb, enough of it to make me weep. (I've always believed I had a heart.)

Except in his manners, he wasn't a jazz man, and would resist my lighter moments of specialist babble about the melancholy landscape of blues, suffering glumly one track or two of forced listening until the genuine anguish on his face made me repent. I felt this was what might have helped him now—the nodding *mea culpa* of the head acquiescing to penitential rhythms—but he pooh-poohed my diagnosis, and baffled by his lack of catholicity I wondered how he could understand Holberg or many of Holberg's musical buddies who, while experts in the serious manner, fondling their cellos, their flutes, their clarinets in the approved positions of musical Kama Sutra, could nevertheless indulge in the horsing about of rape-packs—the uh one uh two uh three uh four.

"Oho!" he jubilated as he limped across to turn the record over, unable, thank God, to decode my thoughts. "You've got to listen to this side. There's a little section in the middle of the second movement. . . ." And he waggled a trembling old joy-finger at me.

"Holberg," I said, "is working on a sinfonia for sax and trumpet. He's calling it 'Gold Coast Trip.'"

Bathgate's record trembled suspended over the turn-table. "Is he, by God? I can't bear the saxophone. Vulgar whore of an instrument. One of my students has a couple of teen-age sons—big bear boys, all shaggy hair and jeans but quite a bit of musical talent, you know. Quite a bit. Spent a fortune on buying one of them a really first-class flute and the other a clarinet, but they put on temperament turns. The younger oaf gave up because he couldn't play 'Rhapsody in Blue' after three weeks and the other because he couldn't manage 'Shepherd on the Rock' in three days. Pity. They're both playing sax now. She told me they raced round the house whacking wind instruments on window-sills trying to smash them in halves." He gave his three-note guffaw. "Of course that's bloody hard to do. Now listen to this. Did you really say sax, old man? I'm frightened Jack will turn into nothing but a cheap sensationalist after all."

"It's what's getting them in!" I shouted through baroque. "It's of the time."

"Listen!" translated Bathgate ordered, ignoring me. "Just listen to this."

But I see as well. Listen and see. Cyclops Vesper rotates his great dial of an eye, its retina a little clouded by too much alcohol, its pupil dilated by nervous debility and sleeplessness, but still functional I assure you, still swivelling like a radar dish in its quest for the rapturous coincidence. This sunny hopefulness. Brisbane is drenched in light, too much of it, so that every leaf, wing, label, fractured can, car-hub, refuse bin, discarded peel, stands out with authority from all other leaves, wings, cans, hubs, bins, peelings, inscaped, instressed, to the point of mania so that I do not merely see the one leaf wing label etcetera, but all others as well, acute with self.

Three months go by.

Slum and Ilse write that they are coming south. Only a visit. Only only only a visit.

My hormones sparked up a little at this. The two of them had some loose marital arrangement the legality of which I never questioned and Ilse would give me at times a flip throwaway physical consolation that relieved physical pressures only. If Slum knew he said nothing. We were just one big happy incestuous family. There we are, the three of us, wandering hand in hand among the groves of *Chamaerops excelsa* in the sun-scuttled gardens. We chew caramels shared from a paper bag. We leave a little trail of screwed-up wrappers behind us, past the phlox, the baboon cage, the lovers only half hidden under the fig, the mind-blasting regularity of zinnia parterres, the park photographer. "Hold it a moment folk! There. Ready in a week." Ilse slips the ticket into a battered purse where it mates instantly with jack-dawed theatre pass-outs, lay-by dockets and a scattering of hairpins. After she has snapped the clip, the smell of spilled powder lingers.

I throw a welcome party: Bathgate hooting fruitily and snaffling the savouries; the goose-girls hissing in a corner; Holberg seated squat in his burgeoning fame in a corner of the room that still managed to dominate the rest; Slum neurotically unable to sit. And how was Freckles? I asked. And Taurus? Had the breakwater collapsed yet? It shouldn't be long now.

No, Slum had said, dropping his voice a third as prelude to disaster. It was still holding. Personally he hoped it would collapse with Taurus on the end of it so he might enjoy the final writhings. He was wearing snappy shorts and sandals. I speculated on his anger and the sadness of his tubby thighs. Freckles was dead. He gulped more gin and my heart missed three beats. She had become pregnant at last, not surprisingly, he supposed, and there was all sorts of scandal at high levels. She had been found strangled in her cheeky red car beached in a tangled bay of sunless tea-tree in the hills outside town. Last look at the ache of sea. So long, Freckles! *Slàinte!* Everyone was suspected. Everyone was third-degreed. Nothing was proved. Hitch-hikers? Bush-lurking pervert? Guilty boss lover? I dismiss this late-evening headline with the dégagé fatalism of a reporter or a copper, but my hands even now keep hitting wrong notes on the typer with the same carelessness that they had bashed out variants of piano tunes, the slight edge of alternation that pink-shears the nerves. I've had some fine effects that way in the ports-have-names-for-the-sea manner.

We had another drink and I put my shock aside for further reference; it must be examined only in privacy.

Ilse looked older. Recovery had done that much for her, chipping the flesh away ever so little more from the bone. As if she had moved spiritually from the kitchenette, she was sitting literally at Bathgate's feet while the entranced old boy raved on across the glistening lawn of her skull. Her upturned disciple glances skidded just off his blood-pressure to deepen their hues on sombre Holberg reacting to Bathgate extravaganza, and I was watching, goddammit, watching and noting everything: Slum checking Ilse and Hilda (blandly) checking Holberg—a suspicious social conga. Da dada da *bum,* da dada da *bum!* Great meaty lumps of laughter came out of my throat.

"But, my God, Paul," Slum was protesting, outraged, "it was a tragedy!"

"The real tragedy—" I began. "Oh, skip it!" I attacked a shop pizza that Ilse had been unkind about.

"No. Go on. Do go on, Vesper. You always were stinking wise."

Slum's intellectual recesses were tracked with the muddy spoor of his reading, countless thrillers with interchangeable situations that sparked off in him only the most lurid of possibilities. His eyes were gleaming at the thought of decay-glitter of explication.

"The real tragedy," I said slowly, picking an olive carefully from the dried cheese, "for some of us, if you follow me, Nev, is going on living. The rut-dwellers. Us. You and me sitting flatulent in our offices and sending the sun down the sky each day with no sense of achievement at all. 'I wept as I remembered how often' etcetera, etcetera, if you know the poem which I'm sure you don't."

"You need a punch. I'm no bloody rut-dweller. I've got Ilse. I enjoy the job."

"We've all got Ilse." The thick fellow missed that. "You haven't let

190

me finish. The non-tragedy among us is him." I waved a piece of pizza at Holberg, who was fooling round on my guitar—yes, I'd taken that up, too. "He alone does get enormous satisfaction from everything he does. Haven't you watched him?"

Sulky Slum stuck out his lower lip. "I've only met him once or twice. Jesus," he added, lowering his voice, "I'm sorry for him!"

"You're a fool, Nev, with respect. He's achieved more than any of us."

"A few piddling bits of music?"

"You rotten Philistine," I said. "Try the mortadella."

The party's outlines shifted. Different forces crashed against each other. Holberg, his great hands working over chord positions on the guitar, was explaining to Bathgate some subtle intention in the work on hand, both of them as absorbed in mechanics as horse-trainers or company directors.

"I'm hoping it will be ready by Christmas," Holberg said. "Performance in the new year." He never suffered doubts about his genius. "I expect it to cause a bit of a stir. Though the wolf-pack will be onto me. Bite and snap till you've made it, then fawn to the very end."

Sometimes I wondered whether the weight of his talent might crush him finally, if he would just give up under the water-grasp of it all; but he was stronger than any of us. He had begun, Hilda confessed to me with a little petulance, to shut himself off for days at a time, seeking, I suppose, a spaciousness of invention. She pulled me back a little from the others into the kitchen and speaking out of the corner of her mouth told me he was living off crackers and cheese. Her mouth was caught down at the corners by guilty disloyalty. Her beauty was vaguely intimidated.

"The rich people are starting," she said, "and soon, I imagine, the girls."

Coming back to a familiar town at night, the tear-ducts stimulated by absence, the car paused muttering between slivers of dark, how explain the tenderness of the hills, the distant watered lights that seem also to be blinking away their own emotion. I've known this once or twice, watching fifteen miles away the quivering live line of light-stir through the dampness of the dark and of my tears, and when at last I set my feet onto hard asphalt under hard neon and smell the river and the dust and the packed lascivious scents of inner city, the tenderness hardens, the lump remains, but it negates the melting perimeters of expectation. The sadness, the importance, are replaced by tram clangour, the carnal stink of hamburgers. So now.

I inspected Hilda's older face, still cream-cheese but soured somehow by the trivia of marriage, and I forced her eyes to meet the wallop of my curiosity.

"The girls?"

"He's been fêted, of course," she said, "in a small way. But fêted. There are cocktail parties and receptions and lion-hunters who don't really want to know me and some who don't even want to know him. Just the idea of him." Blindness is the gift of tongues.

I said fatuously, "He is devoted to you. He's told me."

"I arrange a clean house and lay out time in slabs for him. I feed him and sleep with him and all the time, Paul, I sense his restlessness spreading like nettle rash. Like this: once or twice in the last year I've wakened and it's been pitch dark and he's been gone. I rush all round the house, the part of it that's built, that is, looking and calling and looking, flushing dark out with light, and then I find him—he won't ever answer me—quite still, like some tree growing out of the terrace and his face is turned up in starlight, listening."

Her own face parodied for a second that blinded face.

"An accident," I say. "You must be terrified he'll have an accident."

" 'Listen to that bird,' he says as I come up to him, though I've moved so softly no one could humanly hear. 'What is it?' he asks. And his face has the look of a foreign country I'll never visit. I say, 'What bird?' and he says, 'Come inside, Hilda.' And he sighs. From the pit of him. 'Come back to bed.' "

"You're talking about me," Holberg stated, poking his shaggy top round the door jamb. "You're mincing my foibles."

"Only with the greatest reverence." I reached out to take his arm and steer him in, but he hoisted himself away, tall against the kitchen dresser and rocked a whole row of casseroles and spice-racks. His meaty face swung on us both.

"Matey, who is that tiny sexual maniac with Ilse? I know I've met him but I fail to get the connection."

"What connection?"

"His connection with my other goose-girl."

Hilda said coldly, "They're married."

"Married!" unbelieving Holberg protested. "They don't feel married to me. Where's the tiredness? Where's that sense of deadly inevitability, eh? I have a nose for that sort of thing."

Hapless Hilda. She suddenly looked incredibly weary, her features smudged in across her face as though Holberg were gradually painting her out. Bathgate was doing one of his party tricks at the piano while Slum and Ilse watched, she with her music face on, he with the acceptance of a telly addict who longs for a commercial to rupture the screen. I put a Vesperish hand on Hilda's fragile shoulder and to her horror and mine Holberg, attuned to the slightest of air-stirs, leant forward, fumbled a little and plucked it away.

"Now there's no need for expedience," he said insolently. "She knows I'm joking, don't you Hilda love?"

Holberg's aunt is seventy-two. Six years ago she bought herself a red wiglet and took up vibes. She's a jazzy elastic lady of tiny proportions but her force is tremendous. Holberg adores her. Dumped on her by his carefree begetters, he was mumma'd through two husbands who finally succumbed to her vitality, and having buried Jim (collapsed at sixty-eight on a fun-fair roller-coaster), she snapped her chipped plum talons and set about the business of living. She played Manilla poker and the stock exchange with the deadliness of a Chicago mobster, her small wrinkled face alight. ("But never common, dear," as she raked in the chips. "I'm always a lady," she said, upping the stakes or selling at ten per cent or closing a land deal.) Half a dozen evenings a year she could be seen making guest appearances with a group she had sponsored called the Jimjams at Surfers, her zany stick-like arms beating hell out of "Like a Lady." "I like the sweet stuff best," she would say aside to the rest of the group, tugging her lamé and giving an aged evil wink; and off she would rip on "Royal Garden Blues" while the audience stamped and screamed. "What's that nonsense you're writing?" she would querulously ask her nephew every time they met, but she was proud of him and could be seen loitering round foyers in outrageous slack-suits or hideous concoctions of tulle over whose welter of surf her face would crest with the *brio* of one who could not be drowned.

After the mausoleum was completed she would racket up to visit them at a cracking pace in her yellow roadster and once there, sedated by the blandness of rooms that were awash with tree-light from the slowly growing gardens, she would extend her stay, spading at a patch of silver-beet and egg-plant she had dug at the rear of the house or practising her vibes on the terrace. She wore Bermuda shorts and a Stetson and refreshed herself constantly with chipped ice and a stomach-ripping plum brandy.

At eighteen she had thrown Holberg out. "I love you, boy," she said. "But I'm not going to have you a bludger. And if you trade on your blindness I won't raise a finger. Not a finger. Get out and make something of yourself. I'll send you a hamper at Christmas."

Age only served to increase her rapturous follies. With every letter she wrote, including those notes that dropped monstrously scented into my letter-box, she would include two Roneo'd sheets of advice on what to do in the event of nuclear attack. These found their way into acceptances to weddings, christenings, funerals, art openings and payment for gas and light. She was a careful dater, too: 11.15, 47 seconds A.M., 12th December 1948 (and so on), she would write meticulously at the top of each piece of correspondence. I always made a point of answering her with the same mind-boggling attention to detail.

We made an odd couple. She had a passion for ice follies and League football and dressed, *pour le sport,* drained the mind of reason. She wore a twelve-foot scarf of club colours and screamed, "Kill 'em! Kill 'em!" as she strained at the tackles through a pair of beribboned field-glasses.

"She must get weaker," Bathgate murmured hopefully after a particularly trying Test. All day his gallantry had been tested to its quavering limits as she alternately raised wrath and ribaldry from three lug sailor barrackers directly in front of us. "Go home, lady," they kept telling her. "Go home and knit something." She gave up feigning deafness for one dazzling moment to screech at them, "Why don't you go back to the cruel sea?"

"I feel," she announced settling two yards of scarf across the back of my car-seat, "as strong as an ox. Let's go and have a snorter."

Bathgate made silent frantic pawings. "Not at my place," he hissed in my flapping ear. "Yours. Em's back, you know, and she's bloody jealous of Sadie."

So we found a city lounge with a juke-box, where high on pop, she drummed her glass and cracked her fingers and remained entirely unaffected by five vodkas and lime. Dear Sadie. I could easily be your thurifer but I am committed. Do I know this now? Is this some proxy beadleship, this trailing to sports-fields, concert-halls and theatre-galleries with ancients? They raise their choppy fingers and I come running. Am I a freak, an extraordinary biological sport? Still I insist on the ordinariness, the banality even, of my upbringing—one of nature's fags.

I gazed at my two aged pals, one of whom was strangling in her own scarf, not absorbed in the Anouilh manner with the beauty of an incomparable gesture, but abradingly alive, giving the head to her own vitalism.

Bathgate said, grinning reluctantly at his last drops of Scotch, "Must be off, must be off, boy. There's a lady neighbour looking after Em, but the old girl will be starting to worry."

Sadie gave a dismissal wave. "Off with you, gents! I'm having another and then I'll get myself a cab."

"You can't stay here on your own," Bathgate said. "Drink up, there's a good girl."

"Why not?" She became sharper and beadier at that. "I'd *like* a masher. You get along, you two fussers, and let a poor old lady be." She hooked her bony legs defiantly round her stool.

Bathgate and I drove home silent because something alien to us in its aliveness had been left behind. Six o'clock trams freighted light, people. Tickets blew along gutters. Paper-boys screeched like gulls in the dusk. The park, palms, river held the sadness of souvenirs. When we had sent the neighbour off and I had accepted an invitation for a quick bite, Bathgate vanished from me for so long I tiptoed after him to the bedroom to see what was the matter. Smudged words were padding the air—Emmie's disease had affected her speech ("She can only nag me in glottal stops, now," he used to joke, putting a good face on it)—and there he was sponging her down with the gentleness of a martyr, dipping the face washer into an enamel bowl, wringing it out and dabbing delicately, persuasively at the wan emaciation of his wife. I remembered his coarse-grained protest and knew he had lied out of humility. When he turned at my hesitant shuffling, his face was stuffed with something I could not analyse. "There," I heard him say to her as he adjusted her nightdress and straightened the rumpled blankets. "There. And we'll have some soup ready in a little while."

She said something crumbled in my direction and tried a smile that lopped off to one side. So I went over to the bed and squeezed her chalky hands lightly, lightly. What else could I do? Bathgate, Aunt

Sadie, Em—they reduce the distance in the heart. They curb the wind at the door.

Slocombe grew tired of avocados, too. He collated all the unfavourable data of the tropics and presenting it as an *argumentum ad rem* to the Board had his grievances decoded by Taurus who performed one of his long-sighted kindnesses and transferred him south. The distances in the heart were reduced again although geographical spaces limited this usefulness. They took a patchy house in one of the newer suburbs to the south and became the circumcentre of Holberg, Hilda and Vesper. There's something about mathematics—I could have evolved some theorem from all this years ago had I applied my natural talents instead of cruising round the concert-halls and slumping over the record player. Humans move into positions of natural symmetry, have you noticed? Have *you* noticed, Holberg? Have you? The months travelled over them lightly; Ilse swelled with a new life and a look of satisfaction that became intolerable to all of us, while Hilda seemed visibly to shrink. It was as if something were peeling away her resources—not her beauty, which remained a terrible constant, but her confidence, the assurance that had been able to tell me I was too old in the mind. But it's all one enormous cackle.

Bathgate had his first stroke later that year and sharpened a semitone. Sadie was arrested for speeding and using offensive language to a police officer. She appeared at the magistrate's court dressed in the cow-girl's outfit she had purchased from children's wear and had taken to wearing constantly. "How do you plead?" the humourless fellow had asked. "Darling, I'm guilty," she said. Emmie died a week later, and a week after that Ilse gave birth to someone's son.

Look, I lump all these things together—slob art. Whack this at the canvas, or that, or tack on a bit of jam-can label, the bicycle pump, an empty can of beans. Framed, the whole thing will give you some sort of an impression and that's all I can offer, for, being affixed myself between gobbets of Pammastic, I can hardly evaluate the totality. Whacko, I say to the mess of it all; and through my neurasthenic tears I play Dag Wiren's serenade, now dreadfully worn, and accept my failure.

Holberg returned from a southern tour of four capitals where he had conducted his second symphony to a pack of uncertain critics, each waiting for the other to make the spring. Hilda patiently pasted their cautious reviews and half a dozen cocktailing photos of him into a clipping book that she touched as if it were the Song of Songs and we all sat reunioned round Slum's dreary fibro living-room while Ilse did a madonna with child, feeding it *au naturel,* her spread lap a mass of wool wraps and safety pins.

I see us now. The big blank eye of the picture window leers blandly at the unmade lawn and next-door's car beneath which the owner is prostrated at Sunday worship, anointing its parts. A sprinkler transmits maddening Morse from the back and somewhere there is the indelible whine of a motor-mower. The five of us sit uncomfortably in imitation Swedish chairs and carouse on bulk sherry. Everywhere there is the stink of napkins.

After Ilse has finished with the child—we astigmatically refuse acknowledgment of that co-operatively owned breast—she rewraps it tightly in one of its small rugs and hands the limp meat roll round for our delectation. Slum drools over all of us as we awkwardly take it in turn on our laps and examine its sated sleeping face. Ilse settles back with a lemon squash—she is taking maternity seriously.

We place the child at last in Holberg's arms and he cradles it a moment then lowers it carefully into his lap. Delicately he runs his finger across the closed face, pausing a long time over the pulsing violet lids, learning the curve of the nose, navigating the tiny coastline of the mouth. He raises his head at last and the others, who do not know, fail to watch his mouth.

"Just like his father," he says. "The spitting image, matey."

There are only three other faces for me to watch.

Am I suiting the interpretation to my wishes?—the tightening of Hilda's still pink-prawn lips, the Giaconda prior knowledge on Ilse's, the fatuity of Slum, the tenderness of Holberg? And what is my own face doing?

"Look at me!" I cry sharply to the three of them. "Look at me! What's my face doing?"

It's the first time I have cracked. Leave it at that.

"I think you're having a breakdown, old man," Slum says after a calculating pause. He made a joke of it. "You need rest and care."

And then, gay as all get-out, Sadie drops by one Saturday midmorning on her way to the races, a mass of fringe and fake suede. Her cow-hand boots are killing her but she won't give in. Her Stetson is rakish and has pushed her wiglet askew. She rattles wooden beads at me.

"Have you heard the dreadful news?"

"What dreadful news?"

"All news is dreadful. Give me a long drink. Jack's in hospital."

"When? What's the matter?"

"Yesterday. Where's that brandy, there's a dear boy? Yesterday."

"But what's the matter? What on earth has happened to him?"

"I can't hear you. And no ice."

I play this game, too. "Soda?" I ask. I can veer away myself. I didn't mention it before, but once I visited Huahine. One of those freak things done spontaneously during an annual leave. Its twenty miles of coast have lain at the back of my mind ever since, a personal lotos land where I see continually a thick geometry of palms bending sideways under rain. There was a tiny pub near the beach and through the rotting timber louvres I would glimpse slow segments of reef water spilling into Fare. I've wanted to go back, again and again I've wanted that, seeing it as the place where for a little I pursued my own identity. I was the only visitor. And there were brown faces and smiles and curiosity in me. I craved that. And the shyness that went with it. And a week went by, wandering between the coffee and the arrowroot plantations or the one village street shaded with breadfruit-trees (is this all too much?) or smoking musingly among the decaying buildings of the vanished mission. And another. And then another. And I came back to all this white-skinned indifference and savagery of conformism and I was no one at all in a flash.

"What was that?" she asked sharply.

"Soda?"

"Yes, I said ice."

We smiled at each other over our drinks and I waited. Sadie began to shift irritably because I failed to pursue her carrot. I commented on the thunderous nature of the weather, the condition of her car and mine and my plans for the evening.

"He's injured his right hand," she admitted finally, ignoring all I had said. "Crushed every bone and severed the tendons."

"My God, how?"

"What?" Sadie reached for the decanter and topped up her glass. "I'm not hearing well today, Paul. You'll have to speak up. He pulled a rock on himself."

198

"A rock?"

"He goes rock-hunting, you know. Collecting pebbles in the falls behind the house and he was levering away with his stick at some great slab, the fool, and it pinned him down in the shallows. He'd have been there all night only Hilda found him just as it was getting dark. His whole arm was wedged in and he couldn't move."

I felt it should have been one of Ilse's failed cakes that had dropped its wild justice on him, so I said.

She heard that immediately.

She couldn't help giggling just for a minute and then, "This is an absolute tragedy," she reprimanded shaking masses of fringe. "An absolute tragedy." And the poor old thing began to cry.

For the moment I couldn't see beyond the immediacy of the event. I've never been one of your symbol hunters. I'm hopeless at chess despite my play with mathematics. It's only since I've been absorbed by the arty parasites that nudge their tiny proboscises into the skin of Holberg's talent that I realize my deficiency in a whole world of experience. Doc, what's up with me? I simply don't see trees as dicks thrusting into the gaping uterus of the sky. I see them as trees. I need help. Here's a whole acre of people who live in a world of phalli ("Sockets and spigots!" says rough-hewn Slocombe. I love you Nev—), of gulping labia, of fourth-form interpretations of cars, whales, telegraph poles and mammalian light-bulbs. Look, doc, there are only two possible continuous lines—straight and curved. Do I *have* to see them as genital substitutes? Do I? It makes eating an ice-cream cone difficult. You take my point, doc? My low-grained sensibilia apprehend cars, whales, telegraph poles and light-bulbs. I lick *ice-cream,* feller. I munch a flour-and-water wafer cone. I am not homosexual. I like girls in moderation. I don't want to bite off anyone's tool or switch on a breast or impregnate the Pacific. I am still the clean-cut fifteen-year-old now lumbered with twice that number of years who won two cups for running and I can't get into the team. I can't cry along with my pouched debilitated mates suh-hex! suh-hex! I don't want to. Doc, am I normal? I want tea-pots to *be* tea-pots and cups to be cups.

So I switch on the jug and dab at Sadie's screwed little red eyes with my big male comfy hanky and put an arm about her brave skinny shoulders. She thinks she has failed. It's her achievement that has collapsed. Holberg is her production.

199

"Drink this," I order, because she needs ordering as much as I need to order. It is our occasional medicine. "And have two sugars."

She becomes a grotesque baby in a cow-girl outfit and a Stetson. And we brood over our tea and chew at every side of this stick-jaw possibility and I keep assuring her over and over that whatever happens he can still write, for God's sake. It will be a question of adjustment and it mightn't be that bad at that.

It was that bad.

The goose-girls made it worse by acting out their valkyrie grief over the injured limb. The bones were reset, but there was not much to be done about damage to the nerves. After a while, the sober specialists kept saying. With exercise, constant exercise, a certain amount of control could be achieved. They didn't guarantee anything. He would have to co-operate. They kept saying this and they kept saying this and all the while Holberg's hand dangled limp and twisted at his side. After some months he managed a modicum of movement in the fingers, but it was stiff and non-fluid. Hilda brought him down, an irascible patient, to see me one week-end (sunny patches, clouds, beach-traffic) and we got quietly and sadly drunk and Hilda pleaded at me with her pink-prawn lips to spend my gasping annual leave with them (Huahine Huahine) and perhaps give Holberg a little help, just a little help with the scoring of his Gold Coast sinfonia. He was two-thirds of the way through before the accident and was finding it impossible to go on. Did he want to? I asked fatuously. Holberg said, matey. And rested his crippled hand on my knee. We'll make a team, he said. If you could just keep score, he said. At the moment he couldn't cope with both.

Am I naturally wrung by the disasters of others or am I the too reliable friend or—more likely—am I simply desperate?

I went up for a week-end to ascertain the probabilities of our working together. We had a couple of five-hour sessions and I ob-served with wonder how the man changed at those times into such a concentrated being the natural world of outer sounds and scents shrank to a pip. His left hand was useful enough and we were able to discard the braille manuscript and I notated as he played dictated altered played dictated. Ten hours and only forty odd bars flowered from our spade-work. Tougher than breakwaters, bridges, dams! He would explore the entrails of every possible harmonic combination and occasionally

200

There are one or two farms a mile or so up the road and a small township a mile below us with two spotty shops, a timber-mill and a nondescript branch of some even more nondescript bank. The locals regard us with reserve. Holberg tapping his white-sticked way along dusting roads is pitied and admired and shied clear of. He shouldn't be. He likes people, but they resent his house and his mode, the odd assortment of visitors that tweed and leather-patch their time away on our sprawling terrace or nod their critical way into the fly-hazard of the mixed goods.

I haven't been back to Grogbusters for years although it's only four gallons away. My parents two years ago debated the right of way unsuccessfully with a lavender cement-mixer and I can't bear to see the house any more, not with its new Apex Club owner and his clutch of nose-picking children. I fact I removed only one thing from it— the tin tray with the parrot—which is now propped on a mantelshelf in my own glass box towards the end of the house. It's the purest memory of our relationship that I have and only Sadie understands.

The cement-mixer left me with an income, not elaborate but sufficient to maintain my independence, and I'm here as a fixture, a peripatetic fully clad statue to match up with the garden nymphs. Holberg really cannot do without me: I am patient and long-suffering as an amanuensis; I mow the slippery acres, help Hilda fetch in stores from Glitterlights in the panel van and look after the correspondence. Sometimes I kiss Hilda, briefly as befits my role, on our shopping sprees; and sometimes at the ever-increasing number of dinner parties we seem obliged to attend I say to the hostess (impatient to devour Holberg before the cocktails) when she says to me, "But how lovely you could come!"—I say, I repeat, "You have to have me. I'm the chauffeur." But that's merely a minor lapse. On our own Holberg and Hilda appear to complete the circle of my life-style with a Giotto neatness that exults while it destroys. His arrogance, his impatience, his rudeness to fawners are mitigated by the private man who is funny and generous and at times so tender I am overcome with love. "Why is Holberg such a bastard to me?" this hostess or that host will ask me privately at one end of a packed salon of worshippers. "He's a genius," I explain without apology and they accept that with sudden smiles of recognition and comprehension—Christ in the burning bush!— and charge in for more scorching.

To be really outrageous, he removes his glasses.

But the older women came first.

In those buck years Holberg was still young enough, unsure enough to affect the mothering glands of Arts Council wives. They would swoop on him like social rocs carting him off to mongrel gatherings of the rich and influential; race across home-coming tarmacs to greet him with casseroles (Hilda feigning delight!); drive all the dedicated miles to Plateautop to air the shrine when the idol was absent for a stretch, performing menial domesticities with the joyous dedication of Carthusians, then driving all the way back again to prepare the *canapés* for his welcome. Bonnie Coover was one of these. She was a spectacularly plain woman, wrestler-shaped, whose skin had been varnished by too much sun and too much liquor. A place-dropper of distinction with a passion for head-waiters, she also dropped names. These stale dung-pads littered her conversation with the comic effrontery of an outrageous stage-prop. Glyndebourne? Three years ago. Ralph, remember Ben and Peter. Edinburgh? Ralph, wasn't it too much when Muriel . . . and afterwards at that party . . . what a sweetie! Salzburg? Knappertsbusch? Hans told me . . . and Zakin funning on his gorgeous big black . . . and Oh Ralph, that fabulous too much *bierkeller* where there was that marvellous Nikki? *Not* Salzburg, darling, *Mun*ich! Remembered me straight away after five years. (And why should he not? queried suffering Holberg too softly for her to hear.) Once, tentatively, I mentioned Huahine. She had known the head tribesman.

She made a fetish of her straight-from-the-shoulder dealings—"She's good value, the old Bonnie," her loyal pals would say, and she could always say fuck with the best of them, manly and direct. They were the sort of people you met at air-port terminals, on sugar freighters trundling down to Georgetown and on Lake Titicaca steamers, and they were always clutching glasses, talking feverishly about the quality of the wine or the food with the jargon phrases that made up in volume what they lacked in expertise. At least Bonnie talked, constantly addressing her friends in the vocative. But Ralph was a silent man and much prettier than his wife. "I can see *him* in bubble nylon," unkind Ilse whispered in the infant morning after a particularly terrible reception dinner at the Arts Council.

I glanced across to where Bonnie was pinning Holberg against a wall. Hilda was still going though her peasant vogue and propped wearily against a feature wall was backing slightly from a middle-aged blonde who collected writers, painters and musicians indiscriminately for her own dinner parties even though she knew next to nothing about their media. Her conversation was spattered with words like adventurous warm experimental symbolic innovatory accompanied by hand-clutches (to rip away a little of their talent—relics of the saints!) of approbation. It baffled me how she got away with it until I heard Holberg say once to Hilda, "Let's drop in on Faith. I'm busting for a pee and a grog."

Don't, listen, don't for one eyeball-searing second imagine this is going to be an analysis of the artist in *angst*. We're the ones—Bonnie, Faith, Vesper, Ilse, Hilda—who are the interesting cases, the fringe-dwellers in the suburbs of the great man's genius—any great man. Holberg is my cross and I'm nailed to him and you wonder why it is I don't wriggle off and walk away? The rips in the soft pads of my pander hands, perhaps. The rags of feet. *I'm* the mini-Jesus!

True, after a year or so, Holberg did regain substantial muscle-play in the right hand, enough to demonstrate but not to perform. And I'd become a habit to him as much as he to me. Dad, I confess, churl ploughman of Lamington, I never did like bridges. Roads were worse. Twelfth man again, I hear him sigh when what he wants to say is "gutless" and my hurt mouth tries to protest to explain that for me at least there is a family sense, the excitement of being close to crea-tivity, but it all sounds phoney and I wonder if at heart I'm no better than Faith who has lined her lavatory with wallpaper printed out in the first motif of the Beethoven Fifth. What a scream, her gaggle friends would chirrup as they knocked on the door. What a what a what a scream! Are we in it for the ambience, the tiny stench dab that a Presence puts on the pulse-spot of our wonder? Here we are, a hideous Greek chorus of yes-men who can't do a thing ourselves, even write our names in Runic, but, because we know someone who can, find our personal failures glossed over. We pay for our dinners, our drinks, our leaks by letting fall a story here, an incident there. Not to be repeated too often. So, poor bloody scroungers that we are, we're constantly on the fossick for new and exciting rencontres, our black-edged entry cards to a world packed with the poor relations of genius.

Sadie, of course, didn't give a stuff.

She was rich and would have loved her nephew if he'd got no farther than playing chopsticks. She hated the parties and hated the sycophants and could be heard being rude to them in turn from one end of a reception hall to the corinthian other. They loved it, the bastards. Loved it. Because she was an original. A character. Characters and geniuses were acceptable. And the truth of the matter was that Sadie acted with no *arrière-pensée*. She had the gift of being truthfully herself. I think that must be one of the advantages of age for the genuine—there is no fash about cultist behaviour indeedie and this is where screwballs come into their own. Sadie makes my mouth water for the twilight years when I won't have to bother any more with the tedium of social ampersands. Could it be that is why and where I am now?

The trouble with you, I hear through all those long refracted summers, is that you're too old. Too old too old too old. And I look across the drink-swirling room at Hilda and see us both as ancients, servitors sucked dry of youth while Holberg, self-regenerating with every bar he writes, grows fat with procreation.

He doesn't need either of us for the moment; they are virtually queuing to get at him, even the critics who want to explain to him just where he went wrong in the *adagio*. Fans on the outer circle were giving translations of pain or ecstasy for anyone who cared to listen.

"Come outside for a bit," I said to Hilda. "It will be less frenetic on the veranda. This cocktail party is like being buried before one has died."

"What I had intended at that point, matey, despite that bloody pianist who plays as if he's wiping his fingers," I could hear him saying . . . he had stuck with that offensive term especially as his image enlarged, and they loved it, took it in their strine . . . so Hilda slid from under the blonde who was blazing at him quite unhingedly with adoration and tucked one feeler into my arm.

"How did they like it, do you think?" she asked. The veranda outside the concert-hall looked down on the dark vine of the city. Lit bugs crept along every branch.

"You mean musically?" I always worked on an accepted first premise that she never found fault with his composition. "Or do you mean the razmataz in there?"

"The music."

I was surprised. It was his sinfonia, the "Gold Coast Trip" he had been working on for the last two years. It was written for lady-choirs of violins, clarinet, trumpet, tenor saxophone, tiddly piano and beer glasses. Holberg had employed a compositional device that he liked to call asymmetric growth—parts of the opening material were transposed down a semitone at each successive repetition while other parts were transposed up a semitone and others remained unchanged. The three layers of music symbolized tourists leaving, arriving, and the solid drab fish-smell of town-dwellers; and these three textures themselves involved the use of three different modes, sonorities and rhythms. Programming is a bastard device, but here it had a point. There were the shocks of dissonance and jazz idiom imposed over a steady deployment of mournful sea-surge of, I suppose, conventional enough pattern.

"I am," Holberg had said, "tying time to space. It's Goethe's Ur-plant. The root is the same as the stem, the stem as the leaf, and the leaf the same as the blossom. Even if I stick to classical forms for the structure, the whole organism is based on a series of developments through variation."

"I don't think," I said, picking my words careful as fruit, "that many of them got the idea. But they're such a claque, they'd cheer loudest when they understood least. Well, look at them now."

Looking back through door-glitter. Some plummy-mouthed musical scout for the cultural C.I.A. had Holberg cornered and was struggling to maintain condescension.

"Who's that?"

"That's Neilsen." Sad. Accepting.

"You know them all, Hilda. Who is he?"

"A critic. A vulture flying north for the season. His reviews are in prose wondrous."

Prosit, Hilda! Hi! You've come a long way though the vales of tears and irony. You are still slender and cream-cheese and pink-prawn, but the softness looks bruised as you lean against stone bolsters in your deliberate cotton folk demure. Your tongue, your mind have taken a fork in the road and this is the results of true education—the unknown countryside in the dark, the foreign petrol station with the bear of a pump-boy, the new-whistle-stop township lined with shuttered doors—and the natives unfriendly.

"It will be interesting," I said, "to see what he has to say tomorrow."

She was the true apostle. "Ultimately, it won't matter," she said.

Men can shrivel women in a marriage. I've watched Hilda shrivel. Women seem to have a need to touch even when the carnality in their blood stream is down to .08 per cent. It's a primitive expression of warmth, I suppose, a hangover from the baby-dandling days. Hello, they cry rushing up to hug the just-home business suit. Not now, dear, they say. Wait till I've changed. Hello, they cry, hugging at the sink. Just a minute till I've poured my tea, they say. Hello, they cry at extended newspapers, garden-shears, the cigarette-rolling fingers, the disc revolving at thirty-three and one-third per minute, the raised whisky bottle. I'm reading, smoking, listening, drinking, they say. Just a minute.

What a sad litany:

> Head of the house!
> *Just a minute.*
> Provider of funds!
> *Just a minute.*
> Father of my children!
> *Just a minute.*
> Partner at meals!
> *Just a minute.*
> Mender of broken fuses!
> *Just a minute.*
> Mate of my bed!
> *Just a minute.*

I wrote that down somewhere once and Hilda must have nosed it out, read it to him, for later Holberg set it and sang it to a fascinated roomful at one of her birthday parties. And she took it on her Teuton chin, just as Bonnie Coover might, and went round doling out the chicken fricassee.

Just to square matters now, I took her hand in mine, pressed something of me into it, a *lied*-sob wrung from lost years of romanticism, and forced her to turn her eyes away from the door, the applauding room, the master at bay behind his lenses.

"I love you still."

"Holberg's what matters."

"Holberg Holberg Holberg. This is mutiny, Mrs Bligh!" (She missed it.) "Has it ever occurred to you, Hilda, that you and I are gradually becoming nothings except insofar as we minister? Like the slaves who built tombs for the pharaohs."

"You're talking nonsense, Paul." But she looked doubtful. "You were just as lost building your bridges or your roads even."

"I had a little more hand in what went on."

208

"You madden me!" Hilda said. "You chose this. You didn't have to choose it. But you did. Why?"

Why indeed? Do I have to confess bless me father to a sneaking liking for the verdigris of glory that rubs off on me? (I am all greenish stain!) I could put it down to the rationalization that I am necessary, a concomitant part of his creativity, yet even as I write those words with my apologetic hands I know it stinks. I'm the natural tick parasite necessary for preserving the ecology of culture. That's all it amounts to.

So I told her. And I told her I thought we might be saved if we made a break for it. Let's go, they say in the thrillers, the westerns, the social documents, the domestic comedies. *I* say it and she says, "That's not loving. That's self-preservation."

"Well, what's wrong with that? A microscopic part of me asserting its manliness at last?"

"There's Ilse for that," she said bitterly, toppling my dementia.

I wanted to say, "But only that," but it sounded too limp.

Shrimped out, the lot of us, beside the pool. Rubber Lilos. Striped shaggy rugs. Holberg was resting on his stomach listening to amplified music crash down from the speakers he had graped along the eaves of the house. Halfway through the Cantata for the Twentieth Anniversary of the October Revolution, Aunt Sadie stalked out of the dining-room and asked, "Will I open up the tin of salmon now?"

Fey, feyer, feyest. She had given up appearances with the Jimjams but preserved a cut in their touring profits. Sometimes she still set her vibes up beside the pool and gave us a couple of hot numbers just for the hell of it, her nephew crushed double with laughter. Her increasing years were taking slow bites from her memory. Only a week before she had tottered down to the village at three in the morning with her canvas shopping bag swinging from one skinny arm to buy some sugar. The closed and darkened doors of the store outraged her so that coming back she paused to complain to a second ancient leaning over her front gate. "Everything's shut," she said querulously. "Shut!" "Shut!" the other echoed indignantly. "Tom's gone for tea. He's been gone half an hour." You see, this really is the country of the blind.

Hilda was turning over the noisy morning papers. Under the crash of Engels maxims she tried to read review sections aloud to me—insolent rejection of common sense . . . broad chromatic figures ex-

tended into ascents and descents . . . whole-tone scale of the last movement with its insistent percussive rhythms becomes a knotted mesh
of bones. . . .

"What," Holberg demanded, rolling onto his oiled side, "is a knotted mesh of bones? Sadie, switch the damn thing off and open the
salmon. Now read that again, Hilda, pausing over praise."

"There isn't a great deal of that. Unless, of course, the fact that he
is taking it seriously is praise enough." She began to read in the insect-
silence left with the plunge-down of the speakers. " 'The frenzied
schizophrenic quality of the scherzo adequately made its point though
it is doubtful whether the listeners took seriously the beer-glass witty
cadenza of the final provocative movement. A more skilled scoring at
this point might have made the effect less undergraduate in its results.' " She looked up piteously. "Do I have to read more?"

"Of that rubbish?" Holberg grunted, lazily switching sides. "What
is remarkable is that all these bastards have their jargon phrases and
some of them see themselves as cultural pointers. We're their fall-
guys—feed them the material and they proceed to ring out their tinny
little comments. I say I say I say: whose concerto did I hear you with
last night? That wasn't a concerto etcetera! Ultimately of course their
names are wrapped round the meat."

"Wouldn't know a triad from a trilobite," Bathgate snorted. "Don't
give it a thought."

"The trouble is," Holberg went on, burrowing his nose into his
sun-scented elbow, "that these ignorami—Paul, get me another beer,
will you, matey?—make or break us."

"Nicely pluralized," I said. "And keep in mind that this particular
gent was a sports writer before he got culture. The Greek tragedy of
League and the catharsis of the scrum."

Holberg sat up and stretched his arms out in an embracing gesture.
"My dears, my friends, my loyal ones," he said. I watched those screwed
up eye-holes and I knew he couldn't weep, because the tear-ducts had
been damaged as well, but his mouth caught at shreds of pity in all
of us and I felt disgust at my emotion, for he had the advantage of
everyone, even fame-bitcher Neilsen.

"Lie back," I advised. "There are others and better. Let me read
them to you."

Compresses of leaves. The eucalypts crackled in hill-clefts above us
and the silence was torn by birds. A noon-time filled with smoke and

cloud. Sadie brought out a crippled trolley of wobbling luncheon plates and stood there crowing and crying for the midday stoop, the wild old girl.

It was a mumbling affair, that tuna, as we lay around dampened by inner rains though the sun was vertically sharp. Holberg, less interested these days in the independence he had made such a fuss about ten years before, ordered more frequently, I noticed, made a score of demands that implicated the lot of us, even old Bathgate who was staying the week while he convalesced from a bout of pleurisy. He was hobbling off to fetch more Scotch from the second glass box when he hesitated, rocking on his old pins, to peer straight through the non-private building at the front driveway, and announced that we had visitors. Some long gleaming metal slid into our groaning resenting view and crunched its way to a stop beside the terrace, its metal snout plunged into a banana clump. While we all tensed, Holberg developed a bestial limpness, his head snoozing uninterested half an inch from a tuna mess and a scribbling of munched-at lettuce. I knew that ominous lethargic quality that could take over a whole room like gas.

"They're coming round," Bathgate informed us as he rummaged in the drink cupboard. "There's two of them, ooh ever so tailor and cutter."

He ambled back with fresh glasses and bottle.

"Goddammit," Holberg yawned through curl and flesh, "why can't one of you bring them through?"

"We're waiting for the divine command," I said petulantly.

The suddenly swivelled head glared its sightlessness at me.

"Then say I'm not in." He grinned.

"Stop your nonsense!" Aunt Sadie said. "They're just coming round the end of the house. My! What style!"

Rickety cow-girl, she was away, cantering between the pampas grass and the terrible yuccas to lasso this tussore and gaberdine, steering them back like cattle. Mustered, they champed in sun-dazzle and surveyed like nervy ruminants the landscape of wine dribbles, the scattered leaves of summer presses, the draggle ends of lunch.

"Let me introduce myself," the tussore gnome began.

"Stop him!" Holberg's lips were commanding sky. "Stop him, someone."

I started to laugh and the choc-bit lady who would, I learnt later, withstand any amount of offensiveness to achieve her social invasions, said with cultivated musicality, "Lance, we're intruding."

"He's not here." Hilda stepped protectively in front of the sprawled husband.

"Now this won't do." Aunt Sadie dug her booted stick legs firm into a border of Sweet Alice and drew a toy colt revolver from her hipster belt. She waved its tiddly nozzle at all of us. "I insist that we be nice to these weary toil-worn travellers. What's your names, dears?"

"I'm Lance Shumway," the biffed buster said, but his ponderousness had gone all oblique. "And this is my dear wife Georgie." She gave a diamante smile that failed to reach the indigo frames of her eyes.

"I'm not here," Holberg roared suddenly.

"You should have rung, you know," Hilda reproved in the dreadful sequent silence. "We like to get warning."

"If we could just sit for a moment," Mrs Shumway said firmly with poise. (She was chorus with class.) "It was a very long drive."

"Do you drive standing?" Sadie asked innocently.

"I should explain," Mr Shumway began, and I could tell at once by his drawling basso that he was a raconteur of impressive tediums, "that we have come solely on a business matter. We have been trying to ring for the last three days. Perhaps you had cut the wires?" He smiled lop-sidedly and won my respect.

Holberg had turned his back on the sound of them and sat with feet dangling into the pool, kicking now and then insolent water-furls across its surface. Up here we were cut off and alone with the jackals.

Aunt Sadie was ploughing on with introductions, obtaining an ironic buzz from it all. "And that, up there"—she pointed at her nephew's ham-pink back—"is Jack. He's in a filthy mood, dears, and there's nothing we can do about it. I know. I changed his nasty little napkins."

"I would love a drink," Mrs Shumway decided. She smiled meltingly and regretfully, this time on all of us. "Dear Mr Holberg, may I beg one teeny piece of gin?"

"Have a Scotch, my dear, have a Scotch," bumbled Bathgate who was always overcome by a Reubens plenty, poor old gaffer. Slopping it recklessly over ice while Holberg rising said, "Is this or is this *not* my house?" and dived straight into the deep end.

They went away, the dupes of art, but tried again some weeks later, manoeuvring cunningly through Bathgate whom they discovered and

212

courted in Brisbane, making gestures so persuasive that Holberg gave in. As a last small piece of defiance he had Ilse up to ruin the meal, which she did with aplomb while I wondered how far Holberg's mischief could extend in these retributive processes that forced his beloveds, his disciples, to break bread with him.

"Bring the boy!" he commanded expansively, and dumb Slum drove his wife and child, who was now a fractious five, up the winding tree-aisles of the lower plateau to ruin Sunday for the Shumways. I suppose they deserved it.

While we poked round at a peppery *chili con carne,* Holberg, having discovered his guests were practically tone-deaf (she sang, but reading between the notes as it were) punished their cultural lip-service by playing a Schönberg quartet at ear-rending volume as they ate. He was such smiles and such gentleness and so attentive as a host I feared some collapse in the high-shriek quality of his mannered concern. I hate to say it: he overacted his blindness, feeling his way gently down the table, courteously passing the wrong dishes, forcing and forcing them. "Listen to this little passage." And over he would fumble blindly to the record-player and swing the needle back a track, then come to stand behind them both, a guiding ghostly hand on each shoulder while they took it and took it. "Boy! Can you take it!" Aunt Sadie said admiringly, and while Slum and I rocked into our drinks, the etiolated guests leant, wilted, against the most brutal buttresses of sound and kept their faces pensively intelligent.

There was some cheap stuff, too. I thought better of you, Holberg. When they made approving noises after it was all over (the coffee-liqueur collapse!), Holberg expostulated but still gently: "But you *liked* it? Truly? Oh, you missed my point altogether. I was trying to explain just how . . . it's really pretentious rubbish, you know."

And there they were, forced to stick to their melted guns.

Drenched in the worst possible custard.

"He's a devil, Jack!" Aunt Sadie cried. "Why, when he was little. . . ." And away she prattled, inadvertently curbing the words that Mr Shumway had by now need to spill, his face contorted with pressure. But I'll hand it to his lady-wife: a lavender-rinse equipoise of *bouffant* cool, her horrible snap-blue eyes dancing with superbly feigned lip-hanging interest on Sadie's wizened countenance while Holberg moved up to complete the happy picture, placing his arms round Sadie's urgently lean shoulders. "This is the woman in my life," he announced, hugging. "Hilda knows what I mean." I watched Hilda trying to know. And Georgie leant her dramatic bust across the cheese-plate and said, "But how adorable!"

Later in a patch of shrubbery half a mile up the forest slope, Mrs Shumway tried also to become another woman in Holberg's life. Determined to take the electric shock of cultural exposure, she had experienced with him the quality of leaf and flower shape, the vanishing cries of birds, the explanations of rock and stone. He was busy learning her by heart when I crashed, irritated, through the scrub-barriers, to call him back to the phone for an interstate call. She regained her composure as rapidly as her clothes and, to my private cautionings of his mere ruthless curiosity, she could only repeat in a numbed kind of way, "This has been the most lovely of days. The most lovely."

Have you noticed as I've noticed that since the taking of vows my style has been bruised? I think back to the bauxite and the bananas and the selving of those years and find that the mind's muscles have relaxed. There used to be some ability to construct a pattern of reasonable comedy within my private hours. Now, there is no privacy at all. The clarity of my thinking and absorbing is blurred and the metronome sweep of my wordy wind-screen wipers only spreads but does not remove the fungus. Look! Even my prose style. . . .

It has been seven years now and I know less and more people than ever before. "Animals are nicer than humans," Hilda says despondently one day as we drive our month's grog supply back from Surfers. Is this the beginning of the crack-up? We ponder the Shumways for five miles. They were Bonnie Coover's find—lumps of polished quartz that glistered again and again behind her drunken smorgasbords. Shumway was a writer of sorts with that vice often peculiar to writers, talk. He dissipated his strengths over dinner-table walnuts and in his frantic masturbatory way solved everyone's problems but his own. He had published an indifferent novel, two social documents and any number of critical *essais* in academic journals. This total, as I sourly and mathematically deduced for Hilda, brought him an annual return of twenty free dinners, a score or so of theatre tickets and a couple of dozen review copies which he later claimed for in his tax return. His twisted gnome smile appeared on panel games penned in by thirty-

214

year-old beauties where he was the last, but the last, ponderous word. Now he was writing a play, tackling his last literary Eiger, a non-play defying all possible conventions of theatre and incidentally of sexual good taste. He wanted to rope Holberg in on *entr'acte* music.

As Shumway grew older he found predication harder and harder to achieve, postponing the period with every variety of complementing subordination and appositional parenthesis in a way that amounted to neurosis. He had been working himself up into a cadenza for the last seven minutes.

". . . and as I see it you have a quality of outrageousness that is exactly what this play demands . . ."

Holberg had been listening patiently through ten periodic sentences.

"Help him, someone!" Sadie gasped.

"But you don't like music," Holberg obliged brutally during a pause-sip. "Do I need your play?"

"Lance Shumway's play is brilliant," Georgie stated, who always made her husband a public figure by using his prae- and cognomina.

"I see it this way," Shumway went on, ignoring them both now he had the assertive confidence that came with the entrée, "that the delicacy of each will enhance each. The whole structure—and it is a highly integrated and balanced structure, a Parthenon, if you like, of design and organic rhythms—and rhythms in the mod as well as the classical sense, may I add—that requires music and dialogue—and, believe me, the dialogue has its own sets of tonal variations—to be complementary."

"I don't write musical comedy."

He was shocked into the simple sentence. "But, my dear fellow, that isn't what it is at all. This is a serious work of art."

"So is your wife."

My radar dish absorbed Georgie's snap and tighten. God bless you, Jack, I prayed; this is why I stay, I suppose. I suppose. I am the schoolboy fag for the hero of the sixth, God love us, and I will do anything at all, anything, lick your boots, replay and replay your phrases, cart you beer, accommodate your wife give me half a chance. The lot.

"You'll simply have to read it, Holberg. Simply . . . actually, the braille society is preparing a copy and I think you'll admit then. . . ."

He read it. He admitted nothing of the kind. He said loudly right down Bonnie the Vocative's monastic dining-table, "I find it anti-aesthetic."

"O Holberg! But isn't he the most fabulous reactionary!" Bonnie hissed at geese dining-neighbours. "Dear Holberg is such a rebel!"

Shumway put on his patronizing face. "My dear fellow! Surely you weren't shocked! Don't tell me you believe in censorship!"

"Listen, matey," Holberg said, tackling his *boeuf en daube* manually, "you can have your sex on stage, the lot of it. What stinks is your dishonesty."

"Now I do—I must say this—resent that," Shumway protested. Conspirator, he smiled all round the long room safe in Holberg's blindness and our ship steered into a calm and a silence of tactical responding smiles uncertain which side to barrack.

"This is your dishonesty." (Holberg, there's gravy dribbling down your coat, you are facing the wrong way, your elbow is on Bonnie Coover's bread roll, but there is a magnificence about you.) "If you want total theatre, matey, then I'm with you. But I want urination and defecation and vomiting and nose-blowing. The lot." People stopped poking at their doubtful brown servings. "I want diarrhoea and spewing and mucus and none of your bloody plastic turds, matey. If that actor can't turn on a good crap at ten past nine *every* night in Act Two then I want him drummed out of Equity. I want stench and fartings and blokes blowing their noses between their fingers and spitting great gobbets into the orchestra pit and then I'll be with you. Then I'll subscribe. Then I'll deliver you some incidental music that you'll be incapable of assessing anyway. But I'll respect your motives. You funny man! You seem to think the cerebellum is located in the scrotum."

The chaos of it! Mrs Shumway pitched a loyal glass straight over him and Holberg sat there roaring with laughter through the capillary trickles of claret. "You pretentious oaf!" he kept saying. "You utterly pretentious oaf!"

We should have lost a lot of friends that way. These things work in reverse for the sucking fish, however, and Holberg's social monstrousness brought out the masochist flagellant in all of them. Except the Shumways. "I want my enemies to be worthy of me," Holberg used to say. But Lance Shumway was never that. Though he was certainly an enemy.

216

Holberg had reverted to the use of braille manuscript. Imagine that darkness! Imagine that awkward moving in a world of angles and spikes that could never really be ascertained. A terrain of no-colour and no visual dimension that his white stick poked into, regardless of sun-rise or -set, of cloudlessness or cloud, of distant hill-line or plain-scorch. I would shut my own eyes for a few minutes and try to understand and I couldn't take it, not even for that short time.

There were whole days when I wouldn't see him except for the evening meal and even this might be missed. Physiotherapy had bolstered his right hand; he was playing with reasonable fluidity again, able to play and transcribe as he worked. His testiness when we were all together acted like an itch that had us all scratching at the more tender spots in each other's souls so that I was glad to be baker boy, grocery man, gardener, fetch and carry jackabout. Most of my time went in re-scoring the braille and playing back to him at week-ends the draft of the section he had been working on during the week. I was puritanically accurate and the only time I made a mistake, scoring in a cello passage two bars early, he ripped the manuscript off the stand and tore it into savage pieces. We swore viciously at each other in the sound-proofed room.

"You're a bloody selfish bastard!" I shouted. "You've got the lot of us running like cut cats all over the place on your behalf, homage droppers, saying the right thing, watching our goddam tongues, careful never to rub you up the wrong rotten way. A bit of it would do you good. I honest to God don't know why I stay."

"Why do you?" He was leaning against the piano, his face suddenly white, his lips trapped in on each other.

"Jesus," I complained bitterly, "I don't know. I don't damn well know." And went away, firm as a saint, to pack a bag. He came fumbling after me, his arms groping like antennae, quicker than I would have believed and then I heard him crash across a chair Hilda had switched round on the terrace, the flab sound as his great body whacked the concrete and the cry of pain. The saint in me turned back to the tangle of canvas and flesh and hoisted it up while incoherence shook our limbs. We faced each other and only I could see. Through my trembling. You're older, Holberg. Less physically assured. There's grey in the women-slaying auburn and deeper lines from nose to mouth and mouth itself has thinned a little, drooped a

217

little, the corners of your innocence dragged down by the weight of success.

"Don't bust off in a rage, matey," he pleaded, placing the words on my arm with his fingers whose contact acted at once on my pity glands. "We do need you, Hilda and I. Hilda needs you more. I'm a bit of a sod."

My eyes grazed the sunny acres, guilty for their good fortune, past trees inexpressibly dear, the crammed fertility of the outer slopes. Sea swung gelatinous and blue on the rocker of the skyline beyond and beyond the green light of the Tweed. The green swell in the havens dumb and out of the swing—that surely was it, the haven quality of it that kept me, the explicit quiet of days filled with the drunkenness of grass and insects and the mathematical absorption of music structure (something mischievous uttered, *"pons asinorum"*) and Holberg's very capacity for exploding further and further cells within his harmonies.

I said slowly, my voice pushing heavily against tide, "I've tried to work it out. Sometimes I've wondered what it's all about. You don't really need me, you know. Not now." Should I confess that years of this conventual existence had broken my resource? I was unfitting myself for everything. Twelfth man, I hear my father reproach in a whisper all the way from the neat masonic patch at Grogbusters, and I let the self-pity maudle out in tears, gloating that Holberg could not see. He told me he had never cried, could never cry. When he first discovered this wetness on a playmate's face he had marvelled, accusing the weather and then envying the explanation. "Is it like your heart running out?" he once asked me. "Is it?" Is it? I ask myself then.

"Perhaps it is for Hilda that I do stay," I replied. "I love her with more courtesy than you."

And there she was drawn by the crash and listening just outside the glass doors watching both of us.

She came to my bed after that. Sometimes on hot afternoons when Holberg was locked in his study hammering away at the metals of a third symphony. He had reached the *adagio*. Something comic in that? Ah, there's the old Vesper! Hilda wept as I made love. She didn't really want me. "This is folk demure, isn't it?" I asked her.

"What?"

"Just a private joke."

Sometimes in sweltering evenings behind the hairy and mosquito'd privacy of the creek. Once one early mackerel day of scudded pink. I

218

bit off my conscience with the memory of Mrs Shumway. We managed a day and a night down the trashy coast where, looking sentimentally for our old sea-bitten pub, we found only a high-rise block of vomitous red-brick in its place with forty-two letter-boxes. "It's fifteen years!" we admitted in a sad chorus and drove on to the windy border where at breakfast in a glass and plastic pleasure-dome we found Georgie Shumway glinting bluely at us across the rubber plants, a forkful of scrambled eggs threatening to drop in her excitement.

"It must be reprisal," we heard she gabbled later to Bonnie Coover, "for that forlorn little flautist he scooped out of the ballet orchestra." Memories at this point of a terrible Christmas and New Year when the raped child moved in after a summer school Holberg had been lecturing at. Slogging at it—at something—in his studio, the surface excuse a sonata for flute and piano wittily called "Pipeline." The old swinger at home. Hilda had learnt to knock before entering and that the child took sugar but no cream. Was that really the reason now I found her compliant in my arms, the body no longer expectant?

I'd like to point out that I was a fixture at junkets. You'd gathered this? I used to rope in Sadie's and Hilda's and Ilse's eyes—never mind Slum!—and say wittily, "We're the planet suite." Making the best of my social thrips, you see, until one evening at Faith's just as I was about to vacate her cultured bog-house I heard from the other side of the *leit-motif* door a fruity documentarian explaining me away to a nonsense blonde who was working her social way up from the libertarian pubs: "He's Holberg's eunuch."

Those are hard words to hear. Our drive back was sustained as much by petrol as requited malice therefore. Malice? Too vigorous. I'm not a malicious man, but the harshness of it had rubbed me raw and I can't be blamed for enjoying a small dispensation of redemption. Some dragging sweat lifted from trees whose custom had made me as unseeing as the master. Liberated, I tasted all the beatitudes of early hours country and the champagne quality of adultery, so that when Sadie met us on the terrace with one choppy finger to her tear-twisted mouth and said, "Bathgate's dying in the living-room," not even then was the bubble fizz of my redeemed self quelled.

He'd had a second stroke while roaring with laughter over one of Holberg's stories. A better way to go than Ben Jonson's. Lying now, the colour of milk, on a sofa of ominous blood-red, breathing in snorts and blowing tiny bubbles of saliva at the edge of his mouth. They'd rung for a doctor and ambulance and there was nothing we could do but hover, all of us stilled and somehow shrunken at this wrecking. Sadie was pitiful. I hadn't realized how much for her he'd curbed the wind at the door. She dabbed away each bubble as it formed, her own eyes spinning chains of them that beaded away unchecked onto the fake suede fringe of her cow-girl jacket. It's hard to come such a long way through living and discover worth-whileness at the end for such a short time.

After two white-coated men had removed him through all those shoals of summer, we sat around in our depression and held a wake for him, a recounting of his best stories sauced with the best whisky just as he would have liked it. After all, they might still pull him through and we drank to the hopelessness of it. Holberg kept saying over and over, "He taught me all I knew."

We all slumped there in banana light watching the grieving coast, timing his arrival at points along the champagne road I'd whacked up two hours before. At this place that place this place by now by now by now until finally and intuitively, give me credit, I went deliberately over to the record-player and gave him, all those fifty miles away, my last tribute in a new pressing of the Dag Wiren he'd bought me for Christmas. Fred, I know you thought it was cheap prom pop and I know you thought it amateur and patchy at that, but you knew it spelled something for me and I'm offering it back as the first thing that genuinely promoted my doom. *Vale,* Fred, have you heard this one?

There weren't many of us to mourn. My parents had a traffic jam of Country Women and Masons that cut my private anguish to shreds. Out of the longest car comes the shortest sorrow. Stale tributes, while all the time during the clods and the neat eighteen square feet of plastic lawn, my father punted balls across the frost-browned oval and my mother sewed endlessly my taped name onto my boarding-school underwear. "They were just parents," I said to the drongo minister who backed away from me in horror. "Just people. When I was young I used them shamefully. As I got older I grew to like them. But I must have been twenty before that happened." "I understand, my boy," he consoled with his blank eyes. "I do understand." I envisaged him explaining away my unnaturalness as shock. "I loved them," I said, "for the tin parrot and the golf cups needing a polish and my

220

mother's grease-baked stove." Then I got into my car and drove out of the town and never went back. And I mourned Fred, too, for the things that weren't stated at his funeral by the well-suited chairman of the conservatorium who had come reluctantly to represent his buddies: for his execrable Burne-Jones prints and the sight of him washing Emmie and the simplicity of his frightful guffaw and the fact that he died of extreme youth at the age of sixty-five. "Killed by his innocence," I whispered to the six others cramped in orange polish pews in the crematorium chapel and one of the attendants came fussing up and said, "Please, Mister eerrr, the casket is just . . ." and I had to get up and leave at that point, seized with a nervous giggle for, observing Ilse's pallid seriousness, it had just struck me that here indeed was a job for her, channelizing the cooking, and how much Bathgate would have laughed.

I'm collecting last words. The last words of the working class, that is. There's no bravura about them in the aristocratic manner of the privileged. I've checked around. Bathgate once told me his own father, after forty years of service in the one firm, whimpered, "Where's the money coming from?" and finally closed his eyes. At Surfers a chipper nurse informed me Mr Bathgate had rallied once to say, "What about the rates?" Going out to a tucket of piccolos.

Holberg will have something good put aside for such an occasion. He's designed for the grand manner, I suspect, though when I asked him about it he said with complete simplicity expunged of all vanity, "I don't need last words, matey. This"—whacking the manuscript on the side table—"is my last word." "You think it will go on uttering for you?" "Well, I hope it might. I think it might." For me there'll be some surd-like harmonic of top E.

We attended to Bathgate's poor little affairs, wrote to his one surviving relative, cleaned out his flat and removed the records and sheet music which he had bequeathed me. As well, I stole the worst of the Burne-Jones prints (denying his distant indifferent cousin) and as a *memento mori* propped it for friendship's sake alongside the tin tray. Sadie began to shrink. She moved up with us permanently and we watched her ebullience become muted: an occasional half-hearted bash at the vibes which Hilda put for her down one shady end of the blinkered house; a feeble spade-thrust at her old vegetable patch up the back which was running to luscious weed. She betted by phone now and played poker in the evening with only a fraction of her former

221

deadliness, Bathgate's royal flush being gone for ever. Take four points, A, B, C, and D, and join them with lines that connect but never never never intersect. You have us, a trapezoid of needs that pass from point A to point B to point C to point D and that is all. Soon we will be only a three-pointer.

I am becoming more disgruntled.

Holberg's affliction is making too many demands as he too grows older and edgier. Vesper, he roars, stranded in the shower, come and find this damn soap! Vesper, cut down to the village, matey, and pick me up some fags. Vesper, run me up to town, will you? I must see Neilsen while he's here. . . . We are having one of our man-to-man days in the city where, it seems to me, I am becoming too much of the pander and think sadly of Hilda, palely tying up the bean plants and the sweet-peas or flicking the repetitive leaves that keep gathering on the terrace. I run him to rendezvous with a violist (the flautist has long gone), a charming girl coloratura (where's the violist?), the female lead in Shumway's play (he wants to ruin something for him). I spend my chauffeur waiting-hours mooning round libraries and watching English supporting films that end just in time for me to pick him up and tote him back to the patient Griselda.

I hate myself.

His guilt makes him bloom. "No comments," he says, easing himself into the waiting car. "No comments, matey." And he sucks lingeringly on a sated fag, his face a replete sample of a man who has achieved some kind of satisfaction. I make no comment. I let in the clutch and edge out of town with my jaws set tight and he says, "You disapproving bastard. I wanted a pal, not a Baptist minister." So I exceed all speed limits as we whirl back and not even that frightens him, for he cranks down his window and exposes his blind face to wind-rip and I think what can I do, what in God's name can I do?

Into this sobersides caesura marking Bathgate's death, Ilse and Slum and the boy came, sometimes, to ease the weight of hills behind the house and the pressure of space before it. The child was now seven, personable and alert. Holberg would place his hands firmly on the tender shoulders and then stand in such stillness the boy got the wriggles, shunting from one foot to the other. Take last Sunday, I mean that last Sunday.

"Look at me, Jamie," Holberg says. "Look right at me now and I'll tell you what you're like."

The boy giggles. "You can't," he gloats, brutally innocent. "You can't see."

"These see." Holberg flaps his hands up and down on the boy's shirt then puts them on his face, which shrinks, I observe, then tightens with braveness. "You've got straight hair, thick. Slightly pop eyes. A cheeky grin—"

"What colour are they? What colour are they?" screams the kid.

Holberg hesitates. The wind stops for a minute. "I never give colours."

Jamie squeals, "See! You don't know, you don't know!"

"I know."

"What are they then? What are they?"

"They're blue."

Jamie springs up and down, up and down, at the cleverness of this party trick. "How'd you know, Uncle Jack? How'd you tell?"

"It's genetic," murmurs devious Holberg. "A gift. Now look at me. Right at me, Jamie." Hilda begins to move in protest, but Holberg has his glasses off before we can do a thing and he propels the child's head firmly with his hands until it is pointing towards him. "There," he says. "There."

Holberg, I always believed, a maths moron, that you had accepted the illogicality of that first premise and deduced your life-style from there. I didn't know it mattered so much. Jamie is staring with horror. He has never seen his uncle unblinkered before. This is the first time.

Finally he finds words.

"Does it hurt?" he asks. His soft muscles are contracting to back away.

"For forty-seven years," Holberg says.

Later, when Jamie is absorbed with a rubber walrus he is biffing along the pool's scootway, Slum, in his fumble-bum way, remonstrates.

"I don't think you should have told the boy that. After all, he doesn't understand. Not yet."

And what does Jamie understand? I have watched him sporadically for his seven summers understanding food pushers and plastic bricks and clockwork cars and the large print of purged readers that he will let drop without ceremony to sprint after a pegged ball or a racing dog. He understands all those things, which is a lot, I tell myself, who understand not a fraction of that, especially the pegged ball and the racing dog.

Arrogant Holberg says coolly, "But he will. I'm aiding the maturing process. Later on, matey, much later on, he'll remember and understand the matter of it, not the accidents."

Disaster comes out of the most sheltered places.

The afternoon began to lean over in great blocks of lilac shadow. Redheads were idiotically busy along the garden fringes. Over the speakers came softly the large melodic spans and rocking rhythms of a Berlioz-Gautier mating. *Dites-moi, la jeune belle,* sang a voice that had nostalgic recapitulations for the master, *où voulez-vous aller?* The sails are set, the breeze is rising. The oar is of ivory, the flag of silk, the helm of fine gold. For ballast, I have an orange, for sail, an angel's wing, for ship's boy a seraph. Tell me, where do you want to go? The Baltic? The Pacific? (Oh Huahine!) Java? Norway? Take me, sang the insidious voice, to the faithful shore where love lasts for ever. That shore, comes the reply, is little known in the country of love. Warned, I stretched my monkish legs out into the last drains of sun, watching through glare-narrowed eyes the naked and beautifully brown child smack shafts of water up with his hand. Her head back, resting against the canvas sag of her chair, Hilda was exploring peace.

"I think," Ilse announced in her laconic way as the music came to an end, "that Holberg might tell his own child what he likes."

Every body jerked and then, because we are mature people, stiffened into polite tenseness. The fish gammoning dead. Except Slum, poor old Slum, who crumpled, dragged at the hook, and flung himself against the steady pull. Holberg, I wish you could see. Your fingers are caressing ever so gently the wooden struts of your deck-chair. Your mouth has tightened and relaxed, perhaps with the relief of it after all as you feel the air thicken round the courtyard. My mother once told me, moved by too much dry sherry, the poet in her, that when I was fifteen or so she had been working downstairs and heard me in my room singing in a voice crumbling and cracking on the uncertain edges of manhood, and she was so overcome by the shattering distillation of parenthood and tenderness for this product of her blood, that she kept smiling like a fool into the dinner-time pie. I'd blushed for her. Looking now at Holberg, at Slum, at Hilda, at Ilse, the symmetry of her reactions was explained as I assessed the gain in one, the loss in others. I remembered a score of things—my mother's smile as I wolfed an éclair that had rightly been for her but sacrificed to me, my father's pleasure when I fluked a six, the sheer unending outflow of their delight that drowned and lost itself within my own selfish devices.

Someone should have protested. No one could say anything. Finally Slum managed a mumbled, "What do you mean?"

Ilse—was it too early for menopause?—repeated her remark. And again to our stoniness, chipping away for some ore of response. "He's Jack's child. Jack's."

"I never did like you," Aunt Sadie was complaining in a creaking voice and struggling with canvas valleys to climb to the whisky, when Slum staggered abruptly from his chair and wobbled away through the glass coffin (no wonder Gautier called it *La Comédie de la Mort!*) of a living-room to the front driveway. Jamie it was, sucking and peeling his own ballast of an orange, who found him an hour later sprawled out at the feet of a plaster dryad, degutted by pain and muffling his tears with leaves.

He didn't miss his tree.

"Why did you have to say it?" Hilda kept asking her afterwards. "Why? Was it so important he should know?"

Slum had tried living with his enlightenment for a few bravado months, but one drunken evening on his way home from the city illuminated like Cythère had piled his car up at a corner of the branch road. He lived long enough for them to remove the steering-wheel which had stamped itself resolutely on his breast in a crushing circle of completed fate, and through an ether haze became conscious long enough to say to our bedside concern, "Nothing."

VI

IT'S ALL a mess, a highly organized garbage-tip of human relationships and pardon the stinking journalese of that. The only rock-firm untroubled monolith is Holberg who, since Slum's death, has more or less withdrawn into the shiny glass study where a belt of shelves bears stocks of his emotional needs: barbaric lumps of rock, pottery forms, sophisticated enamel bowls, figurines. He is nearing the end of this third symphony and when he is not working he moves round and round the room, picking up, feeling, his hands like antennae, replacing, moving on, picking up. I'm used to it. I wonder how an outsider would react. With pity? I feel the pity. But I wonder how an outsider would react to me also. Mostly he is working, bent questioningly over manuscript onto which he is transcribing the tiny continent we have made on this edge of the rain-forest. There are days when dictating directly to me he barely leaves the piano except for one of his endless cigarettes, grunting when Hilda interrupts for food, so that I have taken to bringing in a small jug and making coffee for us unasked while we work. It is as if I had taken solemn vows. I play the scherzo for him as far as we've gone and am conscious of hearing Jamie and Ilse and Slum, in *accelerando* domesticities and argument. It's all there. He grins while I play and interrupts constantly with alterations, transpositions, modifications of chords and then a whole set of minor variations crematorium-geared to changes in the old *status quo*. The sadness, the gut-disturbing sadness of those blues harmonies that without apology to Sadie he inserts during passages of almost classic exposition! I grow wary and find Hilda and me, Hilda and me

226

and the muted quality of our love-making trapped in sunless places across the hill.

The icing is licked a little thin.

Holberg sees us only as shadow minions pussy-footing round the vast halls of his domain. There's a dark-haired cellist, now, a long mournful swamp creature who appears regularly at week-ends to liaise (it is her word) between Holberg and some student group she is representing in her practical fan-club fashion. It is mid-week. I am nodding in the small hours with my finger still marking the unread page. The master's bedroom is next door, the door ajar. It is their voices, I swear, that wake me to three o'clock dark and I am no longer one huge eye but ear flapping at the threshold of revelation.

They must have been arguing for some time because Hilda is now sobbing in little triplets, scale of D.

"But why," she is persisting with the idiocy of females, "why all these women?"

Unscrupulously I pressed my blazing head back to the wall and listened.

"All what women?"

She began naming them.

There was only silence to listen to.

She named them again.

"You really want an answer?"

"It might help me."

"Me," he said. "Me! But it won't satisfy you, will it? Nothing satisfies your sex but the inside turned out, the glistening bowels of me and the small white pip of a soul. And then you'd want to carve your name on the pip, even, no matter how tiny. Isn't that it? Isn't that it, eh?"

She resorted to silence. "Nothing I say would be any good," I heard him go on. "The explanation might satisfy me, but it wouldn't satisfy the situation for you, now would it?"

"I could try to understand."

"Understand! Jesus! Look, Hilda, I can only hear or touch." She begged him then to lower his voice and there was a furry silence. "Do you want to hear me or not?" he went on. I pictured her tearful passivity and it was too easy. "Well, do you?"

She must have murmured yes for I heard him say in a moment, "When I've done too much of one, hear, I mean, I must have the

227

other. Can you understand? You work on three dimensions. I've only got two. Can't you see?"

You'll have to believe me that suddenly I couldn't bear it.

Slinking, clad, away through the insinuations of the indoor plants with their inquiring tendrils, to lie booted on my bed where Hilda was now only a memorable whiff between the sheets, and ride the dolphin's back into my own nothing, Slum's maxim mine for all time to be writ foot high on my humble headstone.

Nothing to Hilda. Nothing to Holberg. Nothing to myself.

A month saunters by.

We have worked ourselves to a standstill for the moment and Holberg has gone south with Hilda as luggage porter while Sadie and I, like a couple of baronial retainers, potter about the house, the garden, or drive down to Glitterlights—she still has a craving for night-clubs—and get happily molo. Jaunty. Gin-swigging at the Jolly Frog where Sadie, her latest wiglet oblique, hoods her macaw eyes at the band and jounces on her seat in envious nostalgia. I eye myself off in passing mirrors where my sad twin, thinning into early middle age, rejects those noticeable signs of wear—the hollowed eyes, the mouth-sag, all the stigmata of endurance. Do you think, sport, that I only have pity for me? Truly, I have felt for Holberg, tried often to estimate the interminable absence of light, but when you live with a thing you accept it without analysis after a while. And most of the time he himself acts as if there were nothing different about him at all. Except once, some days after our last town trip to ruin Mr Shumway's leading lady, we were working together in the study where I had just finished playing back to him a particularly beautiful *larghetto* passage that moved me to praise aloud. I was being given a glimpse of reasons for servitude. I confessed ebulliently, "It *is* worth it!" Holberg didn't answer, kept his head turned away from my voice and after a while asked, "What do you do with yourself when you take me down town?" Do? "Window-shop, see odd movies, go to the library. Why?" "I'd like to be able to do that, too, matey. Window-shop, go to the odd movie. What's window-shopping really like, eh? If it's too much of a feast, you'd better not tell me." I couldn't tell him after that, though he pressed me when we were next in the city's main street. "It's a lot of gimcrack rubbish," I said, hesitant outside a picture gallery. "Loud brassy tawdry." "You're a loyal old liar," he said, pressing my arm,

228

and I thought about that now trying to keep my lines straight on him.

Sadie has asked me twice about Ilse and I haven't heard a word. In my case the deafness is genuine.

She smacks my wrist with a shiny evening purse that is nearing full term with a wad of T.A.B. takings.

"I said what's Jack doing about the boy?"

"Ilse's boy?"

"Are there others?" asks zany Sadie.

"I don't know. There could be. Does it matter?"

"I don't hear you," Sadie says glitteringly, her eyes glued to the snack menu where her taste-buds have been enraptured by chicken livers in Marsala. Dear Sadie. She is, like most of the old, a tiny glutton who drools through the hours between meals, reliving the luncheon delight or planning the dinner-time ecstasy.

"I think it will be boarding-school soon. Holberg is financially culpable."

"He's too young for it," Sadie snapped. "Order me those livers, like a dear boy. He's only a child."

"And he has toyed with the idea of moving Ilse up to the plateau."

"I don't hear that either," Sadie said, her eyes full of fright.

"Ilse. To the plateau," I repeated loudly, and she went yellow and said, "And just a little rice to go with them."

But it was not to come to that yet.

Through the social mazes of half a dozen kultur fests it became known that Georgie Shumway's dearest friend ("I can't begin to tell you what he means to Lance!") had been accosted in an amateurish fashion by Ilse, who was making ends meet at Valley Junction. This *frisson* rippled itself out to the farthest edges of our stagnant pool, while Holberg could only laugh, then argue irritably that if it were true, though he doubted anything a turd like Shumway might say, she would certainly have to be brought to us. "To do it here?" Hilda cried unreasonably. "We've tried it once." Protesting because she remembered Ilse's oppressive mouth translated into meal-time damnations. Holberg crashed, whooping with rage, through the decaying landscape and wrapped himself in a bracken salve until dinner when, bringing all his fraudulence to bear, he persuaded the three of us that nothing at all had happened.

Yet afterwards and to me alone he confessed with a kind of rancid honesty, "I did truly want to discover my son. I wanted to know the exactments of parenthood, matey."

There was wind, and had been for days, from the coast, a scurrying dark concussion of branch and leaf-strop.

"So that you could use them? Translate them, I mean."

"How?"

"Into whatever you're doing."

"Am I that distanced?"

"I think you are."

"But what's wrong with it? Doesn't it reduce the distance?"

"It's a point, I suppose."

"Well," he said, doing the palms-out gesture of resignation (how did he know it?), "what to do?"

"And Hilda," I added, pushing like a probe into his private dark, "is another matter."

"Is another matter for what?"

"For your concern."

"I thought you were dealing with that, matey." Without rancour, mind you! "I thought you were the more than general factotum."

If it hadn't been for his affliction we could easily have ended by mashing each other's face, made a tolerable physical jab into ethics that would have satisfied our general hunger. There'd always been barricades between our offered friendship.

You see, it wasn't working. Not any of it.

At certain times of the day Hilda had begun to feign blindness, a private vice she tried to keep from the rest of us.

Three or four times now I had seen her, eyes closed, fumbling her way across the garden to worry at the roots of plants, and following her on the last occasion found she had half filled her gardening basket with ranunculi instead of weeds. Seeking redemption in her own intemperate zone, the poor cream cheese, trying to achieve that handicapped parity. Rallying all her guilt on his behalf or non-comprehension of him, she would blank out the world for say a half-hour stretch, a true and practising penitent, and during this ritual, for that is what it became, would find that every object, every buddy pot and pan and cup and plate, the favourite chair, the standing-lamp, had alienated itself. Well-known teguments became foreign with loss

230

of colour. Yet by her actions she embraced the parodee with a tremendous love that I understood and Holberg never knew about. Perhaps he wondered at the crashings from kitchen and garden, the unmusical shards of pottery and glass that processioned her sacrificial periods. Sadie went round picking up after her the horrible damage of affection.

It has been going on for a fortnight now.

Holberg is closeted with a librettist. They are tacking together the choral section of the symphony, a movement which intends to explore the use of three voices. There will be words and instrumental synonym and I think as I watch Hilda blundering away from the house in uncertain movements towards the rain-collaring trees, "He's never had a contralto. This will be something new." The rotten solipsist, I say. As if every stray stuff amniotically nourishes his latest brainchild.

I offer tactful time, watching her blue frock trip and right itself, and then follow through the wet cantankerous shrubs across squelching mould her staggering imitative spoor up the high rise towards the creek head. Still through the gentler verticals of rain beating boyhood in. I smell the drunken soddenness of bark and grass and football fields along the river, and Traill and Mensch and Sibley and Yuill pound over the mud flat in their stained football shorts (fuh-hirsts, fuh-hirsts!) past me trembling and avoiding the ball and bring down like Whalan the wrecker some monster-gut from Churchie who has been zooming in for a try. And there is Hilda just ahead of me collapsed in a vine-trap and dragging her muddy legs upright through leaves.

She opens her eyes to me.

"And how long," I ask with my comic plastered fringe and my water-fuzzed clothes, "are you going to persist in this?"

Her damp wretchedness fights back.

"I've no idea," she says, vehement, "what you're talking about."

We hook on to each other's eyes. I feel mine might be countersunk in this grieving landscape. And I almost say, Do you think I'm blind? but gum up on the last word. A branch drips viciously down her neck. Years ago I pondered love as a punitive process, and here it is with nature adding those extra refinements that harry the already hurdled soul.

"Oh come *on* Hilda, I know what you're up to. I've been watching you."

"Watching?" Those drops will eat a dimple into the gentle base of her skull.

"You're miming the master," I accuse.

She does it again, involuntarily so I bend forward causing a tree-shower and mildly prise her eyelids open.

"Hilda," I ask, "why are you doing it? Tell me why?"

I know of course. He motivated her one early-morning dark with his admission of loss. I think if she had wept at that point, aggravating the condition of this moist September geography, I would have smashed her back into her self-scooped hollow and left her. But she smiled with the old effrontery and said, "I'm trying to understand him, don't you see?" (Of course I see.) "I want to know what it's like. How hard it is."

I smeared a sleeve over my dripping face. "But you can't," I replied. "You'll never know. It's easier for him, truly, because it's the only thing he's used to. You only have to raise those blinds of skin and you're back where you started."

She blinked wetly. "I want to know," she explained, quoting from an eavesdropped dialogue, "what it's like to be able only to hear and touch."

"You *can't* know," I bellowed parting the hair of rain for a second. "Not ever. Not like him. You've known the other thing he's never known. Give over, you goose of a girl, before you drop down a cliff or electrocute Sadie or serve us detergent salad dressing."

The blinking eyes. The tapes of yellow hair. The damp sleeve scraping away at rain on the cheek. We hadn't made love for a long time. Holberg, the All-seeing Eye. So I push her higher up the slope at that point and in the shelter of some rocks where we once scraped our climbing shins I worry her frantic flesh into a temporary forgetfulness. Sorry, Hilda. It is all I have to offer.

My mouth is full of the taste of burnt plums. This is a spiritual malaise as well as a condition of dining with Ilse at the circumcentre, what used to be, rather, years having repositioned the loci. We have sat through the first half, familiar smells of leather, organ-pipe bright-stripe, Georgie Shumway's Judas kiss still corrupting my cheek (you know, Hilda, I don't think she really likes me; Paul, you never do know until she kisses you) and the old old snaky programme rustle between the discreet compulsive coughings and the straining of the

232

constipated music mugs. We sit, a chained line of disciples: Hilda, Ilse, the boy (writhing and longing for the lemon-sucking foyer half-time to be repeated), Sadie, unspeakable and marvellous in a leather bikie's outfit. Under the dousing of first-night perfume, too much of it, sneaking across the chemical trails of dry-cleaned dinner-jackets.

The enemy is scattered. Five rows away I glimpse Georgie Shumway gaying it with a rotund fellow on her left. "Who's that?" I whisper urgently at Hilda who is sitting with her eyes closed. There is a potency about the built-out shoulders and the continual flickering assured smile.

She unwillingly releases herself from darkness and glances across the hall. Does she, as I, suspect plot and counter-plot?

"One of the abominable knowmen," she whispers back tiredly. "Neilsen's counterpart from *Up Beat*."

Then she closes her eyes again.

The Coovers are somewhere on the other flank preparing rave-phrases for the frenzied backstage dash. I long for Bathgate and the genuine ear, the sheer precision of the man who was worth every one of the sycophants and these devious flies of art. Holberg, steered back from the foyer by an attendant through crowd-stir interest-ripples, gropes into the empty seat between his wife and his son. Ilse feels shamelessly for my reluctant paw as the lights drop in the first woofings of applause, and Crumthorne comes out to the rostrum and bows to the right and sucks it all in and bows to the left and does his baton rap and my tension moves out and meets that of the poised and waiting players.

Look, I love this work but I know it too well. It has gnawed its tedious way through the wood of my days. The worm in the timbers. The only section Holberg has not shared with me is that choral surprise whose lyrics he has promised, with the manner of a trump card held up the sleeve, as something in the nature of a sweetmeat. Perhaps this is the right back-drop for it at last, not the glass study, but wall-soar and society perfumes and rustles and coughs, for it mounts in full performance through one felicity after another like the sequences of a theorem and I hear its beauty and practicality for the first time as it becomes a communicable thing translated by lip and finger muscles with its spoof, its dandysim, its blocks of barbarous harmonies. I steal a look at Holberg, at Hilda. He is *seeing* through those ruined eyes and Hilda has gone deaf through her deliberately shuttered lids. It's true. The sighted hear better with their eyes open, did you know? And I test for a moment closing my own so that I can come back to my true aural sense with my eyes catching the anonymity of the shadowed rows ahead.

They're baffled, half of them. I detect the undertones of puzzlement when timpani spell out—is it ten bars too long?—the rubber-steel frenzy of trippers (he's used this before: it shouldn't puzzle them) in quest moving down to an overriding sea that swoops continually behind the string-surge and cor anglais gulls; and their polite muffled relief of recognition of spasmodic night-club ribaldry (thank God it was programmed!). My dear, it's a fun thing! He's got them boxed with a *passacaglia* arrangement of "Home on the Range" not entirely recognizable yet irritatingly, abradingly familiar, too clever by half as I warned his arrogant truculence. They wriggle with is-its? Holberg is sinking into limpness as the second movement fades into tall intervals of the cedars backing the glass boxes, backing the town and its canvas ghettos. *Entr'acte* for coughers careful not to clap. And the *larghetto* paddles into the mournfulness of the camping area, the caravanserai with its communal toilet facilities under the dunes as those whores of park-managers have it, with the washing strung between piccolo lines and the strips of kerosene light between the cooking smells and the sea smells and the flute cries of children at dusk after the pipi hunters, the clanking of bait tins and the slur of can-openers in after-dark darkening into the endless sea-wash and the stretch of canvas melancholy. The melancholy. I shouldn't be moved, but I take Hilda once again in a sea-anted hotel in my arms wondering as I watch is it proper for her to keep her eyes so open and know now that every time, every time she blacks out her sight to my questioning mouth, it is that bulky parodee two seats away who is possessing her. I could howl lewdly, there and then, but rotarian dad whispers all the way from Grogbusters, "Take it like a man." The doctor says blandly now this won't hurt a bit, son, and I clamp my jaws and he puts in one stitch, two, three, four, five and it does hurt outrageously. And in revenge I strain *my* Cyclops eye at portly knowman, only to see him making, surprisingly, yes-faces at Mrs Shumway's violet noddle.

The singers slide from their unobtrusive seats to one side of the orchestra where we have all had our eyes on them nevertheless, and they are doing their nothings during the twenty-eight bars of declamation that prepare us for the voices. "What the hell does a singer

234

do," Bathgate used to ask, "during the largo ending to '*Morgen*'? Eh? What the hell does he do with his hands?" "He has a little scratch," Holberg said roaring with laughter. "Picks his nose or rubs his arse, matey. Otherwise he'd feel a right galah standing there with all that lot gawking at him." No noses. No arses. Unmoving as the statues loitering in the banana thickets that once, once, I had caught Holberg molesting. Which of these? The contralto had curves about her face, small sensual parabolas of experience that might catch anybody's breath. His? Her name had grown its gradual lawn across our days that Hilda made frantic attempts to mow. Raking the clippings I would pause to watch her understand the dangerousness of grass.

The baritone stood at her right, the counter-tenor at her left. It was only now, seeing this trinity, that I suspected, I suspected through the mad whorls of my mind that we were all sitting on the edge of some deformed revelation. All that crepuscular respect about me, even Jamie placated with a jaw-clamper through which his small white teeth were working like juice extractors. The contralto had slid in behind a banking of violins and her voice reached us before we were aware she had begun. The words? I must catch the words? Cagey Holberg had kept them from the programme with only a précis of their matter, and although I had difficulty in translation it hit me like a bomb blast that it was we three who stood there: Holberg, Hilda, me. Joined by the baritone, tangling in duet, her voice pitched like a trident whose prongs of notes were worrying a net the baritone flung all about her in movements of self-preservation. Then the voice from her left, male rotted with female, wordless sounds of expostulation darting in and out between the pair of them like hands that would tug at trident or drag at net. Holberg's eunuch! Am I deranged supposing this? The hall is so shadowed, so still, no one else is aware except me and the master two seats away who has at last made public-private the sweat of our days.

Something is making sense. The baritone is coming to me in gusts:

> . . . into the blind
> sunlight
> the opened pores like eyes
> that suck the wind
> new flesh of leaves or girls
> touch truth half ascertained in stone vein pebble . . .

The contralto:

> limited limited limited
> not the god of the high hill
> servant limited by service,
> hands that do not feel,
> ears that fail to hear,
> eyes that see beyond the actual to the false . . .

The counter-tenor:

> driving to harbours superplazas
> storeman mechanic
> quill for all occasions
> for master servant,
> thrust of the quill
> writing proxy poems on flesh papyrus
> real papyrus
> all translations all all all.

Then in trio *aaaaaaaaaaaah aaaaaaaaaah,* a winding of ironic other-sustaining harmony where each voice engendered the next voice's comment as phrase after phrase settled on the querying cadence of the sub-dominant where its non-reply was taken up by the next voice or both voices or even all three.

My hands tingled with anger on my servant thighs whose prickling apprehension sensed Hilda bend forward on her seat in all the electric flush of new knowledge.

"Are you ill?" I heard Ilse hiss in my ear. "Are you all right?" The unsubtle girl.

Only the light-spots on stage, the thrust of black arms spelling my inner giddiness, were supporting me into the long wave of the beating smacking hands. All round us. All round. Holberg was smiling like some rubbish-tip saint.

The reception room was jammed. Crumthorne lumped a paternal arm on Holberg's shoulders and steered him to the right people. Who? Where? Here everyone was a god and the scatterings of worship could unhinge a truly ecumenic devotee. Amid these proliferations of homage Crumthorne could be heard deliberating the uses of critics. His powerful hook nose lingered above each spaded-out summation.

"These men," Holberg interrupted, "have gardens full of tidy shrubs. But we're their jungle."

"Oh, very good, dear fellow! Very good!"

"It's in us, in these places," Holberg continued, warming to it, "that confronted by exotica, matey, they've never seen before, they either break into their thin cries of wonder or coarse guffaws of derision."

"But I liked it," Neilsen said coming up behind his careful smile and propelling his plump counterpart. "Tremendously."

Holberg took his glasses off for the introduction. But Neilsen took it like a man. He knew when he was onto a winner. The ponce. McCosker remained benign.

"Most exciting," he said. "Most."

"Did you indeed?" Holberg said to Neilsen, ignoring the other voice altogether.

"A work of superlative freshness, particularly in the last movement. The use of voices in that manner . . . not oratorio . . . not quite Mahler . . . a parodic usage that has an originality all its own."

"Parodic?" questions Holberg, running his feelers through air, overplaying his blindness.

McCosker kept smirking with a prior knowledge.

"Well, that's merely an impression. Musical parody, of course. Not the text."

"Ah!"

"By the way, where is the texter? Not here, is he? I wondered if you'd given him any guide-line on what you wanted, which came first sort of thing, chicken or egg, you know."

I touched Hilda's perspiring hand to tip her away from this and Aunt Sadie croaked across the room, inspecting Neilsen and his colleague behind her granny lamps, "Why, it's the think-tank!"

"Isn't she outrageous? Isn't she gorgeous?" Bonnie Coover screamed. Bonnie the Vocative. "O Mrs Buzzacott, you're a wild old thing!"

"Are we contemporaries?" asks Sadie, ruthlessly laconic.

Sadie was shrinking, in her leather gear, one of the seven deadly dwarfs; she was drinking double whiskies without a care in the world. Patting Ralph Coover on his silent arm she edged him away from his shrieking wife towards a sofa by the wall. ". . . and back home afterwards!" Bonnie was crying after her. "Afterwards?"

237

Sadie murmured to no one in particular, "I'm getting good at deafness" and sent Ralph away in search of *hors d'oeuvre*. Soon she was surrounded by those disciples who could not get near Holberg. Proxiness was better than nothing. Georgie Shumway, angel of light, sat beside her and started the smallest talk. Sadie yawned in her face. "You bore me," she said after ten minutes. "Is it true that Mr Shumway wears ear-plugs so that he won't hear his listeners' cries for mercy?"

I laughed out loud and it was my face that Mrs Shumway cracked with her vulgar painted hand.

"You pathetic little man!" she hissed. People were swivelling on their nicely polished footwear to observe. "Oh, we all got the message, my dear, in the last movement. We got it all right. Do you think we're all fools or deaf? Holberg has certainly made mince out of you!"

"Back row of *Flora Dora*," Aunt Sadie commented with a kind of saccharine disinterest. One of Mrs Shumway's hands whipped out of the lamé like a claw.

Hilda warned softly, "If you touch her, just touch, I will rip that disgusting dress off your lion-hunting body. But you wouldn't mind that, would you?"

"Paul dear," Sadie orders blandly, "do get me another Scotch. They're terrible wine-bores, these people."

A gassoonist intervened. His right hand took soundings of Mrs Shumway's bare arm and in a minute she was a mass of hard dimples directed away from our ruin, putting to best use her capacity to allow handlings while pretending by the lightest weather-talk that nothing was happening at all. Sin was only ever in the mind of the holder. She allowed him to steer her back towards the centre of the room. "Were you aware . . . ?" we could hear her asking.

Hilda turns on me with one last blaze of blue, drops the blinds across her eyes and with arms slightly extended moves her tiny terrible juggernaut commenting body across the golden room, through the door and out. Lurching past the supper tables she sweeps a tray of savouries with her.

She refused to open them.

Crashing from bedroom to bathroom to kitchen to laundry leaving a trail of corrupt food and clothes, the by-products of her phoney affliction.

I tried reason. I tried love. I tried lust. She lay like lard in my hands.

And was it all worth it?

You've been over this before, I tell myself angrily as I say aloud to the blinkless ladies on the terrace: the ruined people. That's what we are. The ruined people. After those lyrics, how can I (or he) achieve redemption? Is it only to scrape up a little of Holberg's exuded genius, like slime, I tell myself now? Like slime? They refuse an answer and I smack their plaster rumps one after the other and go back into the living-tomb to find Holberg bent gently over Sadie stroking the near-bald unwigleted head. You see, every time I convince myself of injustice being done in high places, he confounds me with simplicities. She is exhausted, perhaps from clearing up after Hilda's blind accidents, perhaps from the situation with its incoherencies swooping wild throughout the sunlight hours. And she is old and cursed with loyalty.

Holberg has not heard me, is not yet aware of me. Sadie, a sickly yellow, is lying back breathing so lightly that for one moment I am almost sick with dread, for she has reduced the distance in the heart, curbed the wind at the door. Beyond the room, past the pool, I can see Hilda moving awkwardly between the clothes basket and the line, her eyes screwed shut, pegging the washing upside down. Holberg keeps dabbing at Sadie's relaxed old face with a dampened grubby hanky.

"Lovey," he is murmuring. "Sadie darling. There. You've got to take things easy. . . ." Then he is aware of me though I have done nothing more than breathe. "Only a faint," he says. "As far as I can tell. But I think we'd better call the doctor." And his hands keep stroking the vestigial hair from the meagre skin.

"You'll need one for Hilda, too, while you're about it." I had just seen her crack her forehead against the rigid pole of the hoist and my tenderness was torn two ways.

"Hilda?" His frown was tepid, evanescent.

"Don't pretend you're unaware."

The phone began to nag.

"She's not well."

"Not well! You're crazy, matey. She's plumper, juicier than she's ever been." I wanted to vomit.

"It's the mind, I'm talking about. The mind. It's galloping her out."

"Will you answer the phone?" Holberg roared. "I can't answer the phone *and* attend to Sadie."

Standing my ground. Oh well done, boy, dad whispers. Holberg lumbers across the room and the phone goes sullen in his hand.

"You might as well," I say, "while you're there, ring for a doctor."

It gets tiring, this worship. I am beginning to find it curl at the edges. Who *is* the bird on the golden bough, eh? Who? Hilda comes into the room tripping over the wire mat and Holberg reaches out at the thrust wind of her presence, straightening her. Steady, goose-girl. Steady. You're getting as bad (the ultimate accolade?) as me. Was he pretending unawareness, rejecting the most consummate of prostrations under the appearance of blind and fine? *She* blind-buffs it across the room to Sadie and tries to offer her a glass of water which she tips and slops over the old woman's blouse.

"Oh God, Hilda!" I protest and run forward. Rallying at baptism, Sadie blinks her eyes apart to confront this monster world and says, before she closes them again, "I've had enough."

I thought that might have roused Hilda, seeing tears ooze through the compulsive shutting-off, but instead she lurched stubbornly to the kitchen, angrily refusing my help, and prepared a lunch of sugared steak and salted fruit salad that Holberg munched dead-pan as we waited for the doctor, a kind gentleman whom I over-read as a vision from the outer world where life happens to be normal.

He takes Aunt Sadie away with him in his zoom convertible to a Glitterlights Convalescent Home for a month's repair.

The three of us are left together.

X marks the spot all right, buster. That was the breaking point.

Holberg on the rest-crest of his present success (the reviewers had fawned rather than admit lack of understanding) let his mind lie fallow, as he put it, for some weeks, tinkering occasionally with a violin sonata that he'd been messing about with for years or playing records or reading. He read a great deal. He would drag a deck-chair onto the hottest part of the terrace and I would watch those skimming fingers move across the weighty braille tomes that valet Vesper collected regularly in the city. Each tip, I imagined, had some exquisite intelligence like a tiny bulb, ten tiny bulbs, and the idea was so horrifying I resisted it for a long time, feeling his unfair advantage—to be credited with those extra cerebral lobes.

Hilda was becoming more skilled at affliction. I think she cheated a little and even I was becoming used to meals confronted by two closed faces.

Aunt Sadie wrote irregular long letters from her twilight zone where she had begun a betting pool of aged biddies who followed both dogs and horses. *Eheu*.

Being only a grocer's gardener's stud boy, I turned back to the cleansing force of technical matters and finding a new joy in my hands—Things done with the hands are the only true culture, pontificated rotarian dad once years ago in the frostbite dawns of Grogbusters as he cracked at the reluctant family car with a spanner—fabricated half a dozen tricksy gadgets that with poisoner's art and dedication I inserted into the domestic litany of the house. There was a sprinkler system worked from my study where, clutching a vodka and orange, by the mere turning of a spigot I could solve and save my morning hours. I developed a remote-controlled motor-mower and would send the rotten little bug off lopping into the shrubbery while I lay on a Lilo by the pool. There were some unfortunate occurrences, of course: ring-barked trees and hewn garden gems and once I lost it and found it throbbing indifferently as it ground the toes of one of the master's plaster mistresses. And all the time I was thinking of Huahine and the long blue transversals of the sea. The granulations of fantasy shake and wobble into the hard black and white of the shaped object. The pub stinks of salt and sand and alcohol-eaten wood. Skins shine. Skins of leaves as well, groggy with excess chlorophyll. Oh the acid light beating down and up. While the gardens receive water, while the grass and plaster toes get munched all without my having to raise more than a finger, I indulge in escapist fantasies as if I were a lifer.

And as a hobby I am making a sling.

Why sling?

I think perhaps it is a testament of my tiny talent; my own bruised virtues must become apparent. And more than that, there are undertones which I do not choose to hear.

Leafing through a battered and sentimentally retained school copy (suh-hixth! suh-hixth!) of *Res Romanae* on an evening of dim and mothy lamp-light and distant music, I found myself paused before the crude line illustrations of aries and ballista. Their rough structures had been improved upon by some wit possessor before me—the battering ram had a superimposed human virility the simple-minded artist had

241

not intended, cock-funny, and the catapult a distressing anatomical flavour. Vesper, the Balearic slingster! Who gives back a little!

For a while, I confess, I had pondered turning my skills to the making of a battering ram. For what? Poking a little fun at the plaster ladies, the glass boxes? With a retractable shaft mounted on the sit-along motor-mower or even a ram's (ram is the operative word here) head, pole-pierced, jabbing out comments, I could race across the shifting lawns of this ungenial spring. Sadie would find it funny. But I knew that even if it were distraction I was seeking, it was no one's mirth.

So I begin the sling.

A delicate affair of tensile steel which, like arteries, will bear an electric discharge of superlative energy down the piston that directs the missile cup. From my own distorted and ironic sense of parody unlike Hilda's mimicry outsprung through love, it is what I please to term a three-part invention and I am nearing the end of the first subject, the monopod base with its wistful deposits of egg-like batteries, its nipple switches and its range-finder which is to my heart a trigono-metrical joy. My inner being, filled with a disquiet so persistent and all-pervading I am stunned I don't get the shakes, warns me to keep my composition secret. I lock the apparatus in my wardrobe, comic Vesper, where it prods metallically at the frayed tails of my shirts. Gradually it takes on personality for me. As it seems given to a ward-robe way of life I call it Taurus.

During the master's absences, I make tentative tests.

For what?

The dry-cell batteries are inefficient. I replace the motor on a lead-acid battery and find the spring-like blow and recoil of Taurus's mem-ber an extension of my most secret and hyperbolic dreams, fragments of which include a surrealist sequence in which I take languorous pot-shots at the house that holds me, destroying it piece by casual piece.

But only the house. As some ruffled chick might view sadly, wist-fully, the shatterings that were necessary to make it live. It and I step delicately over ruptured shell.

The days roll languidly across into the dense rains of summer and the plateau springs into a wild-minded fecundity that brings saplings closer, threatening the lawn outskirts of the house. New ranks of shrubs marshal themselves below the trees. I count the years, banging them angrily and then resignedly along the wires of my abacus. I reach

242

ten and pull the eleventh bead, a glossy black affair, one-third of the way across. *Me miserum!* Graduate in engineering now corner-store bargain hunter, part cook, part gardener, secretary scribe chauffeur and wife comforter. Eleven years down the ladder to this. I draw up a mental balance sheet of debits and credits. On the right-hand side there are people and parties and the dubious by-flow oil of Holberg's genius (is it?). And it isn't enough. I cannot look myself in the face. In fact I am recapitulating the thrips (now nervous) of twenty-seven years before.

I am the tin parrot on the tray and nothing more.

The tin parrot.

Which I now nail to my wall decorated by a typed sub-title: Paul Vesper, aged seven to forty-three.

Bathgate would have liked that.

Mawkish Vesper! Mystically I have outdistanced myself and across the uneasy landscape of my nullified dreams, plans, ambitions, spot this tiny figure that is me stumbling between the cratered dunghills of my achievements. Dunghills? Achievements? Sometimes the wings flap and discordant echoes of echoes of echoes parrot out of my harsh throat. Mother, father, you would not be proud of me. There is nothing my tepid personality has contributed and nothing it has abstracted but faint, growing fainter, memories of heyday Hilda and Bathgate and Sadie in their clotted dotage. A shapeless aggregate of forty-odd years who has rendered only a menial apostleship that underscores and underscores what I miss: the most mundane of things— the logic of yellow windows in winter-dark promising warmth to the floor-shivering shanks, food-smells applicable directly to my slammed farewells and hellos, my choir-boy seed sprouting my own choir-boy face.

The divine resentment carries me without pause and composer flair into the sure swing of my second subject and it is only a month before I have my angelic machine erected in a secret eyrie west of the house, its range-finder and brutal arm directed at the font of my discontent.

Last week in a spasm of dilettante rage Holberg thrust the whole of his violin sonata into the ungrateful incinerator and flung away to rest his forehead throb against the cool buttocks of a mouldering Diana. The non-responsiveness of the coldly shaped stone trapped him for an hour during which Hilda woke to vision (I had persuaded her to

243

cut down her ritual masochism to three thirty-minute periods daily) and fed her concern into ten different phone-calls. These depleted her but brought in response-gorged doom-dabblers who would suck the last secretions of possible disaster. Re-transfused, oxygenated, they subjected us to worrying visits of concern and, when the master refused to see them, even tackled minion Vesper and the old principle of knowing someone who knows someone came into play as they filled me up with lunch preparatory to pumping me. Did all this delight me? Once it had pleasured me indeed, gimcracked mortal that I am, but now, my mind a bright scarlet bead, I tuck into south-flown crayfish and out-of-season strawberries and smooth this neglected aged choir-boy face with the cold-cream of innocence while I absorb them thinking they are absorbing me.

Look, I'm concerned about him, too. I don't want to trot out that old cliché of the love-hate relationship, but that is simply what it is. There is so much about him, in way, to admire and loathe. While I pick at a juicy claw I see you, Holberg, I see you standing, dark-glassed, leaning on your white stick on the straggly footpath up at the plateau. I see you standing listening outside the tiny local school during the squealing lunch-hour to the bird voices of the kids in the play-yard. You'd got into the habit of wandering down there in the summer terms and would listen and listen, a distinctive and tragic figure with your blind face upturned in the sun. "There's one little feller," you used to say to Hilda and me, "who's as funny as a monkey. He bosses his pals around in this squeaky little voice and I bet he's only three feet high." The children had become used to him and would gossip over the wire fence, handing him their marbles and tops and skipping-ropes to examine and to their delight he would set a top spinning for them so expertly they would yell with glee and wonder. You're at your best like this, Holberg, I tell him as I munch a piece of cray. Your very best. Or invited in occasionally—the headmaster knew reverently who he was—would enchant them for half an hour with funny rearrangements of nursery-rhymes on the old school piano or make up descriptive monologues musically backed. "Here's that big tough headmaster," he would say, describing a giant ogre with massive chords, "telling all you naughty kids to get in and start work-ing"—fantastic ripples and scurryings along the key-board—"and one cheeky little feller"—insolent waltz theme at the top of the piano—"says something rude"—hideous discord—"and gets his tail smacked"—

244

series of appoggiaturas—and the whole roomful of them doubled up with their squeals of laughter.

That.

And then I remember the last concert and Hilda bent white over the pain in her stomach and I try to be reasonable and tell myself over and over he can't see he can't *see* and there is nothing to do but put on this false calm—I am cut in half—and work at urbanity.

"But you *saw* the score!" Neilsen was chomping messily and noisily at a bleeding steak. "Was it really no good? You see, Vesper, it's reached that stage where anything at all he writes is of interest, or will be anyway, and it ought to be preserved."

"No. Not that at all."

"Then why?"

"Why what?"

"Why did you allow him to do it? Tear it up like that?"

"Allow?" Resentfully I nibble a celery stalk.

Neilsen took a few recuperative gulps at some monstrous red liquid he had discussed obsessively with the waiter.

"Yes, of course. That's not quite fair, is it? But you could have persuaded him. Got him to discuss it. Something."

"Discuss!" I spluttered rudely and blasphemously. "He *is* Goethe's Ur-plant."

"I don't follow you," said ignorant Neilsen.

"Never mind," I said, all my placating juices busy. "It happened so fast, anyway. No one knew till after. What I mean is that it would be impossible for anyone else to direct or persuade. Even if we had been forewarned. He knows what he's about and any suggestions from me might only drive him to get rid of the lot. He's still got notations about the place. One of these days he might dig them out and start patching them up again."

Neilsen paused before going in for a try. Mensch. Traill. Zacka. Tuh-heem! "How are things—well—with him—personally, as it were? Is he going through a rough patch?"

Rough? Patch?

Neilsen had light eyes, shallow enough for me to see the skitter-fish of his intentions. I dropped my own and smiled wistfully at the sauce-dabbled plate.

"He's a man beyond disaster."

"I don't think you follow," spurious Neilsen persisted. (Oh, but I do. I do.) "How's Hilda? How's the boy? Is everything all right on the home front?"

"When you're not talking about music," I said, "you remind me so much of my father." Rough patch. Home front.

"Do I? Well, that is nice of you to say so, but I won't let you divert me. People have been saying that Hilda's not well."

"She seems to me very well," I lied.

"Oh, not physically, you know. Mentally. Is that too harsh a word? Acting rather oddly at times and that sort of thing."

"Oddly?"

"Vesper, I do wish you'd stop using the interrogative for a moment. You must be aware of what I'm talking about. Last time she came down to see us—she had Ilse and Holberg and the boy—she sat right through supper with her eyes closed but every now and again would make remarks like 'The garden is looking lovely this evening' or saying to my wife—eyes still shut, mark you!—'What a truly beautiful dress.' We could have been offended, my dear fellow, if we hadn't been concerned."

"She's breaking the rules," I said.

"The rules?"

"Aha!" I waggled a finger. "That interrogative! She's suffering from severe eye-strain—actually it's a little more serious than that. A slack muscle. Operable if the therapy doesn't work. She has to keep her eyes closed a certain amount of time each day." It didn't even sound feasible to me.

Neilsen's disappointment in the loss of possible scandal was so tangible I could feel him resisting the palpability of reason. The slumped corners of his mouth held little rivulets of suspicious hollandaise—as well they might.

"But no exercises?"

"Yes. Those, too, of course."

Picking my way through the dandruff of his conversation.

Yet Holberg threw himself at it again with a kind of silent fury for one month, two, three, hermetically challenging distraction. He used me as little as possible and that transcribing I did for him round about the second month appeared like the high-knock theatrics of a Wagner mated with a Stockhausen. The crispness of the former work was blunted and there were strange intervals of silence that puzzled me. They interfered in no way with the total dynamic of the movement

246

and I examined them again and again until it dawned on me that he was parodying Hilda's moments of visual withdrawal. The snide shock of it! How long had he been aware, withholding tenderness for the barked shins, bruised shoulders, the staggering feet that were her final act of wifely prostration? He was letting me know he knew, as he had let me know other things I knew he could never see. So I remained the dumb servitor, doling out the praise-phrase I had become so adept at cooking up, the cold collops of one who has grown a little tired of the effort of apostleship. Still, *still* the gauche butler when the curtain rises, the harem pander, the dusting maid. I pad along the wasteland high-polish redwood of our days to his vitreous sanctum and ask a pertinent question here and make a pungent glory-be there and say nothing of biography, while all the time a little smile plays round his mouth and I know he knows I know. *Eheu.*

Sadie is back with us now refreshed and television addicted from the cure-methods of the twilight zone. She watches westerns and space thrillers and replays of horror movies of the thirties with terrible wigleted zest. Suckers on a pugnacious detective in a weekly series, she sits drooling and gasping over her whisky as the chubby fellow flings his weight about the magic screen saying, "I want them John. I want them." "Boy," she says, "I wish he'd say that to me." "If you'd shut up, he might," I say amiably wrestling with the fragmentations of the plot.

Jamie comes up for holidays still with the child-velvet on his plastic limbs. Once I see his father walking him across the terrace and down the sea-watching slope east of the house while his arm, circulating too much love, presses the stranger boy into his side. It is at times like this that my hate does not know which way to turn or even if it should turn into love, only turn back and away from the heart-break of their wrestling together, laughs, shouts, limb-knots on the summer grass.

For a loser he's very much a winner. God, how I envy him just this.

"He's a nice boy," I say forgetfully at dinner and Hilda winces.

The child is unaware, paddling about in a bowl of mangoes beside his plate.

"The mania of art, matey," Holberg pronounces sententiously, "is that one forgets the genuine manias like this. Parenthood, I mean, or toast for breakfast. The honest dependence of another."

He was thinking of Jamie, naturally, but I wouldn't let him get away with it, smug behind his barricades.

"You've had plenty of that," I offered.

His mouth vanished and reappeared.

"Not of my asking, pal."

"There's something toxically attractive about the lineaments of talent," I insisted. "No one wants to be drawn in, but is. It's not of your making, not voluntarily I know, but it's there and you've had it in great swads."

Deciding to be calm about it he felt his way to the salad and helped himself sloppily. "Too much tarragon." I didn't think I could tolerate longer those grease streaks on his chin. They asserted their own stature. "That's not quite the thing I mean. It's the soft physical dependence of another that I've missed. Oh, there's plenty of the other sort, the folk who feed on whatever scrap of reputation I may have. And that's not vanity. I know it. But the other." He wouldn't commit himself into sentiment for his dark disability, though again he knew we knew and could sense if not see our prickling tear-ducts, our guilty mouths. "And what is more, Hilda," he went on, impressive over the luncheon plates, "I'm getting tired of your fantasy."

Sadie gave a tiny snort and Hilda's oblique eyes skated over Jamie, over me. All that wasted blue you will never assess, Holberg. And now the sour cream cheese a little curded on the jaw-line, the cool length of neck.

Again, "I don't know what you mean." She went scarlet with the lie.

"Don't you?"

Fully opened those orbs looked pitiful.

"It's your withdrawals, I mean. Those fakeries of yours. What are you after?"

Jamie was watching us, engorged with his own surprise. He had a large moustache of mango pulp. "Run outside, Jamie, if you've finished," Aunt Sadie said. The reluctant feet dragged off to the door and Holberg listened to them.

"Look," Holberg said, "do you think I'm deaf as well? Do you? Do you think I don't know the scatter sound of sightless feet? Why, I could notate the intervals for you right now, the terrible slurrings of unsureness. All these months. All these bloody phoney months!"

Hilda had begun to cry without sound.

"And you can stop that gutless snivelling." (The tell-tale vibrations of the table, the chair.) He thumped passionately straight into the salad bowl. "I know what you're doing, but I don't know why."

"It's more of that stinking dependence you crave," I said, losing my temper and reaching for her chilly mitt to give it a squeeze. "She's trying to interpret your own lack, you maniac, you selfish rotten maniac, so she can understand your needs a little better."

He sat for a long moment drumming his fingers. After a while he asked, "And has it helped?" but with such irony he was talking at air, for Hilda had shoved back her chair and was running outside and up the slope towards the trees. He went after the sound shouting, "I can't stand these parodies!" and then I understood at last that he was proud of his scar, flaunted it like the jealous apparatus of his success. I could only go on picking at my ham while Sadie kept saying Christ, the fools, the fools, until from the distance, all warped by air, I heard Hilda cry out once and left everything, everything until I had scrambled through the scrub to find him hitting her (tracked down by sound) again and again on the side of her pliant face, while her torn leg bled redly into the bracken.

"Will you stop it stop it!" he was shouting, punching the undodging skull which he had prisoned with his other arm. But she only swayed before each blow, her eyes jamming out the world. "Oh my God!" he cried. "Oh my God!" when he heard me stumble up to them and felt me tearing her back from him. Somehow we all toppled into the shaggy grass, Hilda's body pressed closely against mine, shuddering from its sense of wrong but her eyes dry. Holberg rolled away from us and lay on his back panting. I was conscious of sun draining itself through branch and leaf and the almost soundless quality of the stirring bush. Propped on one elbow to regard this chaos I could see Jamie at the foot of the hill some two hundred yards away staring up at us with his eyes slitted against the shock of light. He was perfectly still, entranced, his young body caught in the expectation of tragedy, horrified and replete and unsated, all at once. I looked over Hilda's diminished shoulders at her husband. His glasses had dropped off and the one opened eye rolled streakily in his head. He was gathering words with an effort. I could hear his breath taken in and see the heave of his chest.

"Will you stop it now?" he asked. And I did what I still regret: I struggled to a kneeling position, crawled across to him and slammed my packed knuckles onto his supercilious jaw.

Hit a blind man, dad! *Mea maxima culpa.* The pain in my right hand shocked me into apology. I mumbled that I was sorry.

My fist has punched a hole right through the blue. I see nothing but the monstrous rent while the air steadies and the trees cease moving. Flattened grass—this is inversely comic—raises its hackles once more and Holberg, rubbing his challenged skin, says slowly and deliberately, "I won't have any apologies. You belittle me by them, matey." He stalks away through grass, and I do understand. I do.

Hilda's cheek has a different shape and now one eye is genuinely closed, swollen and turning purple. I'd like to think this has opened them at last.

"Well, that should be the cure," I say, not meaning to be brutal and fatuously enough as we sit like macabre picknickers in the despoiled bracken.

"He needs me." Funny, that, with the bulging eyeball and the stretched bruised flesh.

"Like cats need mice. He's put us all in our places."

"Look!" Hilda cries, ignoring me. "He's forgotten his glasses."

She picked them up and began to polish their smudged lenses and through my now sparkling ones I summate this hideously wedded couple, him with his slow deliberate stagger downhill, a length of snapped-off sapling used as a guide-stick whacking the obstructive trees, Hilda votively running after him, and the amazed child, obscenely pure, regarding the three of us. They spiritually collide and I can see but not hear the sounds they are making. Goggle-eyed Jamie watches Hilda slip the glasses onto his father's nose, sees his aunt's circus eye and finding their deformity twinned begins to blubber and scuttle backwards into the house where Sadie has sensibly turned her back on all of us. At this distance they are moving like crabs, obliquely, scattering light tubular poolside bric-a-brac, turbulence in the slow afternoon.

At a limp I arrive beside the two of them, always touching the edges of cyclones, in time to see Holberg run those antennae down the ruptured curve of his wife's cheek and to hear him say, "Poor goose-girl. I'm sorry I had to put it that way."

Will she flood with love, the stupid bitch? Will she? I watch her

250

ruined face harden its planes as she turns her head aside sufficiently to catch me. "It's all right now," she says. "I didn't understand before."

Holberg spends the rest of the afternoon punishing the piano. Ironically he pounds right through the two books for the well-tempered clavier. It takes him until well past supper.

Sometimes I hate his damned logic.

VII

A cure—but with what side-effects.
Our household is split in three.

Holberg has begun a compulsive rewrite on the violin sonata. Between work spasms he joins us for silent meals or bitterly recriminatory ones. Hilda's cheek subsides and the purple fades. Holberg develops some doubtful young friends of dubious sex, orchestral minions who make their cars and persons available for fetch and carry. More and more frequently he spends days in the city and nights and week-ends away at the homes of sycophants over-eager to receive him. The purpose of my being—here, I mean—is now as distant as that long swinging sea-line of blue. We keep the household going after our fashion: there are regular meals and polished floors and sawn-off lawn and an overriding sense of discomfort that this is no longer our home despite assurances of domestic regimens.

These days, now there is all the time and opportunity in the world, we never make love. It's a delicacy and a reticence on my part—yes, I do have those virtues in microscopic portions—that is unwilling to tackle her unsureness. I spend a lot of time in the front of the house baking my thinning legs and imagining funk-hole Huahine across the endless water. Sometimes and sometimes not, Hilda steps from the wings of these preoccupations to make brief curtain calls that add nothing to the unassuaged departures in me. Truly, the flesh is sad and truly I've read all the books.

And I am packing a bag.

Rotarian dad left me reasonably secure. I have a pregnant bankbook, no talent, a tin tray, a Burne-Jones print, no talent, two glowing letters of reference from the old firm, an unused clarinet, no talent and a dinner-suit. I have my conscience camouflaged by sarsaparilla and tree-fern entrenched in a secret place upon the hill. Sometimes I wander up to sit beside it swinging the long arm of my private law and adjusting the range-finder so that it has access to vital organs in the waiting house.

History is no longer the privilege of the wealthy as I read somewhere or other. The lower classes can now make their own. I am on the verge of my own historicity, the soft blind point of the pampered years that have fed this surge of creativity into me. Mere me. My sense of discovery irradiates. Celebrating, I make Hilda a rissole lunch and serve it to her on the terrace in a splother of allamanda. Holberg is conducting in a southern city under the guardian-angel-ship of a hairy bachelor trumpeter who might supplant me. Have I feared that over all these years? Have I eyed off every possible replacer of the soft cop, the satellite of genius? Let me assure you, now that I am opened up by my revolutionary climacteric, that it is not soft. Why, Sibley, why, Traill, why, Mensch, you got it easier in the scrum! There has been, I'll admit, a deceptive character about the *largamente* phrasings of our early days when the nine-to-fivers eyed off my sitting-at-homeness, the envious yellow showing in their eyes. And with such a companion! Ah! The constant possibility of being able to touch the hem! And bring about my own issue of blood? I see this now, too. All the hem-touchers ruined for ever by haemorrhage. A touch of the old Vesper, that! I am back in my thoughts in Bauxiteville with Freckles accommodating on late Sunday afternoons and the sun like lava and the long white rind of the coast superimposed over lost and untouchable dream sequences of Huahine which would be the worse for my revisiting though it still dangles its tantalizing medallion before my eyes and I know anywhere, anywhere at all would be better than this fecund and sterile plateau.

He has asked me to notate the last braille sections of the sonata for him and I browse round his study after the work is done to see if there are any other matters to tidy up. In one of the drawers of his desk there is a thick pile of braille notes he has made over the years, not musical altogether, just jottings, ideas he had set down during the last decade. I've never examined them before, not that he has made a point of their privacy, just that they have always been tucked away in a non-work compartment I rarely go to. They seem to be jumbled about with sections of manuscript, and I sit down to do a sorting, glancing briefly at a few lines—I am quick at transcription by now— and then, tantalized by what I read, curious to see more.

They are self-explanations, a biography of growth and apprehension. The few words I have seen—"red as a berry. I comprehend berry. But what is red? What is it?"—nag at me, reopen the wounds of my tenderness, and shamelessly I shuffle them all together, those confessional sheets, and take them away along with a few musical fragments I will put in order.

Hilda and Sadie have driven to a neighbouring farm to buy avocados. I pack the sheets, my bathers and a towel into the vegetable buggy and head off across the six-mile plateau with its orchards and guest-houses for the coast. And the next twenty miles, *ephphatha,* my eyes are opened as never before to the satin of the day, the growth sheen all about the dusty back road leading to smacking black highway with its slick land-settlement deal signs and the new high-rise sores leading in at last the canal estates they miscall paradise with the hundreds of razed allotments gawping down at drain width of Nerang.

The boutiques. The arcades. The metered girls. The closed-down swingeroo nighteries having their morning nap. The coffee bars and the fish joints and the razzle-dazzle motels each with identical blue pools and litter of cars.

I drove along the front to a beach filling up with surfers and, propping my sun-bake rest chair near one of the withered palm shelters, stared gloomily at the sea and the wave-cutting swimmers. Doing an Aschenbach, conscious of the plague.

Then I opened up my brief-case, took out Holberg's pile of braille sheets and began with the top one. It must have followed on something else for it started:

> . . . was my real difficulty. I could follow tales of action without any trouble, the straight line of A pitted against B. When the writer developed an image, however, I was brought up sharply. With words that drew comparisons from sound or touch I was safe. "Her voice was like a bird's" made complete sense; "his eyes blazed like torches" didn't. "The glass surface of the lake" etc., I have touched glass. It is hard and cold and unbending. I know the feel of water. I have dipped my hands in what I was told was a lake. I cannot understand this; only accept. "Hu-

mans in rows, slow vegetables along the ploughed down suburbs." I ferret out the idea of this, but I don't know, not know what a human looks like! I can hardly believe it: I have a pattern of shapes—head, arms into shoulders, trunk with or without breasts (male, female), splitting into legs. We move. But vegetables have numerous species. They have leaves, or long roots or are dug with the hands and washed of soil. What, *what* do we look like? You see, I cannot even conceive a house or a tree or a bird that I've held and nursed. I have no conception at all of colour and no real idea of bulk or depth or total outline. And my world is as real as yours.

I slipped that page under the others and looked along the beach. Splashes everywhere—orange, veridian, cobalt, magenta, on round tall thin flat high wide. God Almighty! I never really had thought what it was to be Holberg; I had merely taken his condition as a *fait accompli,* seeing him as normal, handsome, intelligent, gifted, lacking only one thing, and because I could see it was minor in my total valuation of him. For him it changed the apsect of everything in the world. Did not change, rather, gave it no aspect. There had been moments when I had tried to imagine his concepts; but they weren't nearly often enough or sensitive enough; could not even touch the perimeters. Holberg, how could I be so blind! A kid punched a ball towards my feet and I gave it a kick back, waving, to a sharp stab of guilt.

Sadie taught me the parts of the world I would use. When I was five we started going to the beach. She took me down the sliding hills to the water. "This is sand," she said, putting my hands in it. "Sand?" I asked. It felt like tiny sugar. I wet my finger and dipped it in and tasted it. Like grit. She began making movements near me and took my hands after a while, putting them on a rounded sandy surface. "Sand-castle," she said. And made me put my arms right round it to feel the shape. I made one, too. Then we walked back up the beach and I felt the muscles pull at the back of my legs as we climbed and I tumbled forward, my arms trying to hold a larger shape than I could manage. "Dune," she said. It was all like that. My body warns me now from habit when I am on hills, roads, bracken, down-slopes, steps—but I have no idea of any of them. Just once to know what everything looked like!

Sadie never used colours. She did not say "yellow" or "blue" or "red" or "green". Her sensitivity wanted to spare me so much. But I learned the words from other children and no matter how they tried to explain

255

colour, I could never understand it. "What's red?" I asked Sadie one day. "Hard," she said. "Not to feel but to look at." And touched off by this defined blue as "soft." That's how I see colours: as variations of texture. . . .

. . . I dream a lot. And of people. Not as you know them but as shadows with voices and personalities. They move through my own sort of landscapes and because they have a true picture of me while I have not of them, I feel disadvantaged. More so as I grow older and the tongues become sharper. I have honed my own. I look so vulnerable, Hilda once told me, when she first met me, the days of the room in the city tenements, the cheapest I could get living off my magnificent pension. Twelve of us, the only blind one me, though the others might have been incapacitated in more subtle ways, living in the partitioned warren close to the centre of the town. I walked right down the nearest street once and there were no trees except a dying cypress. It disconcerts people when I tell them these things. They see it as primitive magic. A friend was coming to take me to a party and brought Hilda with him. She told me when she saw me sitting waiting in the narrow hall filled with paper flowers bought by the landlady's wog lover, that I looked entirely isolate. She meant it kindly, but I don't think I ever forgave her. Have forgiven her. . . . I use a lot of visual verbs. It used to be unintentional. So-and-so's the dirtiest town I've seen, I say. I was looking out front and everything was a mass of paper and dust. I almost feel them wince with the shock or is it the cheek they think I have to make use of words that are their property? They forget I have a nose acute to the scent of a hundred things they miss. An ear, as well. I think these capabilities make me arrogant. . . . When I was five they discovered I had perfect pitch. No one else in my family had any musical talent and this was one of those freak gifts, compensatory. I don't know whether I could have tackled the business older, that conversion through the tips of my fingers of pricked holes into sound patterns that in those early years I would learn by heart. It came easily and I don't understand any other method of communication except by speech. Working on distances and spatial relations along the key-board; that's how it's done. My fingers move like tentrip pilgrims over the patterns of all those old [next page missing here]
. . . afraid of losing my hands. Like cutting out my tongue. That time when Vesper came and acted as right hand, he had no conception of what I endured or what he did for me. . . .

I don't know whether I can go on reading. I am cut in half. Bent over with middle pain on the hot yellow yellow yellow sand. Not that it is anything but coolly appraising; the whinge is mine. But I do read on.

256

. . . stupid to say I would like to see just once. I don't know what see is. Many women have tried to explain. Sadie warned me once that I was personable and that blindness was attractive rather than detractive; a trap for sentiment. Women wanting brief emotional encounters, she said, might find me useful until they discovered the efforts that went with owning me. It's been true. But I've got like Skeeter, a cousin of mine who runs a barrow down by Roma Street. He's a skilled physicist who can lay grapes in a bag so the seepage doesn't show till the customer is exactly two hundred yards away, too far to turn back. That's how I lay my grapes now. Or he counts twenty bananas into packs that later only ever contain fourteen. Great mathematical sleight of hand. He's the genius in the family, and I try to take after him. And I can't say I'm sorry. It's my manner of becoming. . . .

I laugh with relief for him and to my surprise find the laughter is watered down with tears so that I bury my surprised face in my hands, a genuine Aschenbach, and a woman's voice nearby asks curiously, "Are you all right?"

I hadn't seen her arrive to spread her tawny towel a few feet away. She was thirtyish and what my mother would have called common with her bad perm and her make-up-stiff lashes, the tautness of her body just beginning to slacken.

"Yes," I said. "I'm all right. Just something I read upset me."

"Read?" Her eyes were fixed on the pricked discarded sheets by my side.

"It's braille. You read with your fingers."

"Well, isn't that something!" Reaching over for a sheet.

"It's for blind people."

"But you're not—" taking a quick assessing glance.

"No, thank God. It belongs to a friend."

"That's sad," she said. "Sad not to be able to do things like this. Being here on the beach I mean."

"Oh, but he does. Often."

"But the main thing is seeing it all, isn't it? I mean all the people and everything and the water and the flags out along the front and the kids playing."

"Yes, I suppose it is. For us, anyway."

She snapped open a cigarette case and made hunting movements so I did what she expected and struck a match for her. She leant back inhaling heavily and breathing out two grey tusks. "Tell me about your friend," she ordered. I was being picked up. I let myself be. (Typical. Man, woman, dog.) But she listened to all I said, and there wasn't much of it, with a quick sympathy, her eyes lowered over the cigarette, her mouth open a little with surprise that gave way soon to a cry of protest at such imposition.

"How does he stand it?"

"I've just been finding out."

I did the next thing she expected. I suggested a drink.

"It's a bit early, isn't it?" she said, meaning it was never too early.

Sitting in the Caper Bar we exchanged names and held frosted gin glasses while from speakers concealed behind tubs of brassias a voice howled its isolation.

"Here for long?" It was going to be one of those Socratic relationships.

"Only down for the day."

"You from town?"

"The country, Lil. The country."

"Taking a sickie?" She laughed understandingly and lit another cigarette.

"I'm a night-time man,"

sobbed the hidden voice,

"And if that's all right with you
I'll have breakfast at midnight
Till I find somebody new. . . ."

"You could put it that way," I said. "You could well put it that way."

"Cause it aint nobody's business
What I do."

She looked at me curiously with her coarse sympathetic face, and tapped off half an inch of ash with a shining white nail, catching my eyes full on and digging away for my privacies with her own knowing orbs.

"Look, you don't have to tell me," she said, "if you'd rather not, but is something up? You look all cut about, if you know what I mean."

258

"I'm married to two people," I said, and couldn't help grinning.

"Well!" she said, drawing up her big bust, the beginnings of outrage. "Well! I must say one was enough at a time for me. Plenty."

"And how many times have there been?"

"Three," she said. And laughed suddenly so spontaneously I liked her.

"It isn't like that," I said. And I began to explain.

It made me feel better, I must confess, even such a second-rate purgation although she was as intuitively understanding as I'd hoped, this glad-time gal with her brassy beach-wear and her eye to the main chance.

"You haven't had much fun, have you love?" She snapped open her horrible metal-mesh purse. "Let me buy you a snorter, eh? Something to knock your eyes out!"

That was my first communion, ladies and gentleman, the Gold Coast Ripper, four parts tequila, one part lemon, offered in charity's name. No, I'm not making fun. No one before had offered a chalice without forethought. What else could I do? I went back to her back-beach flat (she worked shifts as a motel cleaner) and she whipped up some lunch and opened her last two bottles of beer and I took her to bed where she invited me out of kindness expecting nothing, and all the time I kept telling myself I must reread that bit about the cup of cold water offered in my name yet when I came to my conscious self, staring drained across the room at the striped wallpaper, I was engulfed with such guilt at my betrayal of both Hilda and Holberg there was nothing for me to do but drag myself into my clothes and conceal the cracks in my composure.

"That's all right," she said when I started for the door. "I know. That's all *right*."

God bless you for that, Lil. One of these days. . . .

Holberg returned revivified by change. He was unloaded from a long tourer crammed with clarinets and trumpets. There was instant music-making in the study and enthusiastic quackings through which Hilda and I smiled our sullen smiles and organized our spleen. He seemed a little unhinged by his social successes there and here, talking compulsively about the integration of the arts with a lot of high-flown mystical tarradiddle that boiled down to his admitting at last involvement in a proposed rock festival. He had already jotted down half a dozen ideas for a jazz overture.

I listen to this and I can't take him seriously. And I remember his private notes—and I do. The dichotomy is breaking me apart.

Friday. The air is heavy with November rain, a fatness of monsoon weather through which I lie awake in my room listening to the drum-tap of the gutter overflow against the walk of water across the whole sky. Leaves are gummed to glass in black cut-out patterns somehow fluid, sometimes sharp, but penning me into this bed so overwarm now I can smell my flesh tired and failed. It is two on this sodden morning of summer dark and wet and I have counted three thousand sheep all with my face baulking at wires that are barbed with grandiose notation. Unplayable, I tell you. Taurus squats uphill under his cam-ouflage plastic mac. My bag hunches in a corner and is now bearing as well as a mess of tourist-trash brochures that sedate and excite. Last week Ilse had rung me, her distress a faint and febrile twenty miles distant, and I had driven the grocery van down to see her.

Her kitchen was choking on the stench of burned vegetable. A blackened pot was askew in the sink. And now eyelids like swollen pink prawn bulging over grievance. Across the heated grey hills birds had come bursting and then flickering to the closer uncut sweetness of the grass in her garden where insect din quivered its ragged patterns. Oh, this slatternly cave of her being, a slum of stained hopsack and smoke-filled curtain-weave and wine-blessed carpet across which several cushions had crept in a piteous attempt to escape. Inside her weeping house-coat she had shrunk to nothing and the corn tassels of her hair simply hung.

"He's taking legal action to get Jamie."

I sipped Ilse's version of tea. My days were brown enough.

"He has to have grounds. Has he?"

"He says I'm not a fit mother." Blubber away, Ilse. Blubber for me as well who hasn't a child to be unfit for.

What do I say now? I say, "But you only see Jamie in holiday time as it is, what with boarding-school and so on."

"He's like a primitive god," groans sordid Ilse, head down among the egg-shells and the toast crusts. "He wants everything he touches."

I remember and I can sympathize there, with both of them. Holberg moves, a great swinging gulper blind across the galleys.

"Who pays the fees?" my practicality asks her, moving away to swill her lousy brew down the drains and start again.

"He does."

"He loves him. He's the father."

"You rotten stick-together males!" Ilse shouts. "You're all the same same same!"

"What can you do for Jamie that his father won't do?" Won't this kettle ever reach its consummation point? "On Slum's piddling pension?"

"I've nothing." She hasn't listened to one word. "He's taken the lot and ruined the lot and all we've done is sit around and wait to be ruined." He becomes for her the wrecked hopsack, the truant cushions, the egg-shells, the toast. "Can't you talk to him? Can't you make him let me keep the last thing he's left me?"

This is woman's magazine stuff with a stinking vengeance, the kettle screaming its release, the stuck caddy lid and outside the starlings on the Afro lawn.

There's nothing I could say. I can't tell her I'm leaving. The glassy substitute Huahines glow on the lying handbills and I see a repeat slum collage of littered fruit-skin and dirty coconut-shell drinking vessels accumulating on torn rattan and I can't tell her. This is going to be my redemption and I opt for selfishness like a glutton and pour her fresh tea in a clean cup, dab her eyes, smooth back the corn tassels and act useless.

Being human is a hideous burden.

I want time to examine the slack and the quick of the seasons, the calculus of growth in all the long shires of summer. But not really as a human might, having had enough of that. Ilse, I wish I could see, and at my leisure, the hemisphere terraces of sundown colour painting my receptive bones, the unexplainable mathematics of wing and bud. There's time still as I dry and wither to exult in the gummy newness of leaf-flesh at least. And oh for the pure parasitism of the non-Parnassian!

"And a biscuit, too," I urged. "You'll have to take more care of yourself." That easy concern wrecked her in seconds and I had the grubby lot of her leaning and tear-drenched in my fastidious arms.

She wanted to offer a gift I could only, by giving pain, reject.

I gave it. *Eheu* for that.

* * *

Here we are now on ten acres of sand and scrubland a mile from Glittertops. Blackboys grow along the margins of this reclaimed swamp area still muddied by a creek and two lines of secretive she-oaks. This is flatter than hell, but above the slow terraces of cloud swarm up from the sea. It is mid-December and my cleft mind totters in the tottering strides of the mercury. Black underside, those clouds, plumbed towards earth with warnings as two thousand of us with rugs, trannies, guitars, turn special yardage on the stubble into temporary harbours. It's been going on since ten this morning and the walls of fag packs and choco cartons, of stripped gear and shucked-off thongs grow in dusty piles between the butts and the topless kids screaming into band numbers amplified to such a crushing strength the terrible underbellies of the cumulus swing closer.

Why this? Why any of it?

Even Neilsen had tried to dissuade, had protested that Holberg couldn't afford to do this sort of thing.

Ah! But that's where he was wrong. It was exactly the sort of thing he could afford to do, the giant swinger of them all, with his electronic feed-back crap ready to be dished out by long-haired thumpers. He'd even tagged Jamie along, who dragged behind his mother, pulling gum threads from his speculating mouth and munching them back in. Poor Jamie. Seeing his old folk acting young was the *via crucis* of humiliation: Ilse tidied up into hysteric gig-lamps and Indian frockery, Hilda in gipsy flounce, Aunt Sadie, who had refused to be left behind, toddling along with a frantic knobbed cane, her wiglet like a brave moulting rodent. He kept on the periphery of our activities, rejecting acquaintance with us, while all round the squealing fans wrestled each other's bodies into the grass, flung bottles and cans, blew pot in our faces. And we were the object of their derision as well, reading the braille of their slanted eyes and their slanted mouths. Holberg, I'm glad you can't see.

Swingers Shumway who loved to keep in touch were slumming it ten groups away with salami and rum cokes. With his lovely innocent eyes assessing documentary worth, he was absorbing the dust-gold bodies of the freaked-out young. I slipped away from Holberg and wandered over to them, stepping across sprawlers, trying to catch their ears behind the amplified throb. Georgie was snap and crackle in batik kid-stakes acting half her age and still leaving the kids a long way behind. She was so gay she spluttered, perhaps because of my defection.

"And uh well uh well uh well," Shumway crooned, never missing the gentle moment. "And how is your discipleship? You look remarkably well."

What a liar! Here I am in my seedy flesh, worn down by time and vulnerable to every groping moment. And he can see the pluck and the fray of the fabric. My personality has pulled like some cheap woollen and I am a mass of tiny uncomfortable nodes.

"You both," I said. "And I'm not lying." Their bodies are plumped with successful living, the easy way. They have the smooth sheen of financial success and their only parasitism is for each other. It causes less diffusion. Shall I tell them?

But I was gagged by Georgie's cries of isn't this jolly chaps, isn't this fun, these beautiful youngsters! She's out of her lilac mind, of course, but compensating for the fact that somewhere over that boundary tree-line lies the heavy fact of her middle-age which will later be mollified by a crustacean dinner and her sort of madness-chat as she reviews the strengths of the day.

"And when," she gasps, interrupting her husband's rhetoric, "is dear Holberg's work coming on?"

"With luck," Shumway says sourly, "with some fortunate spin of the wheel—and I mean Fortune's of course—it mightn't. Have a rum, Vesper."

I take his rum. I glance back through the diabolic O's of yelling mouths to see Sadie sitting propped by cushions and knitting as if her life depended on it. Nearby Jamie, lying on his stomach, is reading comics and still working over the same piece of gum. The others have gone. Where?

"Not too long now, I imagine. Can you save your spleen?"

"Oh Paul," Georgie reproves, soft as syrup, but her eyes like acid, "you're terribly unkind. We've been so looking forward. Hoping. He's a great man."

"You truly think so?"

"Of course. Don't you? If anyone should, it's you. Never losing the common touch."

Perhaps I do think he's a great man, but for different reasons from Georgie. She is the sort of person who would barely have noticed he

263

was blind. You could spade away for days in the rubble of Georgie Shumway's thinking.

Her husband blinked, suddenly alert, and nudged his wife's skittish thigh. "There he is out front now."

There was a makeshift stage backed by the only stringybark stand in the paddock, creating the kind of natural tarpaulin the promoters had been aiming at—nature-boy stuff—spoiled in effect by the lianas of mass media whose silver trumpet flowers sprouted fertilely. A new group, all in rock-red shirts and sky-blue jeans, had clambered onto the rostrum and were shoving round an electronic organ, several guitars and a tape machine. There was thunder on the left. Below stage Holberg stood, a strong-arm boy at his side, giving last-minute instructions (where was *I?*) and I feel vertiginous from the shallowness of it all, from the wasting of arguments whose ambiguities have brought him finally to this marshy waste poised elementally between sea and centre. A sudden bloodlessness husks me, swaying like some pendulum estimator between the Shumways just as Holberg, cross-semaphoring with his hands like a bat-swinger steering on tarmac, consigns his soul-beat to the red-shirts.

I can't take this hoodlum cult where every singer projects like a pack-rapist, stereophonic balls and a penis-stylus. The music was of that mind-stultifying cacophony and tunelessness (Bathgate, I believe you, I believe you!) spattered with drum knock hard rock that phased itself right into the mood of the crowd, and during some amphibrachic passage—the train knocking to nowhere, the guard drunk—a tripping girl joined the musicians on stage and began an interpretative rhythmic jerking that divested her of clothes and ultimately, thought Vesper the old priss, of her humanity. Holberg was scoring his point with a kind of musical hypothetic syllogism, if A then B, and this surging field was B with its screams, its hyena howls its flying drink cans and the girl (breasts hair) abandoning the last scrupulous preserves of self.

"But musically, musically," Shumway was hissing into my bat ear, "what do you think? I mean do you think it achieves—that is to say—fully interprets—a total idea or . . ."

"This is not to think," I hooted back at him. "The whole idea of it. The brain shattered by decibels." I have dropped through into a void where ancient stars in the final dark are held eternally hesitant and blinking. Holberg is seated below the frenzy with his arms hunched round his knees like a gnome. He is the centre of chaos. All round

264

us are dancers, screamers. I sense tribal copulation but he is blind and unaware, rising as the players slam into the terminus.

In the after-roar, in between the barbarous throats rasping the afternoon air, the sun split the parentheses of nimbus and scrub and went towards him on its knees.

Ilse has been discovered, bedraggled nereid, in the mud body-hollowed parking lot alongside the creek. The five louts had screamed back into the mob. It could have been anyone at all. It was Jamie who had found her—as he found everything—just as they were finishing with her. He had lost the power of speech; only his shocked and plucking hands had succeeded in guiding us back where, now kneeling in the marshy stanzas of her epic, Hilda kept stroking her slime-mauled cheek. I examined the poignant intervals in the folds of Ilse's hair. Her face was gummed with grass and leaves that acted as a benign plaster to the already swelling and lop-sided cheek bone, the purplish darkening tegument around the eyes. One arm had been bent viciously back under her and when Hilda drew it gently out the wrist hung grotesque and useless. Somehow we got her back to the car and laid her out along the back seat tucked into blankets in which she hid her frozen face. Jamie sat in front staring straight ahead, his hands tensed on the legs of his shorts, his mouth tightened over incomprehensible and constricting lumps of fact. Slipping into the driver's seat, Hilda put an arm round his neck for a compulsive minute and pressed her head into his cheek.

"Get away!" he ordered thickly, and he pulled over towards the hard metal of his own door, pressing himself into it as if it were a fragment of the shell which had exploded him but still remained his final home.

I looked through the window at the three of them. Jamie kept his snub-nosed profile directly ahead and did not look at me, only quivering briefly as his mother whimpered once from the back seat.

"I'll see to Sadie," I said. "I'll get them both back. You know what to do?"

Hilda nodded. She could have been Jamie's mother at that, I thought, seeing profile against profile in the muted storm light. Behind us the crowd roared, the amplification wailed a trapped sax into the first rain-spatters and Jamie's plump lower lip shivered then became bluntly still.

My last urgings were lost in the hiccupping of the old motor and my hand, attempting a last benedictus on her weighted shoulder was brushed aside as the car backed and turned and heaved itself onto the road. I watched it as Ilse had once watched me and no one waved and after it had gone I waded back through the dragging quicksand of my own rage to seek out the great man.

Anger sharpens vision.

When I got through the crowd to him at last he was playing genius to a dozen gullibles whose shickered affirmations made it difficult to connect. Only connect.

"Just a minute, Paul," he said irritably, pushing at my arm, "I'm trying to catch what my mate here is saying."

They turned their resentful dark glasses on me and then he became as truly one of them, though if he had been aware of that circle of protective lenses he might have taken his off.

"This is urgent," I said.

"Give us a break, man." The nearest to me waved a dismissive hand.

"Yeh. Give the guy a break, nanny. We'll look after him for sure."

"Have a grog."

"Piss off."

"Clam up."

Song words. *I'm looking for a hard-headed woman, one who will take me for myself, and if I find my hard-headed woman, I won't need nobody else.*

I put my mouth close to Holberg's left ear.

"It's Ilse. There's been a bit of trouble. She's sick and Hilda's taken her and Jamie off."

He was drunk and he rocked drunk and his face remained bland. "So she's sick. So what do I do, eh?"

I know a lot of fancy dancers, screamed the crowd all round, *people who can glide you on a floor. . . .*

"Listen," I said, "take it straight then. She's been attacked. Injured, beaten up, by the equivalent of what you're with."

The thud of the music was going on and on. Someone was sick a few yards away.

"He's got rhythm," commented one of the circle. "But no style."

"Careful, dad," the beard right under me said. "Careful what you're saying."

Grabbing Holberg under the armpits, I lugged him upright against his terrible resistance, his drunken weight and the other arms that

266

reached out trying to pull him down. I shook him. Against the thud thump. "She's been raped—"

"Ilse? Raped?" His shocking ironic howl. "*She* calls it rape!" He knew all about italics for a blind man!

"—and Jamie saw the lot!"

The cold-water cure. I'm sorry, Holberg.

He stumbled away from me then, pushing out with his hands, his circle of fifths racketing with laughter, but I shoved after him, caught his waving blind arm and steered him through flesh and sound back towards the fence. Rain came large, warm, isolated.

"Where's the boy?" His face was panning about for me in a wild way.

"He went with them."

"With them? Oh my God, you fool, you stinking fool. You let him go with them!"

I said sourly, "He didn't have much of a choice. Between a raped mother and a drunken father. Do you want me to tell you a few more home truths at last? Do you?"

We had reached the perimeter. Sadie was a little way off, forty leagues, under a tree, her knitting asleep on the rug, her eyes closed, her fragile skull exposed to the flicker of summer lightning and the casual rain. Turning, Holberg rammed his face at me in an expanding silence, then he smiled in the rueful way he had, a pucker of admitted guilt at the corners of the mouth. "You're right, of course, matey. But oh my God, what will have happened to him!"

I don't want the drunk's tears, I told myself savagely. None of that spurious saline drip. I prodded him on towards Sadie, snoring gently under rock-beat. "Here," I said. "Here." And guided one of his hands down to touch her sleeping head.

"Does she know?" he asked. "Has anyone told her?"

How sweet is suppliance at last from the one who has always demanded it. But the way in which I was achieving manhood sickened me as I fought back the ecstatic transubstantiation.

"Nothing. Nothing at all. We'll wake her and take her home."

His day had fragmented. "There are some farewells. A few things to clear up."

"They'll have to wait."

As we stirred the old lady some discoverer satellites kept up their oscillations about us, urging the sullen Holberg back or on to this or that elaborate wake.

"Oh without doubt, my dear fellow, without any doubt at all," Lance Shumway kept insisting, catching horribly up with us as we pushed out to the run-about, "that was easily—and I include your serious, well, for want of a better word, classical works—the most important thing you've done to date. There was a solidity about your statements, a final philosophic utterance as it were."

Through all this Georgie kept both her smiling mouth and eyes wide open with that agate innocence of the truly knowing. But Holberg was inoculated against visual venom. And other kinds as well, for most celebrities have the immunity established by their egotism, but the skin of this man's vulnerability had never quite thickened. Holberg, charitably, I'm glad you are drunk.

While we drove back Sadie rallied once to ask how the girls were and dropped off again, sun-doused, her head bumping against the stunning resistance of the glass. Holberg, with thoughts of his own, grew more and more sober though he was slumped away from me in the attitude of drunkenness. I took occasional glances at his profile: the nose seemed sharpened above the considering, too-rich mouth that moved munchingly over a variety of decisions. But it wasn't until we had beached the car and I was throwing a scrap meal together in the kitchen that he spoke.

"The boy will have to move up here. I want to keep an eye on him after this."

I added water to the can, stirred it into the saucepan and pondered the gluey mess. Rain and dark had cut off the garden and the hill where Taurus snoozed. Holberg sat in my way on the edge of the kitchen table listening to the weather, and smoked incessantly.

"I don't know what to do about his mother."

The soup was stirring into sluggish waves, glopping gently. I lowered the heat.

"You see there's the problem of his forgetting what he saw and being reminded all the time by seeing her."

I dished it up into three bowls. I broke bread. We were about to eat someone's flesh.

"My God, why don't you say something? What would be best? How the hell do I handle this?"

"I'd bring the mother, too," I said at last. "He hardly knows you."

That one went home. He whacked the edge of his bowl with his spoon and it splashed right across the table onto me. I have the trained passivity of my lot. I went on sipping.

"What you're implying, matey," Holberg hissed, shoving his jaw in my direction but a few points to the north, "is that I've deliberately neglected him."

"Not deliberately. Inevitably. You simply pursued your own interests." I think of Lil unexpectedly and feel guilty, ripped about.

"I suppose he really is my son. You'd never be sure with a woman like Ilse."

"He could have been mine," I said. "I'll just take Sadie in some supper."

I have a great sense of theatre, but this hiatus I'd stuffed up against his choking irritation was futile. Sadie was snoring baldly and happily and I brought back the tray and set it on the sink.

He was drumming the table with his fingers.

"Not," I added, "that he is, by all the laws of time and probability. But there was a chance once."

Jamie of the fluid downy limbs, the clear blue gleam eye, the purely shaped features of the waking morning. I see big splayed toes of his small-boy feet speed over grass and dirt, skip frantic over tar. They say more than his tongue at his age—like the hands, firm and smooth and deft with string and twig and pebble, making nimble commitments with all the paraphernalia of the natural world. It is as if he has ruptured the stage curtains of tree and sky fold and burst onto the foot-lights of the garish real world and the animals, stinking, snarling, restless, gaze up at him illumined against a backdrop of fantastic azure. Shivering a little, but his slender limbs moving inevitably, he descends step by step from the rostrum and offers himself to the pack.

Moodiness separates us. Holberg puts on a tape recording of his last trio and squats broodingly analytical in his favourite chair while the music examines him and reaches a conclusion; and without even having to think about it I know that Shumway's jabs have gone home.

The headlights of the Samaritan car wobble through rain, catch the inside walls of our cage, but although Holberg cannot see them he has heard the motor's throb long before me. For the first time since I have known him he ceases to hear his own proclamation and, treating the *allegretto* as if it were a stranger, fumbles his way to the dripping terrace and takes his second child into his arms.

269

VIII

I'M INTERESTED in the loss of innocence.

I lost mine, the innocence of resentment, that day when, pursuing the private notes of Holberg's plague, I found an unexpected prognosis for my own.

The Sunday children in pleated skirts and prismatically pressed trousers. The zoo children with their upturned faces and circular eyes watching baboons and tigers and the largo trunks of elephants. The week-day children with their concertina'd socks and dreamy reluctant faces, cracking small fibre ports against their Iodexed knees. I listen to Satie a lot these days, swamped by velvet. Holberg finds him a spineless composer, but while my revolutionary self rages against bonds, externally I capitulate entirely to his style.

I've observed Jamie (he's with us now) observing a lizard on a branch observing him and his whole being turned outward in such purity of experience he is unaware of his chiming body, the tender upstretched neck with its gently beating pulse, his tensed legs. When and why do adults lose this sense of wonder?

He's lost it now, I think. He has been here a week and we've lied and diverted and lied and told him his mother was knocked down by ruffians (reverting euphemistically to a Victorianism) and all the time he has stared at us with his eyes gone cold and his mouth hesitating over something he wants to say but cannot bring himself to utter. Too late Holberg has thrown himself into a razmataz of fatherly interest: they go on bush walks and boil billies and hike for minor supplies down to the village. And all the time Holberg lays his late hands on this destiny, it withdraws. Holberg, I'm glad you can't see. Glad you are unable to watch Jamie observing you with those lucid intelligent eyes, appalled by your affliction, conjuring its processes for the first time, gauging the reactions of others, being ashamed. Surely your antennae sense the swivelling of his flesh when you reach out that matey shoulder-slapping paw, hear the subtle hardening of his replies?

Jamie is playing himself a game of marbles at the end of the drive, his circuit sketched in dust at the base of the loquat-trees.

I walk up to him slowly, but his curved absorbed body does not register my approach though I am sending out clear messages of kicked stones and nonchalant whistles.

"Like to give me a go?"

His thumb nudges a sea-green sphere and scatters a nest of glass balls. The sun has burned a red patch on the back of his thin neck. Moving round his roughly drawn circle, he fires again. I might be a mere shadow.

"I'll take you on. Used to be a—well, not a whizz—but so-so, so-so."

"No thanks, Uncle Paul."

"Try and hit this one." I point out a blue taw with my foot. He can sense its humility and aims coolly in the opposite direction.

This one-way business. I pick a loquat and suck it thoughtfully, its taste as yellow as its skin.

"School next week, I suppose."

At that he squats back on his neat haunches and stares at me from under his sandy fringe with sombre directness.

"I'm not going back. Not there, anyhow."

"You're not?"

"Holberg said I needn't." He leant forward, shot and scattered four marbles across the dirt.

"What will you do, then?"

"Go to the local, I suppose."

He was entirely indifferent and began packing his marbles into a leather draw-string pouch that Sadie had made for him. Click click click click. My nerves twiddled.

"Jamie," I said, "how would you like a run down to Surfers? We'll see how mother is. Have lunch. Maybe a swim."

"I'd like the swim and the lunch," he replied carefully.

271

"And what about mother?"

"I don't think so."

He began walking ahead of me up the drive, swinging his little bag so that the marbles cracked against each other. Light-flash in the shrubbery and a kingfisher left its jet-flight blue streak across the loquat-trees. Jamie watched it briefly then went sturdily up the gravel ahead of me, kicking with his toes.

"Okay," I called after him. "It's okay, Jamie. We'll do just that. Get your bathers and tell Hilda and I'll see you at the car."

"I'll have to ask Holberg," he said.

His eyes swept over me like kingfishers, too. Innocence had fluttered out on the last feather-tip of the last wing.

There are certain days made for recall: the disposition of the weather, a certain positive location of trees all scrupulously leaved, some sea-revealing angle of street—totemics of disaster. Passivists in these circumstances have a wild cell capacity for expecting out-of-the-way miracles—Venus Anadyomene rising from a bed of coleslaw; Triton with candelabra ablaze stalking across the plastic-polish floor of fish-and-chipperies; jug-ear film princes splitting apart their toad skins; trees taking to arms against landscape despoilers—oh, any of that fanciful twaddle that might illumine fly-specked glass-bulb of the moment. We couldn't find Holberg. We couldn't find Hilda. Sadie croaked from her bed that they had gone up to the next property to borrow some conversation.

"Come here," she ordered Jamie. "Come here, boy. And you don't have to give me a kiss. Here's something to spend on rubbish." Propped up against candy-striped pillows, she grinned and struggled past knitting for her purse. Jamie hesitated before taking the note. He regarded her curiously, then with a smile moving round the corners of his mouth, leant forward and hugged her hard against his head. "Thanks, Aunt Sadie," he said. "Thanks a lot. I'll bring you back something. What would you like?"

"You see," Aunt Sadie commented, straightening her jacket and ignoring him, "he's a nice child, despite his maudlin behaviour. A turf guide, dear, I'll place a bet for both of us."

She closed her eyes instantly, but I looked back at the door to detect the slit-gleam of them watching Jamie, evaluating him like a young colt.

The long tides of grass were coming in. We had stopped the car

272

on the river reaches outside the township before the sudden fibro assault. Knocking boats were tied up to sand-staked posts along the bank in such peace and such reflected peace my whole body ached with their longing to lunge out of harbour, the oar of ivory, the flag of silk, an orange for ballast, for ship's boy—Jamie? He had hauled in the rope of one of the dinghies and was scrambling over the side.

Idly watching, relaxed, I smoked half a cigarette and then, "Are you sure," I nagged, idiotic as his aunt, "you don't want to see your mother? We're just at the turn-off. Only for a minute or so. She'd love to see you, stuck in that place without any visitors."

Jamie's face went hard, coldness under December warmth. For half a minute he stared at me and then jumped straight into the water.

When he came up, his blond hair was plastered across his face in strips, his fishy mouth gasping, his eyes blinking. Choking the green river water out, he was, and standing up to his neck in the pulse of it.

"Get out!" I yelled. "Out!"

He glared sullen and wretched.

"Not until."

"Until what?"

"Until you promise."

I lunged at him. He was only a foot or so from the bank but slippery as a garfish. Skittering those scales of drenched shirt and shorts. My trouser legs flapped like soaked washing, boots bubbling. He stood still in another spot and watched me, shivering, his face still firm.

"Please come out, Jamie." I was pleading and added idiotically, "There's sharks, maybe."

"Do you promise?"

An interested carful slowed up on the highway and scarfed heads craned out and pulled back.

"Yes," I said, all my social glands secreting convention, "yes yes yes."

He waded into the beach to stand there dripping miserably when suddenly his eyes matched his clothes, had their muddiness, their leached-out hopelessness.

"You silly cove," I said.

We drove into town and the nearest store, every squelch like a sob, and after both of us had dry clothes on (oh, those shop-assisting curious eyes!—it is good not to be seen or to sense not being seen)

273

I took Jamie to a cellophane ju-jube gummed to the esplanade and bought him the biggest Glitterlights banana-split he had ever seen. Calming through mundanities. We bought Sadie her turf guide and Hilda a bean-stringer (what unconscious prompting behind that?) and then Jamie changed into his skimpy bathers and I lay on the soft sand while he shuttled up and down the argumentative waters of the incoming tide. His body looked so thin against the huge walls of green into which he melted and reappeared like a truculent piece of drift. Drift off. The eyes shut against sun which still plants a gigantic golden rose across the retinae. Holberg, you never know that. He told me once some fool asked him how he knew when he was awake. . . .

Jamie came slowly up the beach towards me through my half-doze, his toes kicking sand-shots, his eyes screwed up against the glare, his face still reserved. Jamie, I thought, I wish you hadn't seen what you did. I wish. When I'm in Huahine, I continue to muse, shed of the lot of you despite the disquieting persistence of love, and not even those irritating fragments of Holberg music-making to scratch my mind—the divine itch which I must not scratch unless it fester—my days will be so fluid there will be reversals of earth and water, the only two things I'll settle for now as having any reliability. Losing their abrading figures (the artist's group picknicking Fragonard fashion, the Dutch ploughman, the Tintoretto saints), landscapes will be as pseudonymous as sea with uncaptained uncrewed ships.

Jamie lay beside me on his brief towel blinking into sky before he rolled over, burying his face on his freckled arms, head turned askew so that I can still see the aunt's mouth, the father's nose and chin, the goose-boy hair split into parallel lines. I pick up a piece of sea-smelling stick and smooth away the loose sand surface until my hand has created just in front of me a flat damp board on which to score. I sense his eyes as I draw with my beautiful skill a large clear triangle.

"Look, Jamie," I say. "Look here. I'm going to show Menelaus' theorem."

You're right, buster! This is a parable. "If a transversal is drawn to cut the sides," I say, "or the sides produced. . . ." Jamie props his sandy skull on one hand while I explain, step by step, and bring the proposition to its exquisite conclusion. "It was time for a tutorial," I say. "About time. You won't have done that one yet. Put you way ahead of the other fellows. Did you follow it all?"

He wasn't listening to a word I said, though I knew he had absorbed the entire composition premise by premise. Somewhere behind us rock music cut the air in a beach-front chippery. Lunch-time bathers pickled in oil sauntered down to the foam and sea-berry line. A lifeguard had shinned up the shark-tower and straddling the perch gunned the sea with his binoculars. There was a smoke-line two miles out.

"Is Uncle Jack my father?" Jamie asked.

My heartlessness and my concern had planned dropping Jamie at a cinema while I called on his mother in hospital, but when it came to the point I couldn't do it, so side by side in the stuffy dark we fumbled in the same crisp packet, listening to gunfire and throbbing hooves until five o'clock found us blinking at the crabbing sun and the metered girls just packing up. I hate this ritz: the fake-wood wineries with their footpath eye-level barrel-butt veneers; the camp boutiques with their violet stretched strides; the compound-eyed tourists widening their bloody-minded terms of reference as the vogue phrasemakers have it. God up there at his heavenly cash-register, and down below the two of us frail from airlessness and sound, squinting at cargleam, the blown gulls of paper scraps between the palms and the hamburger fumes.

"I've got to get back and practise," said ungrateful Jamie, dragging me towards the car-park. Torpid, I resisted a little, dazzled as sunset made plate-glass bushfire. Which sunburnt charabanc? Holberg, between the billy tea and the bush hikes, between the fishing trips and the shopping sprees, had begun to give him piano lessons.

"You'll make a nice little altar-boy," I said. Forgive me for that, Jamie. Forgive, please. I have reached tether's end. Too elongated, like some subservient, some carpet-knight at a board meeting, all the panel stretched out and out on rubber bonds of boredom that resist pull from the centre but can be snapped back in a trice. I hear the words "But what is red?" and to quell the guilt in my heart put my hands to my ears. That's me, letting in the clutch, backing angry over the steaming bitumen and out into the traffic-way, honking a clearance through to the west road back beside the river while the lights behind us break out along the tops of the buildings like hair-dye. I just miss a clot bikie (*eheu*) and cut savagely between two hauliers heading west with me.

"Don't spoil it," Jamie said quietly. "It's been a good day."

"Spoil it?"

"You're angry."

"You can't see anger," I said. "We're limited by our sight, Jamie."
Oh, I was a bastard.

"You feel it," he said. "I'm rather like dad."

Wednesday Thursday Friday.

"We don't need the plumber," Aunt Sadie croaked.

Neilsen shifted his weight and tried again.

"But I'm not the plumber."

"You look like the plumber."

"My dear lady, I am a music critic for two major papers, syndicated
in five. I travel regularly with visiting celebrities, I make and break
artists, my word is feared in five States."

"Jesus," said Sadie. "Maybe you'd better have a look at the washing-
machine then."

He glimpsed me over her aged shoulder sniffing at the news behind
one of the indoor plants and cried for help.

"I think the dear lady has forgotten me. Do explain who I am."

"Bugger that dear lady stuff!" Sadie snapped, hobbling back to her
knitting. "Paul, get me a brandy."

Neilsen gave a wan smile and came and joined me behind the Kentia.
"Darling Sadie," I comforted, "it's all right. Truly. We'll all have a
drink. Perk us up."

This was to be my last drink in that house. Did I know it? Does
the moment, rainbow-blue as this was, with December bubbling outside in the steaming greenery, boiling all those insects tiny reptiles
birds into top-pot scum activity, does it carry the crow shape of its
true self?

Innocuously Neilsen asks, "Where's Holberg?"

He is, I know, cracking his stick against the cedar trunks along the
upper ridge and will loathe this interruption to his day. Since Jamie
has come to live with us, he has withdrawn more and more from the
attentions of Sunday social-par intellectuals. Even his pop-pals he's
abandoned in their own shaggy hair as if he realized at last that they
are their only talking-points. But perhaps it won't last. I'd like to
believe Ilse's disaster has sobered him up. I'd like to believe that. It
has done that much for her at least, for she has come to live with us
now and is a shadow goose-girl pecking gently round the edges of
our pond.

276

It has been a week. Jamie seems to have accepted her occasional *autos-da-fé* of heretic food in the kitchen. He pecks her duty-steered good-nights. He strolls gravely to school with his insolent book-satchel slung across one uncaring shoulder. He hangs on his father's every word and hugs Hilda good-morning with enthusiasm. You see, he has lost his innocence. And I, I have lost all of mine.

That is when boredom sets in. It's the last port of call in the long seas of loss. For a while the sufferer practises the very strokes of his art: becomes a drinks bore, a fags bore, a talk bore. Edentulous, no moment bites back. What is there left for a servant of the lord who has discovered that the idol's hands never move towards the slowly spoiling offerings unless it be to stroke its own stone thighs; that the miracles, the answers to prayers, are only fortuitous reactions? The swaying, chanting throngs bearing the garlanded monstrosity through summer streets will be crushed by their own abasement and *still* nothing will shower down upon them.

Get up off your bloody plinth! I shriek right through the bored-out channels of my empty self to hear the echoes vanishing down those chalk-white corridors and passages of no-happening. Get off get off get off!

"He's gummed to the skyline."

"Gummed? To the skyline?"

"Merely a metaphor." I top up his drink and Sadie belches quietly and closes her eyes in the good fortune of old age. "He's on the plinth of the world. Out walking. He'll be back by lunch."

"May I invite myself?"

Sadie groans in her pretended sleep. "One of those," she mutters. "One of those fringe spongers."

"What a character!" Neilsen says uneasily. "Are you sure it won't be any bother? I won't be in the way?"

Sadie and I unite in our silent refusal to ease him.

"It's a documentary I'm preparing. Televised, of course." He is pondering on. "I do have to see him to prepare a script, get his opinion and so on. I believe he's working on something again?"

Yes. He was working.

For a fortnight he'd been up till three and four writing and re-writing—the sound-proofing still permitted scattered phrases to come in my window with the moon. He was trying to save the afternoons for his son and spent the early part of the day sleeping heavily in the giant anachronous bed he and Hilda still used. Two days ago I caught Ilse looking in at him from the terrace. She had been nibbling a loquat and her lips were parted in that way of twenty years before when innocence still spelt out its expectations, her washed hair dripping like wistful curtains over her shallow cheek. As he rolled sideways in his sleep and threw out one naked arm I saw her catch her breath and involuntarily press her hand quickly against her mouth. I seem to spend my days stooping behind plantains and crotons and the aching throats of hibiscus in bloom. It is simply that we are so trapped with each other. Write an essay, children, called Trapped on a Desert Isle. There were six of us that day, I began, in my unformed cursive, three men and three women. One of the men was a child, really, but already he seemed older than I. There's nothing like an island for speedy development! The oldest of the women was the youngest. Yes, teacher, I'm writing in parables! And we had running water and fresh fruit and a big glass hut. What bound us together was our religion, our unstinted worship of the love-object who was indeed one of ourselves. God and man. It was a terrible predicament for all of us though no one realized at the time the predicament for him. If you can gather his difficulties by gleaning the wispy cobs of my own, the matter will have the ambivalence it deserves. Yes. I wrote it all myself. And as a rider I want to add for your curiosity and my own satisfaction that while watching Ilse of the parted lips and the give-away hand, I discovered that she was regaining her innocence.

Bam!

Startling? I had decided once lost never to be regained. Was I wrong? Oh, the swamp-shimmer hope of it! We, I, could be saved. The packed bag glistened in one corner of my mind with a phosphorescence that was the inner blaze of sainthood. I coughed myself into being behind her and she swung about with a stain of pink where her fingers had pressed this renewal.

I cut through her gasp.

"You're looking a lot better, even in this short time."

"I'm home," she said simply.

I picked and sucked at a loquat myself. "Meaning this is where you always wanted to be?"

"I can't tell you how it was when Neville died."

"The centre you didn't want, you mean."

"Put it that way if you like." I was edging her away to the living area. My decoding for the morning was nearly finished and a bundle of manuscript lay neatly tabulated and stacked on the music-room desk in direct spatial relation to a more explanatory work. But this was good, I had to admit it, a work of solidity and shape. I had transcribed my last bar for him, too, but was I aware of that as I strolled that morning in the papaw plantation behind the kitchen? "Oh, you can put it that way and you can nail my guilt on as heavily as you like, Paul, but for nearly twenty years I have been longing to come home. Nev was a stop-over on the way."

"So was I, I suppose."

She turned in the green light from the leaves, the yellow light from the fruit.

"Yes," she said, "you were. You know you were. Just as I was for you."

"I know," I said. Shades of Freckles and the beddy dunes that had been my stop-over. "We're all home now, for what it's worth."

"I'm happy."

I sucked reflectively on the bitterness of the loquat seed. "But then I'm not. Nothing, just nothing, Ilse, has been what I truly expected. I feel like a parasite. And the more I feed the emptier I become."

"You ought to go," she advised, still in the yellow and green tree-light, "while there's still time for you."

"It's too late, isn't it? Aren't I truly ruined now for new starts? Look at me. Look at my age. It's staring you emptily in the face. Well, isn't it?"

She had always for me been the space between the urge and the utterance. Within this safe envelope she stood and regarded my failure, the stoop on the shoulders, the injury within the eyes (Holberg, viciously, I *wish* you could see!), dejection of my skin which has nothing to do with living but a lot with dying. She put up one careful hand and traced the pattern of disappointment that ran from my mouth.

"I don't hate Hilda any more," she replied, and it wasn't irrelevant, just part of the grace of renewal. Perhaps, my minor devil added coyly in my ear, one can afford to re-love what one has ruined.

"But I didn't!" she protested intuitively to my quizzical sceptical eye.

"Didn't what?" I asked, appalled by her E.S.P.

"Ruin her."

"There's been a host of things. Jamie was the greatest shock of them, done a bit of emptying if the truth be known. Who of the three of us has achieved a thing, got one skerrick of self to show for twenty years' servitude?"

"I have."

"You? Well, you are the genuine masochist goose-girl, aren't you, eh? Your wounds bleed profusely and you display them with pride. The Holberg stigmata, that's what you've got. Maybe you are a genuine saint. What you're really trying to tell me is that I don't love my dunghill, isn't that it? I don't love the crap and the stink?"

But she parted the heavy miasma of my anger as if it were curtains and slipped into the back door of the house.

Inspecting Neilsen now, a true earth-worm in the garden of art, I felt I must feed him more grog. Nourish the nourisher. He smiled ta ever so nicely and we looked at each other through a horrible silence. Well, *he* was uncomfortable. Sadie had begun to snore very slightly but I was totally happy waiting for him to speak first. It's taken me years to get like that. He couldn't take it for too long. There were watch-glancings, sly then open, seat-stirrings, too many quick sips.

Racked, he said, "Why don't we stroll up and find him? It's a lovely morning."

"But he should be back soon."

"Still, I'd rather like the walk. Sharpen me up a bit."

"For lunch?" asked Sadie, suddenly awake.

"You don't need that, old man," I said.

He bit his lower lip, the first sign of genuine weakening.

"You see," I explained, "he won't like the interruption. Things are done by ritual here. It's High Mass at Plateautop. And if I fumble the altar wine, I'm the one who'll cop it."

"Oh, come!" Neilsen cried. "It's not that sacred. A stroll among the trees. I'll take all the blame, I swear." He was up on his expensive feet, twitching. "You just point out where and I'll go up myself. I've some news by the way that will truly excite him."

My long-armed god was snuggled up there in bracken.

It was only as I stepped with Neilsen from the last of the concrete flagging that a vision of Holberg's feeler stick probing it out swept across my mind like rocket-waste and lingered. The crack of wood on metal so foreign in that austral Maeterlinck forest . . . the hands would curve in a question, reach out unsure and begin their search. Taurus

280

would lie passive, but the antithesis of the plaster nymphs, his steel member raised significantly, the ammunition for his thrust the smoothest, most ruby-veined of the river-stones I could find stacked carefully in the long grass. Holberg loved rocks. I had gathered them in remembrance. Holberg, Sadie had explained so long ago in my initiating flat, Holberg loves rocks. In a way they had brought me here, that hunt for their cold perfection. Now, taken from their seminal fluid, the colours had faded, the striations of rose and russet had lost the ripple and lap given by the movement of water under the falls. But they were heavy and deadly and they fitted the cup.

We poked through banana thatch and the untrimmed tassels of Chinese honeysuckle. There was a scent of vanilla and limes. This is the orchestra pit and up on the side of the hill the soloist, briefly glimpsed in white shirt and shorts, is crashing his muscular legs between the trees. Even down here we could hear him whistling—he whistled magnificently, a magpie quality, sometimes manipulating his tongue (Oh you lucky lovers!) so skilfully he appeared to be double-stopping. A phrase from the last variation on which he had been working, done over and over, slowed occasionally and then repeated with interpolations.

"What's that?" Neilsen asked, his skin a sweat-glisten in the sun. "That sounds interesting."

Aren't you ever off the job? my anxiety wanted to roar. Ever?

The whistle became thoughtful, hesitated, stopped altogether.

We lost sight of him as we struggled down one gully full of the stink of summer, hauling between bark smells and crushed eucalypt offerings. I stroked the skin of a blue-gum that held memories of the wife. It was like hardened silk and one eye in its bole wept winy resin. I broke off a dried raised seep of it and popped it into my mouth. It was like eating summer. Hangovers from the nature-rape child years: knowing, carnally, this roly-poly slope, wallowing in it, down it, learning its curves by heart; the half-sunken log teetered along to the ripple cover of the tide, squatting on it, balancing, feeling the salt-scars; conning trees, branch by branch, climbing, hanging, inspecting ant-colonies along the limbs. I chewed, and as I chewed, we glimpsed Holberg again in the wide light of the crest thrusting about the grass at his feet with his white spy stick. He squatted suddenly and as we lost him my heart bounded with guilt. How could he unravel its usage?

Neilsen was asking petulantly what was the fellow up to. His trouser-legs were maps of burrs. Summer was eating him. All round us boulders suspended threats of weight and silence, but unabashed Neilsen began to hail him through the mat of timber with his cupped unaccustomed hands trumpeting urban squawks that faded uselessly through the sap of the scene.

And then something whizzed across sky and thudded fifty feet to the west of us into an applause of leaves.

"My God!" Neilsen was exclaiming. "What was that?"

I couldn't tell him.

Then a stone thumped ten yards in towards us on the other side and Neilsen, giving off the strange smell and smile of fright, managed "We're being fired at" like some dated film cur and headed for the shelter of a bloodwood. Heaving away from him, I crashed through the drag of cling-stems, very dilemmas of lantana, and vine-hauled myself up the hill against armies of resentful trees.

Holberg was crouched above my conscience, his hands tenderly busy, stroking, discovering, and his mouth smiling victory. I couldn't begin to define all the categories of bliss. Here was another. His head swung at the sound of me and the hands which had just fitted his elevenses apple into the indifferent cup, paused, performed a nervous mordent and fumbled their way down to the switches.

"It's you, isn't it Vesper? Watch this."

His thumb depressed one of the keys, the arm swung back, a triple claw rested lightly above the crisp red missile, holding it into place, and then Taurus flashed his arm, the claws relaxing at that specially geared second and we heard the whizz of Eden as it sailed over the startled gully. A splather of pulp and seed.

His face still turned in the direction of my crackle and creak smiled.

"Well, matey?" he said. "Well?" And his good hand slid along Taurus's tense limb. "You didn't let your education go to waste, eh? But what's the purpose of it? Let me guess. . . . Beleaguered by the public and the critics, we aim this pretty thing in our defence. Is that it?"

"It's my mobile," I said. And then, "You've got a visitor. Neilsen. He's waiting down below. Actually he's hiding."

His face brightened. "Really?"

"Don't pretend. You heard him call."

"What's he want? Lunch?"

"That. And other things."

282

"You don't protect me, you know, matey. You don't barricade me from these ticks at all."

I said bitterly, listening to the crash of Neilsen elephanting up the slope below us, his fear back in his pocket, "We've not reached that stage yet. You're still selling your talent." Father Vesper administers viaticum for the journey.

"You shit!" he calls me. "You lousy shit!"

I want to break into obscene cries about his half-baked genius, his gluttony for worship, my pity for him, my latest understanding, my own dismemberment, but I look at him struggling to rise, groping about for his stick, his face redrawn with the shock of truth, and I sense him to be right and me to be wrong, but it is too late for anything like that now. We both munch the eucharist and no grace enters our souls.

Stumbling away from me he calls for Neilsen again and again and I want to lie stretched full length in the chaotic undergrowth and weep for the lot of us.

It is five o'clock. Light is being licked from the room where we sit amongst the intransigent shapes of the carved objects that Holberg loves to touch. Scrolls of music like those distant scrolls of sea seen through the glass wall beyond the doric trunks of trees break and recede and break and recede against the ache that has shifted its gristle from my mind and is growing now throughout my entire body. Jamie has gone nesting into the long acres; his mother is burning something in the kitchen and the fumes, a diabolic incense, crowd their pungency in on us. Sadie is travelling in her sleep four rooms away. "Credible?" asks Holberg, ignoring me and paying his total substance to his cultural middleman. I am truly sickened by him and by myself. Why does he have to ask when he knows its excellence? Why cheapen himself with pander sale? The communion bread which I stuffed down so readily on the hillside rises in my gorge and I chew it again with my blunted irreverent teeth, but it refuses to be swallowed. Holberg, I have accepted your bastardry and your brilliance, and have made full allowance for the reason and the pity of it. And I am cut in half.

Through the newly started rain pin-pointed beyond the sliding grey of the sea I search for Huahine and it is only the dazzle-spot on the farthest of horizons. Look, I was lying about that. I've never been there. But I might have, don't you see? It has been one of the side-chapels of my being. The two of them stroll over to the windows, marinated in self-belief, but my tongue is in clamps, not even released by the crippling sounds of wrecked pottery from the kitchen. There's the sound of Hilda sobbing, only briefly, and Ilse's smarting reproval, and the two men who have reached a check-point in their social chess pause, listen and laugh. "Poor Hilda," Holberg says with just that shade too much patronage. "Poor goose-girl."

It was the laugh that did it.

I forget everything I have ever felt for him in that instant.

Mensch, Traill, Yuill, Zacka—my footwork would amaze you: slipped out of the scrum and heading into the slow rain, uphill for a try.

The water wipes back whole webs of illusion, washing off the last grey strings of my own blindness as I cut panting past the hollow of sodden brush and grass where once I had parted the hair of rain for a moment to bellow sense into Hilda; past the ridge where Hilda's masochist submission had been punched in and proved to me for ever by the operator's card; past all this to where, grim in his bracken jacket, Taurus strains towards the weeping sky.

Blind, I kneel in the grass beside his incurious poise and stack my ammunition in a neat pile. What is it I want to do? Make a last gesture? Fling one last comment? The house is spread out full below me, the glass panes this side gleaming leadenly in the last light through the rain. This is the last light. The last drink. The last exchange. Crouched in the coil of my anger, I select the most venomous of those polished river rocks and place it in the cup. What *is* cup? a distant voice asks. That other half of me cries with despair. The arm is trained on the house, but I must readjust the finder so that it will sling its load in memorable fashion. How memorable?

I smear the rain off the finder and the grief from my eyes and tremble the dial into position so that Taurus is about to discover glass and music. I feed another rock within hand's reach and fighting a sound symphony of accusations press the lever. Goal! From below comes the joyous crash of annealed quarter-inch plate, and, seeking orgasm through the attached field-glasses, I discover I have scored a bull's-eye on the study and carried a fox-brush of pampas grass through to the carpet. My hands shake with the joy and the rage and the pity of it. Don't *think*, you fellows! our football coach used to pep-talk us. Get in there and kill 'em. I place the second stone in the cup and shift the range-finder slightly. Shouts are rising from below as if I'd made

284

a find. Whiiiip! The second window blazes stars and there is a violent gesticulating knot of people on the terrace. I whack another onto the roof for good measure and am just about to launch another and another and another when I see Jamie sauntering into the path of my vengeance, his hands cradling something, his head startled as a bird's. He is outraged by clotted throats and planetaria of glass slivers. There is blood on someone's face—Neilsen's—and Holberg is ramping wildly between his wives like a betrayed sultan.

Wildly I think what a field-day Bonnie the Vocative would have: O my god O holberg O neilsen O hilda! I cackle crazily and remember Sadie.

After all, it was only a gesture I wanted, something that gave expression to my strait, not a crushing flesh-pulping blow into the Holberg brain. Taurus is passive and active at once. Validly at the ready but silent. I take ae fond glance at his steel impassivity and picking up a thick branch clobber his delicate limbs till they lie awry but unbroken. Movement has fled the terrace; they are inside now at the phone, reporting a maniac. Rubbing my hands clean on my handkerchief, touching the corners of my sated mouth, I look once round the cradle hills and the oasis of garden, only once like remembering Huahine, and begin to trot fast, faster and then in a shambling run thread in and out the trees until reaching the lower grassy slopes I come at a gallop to the far side of the pool. There are blood dribbles on the scootway and an icing of glass. I crunch my way round on it and see them jabbing at clichés of horror in the living-room. Maniacal Ilse begins shouting insults—she never could see!—and Neilsen, who is mopping a cut on his forehead (I'm sorry about that), peers up through capillary trickles with a face of such bafflement I begin to laugh. I don't want to but I cannot stop and through my laughter isolated rocks appear briefly between the foam and slash, questions and protests and suddenly, cliff-huge, Holberg crying out, cracking for the first time in all the years I have known him, "I wish I could see! Oh my God! I wish I could see!"

Just standing, he is, with his arms dangling beside him, and his admission catches me over the heart.

Next minute he is clawing his way towards me where I stand rooted beside the piano. My first rock has caught it on the key-board, knocked flat six of its teeth whose ivory chippings lie about on the carpet. There is a terrible wound in the rosewood forehead. Holberg has a cut on one cheek and he lets it pour its protest without stanch. Suddenly I realize he does not know.

This is what I cannot bear—being torn two ways. The Romans did it with sets of horses. I've chosen a more abstract method but it boils down to the same thing. I am thinking all these things and even while my eyes prickle with understanding of his disaster he is screaming abuse. Screaming. You rotten sycophantic bastard busboy! You stinking little stooge! It's true, some of it, of course. While the substance is lies. All lies. I want to scream back my defence but his ego is impervious to reason. It would take a frontal lobotomy. "I'll finish you, Vesper!" he shouts. "Finish you for this." But I am finished. That's what it's all about.

If I'd done it years ago, I mean in those twelfth-man years, built up my own male bull-roar, shanghai'd light-bulbs with Loomer in the beery early evenings at Grogbusters or heaved stones through masonic and rotarian windows, got it out of the system as it were when all my buddies were getting it out of their systems, maybe I wouldn't be here now, the oldest lout window-smasher in the business. He'll see it this way—and *only* this way—one of these days; his vanity wouldn't have it otherwise, I realise bitterly, until finally only *I* am left conscious of my true and grandiose resentment.

And all of a sudden I am too tired to explain. Explanations aren't for acolytes.

Jamie is standing pop-eyed by the terrace door. His terrible interest is more than I can bear. Holberg lunges to where he thinks I am and I side-step (tuh-heem! tuh-heem!) so that he goes staggering forward against his wives who have been plucking at my arms. Sadie, who has tottered down the hallway, leans unbelieving against the arch, unable to curb finally the wind at this door.

Outside rain releases a haemorrhage of water and whole landscapes are wiped out in an instant while only the turmoil under shelter rises louder and louder as Holberg flings himself about and calls on Neilsen for help. Who is pouring himself a careful Scotch.

I cannot speak but their voices go on and become wordless. I can sort no sense from any of it and when I look away from Hilda and Sadie and Jamie and Ilse at Holberg again I see his mouth is working like a child's. Despite those ruined ducts he is crying, crying, and for what loss I dare not hazard.

I run from the room, run down the long corridor with rain ham-

286

mering the glass on one side or pouring through its jagged ports and the dozen mobiles and odd-ball sculptures measuring my flashing paces on the left. I crash my door open and the wardrobe clatters its protest. My packed bag looks as naked and unreassuring as a missal. The proper of the mass.

The room has disowned me, I see in this last look which it gives me as if I were a stranger, but I remember the tray with the parrot. Holding it over my head for shelter and gripping my pilgrim bag firmly, I walk steadily into the rain, the garden, past the raped indifferent statues, out to the battered grocery buggy and wrestle its door open under the sodden-trees.

One foot in the car and someone is calling out behind me as I turn and blink through water that is not all rain.

Hilda is running after me under the long pergolas, her hands outstretched in pleading.

Where will it all end?